WICCHING HOUR

The Sea Wicche Chronicles

Sea Wicche
Book 3

SEANA KELLY

Wicching Hour: The Sea Wicche Chronicles

Copyright © 2025 by Seana Kelly

Ebook ISBN: 9781641972857

POD ISBN: 9781641973267

NYLA Publishing

121 W. 27th St., Suite 1201, NY 10001, New York.

http://www.nyliterary.com

*For the outcasts
know that you are loved, wanted, and have
a special place in this world*

ONE

It's a Talent That I Always Have Possessed

Opening night of The Sea Wicche Gallery and Tea Bar was finally here. I'd been planning it since I was little and saw the abandoned cannery for the first time. At first, I wanted to live here, but when I got a little older and would break in and run around, leaping over stagnant ponds of dirty water and playing with rusty machinery, I saw it for the potential it had. I started bringing my sketches with me, taping them up on the walls.

And now look at me. The cannery was remodeled into a huge, forty-foot-tall gallery with my studio and apartment taking a quarter of the space. The floors were dyed concrete that looked like a deep ocean blue. I'd painted the walls to look like water as well, from deep sea to surf.

If one looked closely enough, high on the wall above the front door, in the deepest part of the ocean, there lurked a sea monster, watching and waiting. The exterior of the gallery told us he wouldn't be waiting long. I'd built thirty-foot long tentacles coming from the water under the cannery, appearing to be pulling the gallery into the ocean. I'd given the local fisherman quite a start when they'd first seen them.

I'd also painted one whole side of the building—the side people would see first driving from Cannery Row—to look as though the gallery was still an old condemned building that had tentacles breaking through the rotting boards. There'd been a number of articles written about the exterior of my gallery, which probably had something to do with why there were so many people packed in here tonight.

On the one hand, I'd done it. Having my own art gallery was a dream come true. On the other, having all these random people touching and judging my pieces was making my stomach churn and causing my head to pound.

I don't do well in crowds. I'm a Cassandra wicche, meaning I can see the future. And the past, come to that. I'm an empath and keep covered neck to fingertip and toe, because psychometry is also a gift of mine. Everyone wanted to shake my hand. I wear gloves always, as I don't want to touch someone and drop into a vision, learning every hidden thing in their lives.

I hadn't anticipated all the people wanting to hug me. Yes, my body was covered, but my face and hair weren't. Hugging meant my highly sensitive skin touching cheeks or hair. I was trying to keep myself safe, so my boyfriend Declan, the werewolf Alpha of the Big Sur pack, and my agent Mary Beth were flanking me, keeping people at a safe distance.

I've been working with Mary Beth for many years. She's half fae, like me, but her other half is human. She's one of the most respected agents in the art world. She has an almost encyclopedic knowledge of all art, no matter the medium, time period, or location. Most see her as a hard-ass agent who knows all the major players and always gets her clients the best deals, but I know her as my slyly funny friend who is my biggest champion, refusing to let me undersell myself.

She'd arrived four days ago because she didn't trust me to price my own art. She was clearly right to do that, as I would have gone much lower. As it was, pieces were still flying out the door and I was going to be set for months.

"Okay, shorty, the real money has arrived," Mary Beth said. "Where did your mom go?" She glanced around and then made a quick movement with her hand. "Mom's on her way." She glared at Declan. "Do not leave her side." She glided off, the masses separating before her.

In my defense, I'm not short. Am I as tall as my six-and-a-half-foot, super hot, bearded boyfriend? No. No, I was not. I was five-three and a half, which was a totally respectable height. Did I usually round up to five-four? Of course. I was simplifying.

Mary Beth's mom is a beautiful Black woman, who is herself an artist. I'd met her once when I went to New York to meet with Mary Beth. Her mom is free and funny and open to the world. She's also a gifted sculptor. I'm pretty sure Mary Beth's father is a warrior elf, given she's at least six feet tall. She has long, white-blonde hair she usually wears up, luminous golden-brown skin, and piercing gray eyes.

Arrowing through the crowd, she stopped beside an elderly couple in windbreakers and walking shoes who looked as though they'd wandered in accidentally.

"Do you know who they are," Declan asked quietly, his arm protectively around my waist.

I shrugged. "No idea."

My mom stepped in front of a wild-eyed man coming straight at me. Her fingers twitched at her side and he turned sharply, wandering off.

"Thanks," I said.

Because it was opening night, we also had waiters weaving through the gallery, offering wine and appetizers. Mom was sipping the wine, but I couldn't handle alcohol on a queasy stomach.

"I worry, darling," she said. "I know you've always wanted your own gallery, but this gives people too much access to you." She moved forward and to the left, trying to hide me. "You know how crazy some humans get when they're near you." She lowered her voice, "And demons can look like anyone. Your cousin's friend could disguise himself as any of these people. With this crowd and all the shielding you have to do to keep their thoughts and emotions out of your head, he could walk up and snatch you before you even realized what he was."

Declan's arm tightened around my waist, as he too started glaring at people who came too close. Shaking her head, Mom flicked her fingers again, clearly sending spells to make others forget they'd seen me. Many patrons either walked away looking frightened or with a vaguely confused look in their eyes.

"That security guard you hired isn't watching people to make sure they don't steal. What is he even doing?" My mom was used to being in charge and I was sure this all felt too chaotic to her.

"You look beautiful," I said. "I told you the blue dress would be perfect tonight." Mom was gorgeous to begin with, with Corey black hair, fair skin, and deep green eyes. It had taken some doing, but I talked her out of her very conservative black suit and into a flowing, wrap-around silk dress in blues and greens.

"You do look very pretty, Ms. Corey," Declan said.

Staring out at the crowd, she said, "Yes, well, that's nice to hear, but I'd rather discuss your security."

"Oh, that's right," I said, bouncing on the balls of my feet. "I haven't told you. Bracken and I created a ward. If someone tries to steal one of my pieces, tries to hide it and walk out—that part's important—it disappears from their pocket or bag and reappears in its original spot."

Mom's focus snapped to me. "What? How—that's amazing. You need to share it with me so I can share it with the family. Excellent," she said, nodding. "No more pilfered goods in our shops." She thought a moment. "So, is your guard just for show?"

"No," I said. "That's Carter, Detective Osso's younger brother." Like Declan, he was six-and-a-half-feet tall, with shoulders even broader than a werewolf's. He was a dark-skinned Black man who, like his brother, wore a perpetual scowl. "He's working on a PhD in Marine Biology. We'll only be open a couple of days a week, so it shouldn't cut into his dissertation time too much. The ward should keep my artwork safe. He's here to watch people."

"Oh," Mom said. "Good. But I still don't see how you can possibly make a living only being open two or three days a week."

"And by appointment," I said. We'd already had this argument a few times. "Collectors prefer private viewings. Anyway," I said, trying to change the subject, "that earpiece Carter's wearing? It's not hooked up to a security system or anything. He's listening to podcasts."

Declan laughed. "Nice."

"Are you sure he can handle one of your obsessed stalkers?" Mom asked.

Carter turned to us from his spot across the gallery, eyebrows raised.

Leaning into Mom, I whispered, "He's a bear shifter. He can handle any of them. Probably all of them."

He nodded and went back to surveying the room.

"Mary Beth's walking them to Cecil 2," I whispered.

"Who?" Mom followed my gaze, studying the couple for a moment. "Oh. Your agent is very good, darling. The Winslows look like middle-class, elderly tourists, but the wife's from serious old money and the husband used it to make them even more. They're very committed philanthropists, so at least they're doing a lot of good with it." Mom elbowed me. "You should feel honored they're here. They live on the East Coast. Connecticut, I believe."

"How do you know all this stuff about them?" I asked her.

"I read an article on the charity work they do. I never would have recognized them if your agent hadn't gone straight to them."

"Aaaand there they go." My hopes sank. Not only did they not buy my five-foot glass rendering of Cecil, they didn't even pick up a starfish paperweight. *Damn.*

Mary Beth moved back to us, the crowd parting to make way for her and then reuniting behind her. "Sybil, that dress is gorgeous on you," she said as she went behind the cashwrap.

My Aunt Elizabeth's kids Frank and Faith were working the cash register, ringing up and wrapping purchases.

Mary Beth went into a drawer and pulled out a roll of *Sold* stickers.

"Did they buy something?" I whispered, hope bubbling up.

She rolled her eyes. "Oh, you sweet summer child, it would be easier to tell you what they didn't buy. Cecil is gone. They've put in an order for one hundred and seventy-five of the large octopuses." At my look of shock, she said, "I explained you'd need time for an order that large. They're planning to give them to their top executives in their companies as holiday gifts. I told them we could deliver by November fifteenth. That works, doesn't it?"

She was referring to the twelve-inch octopuses. There was only one five-foot Cecil. I considered and then nodded.

"We'll hire a team when it's time to ship. We do *not* want them arriving with broken tentacles. They also bought three of the paintings, seven of the framed photos—your underwater series—and assortment of this and that. They want to come back tomorrow before opening so they can browse properly. We'll pull out any of the big pieces you still have in the hot shop for them to see." She stopped. "No. We'll take them to the hot shop so they can see what you do. That's better. They get to feel themselves close with the artist. Ten tomorrow morning. I'll get here first." She looked out over the crowd. "It's going well. Let me get these stickers on. And we have another collector who just walked in. He's going to be very annoyed the Winslows got here first."

She left me reeling, doing math in my head.

Declan picked me up and kissed me soundly. "Congratulations, Ursula. Looks like The Sea Wicche is a success." When he put me down, I had to hold tight so my knees didn't buckle.

"Very good, Arwyn. I guess you were right about only needing to be open a couple of days a week." Mom looked as dazed as I was feeling.

I knew it when he walked in. The air changed. Mom made a noise, and I followed her gaze to the door. He'd come. He'd promised he'd come, and he had.

Dad.

Larger than life, he stood just inside the door, taking it all in. He wore a dark gray suit with a snowy white shirt and a watery blue tie. His hair was cut short, making his aqua blue eyes stand out even more.

I grabbed Mom and Declan's hands, giving patrons a mental push out of the way so we could go to him. Mom resisted, but I pulled harder. She hadn't seen him since before I was born, since she did what the family ordered and broke up with him. To say this meeting was fraught was an understatement.

He met us halfway across the room. "Daughter, I like your gallery very much." He may have been speaking to me, but his eyes were on Mom. "Sybil. You look well."

She swallowed and then nodded.

His focus swung to Declan. "And you. Are you strong enough to protect my child?"

Declan said, "I am," just as I said, "I'm strong enough on my own, thanks."

"That's true," Dad said, taking my gloved hand. "You have a lot of me in you." He tucked it into the crook of his arm and moved us away from the other two. "Show me what you've created."

TWO

A Flutter of Butterflies

I escorted him through the gallery, pointing out paintings and photographs. It was my glasswork that drew him, though.

"I would like something small of yours," he said. "Something I can carry with me."

Other patrons noticed us and tried to approach, but they quickly turned away and moved on. I guess Dad didn't want any interruptions, which was good by me. I took him to the locked display case against the slanted wall. My psychic reading room was behind this wall, not that I'd had time to do readings lately.

"I know just the one." Using a spell rather than a key, I slid open the case and retrieved a tiny, perfect replica of a baby octopus. It had been extraordinarily difficult to get the details right when working with something so small. I was very proud of the transparent little guy, with tiny tan spots and big gray eyes.

"My gift," I said, offering him the baby in my palm.

With a delicate touch, he picked up the little octopus and studied him. Turning his attention to me, he smiled and the room grew brighter, the butterflies in my stomach beating their wings furiously.

"Perfect. I know he's made of glass, but my eyes believe him to be real." With a nod, he added, "I accept this gift from my exceptional daughter." He closed his fingers over the glass octopus, gave me his arm, and we continued our walk around the gallery.

We stopped in front of a painting I'd done of a tidal pool right before a large wave hits. Lots of little sea creatures working in the clear pools as a curl of ocean gets ready to slam into them. Some will get washed away. Some will spin and roll, buffeted by the force, but in the end remain where they were.

"There's a lesson there," he said. "We can't always prepare for what's coming. Often, we need to ride out the unforeseen and then make a new plan depending on where we end up."

I squeezed his arm and nodded, probably getting more emotional than the moment warranted. Look at me, getting life advice from my dad.

"Maybe we should go talk with Mom," I suggested. It hadn't escaped my notice that his gaze kept falling on her.

"No." He studied my gloved hand in the crook of his elbow. "Is this fashion?"

I shook my head. "I'm a Cassandra wicche. When I touch people or objects, I hear thoughts, see memories, know who last touched it. I have my mental blocks up high tonight, but persistent thoughts are still getting through."

He nodded. "Like that man in the corner who's been staring at you, dreaming of being your lover?"

Halfway across the crowded gallery, Carter's head swung to the corner to see who Dad was talking about.

I knew exactly who he meant without looking. I didn't recognize the man, but there was something about him that seemed familiar. I nodded. "Yeah, like him." If I'd had my shields lower, I'd probably have picked up enough of a mental signature to place him, but I was blocking hard tonight. No doubt he was one of the very intense men who'd watched my daily progress on the huge mural on the side of the gallery.

My father stared down at me, his gaze charged with barely contained power. "I could kill him for you, so you needn't worry."

My throat went dry as I shook my head. "No, thank you. I have my gifts to keep me safe."

He gave a quiet grunt of approval and then looked over to where Mom and Declan were standing. "What about that one? Are you sure he can be trusted? Can you hear his thoughts?"

I pulled his arm down as I went up on tiptoe. Whispering, I said, "He's a magical null. I can touch him without visions and voices. I have a little bottle of seawater I carry with me, though, to reset my magic after he kisses me."

Nodding slowly, he pulled me on so we could continue our walk. "Wolves are strong. I can see that he has good sense and loves you. I approve."

Declan and I had never used that word. It made the butterflies in my stomach start up again. Dad stopped in front of my pottery, eyeing a large bowl that came up on one side in the shape of a wave.

"I like that I see myself in your art. The ocean is everywhere in here. As your father, it is a fitting tribute."

I glanced around. I supposed I could see where he got that. "It's me, though. I didn't know you. I have my own affinity with the water."

He nodded proudly. "Of course you do, through me." He looked over his shoulder into the back corner again. "I find him quite irritating."

"Uh, Carter," I said, trying not to tip off the humans that I was talking to the large man across the gallery by the front door. "Can you escort that guy out before my dad does something these people can't unsee?"

Carter moved toward the creepy guy and my father turned his back, looking out over the crowd again like he was surveying his subjects. "I suppose that's for the best."

A thought occurred to me. "I'm sorry. I don't even know. What's your name?"

He stared into my eyes again, a soft smile on his lips. "You may call me Father."

The butterflies flapped wildly. "And while I appreciate that very much, I'd really like to know your name." I looked back at Mom and Declan. "I mean, what did Mom call you?"

Detective Osso, Carter's older brother, walked in the front door and gestured to Declan.

My dad patted my hand. "Walk me out. I need to get back now."

"Oh." My butterflies drooped. "Of course. I'm really glad you were able to make it tonight and see the gallery."

We walked past Mom, and he pointedly did not look in her direction. When we stepped out onto the deck, he breathed in deeply and shook his head. His hair, multi-hued and curly like my own, was long again, hanging past his shoulders.

"May I visit again?" He glanced over cautiously before his chin lifted and he stared out at the waves.

"Yes, please." Butterflies resurrected, they bumped into each other like zombie insects.

"Good. I would like to get to know you, daughter." His perfect suit turned into a toga like it did the first time I saw him.

"I'd like that very much." Hands clutched in front of me, I added, "I always wanted a dad."

His austere expression softened. Leaning down, he kissed my forehead. "You've always had one." He glanced through the gallery windows and then turned his back to me. "I suppose a daughter should know her father's name."

I waited.

"You, little one, must call me Father. Or Dad." His brow creased at that moniker, but he smiled. "If your man needs to ask for me, though, he should use Mac. That was what she called me."

I was pretty sure I knew who the *she* was he was referring to, so I didn't ask. I didn't want to do anything to spoil this moment.

"Mac," I repeated.

He nodded once. "But that's not for you."

"No." I pulled his arm down again and kissed his cheek. I had a moment of fear that I'd see or hear something that would ruin this whole night, but he'd just kissed me and I hadn't heard anything, so I took the chance. Nothing but a strong jaw and a feeling of tentative affection.

The back door flew open.

"There you are!" Mary Beth said, waving me in. "I have people I need you to meet."

Looking around, I realized I was by myself. Dad was gone. "Bye." I waved at the ocean and followed my agent back in.

"Okay," Mary Beth murmured. "The Winslows will be back tomorrow morning. Tonight, I want to introduce you to Miles Cheng. He's a tech millionaire who's an heir to billions."

She took us to a man standing alone, studying Cecil 2.0. He was a few inches taller than me and impeccably dressed in a black suit with a matching black dress shirt.

"Mr. Cheng?" Mary Beth said. "Please allow me to introduce you to the artist, Arwyn Corey. Arwyn, this is Mr. Cheng, entrepreneur and art lover."

He turned, his gaze sweeping over me, before inclining his head. Thankfully, he knew not to try to shake my hand. "How do you do? I'm honored to meet you," he said in a gorgeous British accent. "Your work, as I'm sure you know, is extraordinary. But this—" He gestured to Cecil. "I've been staring at him for a little while now and I swear I see his tentacles move out of the corner of my eye. I don't understand how you make glass fluid."

I felt Declan move up beside me, but Mr. Cheng's eyes stayed on me. "I asked Ms. Peredel if I might speak with you about a commissioned piece."

I nodded. "Go on."

"I'd like you to make me a window. A circle five feet across." He paused. "Are you familiar with *A Thousand Li of Rivers and Mountains*?"

"Yes. Fan Kuan," I said, referring to a Chinese artist from the Song dynasty whose painting he'd named.

Finally, a smile. "I don't expect a replica. What I'd like is a piece of art glass inspired by that painting."

I considered the idea. I'd never done a window of that size. The challenge was exciting.

"I saw the glass ceiling you made for a nightclub in San Francisco," he added. "I must confess, I spent more time studying the ceiling than paying attention to the entertainment. Or my date, for that matter."

"The Bubble Lounge," I confirmed. I'd created a glass wave that hung from the ceiling over most of the nightclub. It was dark indigo on one side of the room, the color gradually lightening through blues and greens until it went foamy white on the other side of the club. The mermaid owner of the club wanted the ceiling to look like the ocean surface seen from below.

"That was a logistical nightmare," I said. "I made many smaller pieces of glass ocean and then had to transport them and fit them all together so the lines couldn't be seen."

"You didn't charge anywhere near enough for that job," Mary Beth said, "which is why I don't let you negotiate on your own anymore."

She was right about that. It was a hell of a job, but I was proud of the finished piece.

"Mr. Cheng," Mary Beth began, "I'm afraid Arwyn has just this evening accepted a commission that will keep her quite busy for the next few months. Can this project wait until the beginning of the year?"

He inclined his head again. "I desire art, not a mass-produced windowpane. I will wait, assuming Ms. Corey accepts."

"Oh, I assure you, Mr. Cheng," I said with a grin, "I've already begun designing it in my head."

"Splendid," he replied.

"Arwyn," Mary Beth said, pushing her long hair over her shoulder, "your mother looks as though she's trying to get your attention. You two go ahead while Mr. Cheng and I agree upon a price."

I said good evening, my head filled with plans. I'd never done a window like that. It would be horribly difficult, but I was excited to get started. After I made a fleet of octopuses for the Winslows, of course.

Declan squeezed me around the middle and we moved through the crowd toward Mom. "Damn, Ursula, look at you." He glanced over his shoulder and then back at me. "How much is she going to charge him for the window?"

I shrugged. "A lot. I saw Osso arrive. What was that about?"

Declan growled quietly. "One of my wolves got into a bar brawl tonight and killed a human."

"What?" I clutched his arm.

Expression dark, he shook his head. "That damn sorcerer is getting the wolves all twisted up. The pack is having trouble controlling their aggression." He blew out a breath. "It's going to happen again if we can't find and stop her."

"We will," I assured him. Somehow.

THREE

Quit Thinking So Loud

P eople lingered longer than we thought they would, which, I suppose, meant they enjoyed the gallery. We eventually ran out of wine, so we had the servers offering tea instead, with nary a complaint. When the last person was out and my heels were off, all I wanted was to crawl into bed and sleep for a week.

"Come on, Ursula," Declan said, picking me up and balancing me on his shoulder. "Time for lights out." He took the stairs to my bedroom two at a time. "All locked up?"

I groggily flicked my fingers, locking doors and windows. As an afterthought, I put the window shields down as well. Declan put me down beside the bed and then helped me undress. While I tossed my clothes on a chair that was rarely used for sitting, he grabbed an oversized t-shirt from my bureau, knowing it was what I preferred to sleep in.

"I still need to wash my face and brush my teeth," I grumbled.

He nudged me toward the bathroom, while he sat on the end of the bed and took off his boots. When I came out, he was already in bed, on the side he often used when he slept over. The routine was new and still exciting. Eyes heavy, he reached over and flipped back the covers on my side of the bed.

"Let's see if you can get a few hours in," he said, "before you have to get back up and see that rich couple in the morning."

I slid in, rested my head on his shoulder, and wrapped an arm around his middle. Legs tangled, we both let out a long sigh.

"Oh," I said, dragging myself back from oblivion. "What was up with Osso and the wolf? I never got the full story."

Declan growled, his chest—and me—vibrating with it. "Having a sorcerer working in the area is messing with the pack. Some of them were barely holding on to their humanity as it was. Logan did nothing as Alpha to teach them how to integrate their human and wolf sides. For some, it's innate. For others, it's like the wolf is constantly fighting for dominance."

He blew out a breath. "Wade—the wolf tonight—was at the Post Creek Roadhouse with some friends. He was more than a few beers and tequila shots in when he was walking back from the toilet. This other guy was carrying three beers and not looking. He bumped Wade's shoulder and spilled the beer on him."

Declan shook his head. "He was just some guy who made a mistake and then he was on the floor being pummeled by an enraged wolf. Osso said he thought the guy's neck was snapped almost immediately, but Wade kept going until the man's face was obliterated.

"The bartender called the cops right away. One guy tried to intervene and was thrown across the bar. Luckily, a patrol car was close. By the time Wade stopped punching and stormed out the front door, the cops had arrived, guns drawn.

"Wade flipped them off and went to his truck. The cops told him to stop or they'd shoot. Instead, he decided to attack and ended up dead in the dirt in front of the bar."

Declan's fingertips had been brushing up and down my arm as he spoke. "He didn't have to die. Neither of them did, damn it." We were quiet for a while, him no doubt worrying about his pack.

I, on the other hand, was furious. Calliope did this. She'd sold her soul to acquire power she hadn't been born with. Small and petty, filled with envy and too many grievances, she'd run to sorcery. She'd chosen the power a demon could lend her over her family, her own mother.

Nauseated and filled with shame, I hugged Declan to me. It felt like Cal was getting her sooty fingerprints all over him because of me. Had she not seen him with me at her mother's wake, would she have targeted the wolves?

"I'm so sorry," I whispered.

Declan kissed the top of my head. "Me too. Now shh. You're thinking too loud. Time for sleep."

Exhausted, I gave up and let myself tumble into dreamless oblivion.

"Wake up," Declan grumbled, his voice deeper than usual from sleep. He kissed my shoulder. "I have to get to work, and you need to get up. Your agent and that couple will be here soon."

I dragged the pillow over my head and tried to burrow into the quiet dark. I'd been working tirelessly for so long to make this gallery a reality and I'd done it. Now I just wanted to sleep.

The covers were ruthlessly yanked off me, but I curled up in self-defense, trying to conserve the stolen warmth. Soft lips and a scratchy beard made their way over my hip and down my leg. Grinning breathlessly under the pillow, I waited to see his next move.

By the time his kisses made it to my ankles, I was having a hard time pretending to be annoyed. A giggle escaped and he wrapped his hands around my ankles and dragged me into the center of the bed.

"Siren," he growled, sliding down my panties.

I tried to take off my t-shirt while lying down and ended up getting tangled in it. A moment later it was tugged off and thrown onto my laundry chair. Declan's gaze was hot and possessive as he took in every inch of me.

"Calling men to your shores," he continued, crawling up my body. "Luring us in only to destroy us."

What that man could do with his mouth should be illegal. "Not all men," I said on a sigh. "I only destroy the bad ones. There are still one or two of you I let live." I wrapped my legs around him as he nibbled on my neck.

"Only one," he murmured between kisses. "Only one of me." He slid his lips over my jaw and then sank into a kiss that had me forgetting my name. Bracing himself on his elbows, he stared down at me, his warm gaze making my insides gooey. "Only me"

I knew what he was asking. I nodded, my hand sliding down his ripped abdomen. "Only you."

When his arm slid under my leg, pulling it up, opening me to him, I expected fierce and possessive. Instead, he was slow and measured, watching my every reaction and responding with the single focus of an apex predator. He had me panting and quivering, but still he worked, drawing out every ounce of pleasure he could until I was moaning his name.

Later, both of us sweaty and spent, he picked me up and carried me into the shower. "No passing out," he said, putting me on my feet. "We both need to get cleaned up and get to work."

While he turned on the water and adjusted the temperature, I tried to stand on jelly legs. *Damn.*

I kind of loved that he always wanted to shampoo and condition my hair. I got a scalp massage while he dealt with the mass of curls. Once we were both cleaned and dried, my hair still up in a towel, he gave me another knee-weakening kiss and took off at a jog. He needed to get back to his place across the road before the workers showed up.

Instead of my usual overalls, I put on nice jeans, a thin, long-sleeved sweater, and paint-free sneakers. On my way to the bathroom to deal with my hair, I heard a knock at the back door.

Flicking my fingers, the shutters went up and I saw Mary Beth on the deck. Another flick and the door unlocked. Mary Beth walked in, wearing a very chic and asymmetrical black suit, her gaze going straight to me in the loft.

"Good morning," she said, all efficiency. "You finish getting ready and I'll get some tea brewing. We have about twenty minutes before the Winslows—George and Rose—arrive. I'll tidy down here. Is the hot shop presentable?"

"I think so," I said on a shrug. The fire room—as I'd named it— was where I did both my glassmaking and pottery. It was large and open, with high ceilings, like the rest of the former cannery, though I'd had my contractor add hinged windows to the roof so I'd have lots of natural light and good ventilation in there.

The door to the deck accordioned open, allowing for maximum airflow from the ocean to help cool the space when needed. The kiln was in a fireproof room with good ventilation that was built for it.

I walked through the workrooms in my head while I dealt with my hair. Had I left anything out that would be dangerous for them? I didn't think so. I got my hair to not-dripping-wet and called it good before putting on some mascara and lip gloss. As I jogged down the stairs, Mary Beth sailed through the studio and into the gallery to get the front door.

The couple were more interesting than I'd thought they'd be. They knew art. They didn't just collect it. They studied and appreciated it. Thankfully, Mary Beth did most of the talking. I just had to follow along, add some insights into the genesis of a project, and then let them debate its meaning and importance. Considering how much they were paying me, it was the least I could do.

As they were getting ready to leave, discussing with Mary Beth the best way to get everything shipped to them, I saw movement on my deck. Detective Hernández stood at the open doorway, hand lifted to knock on the doorframe before she saw the group standing in my studio. I put up a finger, asking her to wait, and then finished with the Winslows. It wouldn't do to piss off the people financing the next couple years of my art.

We walked them out the front of the gallery, where they had a town car waiting to take them to the airport. They'd flown to the West Coast just for my opening.

Selling my art wasn't new for me. I'd been doing it since I was a teen, and Mary Beth made sure I always made top dollar. So, yes, I was used to my work selling. It was normally done through private channels, through galleries in different parts of the world, my work just one of many from scores of wonderful artists.

This time, it was my gallery filled with my work, and it felt different.

As we watched the car pull away, Mary Beth turned to me. "Who is that on your deck?"

"Detective Hernández. We went to high school together back in the day. Not that we were friends or anything. She was cool and popular—"

"And you weren't," she interrupted, leading the way back into the gallery.

"Exactly. Anyway, she remembered the rumors about me, and she was dealing with a child abduction case, so she came to see if I could help. That was a few cases ago. My guess is she has a new one she wants my help on," I said, locking the front door behind us. I let her walk through the door to the studio first and then closed it behind us and headed for the back door.

Hernández was leaning over the railing of the deck, looking down. I wondered if my octopus friend Cecil was saying hello. When I came out, she turned with a smile that faltered as her gaze lifted over my shoulder.

It was a clear, glorious day. "Morning. Detective Hernández, this is my agent. Mary Beth, this is Sofia Hernández."

"Good morning," Mary Beth said. "And how much is the police department paying for your highly unique and extremely valuable gifts?"

Hernández was caught off guard. "Oh. I did offer but—"

"Leave her alone," I said, drawing up a stream of ocean water to reverse the effects of sleeping with Declan. As a null, he messed with my magic. Did it mean I got to touch him without hearing his thoughts or being dropped into visions? Hell, yes. It also meant some of my abilities were smothered. Dad's DNA ensured that, with a little ocean water, I was back to factory settings.

Cecil's tentacle slapped the surface in greeting.

"Good morning, Cecil," I called down before turning back to the detective. "Is there any chance you're just visiting to be social?"

When she shook her head, I sighed. Someone was dead.

FOUR

True. She Is Scary and Hot

Cecil slapped the surface again, taking my mind momentarily off murder. The last time I swam under the deck, I'd found that Poppy had made a safe little den for their eggs with rocks against one of the pylons holding up the deck.

The gallery had been a fish cannery in its past life. Gran purchased the dilapidated building when I was little because she said she knew it would one day be mine. Years later, with money from my first big sales, I purchased the property from her and began remodeling.

Two of the outermost purple-algae-covered pylons were home to my large, gorgeously orange starfish friends Charlie and Herbert. "Good morning, gentlemen. You're looking quite dapper."

Mary Beth leaned over as well. "Hello, Cecil. Thank you for looking out for our girl." One of Cecil's tentacles rose above the water and swirled in a circle before dropping under again. "See?" she said, nudging me with her elbow. "He likes me best."

"P'fft." I scanned the ocean, looking for a dark head to pop up. "Wilbur?" I called, looking for my selkie friend. We played fetch most days, but he'd been absent more and more often lately. He was a guard my father sent to watch me. Perhaps Dad had decided

I didn't need the extra protection. I worried, though, that it was more that Dad needed him back, that something more pressing was brewing under the surface.

"So," Mary Beth said, sitting on a bench, "why aren't you letting the police pay you for your services?"

I turned back to see Hernández watching my agent warily. That showed good sense. Mary Beth was no one to mess with. Hernández, though human, knew that supernaturals existed. She knew her sometime detective partner Osso was a bear shifter. She knew I was a wicche and Declan a werewolf. She'd even met a vampire and part demon. I was surprised she hadn't run for the hills yet. The way she clocked Mary Beth told me she was pretty sure my agent wasn't completely human either.

"Because," I said, "if they're coming to me for help, it means that someone is dead and I refuse to profit off some else's tragedy. Bad juju, that."

Mary Beth thought a moment and then nodded. "Sensible." She stood. "I'm going to put special stickers on all the Winslow purchases. I'll have the shippers come Monday, when you're closed. You'll be here to direct them, yes?"

I nodded, sitting beside the detective. "Just give me the time they're coming so I can make sure I'm here."

"Good," she said, heading back in. "I'll call my contact and set it up." Just before she closed the door, she turned back. "You open at two this afternoon, right?"

I nodded.

She skewered Hernández with a glare. "She has her own work to do. Don't make her late."

Hernández held up her hands in surrender and we waited until the door closed.

"Damn," she breathed. "She's scary. And hot."

I nudged the detective with my shoulder. "Look at you, sharing your hot girl opinions with me."

"Yeah, well, she scared the professionalism right out of me."

Shaking her head, she pulled her ever-present notepad out of her jacket pocket.

"I won't tell your girlfriend," I said.

"Eh." She shrugged. "Andie would agree she's hot. And scary." Shaking her head, Hernández flipped open her notebook. "You're right. I am here about someone being dead. I have two people murdered in much the same way, with no evidence left at either scene. So far, I can find nothing connecting the two. One's a middle-aged woman, a judge. The other's a man in his late twenties who works part-time at the station. When I tell you they have nothing in common, I mean they don't even use the same laundry detergent."

Leaning back against the bench, I thought longingly of my nice warm bed. I might have been able to get a few more hours before opening. Then again, without Declan, I'd have a hard time sleeping.

"They have the law in common," I said.

Hernández shook her head. "When I said he worked at the station, I meant he worked in records. He's a drummer in a local band. The part-time work he did for us was his only stable source of income. As far as I could tell, his path never crossed with the judge."

"Okay, but isn't the *no evidence* thing a clue?" I asked. "That takes some expertise, doesn't it? Maybe your killer is a crime scene cleaner."

"Don't think that hasn't occurred to me," she grumbled, glancing at the back door. "So, can I borrow you for a little while? I'll have you back before opening."

I stood. "Yeah, I guess. I need to be back no later than one and preferably before. I've got a lot of empty shelves in the gallery to fill." I waved her into the studio with me. "I didn't get a chance to eat anything this morning."

The clear muffin box on the counter looked emptier than yesterday. "It looks like Declan took a few. I have a strawberry-pistachio, a salted caramel, and a marbled chocolate and cinnamon. What'll you have?"

"I want the salted caramel!" Mary Beth called from the gallery.

"Okie-dokie." I tore off a paper towel to pick it up.

Mary Beth met me at the doorway to the gallery, the phone at her ear. She took a bite of the muffin while *mmhm*-ing to whoever was on the line, and returned to the gallery.

"I'll take the strawberry," Hernández said. "I had a strawberry one before and it was amazing."

"Ah, thanks. The pistachio adds a nice nuttiness to it. Hopefully you enjoy this recipe too." I offered the pinkish muffin in the box to the detective and then took the last one with another paper towel, not wanting crumbs on my gloves. "I just need to get my backpack."

Taking a bite, I went to the doorway and waved to get Mary Beth's attention.

Eyebrows raised, she waited.

"She's taking me to a crime scene. I told her I have to be back by one."

"Twelve is better," she warned.

"I told her that too." I studied the gallery, taking another bite, while I made mental notes of what needed to be filled in. If I was out of anything—and I was—I'd need to rearrange the displays.

Mary Beth glanced around as well. "I'll fill in what I can. I'm flying back to New York this afternoon. The shipping service will be here Monday at ten. I'll leave you a list of everything they should be boxing up."

"Okay, thanks. I'll be back as soon as I can." I grabbed my backpack from the base of the stairs.

I'd started taking it when I went anywhere with the police. I carried a sketchbook and pencils, so I could draw what I saw. I also had bandages and antiseptic after one harrowing experience when the cuts the victim had endured showed up on my body. I even had snacks and water. The police weren't big on feeding me. And my plastic honey bear bottle that I filled with ocean water. Sometimes I needed a little water fae boost.

Hernández waited for me on the deck. I pulled out the honey bottle, dumped the water back into the ocean, and then held my hand over the waves, pulling up a stream of seawater. When the fountain of water was level with me, I collected some into the jar, screwed the lid back on, and stowed the bottle.

The detective knew I was a wicche but still stared whenever I did something wicchey.

I shouldered the backpack, took another bite, and headed around the outside of the gallery, Hernández following.

"You don't hide that stuff around me anymore," she said, hitting her key fob and unlocking the doors of her very plain sedan.

"Do I need to?" I asked, sliding into the passenger seat.

"No," she said before taking a bite and wrapping up the rest of muffin, wedging it into her cup holder. "I guess I'm just off balance when I see you do fantastical things. It's cool, though. I'm getting used to it." She checked the time on the dashboard. "I'm not sure if we have time for both crime scenes. I'll take you to the first and we'll see from there."

I nodded, finishing the muffin. "Hey, any news on the little creep who killed Christopher and Ana?" That series of abductions and murders was the first time I'd worked with Detectives Hernández and Osso.

She shook her head, flicking on her turn signal. "Still awaiting trial. He's undergoing psychiatric testing. His lawyer is claiming trauma response from losing his parent. The DA and our doctor say psychopathy."

Poor Christopher and Ana. The death of a child, that destruction of innocence and potential, cut deep. Staring out the window, I said, "I agree with your DA and doctor."

"Yeah," Hernández said, her voice heavy. It was hard to think of the case and not be weighed down by it.

She drove us into a wealthy neck of the woods and pulled into a circular drive in front of a Spanish Colonial mansion.

"Nice," I said, noting the lush landscaping and the grand home. The only thing marring the picture was the yellow crime tape at the door.

Hernández climbed out, and I joined her. A prickle ran down my spine. I looked in the usual places and saw lenses. "She has security cameras all over. You guys didn't see anything?"

The detective shook her head and led the way to the front door. Bypassing a special lock, she opened the door and let us in. It was beautiful, with large terra-cotta tile floors, creamy stucco walls, and dark wood beams on the cathedral ceilings. A curved staircase to the right circled up from the foyer to the second floor.

"A lot of house for one person. I assume this is the judge's house."

Hernández nodded. "Her husband passed last year. Their kids are grown and moved away. Friends say she was thinking about moving, of scaling down, but the house held so many good memories, she was having a hard time moving forward."

"Real estate agents know how to clean up and make everything look presentable," I said. "Maybe the killer was someone she'd just met about her house."

Hernández nodded again. "I'm looking into it, but she doesn't appear to have contacted any agencies. A house like this would only list through a handful of firms. This place will go for three or four million." She shrugged. "The responding officer's wife is a real estate agent and that was his guess."

"Given the neighborhood, the property size—wait. Is that a golf course out the back window?" I shook my head. "This place is going for a lot more than that." I walked through the foyer, past an office and a sitting room, into a huge living room with windows onto a slate patio, with flowering shrubs and tall trees. A well-dressed man and his caddy moved into the fairway to take a shot.

Lowering my voice, I said, "Are we sure this judge wasn't on the take? This house seems way fancier than a judge could afford."

"I wondered the same," she said, "but her husband was a surgeon and came from money. There are no marks on her record, no whispers of questionable rulings."

I walked around the living room, easing down my defenses. She had photographs everywhere, some posed, some candid. I leaned in close to study a family portrait. The judge was a beautiful Black woman who exuded reliability. She was not one to forget a birthday or recital. Steady. Her husband was a tall, thin Asian man whose eyes smiled even in photos. He was the one who got her to shake off a hard day and play Scrabble with him or go for a long walk. Their two children—boy and girl—were almost as tall as their father, though the son had his mother's serious mien.

"Can you stand in the kitchen or something?" I asked. "I want to walk the whole house and see what I pick up. Okay?"

"Sure." Hernández left the room, retreating the way we'd come. Lowering my mental blocks even more, I opened myself up. Echoes of laughter and raised voices, tears and shrieks of joy. It was a home.

When I walked past the tall glass doors leading out onto the patio, I felt a chill run down my spine. Moving closer, I felt a wave of barely suppressed rage wash over me. This was where the killer had entered.

FIVE

Probably Shouldn't Have Eaten That Muffin

I took off a glove, blew out a breath, and braced for it.

Fucking bitch thinks she's so much better than me.

A dark-gloved hand reaches for the knob. He pauses to look through the glass door. Reflected in the picture frame on the wet bar, he sees a green glowing light.

He pulls a leather case from his pocket and selects a thin, shiny instrument. Moonlight glints off the tool in his hand as he hunches over to use it. The lock clicks open. Dressed all in black, he steps in, his gaze going to the alarm system. Unarmed. Perfect.

A laser-thin beam of light sweeps the large living room, the artwork and expensive knickknacks. He has no interest in valuables.

Stupid cow is sitting on a fortune here and she's too dumb to turn on the alarm.

Moving swiftly, he checks each room on his way toward the front of the house. He moves in a slow circle, making sure he hasn't missed anything. No cameras inside. Only out on the grounds.

He admits, if only to himself, he'd been scared. He wasn't sure if he'd go through with it. Now that he's here, though, he can't wait. He hadn't anticipated the excitement.

Taking the stairs two at a time, he makes his way to the second floor. Lots of doors, and all of them closed. The tile floors continue up here, but he has rubber-soled shoes and so moves silently from door to door, straining to hear signs of life. He has time. He doesn't need to hurry, and it wouldn't do to pass a door that wasn't checked, only to have her come out behind him. No. He'll do his sweep in a systematic fashion.

Feeling a charge of adrenaline every time he puts his head to a door, every time he gets closer to his target, he realizes he's getting hard. A secret smile plays over his lips. He knows what's going to happen, but she doesn't. He has all the power now.

At the last door, he hears slow, even breathing and he feels a clutch in his gut. This is it.

The door swings open noiselessly. Of course. These fancy places would never stand for a squeak. She wouldn't understand real problems. The rest of us have to struggle. Rich bitch like this is probably getting payoffs right, left, and center. Crooked. She doesn't deserve any of this and she has no right to tell hard-working people what to do.

He moves to the foot of the bed and watches her sleep. She doesn't even know. He has all the power now. Watching, he lets his breathing match hers. They're in sync now. He steps to the side of the bed, heart racing. He wishes he could make it last for hours but wants it done now.

Ready to burst, he grabs her, yanking her toward him. She wakes, confused but alert. When she sees the dark silhouette looming over her, her eyes widen. Before she can scream, his hands are around her neck. She fights, trying to break his grip on her, but that only excites him more.

She's nothing, a washed-up old bitch who isn't even safe in her own house. He has the power now. She looks like a fish on dry land, mouth open, trying to suck up air. Her body convulses and he feels a force race through him. Life and death are in his hands.

He knows when she dies. He spasms too. On a long, guttural moan, he drops her back onto the bed. She's nothing now. He's erased her.

And he smiles.

Throat throbbing, feeling sick, my gaze went straight to the family portrait I'd studied earlier. They'd been such a beautiful family. They were happy. You could see it in the ease and famil-iarity. No tense shoulders or angry eyes at odds with a bright smile. They'd loved one another. Those poor children—adults now—had lost both their parents in the span of one year. It was tragic.

I put my glove back on and walked through the house and out the front door. I wanted air and seawater to deal with the pain.

A few moments later, Detective Hernández stepped out and found me sitting on the stairs. "Hey. I thought I heard the front door open."

Nodding, I stared at the bright fuchsia bougainvillea crawling up the side of the garage. "I needed out."

She locked the door and then sat beside me. "Did you see anything?"

"Yeah." And I told her the ugliness that had happened in that beautiful house.

"I checked on the alarm," Hernández said. "Her kids told me she sometimes forgets to arm it. They said she got into the habit of waiting until everyone was home before arming it because the son's dyslexic and was always putting the code in wrong and setting it off. Now, even though she's alone here, she still waits to arm it until she goes to bed. Unless she forgets."

She pulled her notebook out of her pocket but didn't need to look at it. "The security company confirmed that it wasn't set every night. Maybe once or twice a month, it was left unarmed."

She stood and gestured to her car. "I should get you back now. Maybe tomorrow you can see the second victim's place."

I sighed and nodded, following her. "Yeah, I can do that."

When she turned on the ignition, she said, "So it wasn't random? He wanted to kill her specifically?"

"Not random," I confirmed, kind of wishing I hadn't eaten that muffin earlier. I studied my gloves, black today and so like his, it made my stomach twist anew. "He wore black gloves and rubber-soled shoes that were quiet on the tile. He didn't touch anything other than two doorknobs and the victim herself. He listened at doors along the hall, but he didn't press his ear to the door. It was more like holding his ear close to the doorjamb, listening for her breathing.

"He knew, though," I continued. "He knew which door she'd be behind, knew the master suite would be at the end of the hall, but all the skulking and invading her space was getting him excited."

She stopped at a red light and turned to me. "Excited? As in, *excited*?"

"Yep. Hard as a rock and feeling quite powerful."

The light changed and there was a quick honk behind us. Hernández hit the gas. "The medical examiner determined no sexual assault. You're saying there was?"

"No." I thought about how to explain it. "It was more that the power of being in control, of having her at his mercy, got him stirred up. I didn't pick up any thought to rape her. Strangling her, though, her death throes sent him over the edge. He came in his pants and groaned like it was the greatest sex he'd ever had in his life."

Hernández pulled over to write in her notebook. "The other victim is male. I believe it's the same killer. The manner of death is the same, but again, the victims have absolutely nothing in common, so I could be wrong. That's why I want to bring you there. You can tell me if I'm on the right track or if it was his landlord, pissed that he'd missed rent again.

"If it's the act of killing that excites him," she continued, "that might be why he switched victim genders. Killers—serial killers, anyway—usually stick to one gender, often one race, for their preferred victim."

We were quiet most of the drive back to the gallery, each lost in our own thoughts. I kept circling around an idea, though. "I think he knew her and that she'd done something to make him feel small and powerless. Having power over her was very important."

"Okay," Hernández replied, nodding. "Maybe she ruled against him. I'm already doing a search on any convicts who were tried in her court and are out of jail now. I'll focus on that."

She pulled up in front of the Sea Wicche at twelve twenty.

"Thanks for getting me back on time," I said, opening the door and hefting my backpack.

"Listen," she began, tapping the steering wheel. "Your agent's right. We've gotten into a bad habit of just showing up and expecting you to drop what you're doing and go with us. We really appreciate your help, but you have your own work to do. I'll try to be better about calling ahead and checking if you're available. Okay?"

One leg out of the car, I turned back to her. "I know I fought against doing this at first. Psychically and physically, it's tough on me, but I've begun to enjoy it too. I like solving the mystery and helping to catch the bad guys. Mostly, though, what I need to focus on is finding and stopping my cousin. Once the sorcery stops, a lot of this weird, out-of-pocket violence you two investigate will stop with it."

"Hopefully," she said.

"Hopefully," I echoed.

I got out while she picked up the wrapped muffin. "And thanks for this. I'll eat it on the way into the station."

"You're welcome." I slammed the door and waved. As she pulled out into traffic, I jogged up the steps of the gallery, my mind switching to what I needed to do before we opened.

SIX

Families Are Complicated

When I went in, my teenaged cousins Frank and Faith were already working on filling in the shelves and my Aunt Elizabeth was standing at the tea bar talking with my Aunt Hester. Elizabeth was Mom's only remaining sister. Bridget, Abigail, and Sylvia were gone now. We'd learned recently that Abigail had been a sorcerer as well. She'd been the one to train Calliope when she was young. She'd also been the one to kill her sister—Sam Quinn's mom—Bridget. My cousin Calliope brought about the death of her own mother, Sylvia.

Sometimes it felt like we needed a chart, some kind of messed-up family tree, that showed which of us had become sorcerers and killed off the others of us.

Aunt Hester was divorced from my Uncle Roger, mom's brother. He was a tool and didn't live around here anymore. Their daughter Pearl had been killed recently by a shitty human serial killer and Hester had been having a very difficult time wanting to live a life without her daughter in it.

Consequently, I'd been nagging her to stop by for tea and snacks, even talking her into working here a little to get her out of her very sad house that was filled with pictures and memories of Pearl. I was glad to see Elizabeth and Hester spending more time together. They were both incredibly kind women, and no doubt benefitted from talking with someone who understood loss.

My mom Sybil would have been a potential member of this club, but she was too rigid to admit weakness. She carried the weight of the Corey coven on her shoulders and had since she was a child, when she'd been tapped to eventually take over as the head of the family. Knowing my mother, she'd done what she could to put the recent death of Sylvia, her sister and best friend, out of her mind so she could carry on with her duties. Mom was so like her own mother. Neither Mom nor Gran showed weakness. They were women who were trained to rule, and they did not break.

They'd decided, as two-thirds of the Corey Council, that I would be next in line after Mom, but I wasn't like them. Not better or worse, just different. Mom had Gran and Great-Gran as her mentors and they were tough as nails, always putting our family's safety and prosperity first.

I was different, though, the powerfully magic half-fae wicche who couldn't touch someone without reading their innermost thoughts or having visions of their future. They knew I was an asset to the family but weren't sure what to make of me beyond that.

Mom—in her own way—was as indulgent as Gran had been when I was little, though perhaps for different reasons. As a scary-powerful half-faeling, I was treated differently than the rest of the family. Wicches, Coreys especially, can be quite bigoted about pure blood family lines. Great-Gran distrusted the hell out of me. Gran seemed to see me as more of a powerful weapon in the family's arsenal. Mom, I believe, saw me as a little replica of her great love, the one she'd been forced to give up. I was the only one who was truly all hers.

Gran saw my potential to help the family. Mom, though, wanted me to live up to my own potential. I'd misread them for most of my life, thinking Mom saw me as a major disappointment. It turned out that I'd predicted something heartbreaking when I was quite young, and Mom had never really gotten over it. We were working on rebuilding our relationship, and I was secretly working on getting Mom and Dad back together.

"Here she is," Elizabeth said as I leaned on the counter beside her. She gave me an air kiss, knowing she couldn't touch me without causing problems. "I was just dropping off the kids. What time should I be back to pick them up?"

Hester slid me a cup of tea. "Thank you." I inhaled deeply and then took a sip. *Mmm.*

I turned back to Elizabeth and said, "Seven should be fine. They shouldn't need to stay later than closing." I lowered my voice and said, "Do they like working here okay? I don't want them to feel obligated if they hate it."

"Are you kidding?" she said with a wave of her hand. "They love it here. It's much cooler than any of their friends' jobs and they're getting paid more. Faith loves working on the ocean and has been running out to say hello to your Cecil."

Elizabeth tapped the counter and said to Hester, "This week, okay? You pick the restaurant and we'll get lunch."

Hester nodded with the hint of a quiet smile.

"Now," Elizabeth said, linking her elbow with mine, "walk me to my car. I need to ask you a favor."

I dropped my backpack on the floor and walked with my aunt out the front door.

Patting my sleeve, she said, "That was a ruse. You were supposed to contact us for dinner so we could help you find Calliope. Remember, my little family has some unique gifts in the Corey clan, gifts Cal isn't aware of because she was never particularly interested in me or my children. In the larger Corey coven, I think I'm seen as the innocuous one," she said on a laugh. "I'm the Jane Bennet of this family."

I laughed with her. "Meaning you're the great beauty who marries well?"

Grinning, she replied, "I did marry well. Robert is a wonderful man. Your mom and Bridget are and were the powerhouses in the family. My gifts are more quiet and unassuming and my children…" She rolled her eyes. "It would be better if they told you. So, will you allow us to help?"

"Yes, please." I felt like such an idiot. "It's all been so crazy, I completely forgot that we were supposed to get together and plan. I need all the help I can get. Does tomorrow night work?"

She thought a moment. "How about Tuesday? Robert works late at the hospital on Mondays and he'd like to be a part of this discussion."

"Absolutely. Do you want to come here? If Bracken is feeling up to it, he can join us," I said, walking her to the driver's side of her SUV.

"Perfect. Six?"

I nodded.

"Good. And can I just say, I love that you've let Uncle Bracken live beside you." She stared down at her shoes a moment and then said, "Mom is—well, she isn't usually kind to her brother. He's always been a gentle soul who was a little different. Mom respects strength, so I'm not sure she knew what to do with him. In her defense, though, my Gran—your Great-Gran—was a merciless woman who had no use for her youngest son."

Shaking her head, she hit her key fob, making the SUV chirp. "None of that matters now. I just wanted you to know that Bracken's life hasn't been easy, and it means a lot to me—and him, I'm sure—that you're giving him the space and understanding he needs, as well as the family he wants." She took my hand and squeezed.

"I love having him here too." With a shrug, I added, "I mean, it's no secret that most of the family doesn't like or trust me. Having my great-uncle living next door, visiting for tea and a muffin, helping me research where Calliope could be hiding, it's lovely and helps me feel not so alone too."

Elizabeth reached out her open window and held my gloved hand. "I'm sorry. I will say, though, that those who are standoffish with you are mostly afraid of your mother—and you, come to that.

There can be insecurity and jealousy in any family, but it seems particularly bad in ours."

"As evidenced by the number of Coreys choosing sorcery," I said.

"Precisely." She shook her head on a sigh. "I would offer to bring dessert to dinner on Tuesday, but given who I'm talking to, that seems silly."

"How about an hors d'oeuvre?" I suggested.

She tapped the car door. "Perfect. I'll do that and I'll get out of your hair now. I know you have a lot to do." She gazed up at the gallery. "It's remarkable what you've accomplished here. We're so proud of you."

My throat tightened. It was such a simple statement. Why did it have me tearing up? Blinking, I looked down the road toward Declan's place. "It's clear. You should go before we get another long line of cars."

"I will. See you soon." And she pulled out onto the road and drove away.

I had to stand for a minute in the sunshine and breeze. It had been a pretty big twenty-four hours for me, which was probably why her approval hit so hard. As I struggled with my emotions, trying to force them back into the box that had served me well most of my life, I noticed a car parked along the side of the road. My sight wasn't as strong as Declan's, but it was still quite good. A man who seemed vaguely familiar sat in his car with his phone up like he was filming me. *Great.* I gave him a magical push to leave and then went back in to get ready for opening.

SEVEN

The Power of a Disapproving Look

Hester handed me a letter from Mary Beth, explaining in detail what the Winslows had purchased and how it all needed to be prepared for the shipping company tomorrow.

"Thank you for this," I said, holding up the note. "I didn't get to thank you last night. That was very kind of you to jump behind the counter and start brewing tea when you saw the wine was running low."

She waved away my gratitude. "It gave me something to do," she said, walking back behind the counter. She was wearing a blue-gray blouse and black slacks today, which was definitely better than the full black she'd been wearing since her daughter's death.

"I like your blouse. It looks pretty with your eyes." Hester was a Corey by marriage. Where most Coreys had black hair and green eyes, Hester, born a Goode, was pale: light blonde hair, light blue eyes. The black clothing had been so harsh on her, as was the mourning itself. Hopefully, the lighter top was a sign that the grief hadn't pulled her under.

Embarrassed, she turned back to the counter, rearranging her brewing supplies. "I just ordered some new clothes so you wouldn't have to see me showing up in the same three outfits all the time."

"Well, you look fabulous. Doesn't she, Faith?" My cousin was walking by with two vases from the back.

She paused, caught the context right away, and smiled. "You do, Aunt Hester. I like that color on you." Faith then turned to me. "Frank and I weren't sure. Should we bring it all out or do you want us to make the displays a little lighter, since it's not opening night?"

"Excellent point," I said, walking her across the gallery to the display tables and giving Hester a break from all the attention. "I think I do want the tables and shelves lighter. It should look like an art gallery, not a souvenir shop."

"Told you," Frank said. "I've been putting things into the back, not bringing more out. Faith was worried you'd want the opposite."

I took a moment to study their work. "Which of you is the artistic one?" I asked.

Frank grinned, while Faith pointed at her brother. These two were over a decade younger than me and were by far my favorite cousins. How different my childhood would have been if I'd had these two to hang out with.

Working together, we moved some pieces in, a lot of pieces out, and set up the gallery for opening. It was real. Last night hadn't been a fluke. My art gallery was open for business. Glancing around, my heart swelled at the ones here, helping me make my dream come true.

The youngest, Frank and Faith, were a beautiful combination of their parents, with light brown skin, green eyes, and ready smiles. Frank kept his hair short, like his father's. Faith wore hers in thick braids that fell to her shoulders, but both were currently dressed like waiters, wearing black pants and white shirts.

I pointed between the two. "Did you guys create your own uniform?"

"That was her," Frank said.

"I wanted it to be obvious that we worked here," Faith explained, putting the vases down on the display table. "I had Mom order us matching shirts in a bunch of different colors, but always black pants and black shoes."

"We look like waiters," he complained. "And she's been looking at name tags online."

"Just for ideas," she explained to me. "I figured you could make us something much cooler than anything we could find for sale."

"Would you want that?" I asked. "You don't have to dress alike or wear names tags if you don't want to."

The two shared a look and then Frank said, "Faith is right. If it's obvious that we work here, then people won't be giving us a suspicious side-eye."

At what was no doubt my expression of outrage, he held up his hands. "They were okay last night. There were only a couple of people watching us a little too closely, double-checking their receipts." He shrugged and then gestured to his sister. "If we have to go to the mall, we always end up with security following us."

Faith grinned at her brother. "Until Frank creates a distraction that pulls the guards away and gives us some breathing room." She shrugged in almost the same way her brother did. "That's why we prefer shopping online. Anyway, I was looking at different name tags that give hometowns or interests or whatever, but we think just names."

Seething that these two already had to have strategies to avoid bigots made me want to go out and punch everyone. I kept it under wraps, though. I didn't want them to feel like they had to watch what they told me.

"Speaking as someone who has had to deal with creeps my whole life, I say no names. Don't give them any personal information. You guys are here to sell my artwork, to clean and arrange. You're not here to become besties with the customers. They don't have any right to your personal information, okay? Polite doesn't mean you make yourselves vulnerable to people with ill intent."

They both nodded, their expressions more mature than their years.

"I'll make you badges with the name of the gallery, but not your names. And if anyone—and I do mean anyone—ever makes you uncomfortable, you let me know." I wiggled my fingers at them. "There's a reason the whole family is scared of me."

They both grinned, though the look in Frank's eyes turned speculative, like he was looking forward to seeing exactly what I could do.

"And don't forget me," Carter said, walking in from my studio. Carter, like his brother Detective Osso, was a bear shifter. "Just because I have ear buds in doesn't mean I can't hear you. Call me and I'm there. I got no problem throwing assholes out."

"I'm here too," Hester called. "I may not have Carter's strength or Arwyn's very powerful magic, but I have perfected a painfully disappointed and disapproving look."

The kids laughed.

"It may not seem like much," she continued, "but it has shamed many a creep into quietly moving on."

"A superpower, indeed," I agreed.

Hester handed Carter a cup of coffee and he went to his spot by the front door.

I surveyed the work Frank and Faith had done and felt my unease settling. "This looks perfect. I worried the police stuff was going to make me late and I wouldn't be happy with how the gallery looked when I opened. This," I said, gesturing around, "is exactly right."

"Like you said," Frank began, "it's a gallery, and I wanted every piece to look special, not like it was mass-produced and we had boxes of it in back. We knew you needed to fill everything for the opening. It was crushed in here."

Faith nodded. "It was."

"A regular day shouldn't be like that," Frank continued. "Right?"

I shook my head. "Let's hope not. My goal is for us to work a couple of nice, easy days a week and call it good."

"I heard that," Carter muttered approvingly before taking a sip of his coffee.

Faith, who I could already see was the worrier, said, "But can you afford to pay us if you don't sell your art?"

Pointing around the gallery, I said, "Do you see all the pieces with the green stickers on them?"

They nodded.

"All of that has already been purchased. It's being boxed up and shipped to the East Coast tomorrow."

The kids eyes got big as they spun in a circle, hunting for green dots. Carter blew out a low whistle.

"Oh my," Hester breathed. "I guess your gallery is a success."

"So far," I said. "What that means, though, is that everyone can relax. If we don't sell anything today, it's cool. Everyone's getting paid."

The teens grinned at each other.

"What do the white dots mean?" Hester asked.

I looked to where she pointed and thought back. "They mean I need to call my agent and ask. I think those were sold to that other collector last night." I shrugged. "I was talking to my dad at the time," I said with a big grin. "And that is a phrase I have never before used in my life."

"I was going to ask you," Faith whispered. No idea why. "That man is your dad?" She glanced at her brother. "You were right."

"Mom had always told us that no one knew who your dad was," Frank explained, "but there was something about that guy. He gave off immense power and you have the same eyes. Hair too."

"His eyes are a bright blue. Mine are green," I said, confused.

"Yeah, but the shape is the same," Frank clarified. "And you don't have Corey green eyes. Yours are a brighter color, like if you mixed your mom's dark green and his bright blue, you'd get your light green that sometimes looks almost teal. I don't know. It's also the shape of his face. Our moms have heart-shaped faces. Yours is more angular like your dad's."

The butterflies from last night returned. I looked like my dad. "Cool."

I checked the time on my phone. "Okay. We have ten minutes until we open. Everybody do whatever you need to do. Remember, there's a bathroom in my studio. Feel free to use it whenever you need it. Even if I'm working in there, it's fine. I don't distract easily."

I remembered what Elizabeth had told me about Faith. "And if anyone wants to say hello to Cecil before we open, meet me on the deck in a couple of minutes." I grabbed my backpack, took it into my studio, and left it by the steps to the loft. I ran up and used the full bathroom, leaving the half bath downstairs for whoever might need it, and checked if I was presentable.

I brushed my teeth again and then went downstairs and out the back door, finding my whole staff on the deck, looking over the railing.

Leaning over with them, I called, "Hello, Cecil!"

His tentacles slapped at the surface. I heard a quiet gasp from Faith and a chuckle from Carter. I glanced around for the tennis ball and saw it sitting under a bench.

"Don't go anywhere," I called, running into the studio for the orange ball flipper thing. I used it to pick up the soggy ball and then went back to the railing. "Okay, everyone look out at the water." I reached back and flung the tennis ball, sending it sailing over the waves.

On a bark of joy, Wilbur shot out from under the deck and went after it.

"You have a pet seal?" Frank asked, eyes wide.

"He's not my pet," I said and then lowered my voice. "You guys know my dad is water fae, right?"

Hester and Carter nodded, but Frank and Faith shook their heads.

"Your dad is fae?" Frank whispered.

Huh. I thought the whole family knew that much at least. Then again, Elizabeth wasn't a gossip, so it shouldn't have been surprising that her children didn't know. "Yes. That's also why I have ocean friends. Wilbur, the harbor seal you just saw, is a selkie and one of my father's guards."

Everyone's eyes got large at that. "So, when he's in his seal skin, we play fetch, but he, just like all the other creatures of the sea, is deserving of your respect. And if you ever see a pale naked guy out here, come get me. It means Emrys—Wilbur's real name—has a message from my dad."

Their varying expressions of shock and wonder cracked me up. I checked my phone again. "Time to open."

I had a moment to wonder if I'd overshared, but then decided to let it go. If three wicches and a shifter couldn't keep a secret, who could? Plus, they worked here. They needed to know who they were working for so they could be prepared for weird stuff.

I was wrong about my belief that it'd be a quiet day. It was not. It wasn't as crowded as last night and there were no big rollers—as far as I knew—but we did a steady stream of sales all afternoon. Unlike last night, when big pieces were sold, today we sold lots of the three-hundred-dollar-and-under items. We also had tons of people just looking around, which was cool.

The strange man who'd been staring at me last night tried to come back in, but Carter stopped him at the door. The guy argued, but Carter was very persuasive. I was standing near Hester at the time and moved forward in case a magical push was needed.

Carter kept it quiet and discreet, telling the man this was private property and he was making the artist uncomfortable, so he wasn't welcome.

After sputtering a few *Well, I never* type comments, the man left.

Carter turned, saw me, and shook his head. "Sorry, but I could see it in his eyes. That one isn't giving up."

EIGHT

Oh, Thank Goodness. The Raccoons Have Arrived

When we closed at seven, there were several groups lagging behind that had to be moved along. Elizabeth came in to collect her kids as Carter was locking the front door.

"I drove by earlier," she said, "and your parking lot was full. Was it a good day?"

Hester took off her apron and walked around the counter. "It was, though much busier than Arwyn thought it would be," she said on a laugh. "Some psychic she is."

"Yeah, yeah." I rolled my eyes. "I can't see my own future. You know that. And I figured anyone interested would have been in last night."

"People have had their eyes on this place for months and months," Carter said. "I have a feeling we'll be busy for a while. At least until everyone gets a chance to experience it themselves."

"Mom," Frank said, "is it okay if we fill in before we go?" He was tapping on the point-of-sale tablet screen, doing the totals and shutting down the software. "And Arwyn, you had a really good day. I sent the day's totals to your email."

"Thank you," I said. "Thank you all. But you two don't need to stay. We don't open again until next weekend. We have time to fill in."

"But you have that big order to deal with," he pressed. "You don't have time for this stuff. Faith and I can do it. I was also thinking. I can make lists for you of which items and which price points are selling the best and if there are a lot of people requesting something you don't make. For instance, Monterey is often linked with otters, but you don't sell any glass or ceramic otters. Oh, and I think you should sell your photographs just mounted on a board and put in plastic sleeves. More people can afford fifty or a hundred or whatever for a photograph that they frame or not themselves than they can afford a thousand for an oversized one already framed on the wall."

He came around the counter and continued, "You know what I mean? Maybe some photos can be sold as individual shots—five-by-seven and eight-by-ten—and the rest of your more spectacular shots are only sold in the larger format with the frame you've chosen for that photo."

I stared at him a moment, thinking.

"I mean, it's your gallery," he said, now seeming embarrassed. "It was just a thought."

Faith glanced between her brother and me, clearly wondering if he'd overstepped.

"I thought I was just hiring salespeople and instead I got a business manager," I said, clapping my gloved hands. "Those are fabulous ideas, and I'd love to know what customers are asking for. Maybe I'll make them. Maybe I won't, but at least I'll know there's a market for them if I do. If you're interested, I'd love to have you talk with my agent, Mary Beth. You two can coordinate on the business end of things so I can concentrate on my work."

Frank nodded, a huge smile on his face. "I could do that."

"Perfect." I looked around at everyone, feeling so blessed. I patted my chest. "How did I luck out and get the perfect crew right off the bat?" I shook my head in wonder and then noticed Hester standing in the shadows. "And you stayed the whole shift. I didn't mean for you to have to work five hours."

Hester waved off my concern. "It was busy. There are lots of people who can't afford your art, but they can get tea and a cookie and then walk around and experience the Sea Wicche. I liked being here to give them that." Smiling wistfully, she added, "It's magical what you've created here. People recognize that, so even though there were times when it was crowded in here, it didn't get loud. They spoke in hushed voices." She shrugged. "It was exciting to watch them experience your art for the first time."

Blinking back tears for the second time today, I cleared my throat and said, "Thank you."

"Um, Arwyn?"

I turned to see Faith staring out the back windows.

"Your boyfriend is talking to three raccoons." She looked at me. "Is that normal?"

I laughed. "It's normal around here. You guys met Declan last night, right?"

Frank and Faith nodded.

"Good. Do you want to meet Otis, Daisy, and Jasper? They're new friends who are no doubt coming to see if I have muffins for them." I looked over at the pastry display case.

Hester went back around the counter and put on plastic gloves. "We have two apple cinnamon muffins, one blueberry, and one strawberry-pistachio left."

"While I appreciate the automatic donning of plastic gloves, the raccoons aren't concerned about germs," I joked. "How about the two apple and the blueberry?"

Frank had moved beside his sister, looking out the windows. Even Carter was watching.

"Okay, sometimes they get a little scared. Aunt Hester, why don't you come out with me? We'll move slowly and quietly. Daisy sometimes panics. You'll place the muffins on the deck and then we'll move back so they feel more secure getting them. Guaranteed, Jasper will snatch his and run. Otis and Daisy are much more polite." I waved her forward. "Come on."

Hester looked a little nervous but happy to be involved. When I opened the door, Declan looked up and the raccoons froze and then scampered to him, hiding under the bench behind his legs.

"I think they caught Carter's scent," Declan said. "They used to do the same when they caught mine. The more they see you and understand you're not going to eat them, the more they'll relax."

"I don't know," Carter said. "It seems healthier for them if they continue to run when they scent wolves and bears."

Frank and Faith shared a surprised look. Apparently, they weren't aware of the shifter status of one or both men.

"It'll be okay," I said, walking out the door with Hester close behind me. "Good evening, Otis, Daisy, and Jasper. Did you have a good nap today?" I crouched down and saw Otis peeking around Declan's leg. "We have some food for you."

Hester moved beside me and crouched, placing the muffins in a kind of semicircle around us. We both stood and stepped back toward the open door.

One raccoon moved out first. He rested a paw on Declan's boot and assessed the situation.

"That one is Otis," I whispered. "He's deciding if it's safe for his siblings to come out."

After a moment of scenting the wind, his gaze darting between all of us, he chittered and the other two came around either side of Declan's legs. Otis went to the muffins, chose the blueberry, and took a bite, eating warily as he watched us. Jasper raced forward and grabbed the other two. Otis made an angry squawking sound I hadn't heard before. Jasper dropped the second muffin but took his to the edge of the deck, farther from us. Daisy finally came and picked up the last muffin, but then ran back behind Declan's legs to eat it.

"They're not normally this nervous," Declan explained in his deep, rumbly voice, "but there are lots of new people and scents tonight."

"Oh, good," Bracken said, walking toward us from the far end of the deck where his RV was parked. "They came to me earlier for something to eat. I tried to explain that I had nothing, but I wasn't sure if they understood."

Bracken was my great-uncle who, at least for now, was living in his RV right beside my gallery. He was a historian, studying both human and supernatural history. He'd written best-selling nonfiction books, and I'd known next to nothing about him before a month or so ago. As Elizabeth had said earlier, he was the black sheep of the family.

I believed more than anything he'd done or hadn't done, the issue some of the family had with Bracken related to his being on the spectrum. That was my take on the situation, but I wasn't a doctor. For ages, wicches had to hide who they were or risk burning and hanging. My guess was that had something to do with our intolerance of difference, of anything that might call attention to us.

Bracken had been shunned decades ago. Consequently, he'd been living on his own, far away from us for all of my life. Speaking as another of this family's misfit toys, I loved having him around. And as I'd said to my aunt, he was dead useful.

Bracken noticed the people in the gallery staring out the windows at him and froze, not unlike the raccoons.

Elizabeth came around the far side of the gallery to pick up her kids. Seeing the crowd, she paused. "Hello, Uncle Bracken. Do you remember me? I'm Elizabeth." She moved slowly toward him, and he stayed put. Taking his hand, she leaned in and kissed his cheek. "I was so happy to hear that you'd come home."

Bracken studied her a moment and then looked at me. He'd told me once that looking at me calmed him. He said my face was perfectly symmetrical and that perfection soothed his jangled nerves. "Thank you." He was talking to her but still looking at me. "My condolences on the recent death of your sister."

Elizabeth nodded and then gestured to the windows. "These are my children. May I introduce them to you?"

"You married a bear shifter? I doubt my sister was pleased with that," he said.

I looked over my shoulder and saw Carter—whom Bracken had met a few days ago—watching all this unfold.

"No," I said. "Carter works security for me. He's an Osso. Aunt Elizabeth is referring to her two children, Frank and Faith. Their father is a Bishop." I waved them out and they slowly came to the door, unsure of their reception.

Bracken, who could easily become overwhelmed by too much new at once, glanced at the teens a moment and then back at me. "It's very nice to meet you both. You have lovely children, Elizabeth. Faith has the shape of your face and your smile. They both have your eyes. I assume Frank has his father's facial structure. He has a stronger jaw and wider brow than most Coreys."

I studied Frank's astonished face and laughed. "You're right. Frank does look a great deal like Elizabeth's husband, Robert. You know, they're all going to be coming here to dinner on Tuesday to discuss our family's problem." Carter already knew. I'd needed him to be aware of a sorcerer issue, but I didn't like speaking her name when we were out in the open. I didn't want the wind to carry it to her.

"Elizabeth and her family have certain skills," I continued, "that most Coreys do not."

He looked at Elizabeth with new interest. I knew that'd get him.

"If you're free then," I continued, "we'd love to have you join us so you can share what you've learned."

His gaze dropped to my feet. I looked down and realized that all three raccoons were with me now, watching Bracken as though they too were waiting for his answer.

The corner of his mouth quirked up and he finally said, "I'll do what I can to join you."

"Good enough," I said. "I don't want to keep you guys any later. You all have a good night."

Elizabeth gave a look that said she understood what I was doing, which was a relief. They all went in and closed the back door, leaving just Declan, Bracken, the raccoons, and me. Bracken's very tense shoulders began to ease.

I went and sat beside Declan, giving Bracken a little more breathing room.

"I originally came over to see if we could take that drive tonight," Bracken said, "if both of you were available."

"Great idea." I popped up, ready to go.

"We need to stop for food," Declan said. "I'm starving. Then I'll drive you wherever you want. I just need to be back by ten or so." At my confused look, he said, "The pack needs more time away from your cousin and her friend. They need to work off the aggression." He shook his head. "I'm really worried about the ones who are married and have kids. I don't want anyone getting hurt. We'll try twice a week runs. If that doesn't work, I'll up it to three times a week."

The wind picked up. The ocean spray hitting me made me feel stronger, ready to take on Calliope. I knew the feeling would be short-lived, but I enjoyed it in the moment.

"What about you, though?" I asked. "You're working all day and now you'll be running all night? What if you hurt yourself with a power tool or fall asleep behind the wheel?"

Grinning, he stood and gave me a kiss. "Don't you worry. I've got plenty of energy." He nudged me toward the back door of the studio. "Go change into something comfortable and we'll go for a drive." He turned to Bracken. "Does that sound okay?"

Bracken nodded. "Oh, indeed. Wolves need a great deal of exercise naturally. When one adds in the effects of your cousin and her friend…" He shook his head. "I've been thinking, Arwyn. We have to destroy the book too. We can't keep raising and nurturing this evil."

My uncle was referring to the demonic grimoire we believed Calliope and a long line of Corey sorcerers had been using over the centuries. He was right. It wasn't just Calliope, as it hadn't been just Abigail. We had to destroy the book and end our family's apprenticeship with demons.

NINE

The Night Owl

After a quick stop at a diner for burgers—plural for Declan—and fries, we started the 17-Mile Drive through Pacific Grove, Monterey, and Carmel. It was dark, so we didn't have tourists to contend with. The few other drivers we saw probably lived along the scenic route.

Declan drove us in his truck. I sat in the middle of the bench seat and Bracken took the window seat. We had both windows open. Declan was parsing scents, hunting for the sulfurous odor that would tell us demons were nearby. Bracken and I had our eyes closed, focusing on the feeling of magic, trying to sense spells and wards.

There was one stretch of about five miles where we thought the house could be. Declan drove slowly, often pulling over on the narrow road to let others pass him, while Bracken and I concentrated. At one point, we got out and walked a section that had the potential to be hiding a secret lair.

We struck out.

Disappointed, Declan headed for home. When I realized we were close to the Night Owl Bookstore, I asked if we could make a detour. We needed more help.

"Do you remember when I told you we'd met an owl shifter?" I asked Bracken.

He nodded. "Of course. You said her name was Orla. I wonder if she's a relation of Cowen." Pausing, he tapped his finger against his lips. "He was a Eurasian eagle-owl shifter, as I recall. Charming man."

I tried to remember. Turning to Declan, I said, "Isn't that what Orla is?"

Declan shrugged. "Not sure. What I remember is the tension with the falcon shifter." He turned off the main road.

"Oh my, yes," Bracken responded. "Raptors do not get along well. They hunt each other. And if she *is* a Eurasian eagle-owl, then she is one of the largest raptors there is. I'm sure the falcon shifter felt very uncomfortable—perhaps even threatened—in her presence."

Declan nodded. "That guy did take off quickly."

"I didn't get fear from him," I said. "It was more like tightly chained aggression."

"Understandable," Bracken murmured. "And you said she owns a bookstore?"

I pointed up the long, dark hill, at the light on top. "That's it. It's an old Victorian house she's converted into a bookstore. I think you'll like it."

He leaned forward, trying to get a better look, and I smiled to myself. The more I thought about it, the more Bracken and Orla seemed quite similar. Perhaps all of Bracken's quirks merely meant he was supposed to be an owl shifter.

One of the side gigs that comes along with being a member of the Corey Council is serving on a committee of supernaturals whose job it is to police other supernaturals. We can't expect human law enforcement to deal with our enhanced gifts.

I'd met Orla recently when we'd been investigating a possible abduction. An almost-victim had been able to break away from a supernatural serial killer and run to the light on the top of the hill, Orla's place, Night Owl Books.

Declan parked his truck to the side of the wide front stairs and checked the time on his dash. "We can't stay long."

"We won't," I said, shoving him out the door.

"Pushy little thing," he grumbled.

The bookstore was at the edge of the woods. The nearest neighbors were at the bottom of the long hill, which meant Orla's home was quiet and private. That was part of the reason we wanted to use it as our crime-fighting clubhouse.

As we walked in, Orla came out from around a tall bookcase. Head tilted, she watched us for a moment and then said, "Is there another problem?"

She was a tall, thin woman—probably six feet tall—with long brown hair twirled up in a messy bun. Unlike those who aspire to the artful messy bun, Orla came by it honestly. She really seemed to just want it out of her way so she could see the page she was reading.

"Not tonight, no," I assured her. "I wanted to ask you for a favor."

She had bright gold eyes with orange flecks, ones that rarely blinked. At all. Clearly not feeling the need to make small talk, she waited for me to elaborate.

"Is there anyone else here?" I asked.

She shook her head.

"Good. First, let me introduce my Great-Uncle Bracken. Like me, he's a wicche."

Orla stared at him a moment and then returned her focus to me. "I know. You both smell like wicches."

"Might I ask," Bracken began, "do you know a man named Cowen?"

Her head tilted to the other side as she moved forward, zeroing in on Bracken, who, strangely enough, didn't seem at all bothered by her intense scrutiny. "Yes. How did you know him?"

Bracken sighed. "*Did*? Is he no longer with us?"

A line formed between Orla's eyebrows. She was a beautiful

woman, whose owllike mannerisms made her seem alien to humans. "My parents both died twelve years ago."

"Oh, my dear," Bracken said, shaking his head. "My condolences. I never met your mother, but your father was such a lovely man. He granted me an interview—let's see—it had to be thirty-odd years ago now. I was researching shifters. Very little has been written about raptors and I was quite interested."

He gestured to Declan. "People seem to believe werewolves are the only shifters." He shook his head.

She barely spared Declan a glance before focusing on Bracken again. "True, but other than my parents, I've never met another Eurasian eagle-owl shifter." Her hands fisted. "Do you know? Am I the last one?"

Bracken's expression softened. "I'm afraid I can't answer that. I, too, have never met another, save your father. If I ever do, I'll be sure to tell you."

She nodded, accepting his offer, though she looked sadder than when we'd arrived.

"I have a favor to ask you," I began. "I have a cousin who's a sorcerer."

One long blink.

"Nick told me that," she said, "but I wasn't sure if he was making a joke I didn't understand. Sometimes that happens." She was referring to Officer Nick Garra, one of Detective Osso's many black bear cousins. Nick was also a member of the Supernatural Justice League and the one who had invited Orla to join.

"No joke, unfortunately," I confirmed.

Her eyes suddenly got wider. "I forgot refreshments. Can I get you something to eat or drink?"

Declan and I grinned. She'd done this the last time we'd been here. She'd said she'd read about offering refreshments to guests in books across multiple genres, so she was sure it was the proper thing to do.

"We've eaten," Bracken explained, "but I would very much like a cup of tea."

Orla nodded and then disappeared into the back of the bookstore.

"Do you still have your notes from your interview with her dad?" I asked.

He turned and gave me a rare smile. "We think alike. I'm sure I have it in one of my journals. I'll look when we get home. I'll make a copy of it for her."

Hearing him call our place *home* warmed my heart.

Orla returned a few minutes later with a mug for Bracken and then she looked at Declan and me. "Did you want tea as well?"

We both shook our heads.

"My favor," I said, trying to get us back on track, "is to ask if you'd be willing to fly along the coast—Bracken can show you where—and see if you see or hear or smell anything off. We believe my cousin is holed up in a house that's been warded to keep it safe from detection. We were just driving the 17-Mile Drive tonight, searching for any kind of magical buzz."

Bracken handed me his mug and took one of his journals out of his tweed sport coat pocket. He most often dressed like an absent-minded professor, with mildly rumpled shirts and worn jackets with leather elbow patches.

He flipped open the journal and took out an old hand-drawn map. "Do you see here, where it says *shades*? We believe that refers to the lair Corey sorcerers have been using for generations."

"Not a terribly accurate rendering, is it?" she observed.

Shaking his head, he said, "It is not. Ergo, our need for help."

"Honestly," I said, "at this point, it would be great if you could fly the whole coastline, from maybe Santa Cruz down to Point Sur State Park. I'm not sure how big of an ask that is." I grimaced. "I've seen a vision of where she is. I know it's on the water and we know that she has to be close to do what she does."

"We also know," Declan said, "that there's been an uptick of violent crimes in Monterey over the last decade or so when one sorcerer—Arwyn's aunt—and then her apprentice—Arwyn's cousin—were working with demons. From what we've been told, when a sorcerer is working in a particular area, the evil seeps into the community, affecting humans and supernaturals alike. Because crimes are up here and not north or south of us, we think she's nearby."

Orla nodded slowly, thinking. "I can close early over the next few days and go out searching. I'll take smaller sections and go over them multiple times. I don't think it would be helpful to fly the entire coastline at once. You'll get an answer faster, but if they've stayed hidden for generations, finding them will be more challenging than spotting a smoking chimney in the middle of nowhere."

"True," Bracken said before drinking his tea.

"If you could do that," I said, "we would all be incredibly grateful."

Orla looked up at the clock over the front door. "My regulars usually arrive by midnight or one. I'll close after that and then begin the hunt." She glanced at Bracken's pocket, where he'd stowed his journal. "I have a better map than that one. I'll make note at the end of each night's flight if I've found anything I think you should study more closely."

"That would be fantastic," I said. "Thank you."

Bracken's attention had drifted to the bookcases. I knew Declan wanted to leave ten minutes ago, but I also loved that Bracken seemed comfortable here.

"We should come back soon so you can browse Orla's books," I suggested.

Bracken's attention snapped back to Orla. "Yes. I'd very much like that. I too have a large collection, though mine are predominantly old histories, not new fiction. Once we have solved our problem, I'd love to come back. You, too, may visit my home and see my books anytime you wish."

Orla, eyes bright with interest, bowed her head, accepting the offer.

"Great," Declan said. "Orla, it was good to see you again, but we need to get going. I have a pack meeting tonight."

Orla stared a moment and then nodded. "It's good to get the wolves away from the sorcerer. You have too much natural aggression as it is." She opened the book in her hand and wandered off, already reading as she disappeared behind a bookcase.

Declan and I looked at each other in surprise. We'd known she was smart, but to have made that connection so quickly was remarkable.

"Let's hit it," I said.

We all walked out and piled back into Declan's truck. He dropped Bracken and me off in front of the gallery and drove off, heading out of town later than he'd intended. The responsibility weighed heavily on his shoulders. He knew the safety of our community relied on him wearing out the wolves.

TEN

A Hard Truth

"I've had a thought," Bracken said, as we rounded the gallery into the parking lot where his RV was situated. "But first I want to know if this arrangement is working for you?" He glanced over and then looked out at the water again. "Do you mind having me living so close, visiting so often?"

I reached over and patted his arm. "I didn't know what it would be like when I invited you to stay."

His shoulders tensed, as though waiting for the blow. For a man who'd been overlooked and pushed away for most of his life, this heartbreaking hope and world-weariness tore at me.

"What I hadn't anticipated," I continued, "is how much I'd love having you here."

In the moonlight, he stopped walking and waited, hope shimmering in his eyes.

"I've been living on my own for a long time and it's fine," I explained. "I know how to take care of myself. I have systems in place for when the visions are too much. I've developed strategies for crawling out from the dark. All that is to say, I don't *need* anyone, but that doesn't mean I don't *want* anyone.

"Having Declan in my life has been miraculous. It's like the

Goddess looked down on me and took pity, giving me a man who could deal with all those dark places in me, who could hold my hand and help me find my way to the light."

Bracken nodded, hearing the truth of my words.

"It's the same with you," I continued, surprising him. "I think the Goddess decided that both of us had spent too long alone and figured out a way for us to meet."

"Through a sorcerer," he mumbled.

I nodded. "She works in mysterious ways."

He smiled, as I'd hoped he would.

"Most people don't know this," I said, "but I think it's important that you do. I've cultivated and maintained a façade of aloof disinterest in almost everything except my art. It's a cover, though, for a bone-deep fear of not being able to survive this gift of prophesy. Most Cassandra wicches who came before me died young, either at the stake or by their own hands. I think part of why I push people away is my dread of disappointing them. If they saw the hesitancy, the hands shaking, the gasp as I shudder awake in terror, I'd become something to pity rather than fear.

"Mom and Gran tout me as divinely touched. The othering has been lonely but also comforting. If I go the way every Cassandra before me has gone, I don't want to leave behind mourners." I thought a moment. "Or maybe I'm worried no one *will* mourn. No," I said, blowing out a breath and bracing myself to speak the horrible truth. "I was clearing the way to check out more easily if it became too much."

"I understand," he said, his voice low and sorrowful.

I gave my head a quick shake. "That wasn't the point. The point was that the Goddess gave me a big kick in the butt, bringing me Declan and then you, helping me to better understand my mom and then allowing me to meet my father. Even with the detectives and the cases they pull me into, it feels like everywhere I look, I see another point connecting me to this life."

I brushed away sudden tears. "Which is a very long way of

saying that I prize the Goddess' gifts, and I love having you here. I love having my family so close. When I have horrible dreams or terrifying visions, I love knowing you're nearby. It makes everything a little less scary."

His shaking hand went to his chest. "Then I, too, have been blessed."

The wind off the ocean tonight was icy and I felt a chill run down my spine. "Good. Now that that's settled, what were you going to say before you asked if I was good with you living here?"

"Oh, yes," he said, wiping moisture from the corner of his eye. "I had a thought. I think I should buy a car. Then we wouldn't need to rely on Declan. The poor man is burning the candle at both ends. This RV isn't terribly convenient for excursions like tonight. I think I need an easier mode of transportation, but that only makes sense if I'm staying for a while."

"Yes!" I clapped, though with gloved hands, it was muffled. "I've been waiting for self-driving cars to hit the market, but this works better. We should go fifty-fifty, since you'll sometimes be driving me around."

He waved that away. "Nonsense. I have plenty of money and precious little to spend it on. Good," he said on the way to the RV door. "I'll research models after I copy Cowen's interview for Orla." Checking his pockets as he walked away, he muttered, "It needs to have good head and leg room for when Declan drives with us." He unlocked his door and went in.

Grinning, I walked around the RV and stepped onto the deck hanging off the back of my gallery. Too preoccupied thinking about cars, I didn't realize there was a man seated on the bench by my studio back door.

Pausing, I lowered some of my mental defenses. Not all or I'd be bombarded by too many thoughts and emotions. Self-preservation meant protecting my mind from the unrelenting noise. The person on the bench was human.

"It's about time," he complained, standing up. "I've been sitting here for over an hour. Where have you been?"

The possessive, angry tone had my fingers moving as I built spells. "This is private property. You need to leave now."

"Big talk, but you don't have your security guard around. No boyfriend either, huh? Looks like you're all alone." He moved forward and a cloud shifted, revealing his face.

This was the creepy guy who'd been standing in the corner of the gallery last night. I'd been focused on my father and so hadn't looked too closely at him. I'd felt his obsession across the gallery but had tried to tune it out, not wanting another creep to ruin my evening.

"That giant boyfriend didn't even seem to mind when you walked off arm in arm with that other guy who was even bigger." He scoffed. "You got him cucked already. You let them all rail you, don't you, whore? But nice guys, ones who would treat you like a princess, you won't talk to us? Is that it?"

I walked forward and his eyes lit up. What gave me pause, though, was the strange tangle of emotions he was experiencing. Yes, there was obsession and a petulant anger at not being given the object of his desire, but with it was a strange giddy calculation. He wanted me to threaten him.

Lowering my mental blocks a little further, I caught gloating. He was recording me. He wanted evidence to prove I was something dangerous, a wicche.

Oh. I had it now. This was the man who'd followed me onto my deck a month or two ago. He'd tried to corner and overpower me but I'd given him a taste of scary Arwyn, using a spell that choked him. Then Declan had shown up and lifted the guy off the deck with one hand, scaring him so much he'd wet himself. The creep had grown a beard since I'd last seen him, so I hadn't recognized him.

Shit. The first rule of being a supernatural was not letting the general public know you existed. I couldn't use magic. Instead, I pulled my phone out and hit the screen for Detective Hernández. "Sir, I'm going to ask you one last time. Please leave."

"Hey, Arwyn." Hernández's voice was almost lost in the roar of the surf.

"Detective Hernández, this is Arwyn Corey at the Sea Wicche gallery. I have a man trespassing on my back deck. He's threatening me and refusing to leave. This is at least the third time he's been here, and he's been asked every time to leave."

"Stay on the phone with me," Hernández said. "I'm calling now for a car to pick him up."

"I need a restraining order," I continued, still staring at the man and slowly walking toward him. Calling for help went against every instinct I had. I wanted to deal with him myself, but if he was recording me, I needed to play human.

"I bet if you looked into his past," I continued into the phone, "you'll find other stalking complaints against him." The quick spike of panic I felt from him told me I was right.

"The detective is asking your name?" I lied. I knew he wouldn't answer me, but I hoped he'd think it. And he did. Brandon.

"Fuck you," he ground out. "This isn't over." He turned and retreated while trying to look tough, which isn't easy.

I followed him to make sure he left. Once he'd turned the corner, he started jogging. A police car pulled up as Brandon made it to the front of the gallery. The cop looked at my stalker and then slowly got out of his car, letting Brandon run down the road to wherever he'd left his own vehicle. The cop turned his head, checked his phone, spoke into the radio on his shoulder, and then slowly started walking down the side of the gallery.

My eyesight might not be as good as Declan's, but I saw that cop let my stalker get away just fine.

"Arwyn, what's happening?" Hernández demanded.

"I'm going to keep the line open," I whispered. "The cop just watched the guy run away. He didn't do anything to detain him. I recognize the cop, though. He's the one I warned you about. The one who resents the hell out of you and Osso, two brown-skinned people who made detective before him."

The cop was getting close so I drew back, put the phone in my pocket, and then pretended to run around the corner, just seeing him for the first time.

"Oh, my goodness! You scared me, Officer." Eyes wide, I said, "Did you see him, the man who was waiting for me?"

He held up his hands. "Calm down, ma'am. No. I didn't see anyone. Are you sure you saw a person? Shadows can play tricks."

The moon had slid behind a cloud again, but I could see his smug sneer well enough.

"Yes, Officer. I'm sure," I said with forced politeness. "He was sitting on my deck, waiting for me. He threatened me. Shadows rarely do that."

Anger flared. He was not happy about the sarcasm. He was a petty little tyrant who handed out sarcasm. He didn't take it. After an extended period of glaring, his hand on his gun, he flipped open the portfolio in his other hand, asking me basic questions in a bored voice.

When we were finally done with the report he was filling out, he flipped it closed and said, "Well, none of what he said or did is illegal. I'll file it, but…you said you didn't know who he was, right?"

"He was trespassing," I reminded him.

The cop looked around at the deck and the tentacles. "This is a business. You invite the public onto your property all the time." He was taking a great deal of joy in blowing off my concerns.

"I see. So if a business exists on private property, it's no longer private? Is this a new law?"

He gestured with the portfolio in his hand. "No fences. No signs. Access to the water. It's almost like you're asking for it, don't you think?"

"Officer Harding," Hernández barked as she came around the corner of the gallery, phone still at her ear. "We do not tell victims of crimes that they were asking for it."

His eyes went flat and mean. He didn't appreciate being reprimanded.

"You're relieved, Officer. I'll take it from here," she said.

He turned on his heel and stalked away. Hernández waited, watching him go. When his patrol car peeled out, she turned to me and shook her head.

Pointing at the back door of my studio, she said, "Let's go in and you can tell me what I missed."

ELEVEN

The Return of Sleepless Baking

I hadn't invited Officer Asshole in because I didn't want that horrible negative energy in my workspace. Now, though, I opened the back door, hit the lights, and invited Detective Hernández in.

"I'm freezing," I said. "I'm going to make tea, if you want some." I went to the kitchen and pulled out my brewing supplies.

"Yes, please," she said, taking a seat on the couch. "Should I assume you're shivering right now because you didn't want him in your space?"

"You're an excellent detective." I opened the freezer door. "Do you like meringue? I have some chocolate-filled meringue cookies."

Hernández leaned back on the couch. "That sounds amazing. Yes, please."

I turned with a plate of magically thawed and warmed cookies and stopped short. "Oh, no. I'm so sorry about your grandmother."

The detective blinked and then sat up straight.

"Shit. Sorry! I'm sorry." I shook my head, disgusted with myself. "Give me a minute." I put down the plate and walked back to the kitchen. Putting my gloved hands over my face, I built my mental barriers back up, reinforcing them.

When I walked back with two mugs of tea a few minutes later, I placed one on the coffee table for her and then kicked off my shoes and sat in my chair with my legs pulled up, holding the steaming cup between my knees and chest, trying to warm up.

"Please forgive me. I wasn't looking. It's on your mind. There's a lot of emotion wrapped up in it, so I got a flash of her in a hospital bed. I'd lowered my mental walls earlier when I was trying to figure out who was on my deck and what was going on."

I closed my eyes and breathed in the steam from my mug. "I *hate* hearing personal things." Opening them, I found her watching me, her brow furrowed. I took a sip and tried to make peace with the death of yet another friendship. I'd really thought this one might work. She knew a lot about me and still liked me. Past tense.

"I don't want to talk about that," she said.

I nodded, staring into my cup.

"Can you tell me what happened with the stalker?" She opened her notebook and began to write.

I went over all of it, including my belief he had been recording me.

"You said his name is Brandon. Can you draw a picture of him?" She asked.

Placing my empty cup on the side table, I stood and went to my computer. "I could, but I have video footage of him. There are cameras all around my gallery."

Hernández moved to stand behind me so she could watch what I was doing.

"There's no sound," I said, pausing the replay when the cloud moved and the guy's face was visible in the moonlight.

"Can you send me that?" she asked.

I nodded, taking a screenshot and then running it through my digital imaging program. It was what I used to clean and tweak photos for sale. Once I was done, the image was quite clear. "When he approached me the first time—a month or two ago—he was clean-shaven. The beard is new."

She made a soft *hmm* sound. "He wanted to look more like Declan."

My hand on the mouse froze. How had that not occurred to me? "There'll also be footage of him last night and earlier today on the camera feed from the front of the gallery. Do you want me to pull that up as well?"

"No. This is good enough for tonight. I can get started with what you've already given me. *But* can you check the other cameras to see if you've got your stalker leaving and Officer Harding watching him go?"

"Ooh, good call." I flicked through camera feeds until I found the one on that corner of the gallery. Unfortunately, it was pointed down so I could document and charge anyone vandalizing my gallery. The outer edge of the video feed caught the police car hood but not the windshield. We couldn't see the cop. The stalker clearly jogged by after the car appeared in the video, though.

"Is that enough to prove he let the stalker go?" I asked.

"No," she said, voice cold as she scribbled in her notebook.

I didn't think that anger was directed at me.

"It's the hood of a dark SUV," she explained. "There are no insignias we can see that mark it as a police vehicle. Can you send me that video clip too, though? At the very least, I can submit the full report, your phone call—I started recording almost immediately—the images, and videos to my captain and see what he says. Harding doesn't have a clean record. I know of at least one suspension."

Turning in my computer chair, I watched her flip her notebook closed before pocketing it with her pen. She took one last sip of tea and said, "Send me what you have there. I'll go home and write it up and then see if I can talk with the captain tomorrow."

"Thanks. I know you're already busy, so I hate adding to your work." And I hated that my comment about her grandmother was weighing so heavily on her.

"It's my job, and that officer just let a potentially dangerous man walk free because he's upset he got reprimanded for pulling his gun on you instead of the suspect in the last case you worked on."

She stared at the plate of cookies, debating, and then took one. "Lock up after me," she said and was gone.

Doing as I was advised, I made sure the doors and windows were locked and then put down the window shields. They'd been installed as part of the remodel to keep the gallery safe from huge storms on the ocean. Monterey didn't get those kinds of storms, but something had made me say yes to the expensive and unnecessary protection. I think in my gut, I knew the danger was far more likely to be from two-legged predators than from a furious storm.

I ate a cookie as I rinsed out the mugs and put them in the dishwasher. Hopefully Declan and the other wolves were getting a break from the aggression Cal and her demon engendered.

Trudging up the stairs, I considered whether or not I should even bother trying to sleep up here. I needed to change, but without Declan keeping the nightmares away, it hardly seemed worth it.

So, after my usual nightly routine, I went back downstairs to stretch out on the couch. I hit the remote, lowered the screen, and then browsed through a streaming service for a nice quiet British mystery with lots of long shots of the countryside. Those always settled me into sleep. How long I lasted before the nightmares started varied.

I sent Declan a goodnight text and then settled in, knowing full well I'd be out before I discovered who'd done it. And I was.

A woman's voice whispers through a phone line. Poison circles the central processor, weaves through circuits and chips, moving out through the speaker and into the ear of an angry man who feels deprived of what he's entitled to. Sneering in his triumph, he grabs a pen and starts taking notes.

It goes dark and then…

A leaf crunches under the boot of a different angry man. He stops, lifting his foot and placing it several inches to the right. His focus is on the back of small house in a row of small houses. The ones on either side are dark and quiet. A light remains on in one room. Understanding he needs to wait, he stands beneath a large tree in deep shadows. A phone rings and it's picked up almost at once.

Lights in the living room and then the kitchen turn on, illuminating the patio. Three flowerpots are filled with colorful impatiens blossoms. He takes out a compact set of binoculars and watches narrow strips of her through barely open blinds, as she moves through the house. He's thinking about being in her house, being able to come out of nowhere and grab her, like you see in scary movies. Grinning to himself, he steps farther back into the deep shadows under the tree and waits for her to finish what she's doing and go to bed.

Eventually, as the night wears on, a final lamp is switched off. Adrenaline floods his system. It's time. Shouldering the bag that's been sitting at his feet, he moves silently in the night, a shadow moving through the dark.

At the sliding glass door, he shines his penlight through the glass, looking for locks. He takes out a tool, picks the lock, slides it open a few inches, and then pulls a slim pole with a hook on the end from his bag. He pulls on the ends, extending it to its full length, and then reaches through the door with it, dislodging the dowel in the runners at the base of the glass doors as a secondary lock.

He slides the door open, moves in, and then closes it behind him. He has the house to himself now. Her things are his. He can do whatever he wants, and that mouthy bitch doesn't have a say in it.

The house is small and too fucking girly. Who the hell buys a floral couch? Gaze barely touching on photos, he dismisses them all, too excited to find his prey in her bed. I, though, jolt awake.

Grabbing my phone, I swiped through and tapped the screen. It took multiple rings, but I finally heard, "Arwyn?"

The breath I'd been holding rushed out. "Are you okay?"

"Sure. I mean, I'm awake and confused, but yeah, I'm fine." Hernández said. Another voice said something in the background, and I knew I'd woken her girlfriend as well.

"Sorry. I had a dream." I sat up, trying to put it all in order. "The killer was waiting in the back of a house. There was a row of little houses backed up against a wooded area. Lots of trees."

I heard rustling and knew she was probably getting her notebook. "Do you live in an area with lots of little houses?"

"Wait. You saw me?" Hernández's voice was alert now. She was up and moving, murmuring something to Andie. "Give me a minute." The sound muffled and I assumed she'd put her phone in her pocket.

After a few minutes, she came back on. "The house is clear. What did you see?"

I started to explain, and she stopped me. "A floral couch? No. That's not us. Is this happening now?"

"I don't know! It could have been last night, last week, three years ago, or tomorrow." It made me crazy. How was I expected to help if I didn't know. It wasn't as if killers held up their phones at the start of visions so I could see the date and time.

"Okay, okay. I understand. Keep going after the couch," she said.

I did until I got to the photos. "That was why I called in a panic. You were in one of the photos on the living room wall."

"I was—*shit!* I know who it is." She hung up and I was left in a knot of jangling nerves.

There was nothing to paint. I had no lingering images haunting me, so I flicked on the lights and headed to the kitchen. Aunt Hester had told me that cookies had sold the best yesterday, so cookies it was. I checked the refrigerator: eggs, milk, butter. I checked the pantry. I pulled out my mixing bowls and baking sheets and decided to make what had always been a crowd favorite. And by *crowd*, I meant large family get-togethers. Chocolate chip cookies with Heath bar chunks it was.

I had just started measuring flour when my phone rang. It was Detective Hernández.

"Okay. We're good," she said. "It wasn't my friend Gaby. What you said sounded so much like her place, but she can't be the only person with a floral couch. If they weren't popular, they wouldn't make them."

"True," I said, though I was still feeling uneasy. The name Gaby gave me a little jolt of recognition. "Are you sure, though? Did she check? That name… I don't know. I'm not trying to scare you. I woke up in a panic when I saw your picture." I thought a moment. "There were big flowerpots on the patio."

Hernández made a noise. "I'm going over myself right now to check." And then she hung up again.

Could I have tried to go back to sleep to see more? Maybe. I'd tried before but it hadn't worked. After nightmares, I was too keyed up to sleep. One time, I tried taking a sleeping pill, but that was a failed experiment. I'd been trapped in horrors, cycling through my brain. I'd learned nothing more and instead had been given more fodder for future nightmares.

TWELVE

We Interrupt This Regularly Scheduled Program for Murder

At a little after three, when I was putting a fourth batch of cookies in the oven, I heard a knock on the back door. With a flick of my fingers, the outside light over the door went on. I'd spelled the back windows a few days ago to be opaque from the deck looking in. I knew the gallery was getting ready to open and more random people would be visiting my property. I could see out, but potential creeps, like the one earlier, couldn't see through the windows into my home or gallery.

Bracken stood under the light, squinting into the dark glass nervously. When I opened the door, he breathed a sigh of relief.

"Oh, thank goodness. I was afraid my knock would wake you up." He walked in, gesturing to the glass. "I understand why you did that, and I agree, but now I can't see light from your windows, so I don't know when you're up."

"Oh," I said as I headed to the kitchen to brew more tea. "I hadn't thought of that. We need to come up with a better system then."

He sat on the couch. "I was taking a break and came out to sit on a bench and be at one with the waves in the moonlight." He watched me plate a few cookies. "It helps me wind down so I can sleep. Tonight, though, I smelled cookies and thought I'd take a chance and knock."

"I'm glad you did," I said, bringing the plate and a mug to the table for him. I went back for my own mug, checked the timer for the cookies in the oven, and went to sit with him.

"*Mmm*, delicious. I thought I'd smelled chocolate." He took a sip of his tea and leaned back. "You've spoiled me." He shook his head and took another bite. "You bring me peace and comfort."

"And cookies," I added.

"Thank goodness," he said. "And thank the Goddess." He glanced up the stairs to my loft. "No Declan, I take it."

I shook my head. "Hopefully, he's home sleeping by now." A thought struck me. "Or maybe he's sleeping in the woods in his fur." I pictured it, nodding. "I hope he sleeps well."

"I must admit," Bracken began, "as much as I benefit from your baking, I feel guilty that you have to experience horrible things in order for me to have middle-of-the-night treats."

Shrugging, I sipped my tea. "The nightmares happen. Why shouldn't cookies too?"

He grinned into his mug. "I believe you have a future as a fortune cookie writer, should art fall through for you."

"It's always good to have options." The timer dinged and I went back to the kitchen area. "I wasn't ready to start blowing glass, so I made a batch of lemon drop cookies, if you'd like one."

"They smell delicious. I'd love one."

It had only been a few weeks that Bracken had been living here, but I could already hear a lessening of tension in his voice. He'd never be what some of the family would consider normal, but the fact that he seemed more relaxed, more comfortable around me, made me very happy.

"Some bakers like to drizzle an icing on their lemon drops, but I prefer a lemon zest-powdered sugar combination." I put my concoction in a special sieve with wider gaps for the tiny pieces of zest. I shook it lightly over the warm cookies. I liked to do two dustings. One when they were warm, so the tart sugary taste melted in, and then another light dusting when they were cool for more of a pretty, powdery finish.

I took back Bracken's empty plate and slid two lemon cookies on it, returning it to him. I grabbed myself a cookie, took a bite, and loved the quick tart snap to the back of my tongue.

"*Mmm*. You are a master, dear," he said.

I felt a little bubble of joy in my chest as I took another bite and then I remembered something. Spooning out more lemon drops onto a baking sheet, I said, "Earlier, you told me Otis, Daisy, and Jasper came to you for food, but you didn't have anything. Did you mean that literally?" I gestured to the refrigerator. "There's always food in there—more than usual since there's a werewolf around. I have groceries delivered. I can add whatever you want to my shopping list. And I can give you a key."

He waved away that last suggestion. "No. This is your home, and you deserve privacy. You have a boyfriend that often stays with you. You don't need me wandering in looking for a snack."

His hand dropped back to the couch, and he said, "But I would like to order groceries along with you. That's one of the reasons I want to get a car. Taking an RV to a local supermarket isn't terribly convenient."

"Perfect," I said. "Make out a list and we can use the app together, so you get exactly what you want. When you get a car, I might even go shopping with you." Once those words were out of my mouth, I wanted to snatch them back. Supermarkets were filled with people who occasionally brushed you as they passed in narrow aisles. The psychic noise could be loud.

Bracken must have seen my expression because he said, "I like to shop in the middle of the night in one of those twenty-four-hour markets. The store is empty except for a skeleton crew of zombies restocking shelves."

"Oh," I said, sliding the sheets back into the oven and setting the timer again. I stripped off the rubber gloves I used for baking, leaving my normal ones. "I'd love to be able to walk the cooking aisle and see everything they offer. Okay, that's a plan. Once we have a car, I'll go late-night shopping with you. In the meantime, we can place an order today."

I grabbed my phone and sat beside him on the couch. "We should just do it now. You're going to go to sleep soon, and I need to get to work."

We used the thirteen minutes the cookies were baking to create an order. I had lots of baking supplies to replenish, and he had a love of pot pies. Who knew? There were frozen individual-serving ones he liked to fill his freezer with. I also made sure he got some fruits and vegetables. When I suggested chips, he told me he never ate them when he was working—and he was almost always working. He couldn't touch old texts with greasy fingers. I suggested pretzels and he said he'd give them a try.

Once we were done, he went back to his RV to sleep and I cleaned up, put on my work clothes, and went into the gallery to move all the items the Winslows had purchased for the shipping people who would be arriving later today.

Using the list Mary Beth had left me, I gathered a great deal of my art into the open café section of the gallery. Remembering, I went into the fire room to get the additional items they'd chosen yesterday morning, wheeling them out to join the rest.

While I was at it, I gathered all the artwork with white dots—a far smaller number of items—for the second collector. Mary Beth had texted me back while I was baking, giving me a list for him and informing me the same shipping company would take care of his purchases as well. She also told me to check my gallery banking account.

After everything on the lists had been double-checked, I clicked into my banking app and about had a heart attack. I sent a mind-blown emoji to Mary Beth, and she responded, telling me that didn't include the big order for the twelve-inch octopuses I needed to work on for the Winslows, nor the window for Mr. Cheng. I still had a couple of months to complete the first order and even longer for the second. When I was done, I could expect two more large paydays.

Bursting with pride, I looked over my gallery, knowing even if I never sold another piece of art, I could take care of myself for life. Eyes welling, my throat tightened. Why was I crying?

I brushed away the tears as I wandered around display tables. I'd done this. I'd created something that others valued and because of that, I never had to worry about being a burden to the family who didn't much care for me, or about having to move in with Mom or Gran. I'd fought to stand on my own, to express what was in me, and enough people appreciated my art that I was making a living on my own terms. *Damn.*

A loud knock sounded at the front door. Startled, I looked out the back windows. The sun had barely risen. The clock against the café wall read 6:20. Who in the world? I pulled up the security camera feeds on my phone as the loud pounding came again, followed by the buzzing of my phone.

Detective Hernández was calling. And Detective Hernández was standing at my front door. I jogged over and opened the original cannery metal door. I'd intended to replace it with something much nicer but decided a fancy door would ruin the abandoned cannery look.

Hernández, red-eyed and somber, gave me a look that told me everything.

"I'm so sorry," I murmured, opening the door wider for her to come in.

"Can you come with me while the scene is fresh?" she asked.

I held up a finger and jogged back to the studio, grabbing my backpack and some cookies in a napkin. When I went back, I handed her the cookie pack. "I know you're not hungry, but you need to eat something. Maybe sugar from a friend will ease the pain a bit."

Flicking my fingers, I locked up the gallery and headed to her car. Hernández put the cookies in the cup holder and started her engine. We were in the car for at least five silent minutes before she said, "It looks like he broke in after I called to check on her."

In the dream, the killer had been waiting outside, watching the back of the house. He heard a phone ring and then the lights turned on. Eventually, they all turned off and he moved in. It hadn't happened yet. I'd dreamt it before it happened, called the police, and still hadn't been able to stop it.

"I'm not sure how to talk to you about this," I said. "She was your friend. I don't want to hurt you."

Her grief washed over me and made my head pound. "It's Arthur's case. He knew Gaby too—she works at the station—but they aren't friends. I told him about our phone calls, but I might have left things out. You should tell him everything from the beginning," she said.

"Of course, and I'm very sorry about your friend." I knew my words were hollow in the face of her grief, but I also felt compelled to say them.

She nodded and continued driving in silence. Eventually, she turned into a neighborhood of small, neat houses, lined up in a row, and my stomach cramped. It wasn't as though I hadn't known where we were headed, but now I was going to have to watch Detective Hernández's friend being murdered.

THIRTEEN

Well, That Sucked

When Hernández pulled up, Detective Osso was standing out front, talking with a man in a white coverall that left only his pale face exposed. Osso walked over and opened the passenger door, leaning in before I could get out.

"Sofia, I've got this," he rumbled in his deep bear voice. "You go home, be with Andie, and try to get some sleep. I'll call you in a few hours. Okay?"

I felt her struggling, wanting to make sure her friend was taken care of, but she finally nodded and turned her head away from all the police activity. Osso stepped back and let me exit, gently closing the car door after me and tapping the roof.

Once Hernández had driven away, we walked up the path to the door. "This isn't like the other one," he said. "He was more violent this time."

The cops on scene watched us approach with expressions varying from disgust to wary hope. Another person in white coveralls gave me paper booties to put on over my sneakers before I entered the house.

"There are too many people here," I whispered, knowing he'd hear me. "It's too chaotic. Can you bring me back later once they've all left?"

He paused at the entrance to the short hall. "I could, but can you try? Everyone is a little worked up right now. Gaby was one of our dispatchers. Everyone knew her. That's why there are so many people milling around."

Five people were standing in the living room, talking quietly. Two were in white coveralls, the rest in uniform. It felt like more in the small space. "Aren't the extra people mucking up your crime scene?"

He tugged my sleeve, knowing not to touch me, and pulled me down the hall, past what looked like a craft room and a small bathroom. "The scene's been processed. Like last time, they couldn't find anything. Sofia said she was going to get you a little too loudly, so now they're waiting to find out what you see."

The officers knew I was a psychic—or that I *said* I was. Most didn't believe in psychics and so thought I was a con woman who'd duped Hernández and Osso, which accounted for all the dirty looks.

"It's a small house," Osso continued. "If you need them out, I'll kick them out, but I'd prefer not to. Emotions are high and distrust of you and now me is strong. I can keep them in the living room, and I'll stand in the hall. All right?"

I nodded and blew out a breath before I walked in. The scene was too fresh. The terror, pain, and anger were already overpowering. The bed had been stripped, but I saw a speck of red on the mattress that looked like blood. Shaking out my arms, I braced for what was coming.

Taking off a glove, I stuffed it in my pocket and then leaned over the mattress, touching a fingertip to the red spot.

The sheets are ripped off and she startles awake, flying up in bed. Her eyes are huge in the dark, trying to see who's there. The backhand comes fast and without warning. The force of the hit knocks her onto her side. Lip bleeding, eyes blinking, she scrambles to the far side of the bed, but he's there. Grunting insults, he closes his fists and begins the beating in earnest.

She knows some self-defense moves and tries to fight him. Her aim is off in the dark, but she manages to smash her wrist into his nose. The cursing gets louder before she takes a punch to the abdomen that cuts off her air and throws her back onto the bed.

He falls on her, his hands going around her neck. Frantic, she hits his arms and then jabs her thumbs toward his eyes, but he sees them coming and has a longer reach. Hands still crushing her throat, he stretches away from her, turning his head to save his eyes. A fingernail cuts his cheek.

Clawing at his hands and kicking, she fights for her life. She feels spittle hit her face as he rages about her thinking she's so important and how she's really trash. She feels his erection against her hip and a new fear tears through her.

When her limbs lose strength, he leans down and whispers, "You're all the same." His breath is hot in her ear. "You think you have some say over me? Fucking bitch! You're nothing. And you're going to die nothing." The last thing she sees as the world goes dark are lips pulled back in a grimace and a crooked eye tooth.

I blinked my eyes open, staring up at Osso, who was staring down at me. What the—

"*Shit,*" he said. "Let me help you up. I'll call Declan. Just a minute."

I couldn't breathe and started to panic.

He held up his hands. "It's okay. I'm going to take care of you."

A trickle of air made its way through my windpipe. Tears slid down the side of my face and pooled in my ears. Mouth open, gulping unsuccessfully at the air, I grabbed Osso's forearm with my gloved hand and held on.

He grabbed me around the middle, making sure he wasn't touching my skin, and hauled me to my feet. What—Oh. I remembered now. Gaby. That was why I felt like I'd been hit by a truck. I slipped my glove back on as Osso led me down the hall away from that room.

A cluster of cops stood at the end of the hall, blocking the front door, staring. "What the fuck?" one of them breathed.

Osso waved them out of the way. "Let me get her outside."

I thought I heard one of them say something about my neck,

which was a concern of mine as well. It felt like it was on fire. The ringing in my ears made it hard to hear anything.

When we got to his SUV, he opened the passenger door and picked me up, depositing me on the seat. If I'd been able to talk, I'd have protested. Then again, I wasn't positive I could have climbed in on my own. Someone ran up with a glass of water and Osso handed it to me.

I tried a small sip but ended up coughing. Osso was talking but I couldn't hear him yet. I held up my hand, closed my eyes, and waited for it to pass. When I felt him take the cup from me, I realized my hand had been trembling too hard to hold it without spilling.

My breathing was finally easing when I heard tires squeal and then Declan was there, shouldering Osso out of his way. His gaze raced up and down, looking for injuries. When he got to my face, his shoulders dropped, and his hands came up to cradle my head.

"Ursula, what did you do to yourself?" he murmured.

"Not my fault," I mostly mouthed.

"I know." He kissed my forehead and then turned to Osso to take the cup from him. "Can you drink?"

I tried swallowing. It hurt like hell, but I did it. Nodding, I held out a hand and he placed the cup in it. I took a small sip and was able to get it down.

"Your neck is black and blue, and your left eye has burst blood vessels," Declan told me.

"If it bothers you," I whispered, "I can use a glamour spell to cover it."

"Don't, please," Osso said. "You have an audience."

I looked around Declan's shoulder to see a loose group of cops watching me. Super.

Osso pulled his notebook from his pocket. "Can you tell me yet what you saw?"

I took another sip. It went down, so I nodded. My voice was a painful rasp, but I eventually got it out.

"You didn't see him?" he asked.

"There was no light in her room," I said.

He thought a moment and nodded. "Blackout curtains for when she works the night shift."

"Then how did he see her?" Declan asked.

Osso looked back at me. "No flashlight this time?" He must have read Hernández's report of the last scene, when the killer used a flashlight.

I shook my head. "I think I was seeing things from her perspective, and it was like the darkness was beating her. The only clear thing I saw was, as she died, his lips parted and his teeth were visible." My fingers went to my mouth as I tried to remember which side it would have been. "His right eye tooth is crooked. It angles left, kind of pushing the next tooth."

Shrugging, I added, "He was taller than her, but she seemed petite. And really, it was more of an impression that the blows were coming from above. He was at best a shadow in the dark."

Osso flipped his notebook closed. "Thank you and sorry about this." He gestured at all of me, but I got it. "If you think of anything else, let me know."

"Okay." I slid off the seat onto the pavement and Declan held a hand out to steady me.

"I'll take you home," he said.

"Home! Shit! What time is it?" I had a shipping crew arriving at ten this morning.

Osso checked his watch. "Seven forty."

"Oh." I blew out a breath and leaned into Declan, who wrapped an arm around me. "I'm good then."

Declan helped me into the passenger seat of his truck and then closed the door. As he walked around the back, I looked out the window at the cops who were still watching me. One of them shook his head and turned his back. A couple of others moved back into the house. Osso went to the man in the white coveralls. The man's whole head was visible now. He looked over his shoulder at me and then, talking with Osso, walked back into the house.

Declan slid behind the wheel, started the engine, and then looked at my feet. "I like your new booties. Did you bring your backpack with you?"

Yes. Shit. Did I leave it in Hernández's car? I tried to remember. "Detective Osso took it off my shoulder when I went into the bedroom."

He patted my knee. "Hold tight. I'll go get it." As Declan jogged across the street, Osso came out the door, holding it. They spoke for a moment and then Declan returned. He put the backpack behind his seat and slid back in.

He took my hand, pushed up the sleeve, and kissed my wrist. "Osso's phone call scared the life out of me," he said, pulling out onto the road. "He's a man of few words, but two of them could have been *she's okay*." He shook his head and turned onto the main road toward the gallery.

"I was driving back from Big Sur when he called. I was close to home, which is how I got there so fast."

"Did you sleep in your fur in the woods last night?" I asked.

He glanced over, looking suspicious. "How did you know that?"

"Psychic. Duh." Breathing more easily, I grinned. "It just came to me last night. I was worried about you driving home on curvy roads when you were exhausted and then I imagined you curled up in the woods, sleeping under a tree."

"You're a wily one," he said.

I watched the ocean pop in and out of view as he drove across intersections. "Back there. I know you were focused on me, but did you notice anything about the cops?"

"No." He glanced over again. "Should I have?"

I went back to staring out the window. "Not sure. Something felt off, though."

FOURTEEN

Necking

Declan pulled up in front of the gallery and turned in his seat to study me. "You look better. Your eye's clear now and your neck only has a light bluish ring around it." His long fingers brushed softly down my throat. "Does that hurt?"

"Not really. It's still sore, but it's nothing like it was." I took his hand and held it in both of mine. "I need the police to stop taking me to the crime scenes of choking victims."

He squeezed my hands. "The last one wasn't this bad, was it?"

I shook my head and felt a twinge. "No, but that one hadn't happened a couple of hours earlier."

Declan's brow furrowed. "Why did they call you in so fast? Why aren't they doing their own investigation first?" His eyes lightened to wolf gold. "You're supposed to be the last resort when they've tried everything else. You're not supposed to be the sacrificial lamb that lets them clock out early."

His grip started to hurt, so I wiggled my fingers and he immediately let go. He shook his head and then stared blindly out the windshield. "Sorry."

I explained the nightmare and the phone calls, everything that had happened before he'd arrived. He listened, his shoulders dropping. He took my hand again, gently holding it on his thigh.

"You saw it before it happened?" He looked back at me, eyebrows raised.

"It happens that way sometimes." Something had been bothering me for a while and I decided to just tell him. "I've been struggling with some guilt about sleeping with you."

No anger, just concern. "Guilt? Why?"

"When I'm with you, I don't dream," I began.

"Which is a good thing," he said. "You don't sleep anywhere near as much as you should. I worry about how little sleep you get before you start working with fire or climbing forty-foot scaffolds to paint walls."

I nodded, accepting the truth of that. "But if I don't see the horrible thing, I can't do anything to stop it. It's not just about you being a null, though. When I joined the Council and had shared visions with Mom and Gran, they saw things I didn't. I've been hiding, trying to put these horrible visions out of my mind most of my life. If I'd joined the Council when they wanted me to, maybe —between the three of us—we could have helped the people that I blocked out."

He flicked open his seat belt and then leaned over and kissed me. When we broke apart, he rested his forehead against mine. "You don't owe the world your health and sanity. You protected yourself until you were ready. That's nothing to feel guilty about."

He pulled off my glove and twined his fingers in mine. "Those other Cassandra wicches that came before you died when they were children. You've learned how to survive this gift—"

"Thanks to dad's DNA," I interrupted.

"Exactly. Which is why pure wicche lines are not healthy." He was still pissed off that Gran and Great-Gran had made Mom give up Dad when she was pregnant with me because he's water fae. They wanted the extra punch of power to help me survive but they didn't want other little half-faelings polluting the family line. Truth be told, I was right there with him.

"So," he continued, "you've had the time you needed to come up with strategies that protect you." He coiled one of my curls around his finger. "Regardless of whatever your family was thinking when they knew a Cassandra was coming, your goddess didn't make you this way to torture you and put you in service to the rest of the world. And she certainly didn't bring me into your life if she didn't want you to sleep."

Oh. That helped. He was right. She wouldn't have gifted me with Declan if she didn't think I needed dreamless sleep. And him. A tightness in my chest eased.

"You are your own amazingly artistic, culinarily creative—"

I grinned.

"—gorgeously magical siren who. Needs. Sleep. Having your own wants and needs doesn't make you selfish and shouldn't cause guilt. Besides," he said, "what am I supposed to do without you?"

He looked up a moment and then gave his head a quick shake. "I don't know what the rules are on spilling my guts like this, but I don't sleep well without you in my arms. If I'm at my place or in the woods, I don't go into deep sleep. I'm always hovering near the surface, awakened by a branch bouncing in the wind or a car driving by. My first thought is always, *Where's Arwyn?* And then I remember you aren't with me. But I can't fall right back to sleep because then I'm wondering if you're okay. Is there a creep bothering you? Are you having a nightmare? Is your cousin up to some demonic shit?"

Grinning, I kissed his jaw. "Thanks."

He rolled his eyes. "It's ridiculous. No one knows better than me just how powerful you are."

"Nuh-uh. It's sweet and makes me feel warm inside. I'm not thinking about death and tragedy anymore," I said, climbing into his lap. I wrapped my arms around him. "Now I'm just thinking about you."

"My plan worked." And then he was kissing me, and all thought disappeared.

After quite some time, during which we ended up reclined on his bench seat with him kissing my neck and growling—which did funny things to me—he sat up suddenly. Looking over his shoulder out the window, he spat, "That fucking guy," and jumped out of the truck, charging across the road.

A car slammed on the brakes and honked, but Declan ignored it. On my knees, I watched out the back window as he went straight for the sedan parked across the street. The guy dropped his phone into his lap and floored it, almost causing another accident trying to get away from Declan.

I needed to talk to Mom and Gran about this guy. Surely we've had creepy humans fixated on us before. How did we get rid of them without tipping off the world to the existence of wicches?

Declan came back to the open driver's door, his eyes wolf gold. "Did you see that? He was filming us?"

"Yeah. I saw." I shrugged. "We're single and dating. We're both fully clothed. He couldn't see most of the kissing when our heads went below the window. I've used spells to get rid of him, but he just keeps coming back. I don't understand—" And then I remembered the first part of my nightmare last night.

A woman was talking, spreading poison through phone lines, as a man listened avidly and took notes. *Shit.*

"I think I know why he keeps coming back," I said.

"Fae blood?" Declan guessed.

"No. I mean, some of it initially. Probably. Now, though, I think Cal's pushing him to stay on me like that other stalker who was going to kidnap and kill me a couple of weeks ago."

Still standing between the truck and the open driver's door, he let out a gust of breath and then grabbed my backpack from behind the bench. He put it on his seat and unzipped it. "Is it wrong that I really want to punch her in the face?"

"In Cal's case, no. She deserves that and more." I watched as he rifled through my bag. "What are you looking for?"

He shrugged. "No idea. Osso said he left your backpack on the floor when you went into the bedroom. He forgot about it as he walked you out. When he went back in, he saw it, went to grab it, and noticed it had been unzipped. The house was filled with cops that don't like you. I'm trying to see if they were just curious or decided to screw with your stuff."

Grimacing, I leaned forward and peered in. "You don't smell pee or anything, right?"

Declan gave me a blank stare. "Would I have my hands in here if it smelled like piss?" He gave himself another quick shake and then kissed me. "Sorry. They make me very angry. You go out of your way to help them—at great physical pain—and they harass you like middle school bullies."

"Yeah. That part does suck." The pocket where I kept my honey bear filled with seawater looked too flat to hold the bottle. I unzipped and looked. Empty.

Declan reached into the main compartment and pulled out the bottle. "That's not where it belongs." He held it out to me.

I reached for it but then snatched my hand back. "You were wrong about them pissing on—or in this case in—my stuff."

Declan growled loudly, his eyes bright gold again. I shoved the backpack into the foot well and knee walked to him, taking the bottle out of his hand and dropping it into the open backpack. "I don't want you to crush that and splash us both in seawater and urine." I laid my head on his chest and wrapped my arms around him. "Sorry."

He growled again. "Why are *you* sorry? You didn't do anything. I'm the one hanging on by my claws right now."

"And that's why I'm sorry," I said, squeezing him tighter. "Cal and her demon are pushing the wolves. My guess, though, is that as Alpha, you're siphoning off some of your pack's aggression to keep them from hurting their loved ones. Meaning you're the one drowning in excess aggression right now."

"Meaning I'm endangering you," he said, his voice somber.

"I'm stronger than the human partners and children." I tipped my head back to look him in the eye. "What's going on right now isn't you. One of the things I found so attractive about you at beginning was your control. When Logan was doing everything he could to rile you up, you didn't rise to the bait. Not once. All you wanted were my brownies."

His eyes darkened. They weren't quite his normal deep brown yet, but they were getting there. "That wasn't all I wanted."

"Yeah. That was pretty sexy too. So," I said, sitting back on my heels, "can I make a suggestion?"

"Of course." He picked up the backpack and put it behind his seat again. "I don't want you touching that. I'll get you replacements and burn that." He got back in and slammed the door shut.

"My suggestion is you take the day off work, crawl into my bed —that smells like me—and sleep all day. Your exhaustion is making it harder to control the way she's poking at the wolves."

He opened his mouth to argue but then pulled out his phone and started texting instead. "I'm already late. Kenji and his sister are on site. They can take care of it while I sleep." He wrapped his arm around me. "You should sleep with me. You only got an hour or two last night."

"No can do," I said as a large moving truck pulled into my parking lot. "The shipping people have arrived."

He growled again, but it was a playful, frustrated one. Those butterflies were taking wing in my stomach again. I was learning the language of his growls.

"Buckle up. I'll park around back," he said, turning the ignition. He stopped beside Bracken's RV, at the water's edge. Pointing at the ocean, he added, "You should reset. You never know when you're going to need your magic."

FIFTEEN

Cookies!

"Good point." I unbuckled and slid out, went around the RV, and stepped onto my deck. Leaning over the railing, I put my hand out, drew up a fountain of water, and let it splash my hand. Shaking it off, I yanked my glove back on. Declan, waiting for me at the edge of the deck, took my gloved hand and walked me back to the people gathering at the truck. A few more cars had pulled into the parking lot.

I went to the tall Black woman with the clipboard. She seemed in charge—and looked vaguely familiar. She had broad shoulders and long braids coiled in a topknot.

"Hello. I'm Arwyn. You're here to pack up my artwork."

She looked up from her clipboard and smiled, two dimples appearing. "Ms. Corey?"

I nodded.

"Good to meet you." She didn't try to shake my hand, so Mary Beth had prepped her.

The woman checked her watch. "I'm Melissa Garra. I'll be supervising the packing and shipping. We know this is a delicate project. I'm using my best people. We're just waiting for one more." A car pulled in and a young man jumped out and ran over. "And there he is."

I looked over the crew of eight and realized why I was suddenly thinking about honey. Well, that and I recognized those dimples. "Garra? Are you any relation to Officer Nick Garra?" He was a black bear shifter and a member of the Supernatural Justice League. He was also Detective Osso's cousin.

She nodded. "Nick's my brother." Gesturing to all the people gathered, she added, "In fact, these are all our cousins, second-cousins, whatnot."

"So, if I were to bake some honey cookies for you, you'd all enjoy that?"

Seven of the eight all nodded eagerly. The eighth, the one who arrived late, raised his hand. "I'm whatnot. Could I have a cup of tea instead?"

I felt a small charge of magic from him. The others all seemed to be black bear shifters. This last one was not.

"I'm a Swan," he volunteered, naming an old wicche family. "Not a very gifted one, I'm afraid. I know all about Coreys, though, and you. Growing up, Gran made sure we knew all the old families." His fingers kept straying to a lump in his front pocket.

"Mr. Swan, I know my family doesn't have the best reputation, but if your grandmother gave you a protection against me, chances are my wards won't let you in the door." I turned to Melissa. "May I speak freely?"

She nodded. "Yes, ma'am." She confirmed what I'd assumed. We were all supernaturals. There was no need to speak in code.

"Mr. Swan?" I gestured him forward. "You and I have the least sensitive hearing in this group. You should move closer." When he did, I felt the gentle push of his grandmother's fetish in his pocket. The Swans weren't a powerful family, but they also weren't riddled with sorcerers, like mine.

"You can call me Milo, ma'am," he mumbled. Most of the workers shared a family resemblance with Melissa and Nick. Swan, though, was pale, skinny, and only a few inches taller than me.

"Thank you all for coming," I began. "You already know who and what I am." I patted Declan's shoulder. "This is Declan, Alpha of the Big Sur Pack." A few eyes widened at that. "Most of what you'll be handling will be very delicate glass sculptures. The octopuses will be the most problematic, given their tentacles and unusual shapes. I've already given them a light protective spell, to make them a little stronger for the handling and packing."

A young woman raised her hand.

"Yes?"

"We'll be super careful, but why not just make them unbreakable?" She looked a lot like Melissa, but younger. Like my new employees Frank and Faith, she was probably still in high school.

"And what happens on the other end," Melissa asked, "when some fancy executive drops his glass figurine on his marble floor and it bounces? Then Ms. Corey is a cheat who sells plastic instead of blown glass."

"Exactly," I said. "I know you guys are going to need to go in and out of the gallery, so I also want you to be aware of a stalker I'm dealing with."

"He's a little under six feet," Declan said. "He has light brown hair, a beard, and dead blue eyes." He glanced around. "Do you know what I mean?"

Everyone but Milo nodded. Milo glanced at the rest of the crew and then back at Declan and me. "Oh, like, his eyes are dead inside?"

Declan nodded and Milo said, "Got it."

"This won't help you," Declan said to Milo before focusing on the rest of the team, "but he smells like stale coffee, cologne, and those fake forest car fresheners."

The bear shifters all nodded, taking note.

"He drives a sedan that's somewhere between tan and gold," I told them.

"Chevy Malibu," Declan specified.

"He's human but obsessed," I said. "I've given him a magical shove multiple times, but he keeps returning. Don't let him in and please come tell me if you see him. I'll be in my studio."

"We'll keep an eye out," Melissa promised, nodding to her crew. "Now, would you like us to use the front door or is there some other way you want us going in and out?"

"I'm not sure how much space you need. I can show you both entrances and you can decide which works best for you." I waved her forward. "Let me show you in."

Melissa turned back to the crew. "Start unloading the packing supplies and I'll be back to tell you what we're doing." She followed Declan and me around the corner of the building to the front door.

She made note of the steps, the double doors, and then went through the gallery to the narrower back door with no steps but with a precarious passage past the RV. "I think we'll primarily use your back door. For the larger pieces, we'll go out the front. That will lower the risk of people wandering in through the open front door."

"Sounds good," I said. I showed her where the two caches of items were for the two collectors and then showed her the door to the studio. "If you don't need anything else, I'll go bake some cookies."

She tucked the clipboard under her arm. "Yes, ma'am. I have my list here too. If I have any questions, I'll come find you. And thank you for the cookies. The crew and I appreciate it."

I left them to it and then Declan and I went into my studio. I pushed him toward the stairs. "Go sleep. I'll be down here baking and then doing some work."

He stared down at me. "You don't honestly think I'm going to be able to sleep with all this commotion, do you?"

"Yes, I do. Go," I said, pushing an immovable Declan. "I've never been so safe. I have a gallery filled with bears right now. You're off duty. Go take a hot shower, throw your clothes in the washer, and go to sleep."

He scratched his beard. "A hot shower does sound good."

"And I got you that beard conditioner I told you about. It's on the bathroom counter. Go. I've got hungry bears to feed."

He reluctantly trudged up the stairs and I went to my pantry to check how much honey I had on hand. I'd need to order more. Which reminded me: I had a grocery order to submit. I pulled out what I'd need for the cookies and then added a few more items to the list before submitting it.

When I heard the shower cut off and then the washing machine start, I relaxed. He wasn't going to work naked. With any luck, he'd be asleep soon.

I was just putting in a third batch of cookies when I noticed Carter, Detective Osso's brother and my new security guard, sitting on a bench on the deck.

After setting the timer on my phone, I finished loading up a platter with cookies and went out my back door, quietly closing it behind me. Carter looked up and stood, coming to grab two cookies.

"If I don't get these first, they'll all be gone," he whispered.

A moment later, Melissa and her crew came out. They took cookies from me first and then very quietly greeted Carter, who was, of course, cousin to them all.

"I know why I'm being quiet," I said, "but why are all of you?"

Carter took a bite and hummed his delight in the honey treat. "Same reason as you," he whispered. "We're trying not to wake the Alpha. We hear he's been running the pack ragged, trying to counter what that sorcerer's doing."

The bear shifters nodded and ate more cookies. I guess the word had spread through the shifter community. Milo, though, came to the gallery door and watched me warily. The fact that the other wicche families hadn't been informed didn't surprise me at all. Coreys were all about secrets.

"Thank you," I said, "but how did you know he was sleeping? He doesn't snore."

The bear shifters grinned as they grabbed the last of the cookies off my platter.

"His heartbeat and breathing are slow and steady," Carter explained. "We know what sleep sounds like."

I looked between them all, amazed. "From out here, over the sound of the surf, you could hear his heartbeat?"

Laughing, Carter shook his head. "I saw the gallery door open, so went there first. Melissa said you were in the studio, but no one —me included—wanted to knock on the door and wake the Alpha. I assumed if I waited on the deck, you'd eventually see me. And you did."

My phone buzzed. "Give me a minute. I need to get the next batch out."

I went back in as quietly as possible, but I heard a groggy, "Arwyn?"

"Yep, it's me," I whispered. "I'm just giving the crew cookies. I'm fine. Go back to sleep."

"'kay." And it was silent up there again.

I took the latest batch out to cool, put a last batch in, and then moved the cookies from the baking sheet to the platter. Were they still warm and bendy? Sure, but the crew didn't care. When I went out, they were all waiting patiently. They took a few more each and then Melissa had them return to the gallery.

Once we were alone, I sat on the bench beside Carter. "So, what's up?"

He pulled out his phone. "You know how I'm always listening to audiobooks or podcasts?"

"Sure," I said.

"Well, I saw there was a new one about witches—or one in particular—and it's local."

He opened his podcast app and turned the screen to me. It was called *A Witch Burning* and featured a woman who looked a lot like me, with a ton of curly hair and a pointy witch hat, who was being consumed by flames.

Unconsciously, I reared back. What the hell?

There was a crash inside and then Declan was standing in the doorway, naked, his wolf-gold eyes on me. "What happened?"

SIXTEEN

No!

"Me what happened? How about *you* what happened?" I stood and pushed him back in the door.

"Did Carter do something?" he growled.

I glanced around, trying to figure out what that big noise was. A couple of bottles and jars had tipped over in the kitchen. Luckily their tops were on. "Did you jump down from the loft? That's like thirty feet."

"Of course I did," he said. "Your heartbeat stopped and then raced. What happened?"

My phone buzzed, so I took out the last batch and then pushed him toward the stairs. "I'll tell you once you lay down again."

He threw me over his shoulder. "Fine, but you can come with me," he said as he took the stairs two at a time.

"Don't even think about it," I hissed. "We're surrounded by people who can hear you breathing. We're not messing around. And I still need to find out what else Carter was going to tell me."

He put me down and then went into the bathroom to move his clothes from the washer to the dryer. "There. Now the next time I have to run to your rescue, I can be wearing pants." He sat back in bed and leaned against the headboard.

I sat on the end of the bed and explained what Carter had been telling me.

"A podcast about you? About you being a wicche?" he asked.

"Carter?" I called.

A moment later, my back door opened. I moved to the stop stair and sat down, so I could see both men.

"Can you finish what you were telling me?" I asked.

"Yeah." He lifted his nose and zeroed in on the cookies cooling on the counter.

"Go ahead," I said. "Just leave some for the others."

He went to the kitchen, grabbed a handful, and then went back to stand near the door. Declan couldn't see Carter from where he was, but I watched him physically relax as Carter moved farther away. Clearly this was a shifter thing because Carter knew to stand as far away as he could while still being in the studio.

He held up a cookie and said, "These are really good, by the way," and then tossed one in his mouth. "There are three episodes up. They all look pretty short: maybe twenty minutes. I only listened to the first one and then came here to warn you."

"Okay. I'm sitting down. How much can he know?" My hands were fisted in my lap. Secrecy was paramount. Without it, we had a history of dying rather badly.

Carter shook his head. "The guy comes off crazed—to me. The pitch of his voice says panic. I doubt humans will pick up on that, though. Anyway, he talked about there being real witches in the world. How they were evil and preying on good, honest people."

He ate another cookie. "At first, I thought this would be a funny podcast. I was hoping that image of what looks like you in the graphic was a strange coincidence, but then he talked about living in a seaside town and it got far less humorous. He said he met a witch who was pretending to be an artist, like the witch in Hansel and Gretel pretended to welcome the children and invite them to dinner."

"Oh, shit," I said under my breath. I had to warn Mom and Gran.

"He said she'd choked him with her magic," Carter continued, "almost killing him and then her vicious monster guardian picked him up off the ground with one hand and threatened to eat him." Carter looked up at the half-wall of the loft. "I assumed that monster was you, Declan."

Declan growled, deep and angry.

"Yeah, thought so," Carter replied. "Anyway, he talked about how dangerous and demonic witches are, how they needed to be captured and burned." He shrugged his massive shoulders. "He's human. I can't go pound him into oblivion, but I'm worried that one of his handful of listeners will decide to act on his words."

"Shit, shit, shit, shit," I began chanting quietly.

"Can you see?" Declan asked. "How many listeners does he actually have? If there are only three and they live in other countries, we have time to deal with him."

Carter ate the last cookie and took out his phone again. He swiped through and said, "I can't tell how many have listened to it, but he has one hundred and thirteen ratings. When I listened this morning, there were eighteen ratings."

"That's a big jump in a few hours," I said. How do we fix this?

"He could be advertising somewhere," Carter suggested, "or be in an online group of like-minded weirdos and they're passing on the information."

I did an internet search on the podcast and found multiple listings for the different platforms that offered the podcast and then saw a Reddit thread about it. There were only a few comments, but one of the posters had named me and my gallery. *Shitshitshitshit.*

"I know you have cameras all around, but you might want to hire proper security. I'm only here when the gallery's open. I think you need someone around all the time. All this *witch burning* talk has me worried about you and the gallery."

"I have an idea about security," Declan said. "Let me work on that. In the meantime, are there any other spells you can do to protect yourself?"

I shrugged. "Mom, Gran, and I warded the hell out of the place.

It should be fine, but I'd be lying if I said I wasn't nervous." I had a thought. "We need to ward Bracken's RV too. He's in danger, being so close to me."

I stood, realized I couldn't go anywhere yet, and sat back down. "Once Melissa and her crew are done, I can meet with Mom and Gran…and we…" My head began to pound and my vision went dark. Oh, no. I was on stairs. I—

Gran is sitting in her living room by the fire, drinking tea and reading a book. Outside, a giant, hairless beast skulks, circling the house, sniffing at doors, peering in windows, waiting for Gran to leave the safety of her warded home. Drool drips from his fangs, burning holes in the patio. It scratches its razor-sharp claws against the window. Gran looks up, but not seeing anything, tugs the warm shawl around her shoulders and sips her tea.

In a torch-lit basement, a woman pores over an ancient, hand-written grimoire filled with the foulest spells ever imagined. A small animal whimpers in the corner as the woman crushes tiny bones with a mortar and pestle. The stench makes me lightheaded. The fur and feathers of previous sacrifices are heaped in the corner. The chanting begins and my stomach twists.

The vision goes black and then…

Bracken is in his RV at his desk, reading over a journal and drinking a cup of tea. It's the middle of the night, but he hears voices outside. When he looks out the window, the RV shudders, like it's been hit by something large. He gets to his feet and is thrown back in his chair. The RV rocks violently from side to side.

He throws a spell, but the RV is already crashing onto its side. Bracken is crushed beneath his heavy wooden desk. Hand up, he pushes his magic against the desk, shoving it off his crushed middle, and then he sees the smoke. All of his books, his precious histories, are going up in flames.

The vision goes black and then…

Hester hands a child a peanut butter-chocolate chip cookie. He takes a bite as his mother pays for it and grins, looking at all the octopuses. The child takes another big bite, thinking about the Monterey Bay Aquarium where he saw a real octopus. It was so cool, even if it did hide. He saw the tentacles come out and it made him feel both scared and happy. His stomach starts to hurt.

His mom is still talking to the lady behind the counter. He knows it's rude to interrupt. He looks at his cookie. It's so good. It'll help. He takes another big bite, hoping the good taste will cover the bad pain.

He drops to the ground, convulsing, bloody foam on his lips.

"No!" I shot up and realized I was being held in place. Declan was sitting on the top step, his arms around me.

"Is she okay?"

I heard Carter's voice, but the waves and wind were making him hard to hear. I turned in Declan's lap and looked down the steep stairs to find Carter standing outside the open door. Melissa moved into view and looked through the door, worry lining her face.

"Everything's fine," Declan growled. "You know she's a Cassandra wicche. That's why your brother is always asking for her help. She's perfectly fine. Close the door."

Carter did and walked Melissa back to the gallery door.

I tipped my head onto Declan's shoulder. "I thought for sure I was going to break my neck tumbling down those stairs. It came on so fast, I couldn't scoot myself back, away from the drop."

He hadn't let go yet. "When you're falling into a vision, your eyes go glassy and vacant. As soon as you lost the thread of what you were saying, your eyes went blank and I was up and diving for you. You were going head-first down the stairs when I caught you." He squeezed me tighter. "Don't do that again."

He stood and carried me back to bed, sitting on the edge with me still in his lap. "You scared a good decade off me."

I kissed his cheek. "Sorry about that."

He shook his head. "Not your fault."

There was a knock at the studio door.

"Come in," I called.

"Ms. Corey?" Melissa asked.

"Yup," I said. "I'm up here. Do you need me down there?"

Declan growled, making his opinion on my moving quite clear.

"No, ma'am. I just wanted you to know that we were done. We're all loaded up. We'll make sure your art is delivered in perfect condition."

"Thank you! Oh, there are cookies cooling on the stove. Please take them all and share them with your crew."

"Thank you." I heard footsteps crossing the studio. "They're delicious. I had a hard time keeping their heads on business once they smelled what you were baking."

I grinned, snuggling into Declan. "Good. I'm glad you all liked them. Hopefully, Milo liked his tea."

"Oh—I'm not sure he ever had any," she said. "Doesn't matter. We hope you're feeling better soon."

"I'm fine. Declan is feeling particularly protective right now. That's all. I'm good."

"Thank goodness. The crew will be happy to hear that. Also, I was thinking. Instead of our returning in November to pack and ship all those octopuses, how about if we come every month and pack up whatever you have ready? You won't have to deal with all the space they take, and we won't have to pack that many all at once. I'm afraid of something getting broken."

"That's a great idea. Let me check with my agent and see if we can do partial shipments early. We'll get back to you," I said, rubbing my hand up and down the arm Declan had wrapped around me.

"Sounds good. Thank you for choosing us, and we'll see you again soon," she said before the door closed behind her.

I waited a few minutes and whispered, "All clear?"

"She just went out the back door…is walking across the deck… and is now being rushed for the cookies. We're clear."

I flicked my fingers, locking up.

Declan adjusted me on his lap so he could see my face. "You want to tell me what you saw? Because you came out of that one ready to fight."

SEVENTEEN

Age-Old Betrayals

"Yeah, but I might as well tell you all at the same time," I said, pulling my phone out of my pocket. I swiped and dialed Mom first.

"Hello, darling. Did your artwork get packed up?"

"Hi, Mom. Yes, it did. I'm calling because I have some things I need to talk with you and Gran about. Do you have time to talk?"

Mom's voice became muffled as she spoke to someone. "All right. Roseann's going to cover the shop for me. I'm in my office now. Did I tell you I was hiring your cousin to help in the shop?"

"You didn't."

"She's smart as a whip, but when she's not talking to customers, she's sneaking away to read. It's currently a contest to see which of us will break the other first."

"My money's on you, Mom. Let me loop in Gran."

The phone rang a few times and then, "Hello, dear."

"Hi, Gran. I have Mom on the line too and Declan is here with me. You guys are on speaker."

"What's happened?" Gran asked, her voice urgent.

"That's why I'm calling. We have a few problems." I explained about the stalker and his podcast and then went into the vision.

When I got to the little boy being poisoned by my cookie, Declan kissed the top of my head and held me tightly.

"Poison again," Mom mused. "How will Cal poison your baked goods?"

"I don't know," I said. "If we can't figure it out, I'll stop selling food."

"I'm afraid you'll have to," Gran said. "And we'll come and help you ward Bracken's vehicle. We can at least get that worry dealt with."

I squeezed Declan's arm. "Gran, that hellhound, or whatever it was, has me worried about you leaving your house."

"Nonsense," she argued. "That girl is not locking me up in my own home."

"And I totally get that," I said, "but what if something happens to you? We'll be back to two-thirds of the Council trying to fight a sorcerer and her demon. I know it feels like the strong thing to do is ignore the threat, but the Goddess gave me the vision for a reason. I don't think it's wise to ignore Her warning."

"She has a point," Mom said. "I think it makes more sense to bring you out when we have a plan for defeating Calliope. Not to waste it for wards that Arwyn and I can build. If her demon puts you in a coma, how are we, as the three, going to finally destroy her?"

This was unprecedented. Mom and I never argued on the same side. Normally, the two of them stood together. Maybe allegiances were beginning to shift.

Gran was quiet for a long time. "Has it been unseasonably cold?"

"No," Mom said. "It's been a normal July. I think it was sixty-eight today."

"Gran," I said, "in the vision, you were sitting by a fire and pulled a shawl around your shoulders. Have you been colder than normal?"

She was quiet again. "Fine. I'll stay behind my wards, but,

Arwyn, you have to find Calliope. She can't be allowed to continue her sorcery."

Declan opened his mouth, no doubt to remind her this wasn't all on my shoulders, but I shook my head. Gran had agreed to wait, and that was huge for her. We didn't need to push. With a sigh, he coiled one of my curls around his finger and continued to listen.

"We *all* need to work together to find her," Mom said, and I felt my eyes suddenly fill with tears.

Declan kissed the top of my head again.

"All right," Mom added. "I'm coming to you, darling. We'll ward Bracken's home and then I'll take you to your Gran's. We need a shared vision to help us know what to do next."

I swallowed the sudden emotion down and said, "Sounds good. I'm here."

After I disconnected, I pushed Declan back onto the bed. Of course, if he hadn't been willing, I wouldn't have been able to move him. "Now will you go back to sleep? Mom is on her way, and you know how boring ward building is to watch."

"I'm all keyed up now. I'll guard you while you work," he said.

I crawled up him and gave him a kiss. "I could always relax you."

Grinning, he wrapped his arms around me. "How long will it take your mom to get here?"

"Not long enough for that," I said, grabbing a hair tie from my nightstand. "This is all about your relaxation." I coiled my hair up and began kissing and caressing him until I made my way down and settled in.

Later, on a final groan, Declan said, "Thank you, and your mom just parked."

The fear of getting caught by Mom didn't seem to ever fade, even in adulthood. I undid my hair, swirled some mouthwash, and was running down the stairs a minute later. "Go to sleep," I shouted as I ran out the back door.

I found Mom standing beside Bracken's RV. "I knocked but he hasn't answered," she said. "Is he home?"

Wincing, I checked his windows. "He sleeps during the day and studies all night," I told her.

His door opened and he came out, dressed in his usual slacks, button-down shirt, tweed blazer, and sneakers. "Ah, guests. How lovely."

"I'm sorry we woke you," I said.

He waved that away. "Nonsense. Would you like to come in?" He waited for Mom's reaction. When he got none, he said, "Or we could sit on one of Arwyn's benches over here." He gestured to the deck.

Mom smiled. It was the first time I'd seen her give him a smile. "You're right. We should go in and talk first, so we can explain what's going on."

He pulled the latch and held the door open for us. Mom looked genuinely surprised by the interior. Bracken had made the RV a kind of beautiful dark wood and green leather study. Mom and I sat on the bench below the window in the front part of the RV. Bracken took his usual wingback chair and then popped back up.

"Tea. How rude of me to have forgotten to offer you both tea." He went to his kitchenette and gathered three cups.

Mom opened her mouth to stop him but I shook my head, and she listened. It was a day of firsts.

"Sybil, your daughter gave me some of your excellent blends, so I think you'll like it," he said.

"I'm sure I will. Thank you." She studied the compact sitting room and then looked down the hall to the wall of bookcases, his bathroom, and the bedroom he'd turned into an office.

"I'm afraid I have no little nibbles to offer you two." He handed us our mugs of tea. "Perhaps next time I will. Your daughter is very kind, always making sure this old man is taken care of." He took his own cup and sat back down.

He gave me such a delighted smile, I had a hard time swallowing the lump in my throat. "I had a vision this morning."

"Oh?" He picked up the journal on the side table at his elbow. "Anything related to our little problem?" Bracken knew not to use names when it came to sorcerers and the fae. Better safe than sorry.

"Yes, and tangentially." I went through the vision with him. He stopped me often to ask questions and take notes.

"You haven't made any peanut butter cookies, have you?" His handwriting was tiny, but I knew it was probably quite clear to his own eye.

"Not in months," I said, "but I keep tons of baked goods in the freezer, so…" I shrugged. "Hester knows where they are, if she needs to fill in the case."

He nodded. "So, this could be prophesy. I'll check everything in your kitchen. I have an affinity for poisons. I believe you were baking earlier today. The workers were quite excited about the cookies you gave them."

My hand flew to my mouth. Had I poisoned half the black bear shifters in Monterey? No. My hand dropped with the understanding that they'd had time to develop symptoms and they were all fine. "I'm sorry they woke you too. They were here to pack up my art and ship it to two collectors. I made them honey cookies because they're bear shifters. Oh, and one wicche."

I turned to Mom. "Do you know the Swans?"

Mom tipped her head side to side. "I know Catherine, sort of. She's the current head of the family. She's your Gran's age. I also know a few of her children." She shrugged one shoulder. "They're not a powerful family."

Bracken nodded. "Though it's not for a lack of trying. I knew Catherine when I was young. She's a few years older than me but I thought she was a friend. It turned out she was using me to get close to your grandmother. She seemed to believe she could become more powerful if she used the same grimoire or if she knew what Mary was studying."

Mom leaned forward at that.

"When I realized what she was doing, I told her she'd never be as powerful as Mary because she was nowhere near as powerful to begin with." He took a sip. "She didn't like that. And suddenly, I was an outcast among my peers." He sighed. "Even my sister had no use for me. Well, I suppose I could have been more tactful." He took another sip.

"Uncle Bracken," Mom began, "I'm confused. Didn't you take the family grimoire and give it to Catherine?"

Bracken's head whipped around like he'd been slapped. "Of course I did no such thing. Where on earth did you hear such a ridiculous story?"

Mom glanced at me and then turned back to her uncle. "It's an old story I've heard from multiple family members. Our grimoire had gone missing. No one knew where it was. The then-Corey Council did a finding spell, and they located it at the Swans' house. Gran and Mom went to get it. The Swans swore they had no idea what we were talking about. Mom said she hit Catherine with a truth-telling spell, and Catherine finally admitted that she did have it."

Bracken's brow furrowed in confusion.

"She went to her room and brought it back to where everyone was standing by the front door. She told Mom and Gran that you'd loaned it to her, and she was just reading it."

The look of betrayal on Bracken's face broke my heart. "I see," he said quietly. "A person who posed as my friend stole from us and then my family all accepted the story of a liar and thief, assuming the worst about me."

His hand trailed to his chest. "It was a very long time ago. I don't know why it bothers me so."

I went to him and took his hand in both my gloved ones. "Because you've spent your life locked outside your family, forever looking in, and no one even bothered to ask you if it was true."

He took in a deep breath and blew it out. "Yes. I believe that's why."

"I'm so sorry," Mom said, rising to her feet.

He waved away her apology. "You hadn't even been born. I,

myself, was still a child. And an odd one, so I suppose they assumed me capable of horrible disloyalty."

"No," I said. "We're not making excuses for them. What they did to you was cruel."

With a sad smile, he patted my hands. "You're such a blessing to me." With a head shake, he added, "What's done is done. You came here because you had a vision of me being crushed under my desk and my books burning. That is far more pressing." He glanced down the hall. "I won't feel comfortable sitting behind it until we fix this."

"Then let's do that," I said, going to his door. I held it open for both of them.

Mom stepped out and glanced around the parking lot. "We're out in the open here." Her fingers flicked as she stood east, south, west, and north, casting a safe spot for us where we couldn't be observed.

I looked over the RV as I slid off my gloves and stuffed them in my pockets. "Bracken? I have a suggestion you might not like."

Eyebrows raised, he waited.

"I think we remove the tires and do what we can to make this a stable addition to the gallery."

I thought for sure Mom would protest, but instead she said, "You could hire Phil's construction company to come back and build a proper in-law unit."

I tried to gauge Bracken's reaction. "We could ask him to make it as close to what you're used to as possible," I said. "If you'd like that."

He swallowed. "That's quite a bit more permanent than we discussed earlier."

"I don't want to push, but I love having you here," I said. "You don't have to decide n—"

"Yes. I'd like that very much," he said, nodding. "Very much indeed."

EIGHTEEN

And Bracken Makes Three

Mom walked to the side of the RV. It had been parked about a foot from the wall of the gallery.

Mom looked back at me. "There isn't much room for it to tip back and forth." Her focus shifted to Bracken. "Were you planning to go anywhere?"

Bracken and I shared a look and then he nodded. "Arwyn and I were going car shopping. I need something smaller for driving around town."

Mom walked back around. "Good, then. Now you know not to take this to car shop."

"I can take them," Declan said, walking around the back of the RV from the deck.

"You're supposed to be sleeping." I poked him in the side and then remembered I'd already taken off my gloves. "Oh, damn." I went to the water's edge and caught a shot of water.

"That actually works perfectly," I said when I returned. "Then we'll know if there's enough headroom for you."

"If you're trying to find a car I fit in," Declan said, "your options are going to be severely limited." He looked at me. "And I'm here because your groceries were just delivered. I didn't know whose was what, so I put all the perishables in your fridge. I figured you could separate the orders when you're done here."

"Good," Mom said. "You can keep an eye on things while we work."

"Please and thank you," I added on an eye roll.

"They were implied," Mom assured us.

Bracken and I moved to where Mom was standing near the gallery wall.

"I think a simple sticking spell," she said, "so it can't be tipped. Then we'll ward against everything else."

"Especially fire, please." Bracken's gaze moved between the two of us. "I've been building my collection for over fifty years. Many are one of a kind books that can't be replaced."

Mom nodded. "Fire will be the priority."

"Okay," I said, holding my bare hands up. "I have no idea what's going to happen. I'm going to focus on protective spells, but shared visions aren't out of the question."

They each took a hand and then—

A man sneers. I can't see his face, just his sneering lips and smoke-stained teeth. His thick fingers wrap around the neck of a bottle with a threadbare rag hanging out of the top. A chunky silver ring in a shape of a heavy metal cross sits on his thumb as he flicks a cigarette lighter with a broken, dirty nail.

A tall flame shoots up and is put to the rag. It catches fire. Adrenaline pumps as the man reaches back and then launches the bottle against the side of the gallery. Old work boots, peeling at the creases, run to a waiting sun-faded blue pickup truck. The edges of the running board and the fender are being eaten by rust. He jumps into the passenger seat even as the truck kicks up pebbles, racing down the dark, empty coast route.

The vision goes black and then...

A boat bobs in the rough ocean waters. It's storming and waves are capsizing over the stern. The boat reads Bishop's Queen. *It's tossed in the tumult. White knuckles grasp the tiller. A piercing scream cuts through the roar of the storm. A young woman, her black braids whipping in front of her face, is thrown against the older woman desperately trying to keep the boat from capsizing.*

The young woman grabs the tiller too and tilts her head into the wind. Faith. Her mother—Elizabeth—grabs Faith and holds her tight just as a huge wave bucks the boat and sends them both overboard under the deadly waves.

Mom gasped and we were standing beside the RV, still hand in hand.

Bracken blinked rapidly and then said, "My. That was extraordinary. Is it always like that?"

Mom shook her head. "At least we aren't on the ground."

I glanced between the two. "It was different because you were a part of it," I told Bracken. "You have an eye for detail, so we were focused on the details."

He nodded. "I got the license plate number. You can give that to your detective friends."

"I didn't see that," I said and almost dropped my hands. "Wait. Let's do the wards first and then we can discuss what we all saw. If this vision was like previous shared visions, we all saw something a little different."

Mom nodded, looking up at the clear blue skies. "I'll call Elizabeth when we're done to tell her to stay off her sailboat for a while."

The magic felt different with Bracken involved. He tempered the strong female power with his own, and he was very powerful. Why had no one ever told me that? Never mind. I knew why. They'd discounted him as a child, and he'd been cut adrift to develop his skills on his own.

The warding went faster than usual. Granted, we were warding a much smaller residence, but still, we were a strong three. By the time we finished, though, my left hand was cramping. Bracken had had a death grip on it while we worked.

I tried my best to inconspicuously shake it out, but apparently I wasn't as sneaky as I'd thought because Declan was suddenly holding my hand and massaging it.

Bracken stared thoughtfully at the water and my mom pulled out her phone to call Aunt Elizabeth. I leaned into Declan, my head sore. A moment later, his strong fingers were in my hair, rubbing my scalp.

"Do you read minds too?" I whispered.

"You have a very expressive face." He kissed me and then led me back to the deck. "Let's all go in and you can discuss your vision."

Mom held up a finger to let us know she needed a minute. Bracken followed quietly behind us.

When we got to the back door of the studio, I turned to my great-uncle. "Is everything all right?"

He looked up from the deck. "Hmm? Oh, yes. Of course. Just thinking." He followed us and then got a new look in his eye. "I need to check your stores for poison." He went to the refrigerator first, opening the side-by-side refrigerator and freezer doors. Closing his eyes, he held up his hands and slowly drew them from the top to the bottom, never touching anything.

When he was done, he closed the doors. "No poison." He turned to the storage closets I used as my pantry. He'd seen me go into them before and so knew where to look. It took a few minutes, but then he turned, shaking his head. "Your stores are clear. So, how will the poison be introduced?" He was talking to himself, but we were all thinking the same thing.

Mom walked in a moment later. "Your aunt says they had planned to go sailing this Sunday, but they're canceling those plans."

I nodded, the tightness in my chest relaxing. "Bracken says I'm poison-free."

Bracken held up a hand. "Not so fast." He pointed to the gallery door. "Isn't there food out there?"

I thought about it and realized I hadn't put the food away yet. Nodding, I followed him into the gallery. He walked behind the display case and slid open one of the doors before taking a step back almost immediately.

He turned to find me watching. "I'm sorry, my dear, but there is definitely poison in this case." He slid open the other door, held up a hand, and then shook his head, sliding it closed again. "That side is fine. The poison is on this side."

Mom stood at the front of the case and looked in. "You have a peanut butter chocolate chip cookie on the bottom shelf."

Bracken, surprisingly spry, crouched easily and held his hand over the cookie. He nodded. "Yes." He checked the few items left in the case. Two more had been poisoned.

I grabbed a trash bag from under the café sink and threw everything in, whether it was poisoned or not.

When I got to the cookie, Mom said, "Wait. If you touch it, can you see who poisoned it?"

"No!" Declan roared.

Mom jumped but Bracken patted Declan's shoulder. "It's not that kind of poison, son. It has to be ingested. Arwyn will be perfectly fine."

I slipped off my glove and Declan said, "Wait." He came over, sat in front of the open door of the display case and then pulled me down into his lap. "You're not hitting the floor." He wrapped his arms around me and then rested his chin on my shoulder. "Be careful," he growled.

I reached out and touched the cookie with my fingertip.

"Come here, child. You remember what I told you, don't you?" An older woman with pale skin, pale eyes, and dyed black hair crooks her finger for her grandson. Milo. "You heard what she said about the power we'll have if we help her." She places a small fabric pouch in Milo's hand. "I spelled it to keep her away from you. We don't need her getting nosey."

"What if someone dies?" he asks, staring in fascination at the pouch.

She waves away the concern. "People die every day. They get hit by cars. They get sick. We have to destroy that half-breed, the whole Corey Council, and then we'll have the real power in this town."

"And the money that goes with it," Milo says on a grin.

"Good boy," she says, curling his fingers around the poison in the fetish bag. "Now hurry up. You're going to be late."

The vision goes black and then…

Melissa claps her hands. "Okay, all. Time for a break, and judging by the smell, Ms. Corey has cookies for us." She waves the crew out the back door.

"I'm just going to grab a cup of tea," Milo says.

Melissa nods absently, following the crew out for honey treats.

Once he's alone in the gallery, Milo pulls the pouch from his pocket, steps behind the display case, and slides open a door, his eyes on the deck. He casts a look-away spell and though he's not a powerful wicche, it's a simple spell. It helps that the bear shifters are completely focused on cookies as well as the arrival of Carter.

Milo sprinkles the poison on a muffin, a shortbread cookie, and the peanut butter cookie. He slides the door closed and then, with the few grains of poison he has left, he drops them in a tea leaf jar on the back counter.

When my eyes blinked open, Declan pulled me to my feet and was then washing my hands in the sink.

"Bracken? Could you check these jars too? He dropped poison into one of them as well."

"Who?" my mother demanded.

Declan was on the third wash of my hands. "Come here," I whispered to him.

He leaned down and I gave him a big kiss. "Thank you."

He took the tea towel from the counter and dried my hands. As Declan had already touched me, I didn't need to worry about seeing visions of whoever had last touched the towel.

"Yes," Bracken said. "This jar has poison in it."

"Arwyn?" Mom was getting annoyed.

I turned around and said, "Milo and Catherine Swan. Cal promised them untold power and wealth if they helped her bring down the Council."

NINETEEN

I've Always Wanted One!

Mom collected her things and left, heading for Gran's. She said she'd call us to discuss the shared vision once she'd explained the situation to Gran. I think she wanted to be with her so Gran wouldn't feel cut off from what was happening. I was also pretty sure she needed to talk with Gran about Bracken.

The first thing I did when Mom left was grab the receipt from my worktable and call Melissa's number.

"Ms. Corey?"

"Hi. Sorry to bother you. Am I on speakerphone?" I asked.

"No, ma'am." I could hear road noise and so assumed she wasn't the driver.

"We have a problem."

"Okay," Melissa said, clearly wary.

"One of your crew, Milo, poisoned some of my baked goods when he was alone in the gallery."

"What?" Her voice was an angry growl.

"It's a lot to explain, much of which I'm not sure I'm allowed to yet. You already know we have a sorcerer problem. Milo and his grandmother are trying to help my cousin. Catherine Swan gave Milo poison to sprinkle on my food. I had a vision, saw a child eat one of my cookies and die. I checked the cookie. It had been poisoned and when I touched it, I saw Milo and his grandmother. I know this probably all sounds ridiculous, but I can assure you—"

"Ma'am, that's not necessary. We all know what you can do and that you're crazy powerful and accurate with your visions. I have no doubts. Firing Milo is easy. What else do you need?"

The tension in my neck and shoulders eased. Declan walked by and rubbed my back. With his werewolf hearing, he always caught both sides of a phone call. "Is there a way of knowing which boxes he packed? If he's willing to kill innocents, I'm sure he's willing to destroy my art. I can't have a box of broken glass arrive at the Winslows."

"Shi—excuse me. You're right, ma'am, and it's the reputation of my company as well." A very loud growl had me pulling the phone from my ear. "We're almost back to the warehouse. Did you sense anything amiss with the rest of my crew?"

I thought about it a moment. Closing my eyes, I sorted through all the others I'd met and fed cookies to. "I keep my mental walls up unless they have to come down," I told her. "No one stood out as problematic—even Milo seemed fine. He was clearly nervous, but I assumed it was because Coreys don't have the best reputation in the wicche world."

"Okay. Each member of the crew has a mark that they put on a box they've packed. Elise and I are going to open every single box and do a quality check."

Even I heard the groan of the driver, who I assumed was Elise.

"Thank you," I said. "I'm sorry I have to ask it, but we can't ship destroyed art to people who paid a great deal for it."

"Absolutely. And I don't want my company's name associated with shoddy work. I'll call you back when we're done."

"Thank you again. Also, can you hold off on firing Milo? I need to hear back from my mom and gran with what we're doing about this."

"Understood," she said. "If it was us, we'd rip his scrawny head off. I get that you guys do it differently."

"Yeah. We try to keep our head ripping to a minimum," I said.

"Which is why you have this problem," she replied. "If you don't mind my saying, ma'am."

Declan laughed at that.

"I'm not saying you're wrong, and please call me Arwyn. Okay. We've got a hazmat cleanup going on here. I'll talk to you later."

Declan and Bracken had finished clearing out the display case and the tea jar while I was on the phone.

I used a scouring spell on all of it, but worried it wasn't enough. The tea jar and pastry pans went into the dishwasher, and I donned rubber gloves to wipe down everything with harsh cleansers. When I was done, I still looked at the case with distrust.

"The poison is gone," Bracken assured me. "It was on the food, not the shelves or glass."

Nodding, I added the rubber gloves and sponge to the trash bag. "I just keep seeing that little boy, so excited for his cookie and then foaming at the mouth and convulsing in pain. My food killed him."

"No." Declan wrapped an arm around me. "Not your food. Swan's poison. And you saw what was going to happen, so that little boy is alive and well."

"The idea of putting food back in there makes me really nervous," I admitted.

Bracken tied up the garbage bag.

"Wait! That needs to be disposed somewhere where the raccoons won't find it." I couldn't have my little friends eating tainted food.

"I can take it with me," Declan said. "My dumpster locks."

Bracken swirled his hand over the bag. "It should be safe now. I strengthened the bag itself and then gave it a highly astringent scent that animals will avoid."

Declan nodded. "It smells like the cleanser you were using. No animal is going to chew his way through a bag smelling like that."

"Thank you very much," I said, and Bracken nodded with a shy smile.

"Do we know how long it'll be before your mom calls?" Declan asked.

I shrugged. "Probably not for a while. They need to go over every possible angle before they tell us what they've decided. They're not big on open discussions."

"But you're a member of the Council," Declan argued, offended on my behalf.

Grinning, I patted his shoulder. "I have not yet earned their trust or respect. I'm getting there, but those two have been working together since Mom was a teenager and joined the Council. I'm the powerful punk kid who ignores her responsibilities. Once they've decided on a path, they'll entertain my input."

I washed my hands again, just to be safe, and slipped on a new pair of gloves.

"Well, if we have time, let's get lunch and go car shopping," Declan suggested. "I'm hungry and that RV isn't going anywhere any time soon."

As we all loved Mexican food, Declan drove us to Mariana's. We'd missed the lunch rush, so we got a table easily. As we ate, we discussed car options. It was decided pretty quickly that it needed to be an SUV if we wanted Declan to fit in it.

"That works better for me anyway," Bracken said. "I'm so used to being up high when I drive. I don't know how well I'd adjust to being low to the ground. Not being able to see over the other cars."

Declan drove past a dealership, and I saw a rig I didn't think they made anymore. "Was that a Bronco? I love those." I turned to Bracken. "Can we try one of those?"

His smiles seemed to come easier these days. "By all means. That one's on my list."

Declan circled around the block and came back around to park in front. I almost crawled over him to get out. It was exactly like I remembered, but new and shiny. There was a guy down the block when I was growing up who drove one and I always loved it. I wanted one, but because of the visions, I can't drive.

I pushed Declan ahead of me. "There's no point getting my hopes up if you can't fit in it."

The price on the window was way higher than I was expecting, but Bracken didn't blink an eye at it. Declan climbed in, easing the seat as far back as it would go so his knees weren't jammed under the steering wheel. He put his hand over his head.

"I've got maybe a quarter inch, but my head's not touching," he said.

I pulled on his arm. "Try the back seat too."

He looked over his shoulder into the back. "I think that's going to be your seat." He got out, opened the back door, and stopped. "If I'm wounded and you need to lay me out, put me in the cargo area."

"Good afternoon." A tall Latino man with short dark hair and a trim beard came around a big SUV, saw Declan, and stopped in his tracks. He lowered his head and waited.

"Miguel," Declan said, walking over and putting a hand on the man's shoulder, his thumb touching the man's neck.

Ah. He must have been a werewolf too. Declan had once told me that when wolves were upset, having the Alpha touch them helped to ease whatever was going on.

The Big Sur pack was all male, which seemed odd to me. I knew female wolves existed, though in much smaller numbers. I had asked Declan at one point, and he told me that he believed the reason the Big Sur pack had no women was because Logan and his inner circle were predatory creeps. He'd asked Kenji and Daniel, his third, about it and had been told that the few women the pack had had felt unsafe and moved to join other packs. Kenji, though, had told him they'd recently received a few petitions from female wolves who wanted to join, which made Declan feel good. He was changing things.

"You haven't been to practice in a while," Declan said to Miguel. Everything was code when we were out where humans could hear us.

"No, sir. My wife is a nurse. She was put on the late shift. I can't leave the kids and go to late night practices." He glanced up at Declan, his head still tilted away. He looked braced for violence.

"I understand. Would an early morning practice work better for you?" Declan patted the man's shoulder.

Surprised, Miguel stood straight and nodded. "Yes, sir. I need to be here by ten. My kids can walk to school. It's only three blocks away and my wife is home by then. She'll be sleeping, but she's there if there's an emergency." He chanced a smile. "That would help a lot. Get rid of all this…" He rotated his shoulders, trying to demonstrate where the tension was hitting him.

"Then that's what we'll do," Declan said. "Does five work? Five thirty?"

Miguel nodded eagerly. "Yes, sir. I know there are a few other guys who also can't do late nights. I think they'd really appreciate being able to meet early mornings."

"Good," Declan said. "I'll send out a message." He turned to Bracken and me. "We're here to look for an SUV for my girlfriend's great-uncle—one I can fit in too."

"Absolutely," Miguel said, a broad smile on his face. "Ford started making the Bronco again in 2021 and it's been really popular ever since. If it was for you," he said to Declan, "I was going to suggest the Raptor edition. It's a little bigger, but also more expensive. This one is the Everglades edition. It's a four-by-four, of course…"

He went on about a whole lot of things that meant absolutely nothing to me. Bracken test drove the first one we saw and then both Bracken and Declan test drove the bigger one Miguel had referred to. Personally, I thought the rear-facing camera was very cool and I loved that the top could come off. The rest? No idea.

Miguel told us we could get a bench seat in the second row, understanding that would be much better when dealing with someone in wolf form.

In the end, Bracken bought the first one we saw, the tricked out emerald-green Bronco, and Declan ordered the bigger one for himself. Given he was now going to need to drive up to Big Sur, sometimes twice a day, he wanted something that worked better than his pickup.

Miguel's body language was lighter with the promise of early morning runs and two big sales.

We had to wait a few as they took Bracken's SUV in back to clean, even though it was already immaculate. I looked between the two men who'd both just dropped a lot of money on a new vehicle.

"Wait," I said. "You didn't both buy Broncos just because I love them, right?" I mean, seriously, what the hell did I know about cars?

They both looked at me and smiled, neither saying a word.

A man in blue coveralls brought the Bronco around and Miguel gave Bracken the keys and had him sit in it so he could walk him through inputting the driver settings and whatnot.

"You go ahead and drive with him," Declan said. "I'll follow you back. I want to swing by my place and see if they need me and then I'll be over. I want to hear what the plan is for these new players gunning for you." He leaned down to kiss me and then remembered I didn't have my backpack and therefore no seawater to reset my magic, so instead, he picked up my gloved hand and kissed that.

"On second thought," he added, "I'll go get you a new backpack. You need to have ocean water with you at all times until we have your cousin taken care of."

I nodded. "I have plenty of art supplies. I just need a backpack and a jar. And, honestly, if you can't find a little one, like I was using, skip the jar. I have empty honey jars I can use. I just liked the little honey bear."

We turned back when it seemed like the tutorial was winding down. The concentration in Bracken's face as he committed to memory every bit of information Miguel gave him made me smile. I tugged Declan's hand. It was wrapped around mine. "How long do you have to wait for yours?"

Declan shrugged one shoulder. "Miguel said it looked like a

dealership in Salinas has the one I want: bench seat, azure gray exterior, all the rest. We'll see. If they don't, he has to order it, which can take a couple of weeks."

"So," I said, leaning against his arm, "does this mean you're doing two-a-day trainings now?"

He let out a gust of breath. "Looks like."

"I know you have to," I whispered, "but I worry about you falling asleep and ending up in a ditch or over a cliff." I squeezed his hand. "Please promise me to be careful and pull over and sleep in your truck if you're tired. Okay?"

He lifted my hand to his lips again and said, "I promise."

TWENTY

Double Vision

Declan walked me to the passenger side, opened the door, and showed me the handle for pulling myself up and in. Even though I wasn't having trouble, I still felt his hand on my butt, guiding me to the seat. Odd, that.

The drive back to the gallery was fun. I kept wanting to push buttons to see what would happen but didn't want to irritate or distract Bracken. When Declan got his, though, I was pushing the shit out of all the buttons.

"Oh, I forgot to tell you," I said. "Aunt Elizabeth and her family are coming for dinner tomorrow night. Can you join us? They want to help us find Calliope."

He nodded. "You already told me. Do you have something to serve, or should we go to the market?"

Hmm, did I? "I always have frozen lasagnas in the freezer now because of Declan. It's also not unusual to find steaks in my refrigerator. I never see him add them, but they're there."

Bracken chuckled. "I've always like Elizabeth. When I was still occasionally visiting the family, I saw she was a kind child. She wasn't the strongest wicche but didn't seemed to care one way or the other, which I found refreshing."

"That was my take too." I put down the sun visor, as my head was starting to hurt. "Lately, though, I've begun to question that. I think she's been hiding her gifts."

Bracken glanced at me and then focused on the road again as he turned onto Lighthouse Avenue. "Really? That's interesting." We got stuck in traffic near where the whale watching boats launch. Bracken hadn't been back long enough to remember to avoid this intersection. "Is it silly that I love the color?" he asked.

"Not even a little bit. I've been trying to restrain myself from touching everything. And you can drive around with the top off, if you want—"

An image of a woman in a topless Jeep superimposed itself over the road we were driving. It was like a strange, disorienting double exposure. She drove down a short driveway, hit a button on a remote attached to her rearview mirror. Her garage door opened and she made the sharp turn inside to park. She stepped out of the Jeep, grabbed a handbag and a water bottle, and then hit the remote again. As the door came down, a narrow rectangle of light was visible for a split second as she walked into her condo.

Feeling seasick, I watched Bracken drive and turn but I was also watching that woman's garage door. A man stood beside a fence across from the garage, out of sight of the street. Waiting.

Curtains in the woman's front room opened. She came out, got her mail, and walked back in as she shuffled through envelopes. Once she was in, he moved toward the back of her unit.

"Arwyn? Are you okay?" Bracken's voice broke through the haze. We were at a stoplight, but I was also watching the killer find a new spot to hide. There was a little copse of trees between the townhouse village and the property next door.

"I'm not sure what I am," I said slowly. "I'm awake. I can sort of still see the street you're driving on, but I'm also watching a killer stalk his next victim. I've never had a vision while I'm awake. I—I think this is happening right now."

"Oh dear." He pulled over. "What can I do?"

I fumbled in my pocket and pulled out my phone. "Can you call Detective Hernández for me?"

He took it from my hand and then I heard ringing over the speakerphone.

"Hello, Arwyn," Hernández said.

"Hey. I'm having a weird vision right now. I'm awake, driving with my great-uncle, but I'm also watching a person stalk a woman. I'm not sure what's going on."

"Okay. Give me a sec." I heard rustling and then— "Ready. What are you seeing?"

"A young woman was in a Jeep. I was thinking about Bracken being able to take the top off his new Bronco and drive in the sunshine and then I saw her. It's like a double exposed image. One on top of the other."

"She's driving a Jeep," Hernández said. "What else can you tell me about her? Did you see the license plate?"

I shook my head and then remembered I needed to speak. "No. It's a black Jeep. The spare tire in back is covered in a pretty rainbow kaleidoscope. I don't think there's any writing on the tire cover. It's behind a garage door now, so I can't tell you." Bracken held my gloved hand and helped me settle.

"I understand," Hernández said. "Tell me about the woman."

"Uh, I mostly saw her from the side and behind. She's twenties, maybe. Tanned with long, shiny black hair pulled into a ponytail. She's wearing black shorts and a white polo. Maybe a waitress uniform or something? I don't know. Maybe she just doesn't like color."

"Rainbow tire cover," Hernández reminded me.

"Right. If I had to guess from what I could see of her, I'd say she's Asian. As for him, I can only see what he's seeing. He hasn't looked at the rest of the buildings, so I can't tell you the name of the community or anything."

"That's okay. Tell me what you can see," she said.

"It's light gray with white trim. One-story end unit. It looks beachy. Not that it's on the beach, just that builders around here make the condos look like they should be on a beach."

"Got it," she said.

"The garage is on the side. She drove down a narrow drive, hit the remote, and made a sharp turn into the garage. The door came down as she walked in. He didn't try to follow her in. He waited by—you know how complexes often have communal dumpsters in a fenced area so it doesn't look crappy?"

"Sure."

"It was like that. The fencing is painted the same light gray as her unit. There's a tall fence at his back. I can't see what's on the other side, but I think it's a house—no idea why. That's just what I think."

"Okay," she said.

"He watched from that spot as she went out the front door and grabbed her mail, still wearing the black and white. It felt like he knew that was what she was going to do, like he's been watching and clocking her routine. When she went back in, he walked down the narrow drive to the back of her unit, where there's a bunch of tall trees."

"Trees again," Hernández murmured. "Is he hiding in them?"

"Yes. Oh, there's a strip of lawn behind her place and then a tall fence with vines hanging over it. It's a weird cyclone fence hybrid with wooden slats going through the metal, so you can kind of see through it. A little, because the vines are blocking the view too. I'm piecing together the glimpses I'm getting, but I think it's a large—I don't know—soccer field, I guess, with a group of buildings on the far side of the field. Maybe an elementary school?"

"Good," Hernández said. "A condo village that backs up on an elementary school. The last unit before what might be a private home. A possibly Asian woman in a black Jeep."

I sighed. "Sorry. That's like a needle in a haystack."

"Not at all. You've given me a lot of angles to work. What's he doing now?"

"Still standing in the trees, watching the back of her unit. It feels like he's waiting for something," I said.

"I'll get started. I'm already pulling up maps of the elementary schools in town. We've got hours before the sun goes down. If you see anything else, let me know."

"Wait," I whispered. "The sliding door just opened. This was what he was waiting for. She's wearing yoga pants and a tank top now. She turned on a water valve and is carrying a hose to a couple of pots filled with flowers. Her back is to him as she waters. He's moving."

"Moving where?" she demanded.

"He's sneaking up behind her. She's finished watering and is leaning down to turn off the valve. A gust of wind is shaking the trees. He's using the sound cover to move in quickly. He's right there. I can see the goose bumps along her arms. She's standing. He's behind her. One hand covers her mouth while his other arm wraps around her waist and picks her up. He's carrying her through the back door."

"*Shit*. He's escalating. He hasn't hit in daylight before. Arthur!" Hernández shouted.

She was filling him in on what was happening, but I was no longer listening. The killer had put the young woman down and spun her around. "Her eyes are so wide. Her pupils dilated," I told whoever might have been listening. I was past caring. My heart was racing right along with hers.

"'Fucking bitch,'" I spat out, his words in my mouth. "'Not talking down to me anymore, huh? Still want to go above my head and file a complaint?'"

"The woman's having trouble breathing. Her lips are parted but her chest is frozen. She's looking up at him, but I don't think she's very tall. She looks petite and fragile.

"'What, you ran out of big words?' He slaps her and knocks her off her feet. He shakes out his hand and makes a fist. A thrill of excitement races through him.

"He's yanking her to her feet. Tears are streaming down her face. 'Please,' she whispers, sounding hopeless, like she knows there's no escaping him. He punches her and her eyes roll back as she flies back into her couch and then slides to the floor."

My vision goes black. I can no longer see my world, only hers.

"He shoves the coffee table out of his way and then straddles her, sitting on her legs, and waits.

"Little flinches, hands, eyes, lips, and then finally her lids flutter open. She sees him looming over her and it all comes back. Terror fills her again."

I was vaguely aware of hearing Declan's voice, but then it was gone and I was trapped in that room again, narrating a murder.

"She opens her mouth to scream and he lunges forward, wrapping his hands around her delicate throat."

I couldn't breathe. My eyes went wide as I clawed at invisible hands strangling me.

"Arwyn!"

The killer was crushing my neck. A heavy pressure sat on me. And then Declan was kissing me and the double exposure was gone. I'd lost the vision and regained my sight, my ability to breathe, albeit labored.

Bracken's fingers touched my throat and breathing became less painful.

Declan was there, holding my face in his hands. "Nice slow breaths in and out. Are you with me now?"

I nodded, blinking back tears.

"Arwyn, what happened?" Hernández demanded. "What's he doing?"

I followed the sound of her voice and saw my phone on the dashboard. I was confused by the question. Hadn't I been speaking out loud? "I told you." My voice was a harsh rasp. "He's killing her."

"And he almost killed Arwyn," Bracken said, outraged. "She's given you everything. She's done now." He tapped the screen and disconnected the call. Shaking his head, he added, "They ask too much of you."

I leaned into Declan, clutching at his shirt. What would have happened if he hadn't been here, his nulling touch dispelling the vision?

"How are you here?" I croaked.

He kept his arms wrapped around me. "I noticed a brand new, shiny green Bronco with temporary plates by the side of the road and stopped to see if there was a problem."

"And there was," Bracken said.

There was something about his voice. I turned my head and found him ghost white, staring back at me. I reached out a hand and he took it in both of his.

"I'm sorry you had to see all that," I said. "I'm okay."

"You most certainly are not. You were experiencing what that poor woman was. You told the officers that he was strangling her and then you stopped breathing." He shook his head. "I felt as though my own life was flashing before my eyes. I didn't know how to help you." He rubbed at his forehead. "And then Declan arrived, saw what was happening, and acted before I could explain."

My phone buzzed, making Bracken and me jump.

"If it's that detective again," Bracken began, but then he tipped the screen toward me. Mom.

TWENTY-ONE

Of Turrets and Sorcery

I let out a breath and tapped the screen. "Hey, Mom. We're on the road. Can we call you back when we get to the gallery?"

"What's the matter with your voice?" she demanded.

"There was an incident," Declan said, "but she's recovering from it."

The line was silent for a moment and then Mom said, "Can you all come here? This is a conversation that would be better had in person."

The three of us shared a look and then Declan said, "We're on our way," and tapped to disconnect the call. Pushing my hair back from my face, he asked, "Are you okay to go?"

I nodded.

"We need to detour to the water first, though," he said, "so you can fill this." He picked up a beautiful ocean blue leather backpack that he must have dropped earlier. He unzipped it and handed me an octopus bottle, like my old honey bear. The tentacles were all wrapped around, so the shape of the bottle was similar. The cap on the honey bear had looked like a yellow cone. On the octopus, it was a starfish that could be pulled up to squeeze out honey—or in my case, seawater.

Why was I crying? I gave Declan a watery grin. "I love them

both." I held the bottle in one hand and the backpack on my lap. How'd I get so lucky?

"Okay? We'll stop at the gallery so you can fill both up and then we'll head to your Gran's," Declan said.

I nodded again. He made sure I was in and then closed the door, heading back to his pickup.

I turned to Bracken, my neck still sore. As he started the engine, I saw the gold sedan out of the corner of my eye. I couldn't snap my neck around to see if the stalker had been sitting across the road watching us. Doing my best to push him out of my head, I asked Bracken, "Is this okay?"

He nodded, merging into traffic. "Do you think they meant for me to come too? They may not have known I was with you."

"They knew," I said. "The whole point of our being on the road was getting you a new car." I studied the octopus bottle in my hand and wondered where Declan had found it. "You don't have to go if it feels like too much, but I think it would be really good if you did." I left it at that.

The earlier excitement of the new car was gone. In its place was death and banishment. The cops were dealing with one of those things and we'd see if Gran was going to step up to confront the other.

Bracken parked next to his RV and Declan pulled in right beside him. I pocketed my phone and then stepped out of the SUV. Declan was already there, taking the backpack and wrapping an arm around me.

"I'm okay," I whispered.

"Yeah, well, I'm not," he responded, walking me slowly onto the deck.

"Nor am I," Bracken said behind us.

I tried to turn my neck, but it made me wince. "Maybe you should get your journal, in case they want to see some of your research."

He patted his breast pocket. "Already have it."

Leaning against the railing, I held out a hand and caught a

directed splash of oceanwater. Almost immediately, my throat felt better. I turned my neck this way and that, rolling my shoulders, shaking off the aftereffects. Yep. All better. Physically, anyway.

"Thanks, Dad." I held out my hand again and slowly drew up a fountain of water. This was harder and required more control. I'd taught myself how to shoot jets of water at my cousins when I was a kid. A slow, measured build was trickier. Once the tip of the fountain was within reach, I unscrewed the top of the octopus bottle and scooped the seawater into it before closing it back up again. Just to be sure, I popped up the starfish and dribbled water over the deck.

"We're good to go," I said, snapping the bottle shut again.

Declan held up the backpack. "Do you want to put a sketch-book and pencil in here?"

"Yes." I jogged to my studio. "I'll just be a minute."

Wilbur's ball was next to my back door. "Wilbur! You're back." I grabbed the ball, went to the edge of the deck, and threw it as far as I could for my selkie friend.

Admittedly, that wasn't as far as Declan could have thrown it, but it still gave me a bubble of joy when Wilbur shot out from under the deck to chase it. Cecil, my best octopus friend, slapped the surface with one of his tentacles, and some of the weight I'd been struggling under lifted.

I went in, opened a door in my wall of storage closets on the hot shop side of the studio, and grabbed a new sketch pad off a stack. I also took a box of colored pencils and one of charcoals. With a sharpener, eraser, protein bars, extra gloves, and a bottle of drinking water, I called it good and went back out to the deck.

Declan and Bracken stood side by side, both leaning on the railing and talking quietly.

"Everything okay?" I asked.

Both men turned. Bracken still looked shaken, but Declan smiled and came to me, taking my gloved hand.

"Of course," he said. "Are you ready to go?"

"As I'll ever be," I responded.

He walked me back to Bracken's Bronco and waited for me to climb in. "I'm going to follow you. I'm not sure how long this will take, but I'll probably need to head back to the pack grounds when I leave."

"Oh." I secured my seat belt and fought off the disappointment. I was hoping he could stay with me tonight.

"I know," he murmured and squeezed my hand as Bracken climbed in.

I pushed my hair out of my face. "Trust me, I get it. Yet another reason we have to find my cousin."

Bracken started the engine and Declan closed my door before returning to his truck. Bracken backed out, using his rearview mirrors while I stared at the rear-facing camera feed. It was so cool.

"Do you remember where Gran lives?"

Still pale, he nodded. "I grew up in the house your mother now lives in. While it's a very large house, by the time I came around, my siblings had all the bedrooms. I was in the turret."

"That was my room too," I told him.

Brow furrowed, he glanced over before returning his focus to the road. "With all the bedrooms in that house, why in the world did you end up on the third floor in a circular room? Wasn't it just you and Sybil?"

Watching the scenery change from oceanside to woods, I shrugged. "Mom says I just started moving my stuff upstairs and told her that was my room."

"Something else we have in common," he said. "I did enjoy the view of the garden."

I nodded.

"And it was quiet up there. Even then, I spent the majority of my time reading, so I think they forgot I was there."

"Oh," I said, turning to him. "I'm sure they didn't."

He gave me a quick look as he turned onto Gran's road. "I've lost count of the number of times I wandered downstairs, hungry, only to learn that I'd missed dinner. Mother always put it back on me, that I should have known it was dinnertime, but a shout up the stairs would have proved helpful, especially as there are rarely leftovers in large families."

I rubbed his forearm. "Sorry."

"When my sister Martha moved out at eighteen, they offered me her room, but I'd become used to the quiet and solitude. Plus, I liked Martha. I wanted her to move back, so I didn't want to take her room." He made the quick turn into Gran's drive. The entrance was hidden, but he remembered where to slow and drive between large, sheltering trees. Declan was right behind us and parked beside Bracken.

"Sam told us about Martha," I told him.

"Sam? Quinn? Bridget's daughter? How in the world would she know my sister?"

Declan opened my door but waited while Bracken and I spoke.

"She told us that Martha and her partner Galadriel, an elf, owned a fae bar near San Francisco," I said.

He sat back in his seat, absorbing that information, and then a slow smile finally brought color back into his face. "She found love and a purpose?"

I nodded. "Apparently, they were together for something like fifty years."

Sighing, he tapped his heart. "Oh, I'm so glad. She deserved happiness. As much as my family ignored me, they badgered her. She wasn't as powerful as Mary, or our mother, or any of our siblings for that matter, so she was treated quite poorly, I'm afraid."

"She was a necromancer," I said. "That was how Sam met her. Sam's a necromancer too. She went to Martha for training. Sam believes that her seeking out Martha is what called Abigail's attention to her. Martha had stayed hidden in the twilight between this realm and Faerie for most of her life and then was murdered horribly a week or two after meeting Sam."

"So," he said, a look of disgust on his face, "Abigail not only trained Calliope in sorcery, she also killed her sister Bridget and her aunt Martha?" He shook his head. "We have to find that grimoire and destroy it. This has to stop."

"We will," I promised, not at all sure we had the ability to destroy an ancient demonic grimoire.

Bracken got out and moved in a slow circle, taking it all in. Declan stepped back so I could slide out.

"How old were you when you moved out on your own?" I asked my great-uncle.

"Hmm?" He looked up into the branches of the trees above. "I left for college when I was seventeen. I returned for short visits after that, but it was clear, even then, that they'd rather I didn't."

"You have a home with me now," I told him as I slipped a gloved hand into the crook of his arm.

He patted my hand, the tension in his shoulders beginning to ease. "I suppose we should go in and hear what they've decided."

When we approached the front door, it swung open. Mom stood on the other side and waved us in. Gran was sitting in her rocking chair by the fire. As we entered, she stood, her gaze on her younger brother.

"Bracken," she began but then faltered. I'd never seen my grandmother so unsure of herself. She crossed the room and took his hand, so I moved back.

Declan pulled me to the side, his arm wrapped around me.

Blinking rapidly, she straightened her shoulders and said, "I don't know how I can ever make it up to you, brother. Please forgive me."

Bracken swallowed and then cleared his throat. "Can I ask? Why did you immediately believe I'd betrayed the family? I know I was an odd child, but why did everyone assume that oddness meant I was traitorous?"

I turned my head into Declan's chest, and he held me tightly. I knew exactly how it felt to be the sketchy outsider no one trusted.

Gran shook her head. "I don't know," she responded slowly. "Mom believed it. Gran did too, so it had to be true."

"I see." He nodded, staring at his sister and then over her shoulder out the window. "I don't believe I was our father's son."

Gran flinched and Mom's hand went to her mouth.

"Research is what I do, you see," Bracken explained. "There have been other eccentrics in the family. Why was I shunned? Given when I was born and my weight and size, I believe I was probably born to term. That being the case, I couldn't have been our father's. Forty weeks earlier, he was in Massachusetts at his mother's deathbed. He'd already been there a month."

He shrugged. "I have no idea of she had an affair or was attacked. Given the way Mother and Grandmother treated me, I lean toward the latter. Nothing was written about it, at least as far as I've found. And certainly no one spoke to me about it, so this is conjecture. I believe it to be correct, though."

Gran, like Mom, looked stricken. I could see the wheels turning as this new information altered her memories. Looking more frail than I'd ever seen her, she stepped forward and hugged Bracken to her.

He stood stiff and shocked for a moment before finally wrapping his arms around her.

TWENTY-TWO

We Were Overdue for a Family Meeting

Once everyone was finally seated, Gran and Bracken on the sofa, Mom in Gran's rocker, and Declan in my usual club chair—he'd pulled me onto his lap to sit with him—we got down to business.

I explained both of the prophetic visions I'd had this morning and then briefly touched on the murder so they'd know what had been happening when Mom had called earlier.

"The shared vision with Uncle Bracken was different," Mom said. "When we've done this before—you, your Gran, and me—we see things from a little different angle. This time, I was watching the arsonist from inside the truck, idling up the road, waiting for him. The gas gauge was close to empty and there were fast food wrappers littering the floor mats. The radio was turned low, a man talking about baseball. The driver kept turning his head, looking in all directions.

"Through the back window, I watched a dark figure throw something bright in the moonlight. It hit the side of the gallery and then flames began to climb up the walls. The driver threw it into reverse, kicking up pebbles as he floored it and then slammed on the brakes. A man opened the door and jumped in, but the cab lights must have been disconnected because I couldn't see the arsonist's face. He was turned around, staring out the back window while he hit the dashboard, yelling at the driver to go."

"It's because Bracken was with us," I explained.

They all looked at me.

I gestured to my great-uncle. "He's the one with the eye for detail. I know the arsonist has yellowing teeth, a chunky ring on his thumb, and cracked and peeling work boots. I don't normally see that. My visions aren't that zoomed in. This gives us some details to look for and report."

"But nothing has happened," Bracken protested. "Why would the police be involved before the fact?"

"Remember I told you that Declan, Orla, and I are part of a supernatural crime fighting committee?" I asked. "We can tell Detective Osso—he's a black bear shifter and our grumpy leader. A hate crime against a wicche qualifies as something we need to investigate."

"Oh, good," Bracken said.

I explained about the stalker and the new burning witch podcast. At first Gran waved it away as a waste of our time, but the more I explained his behavior, the recordings, and my belief that Cal was pushing him, she sat forward, anger lining her face.

"She'd expose all of us?" Gran demanded. "She'd see us all hanged?"

Bracken patted her arm. "They don't do that anymore."

She turned to him. "Given the vision, they still want to burn us at the stake."

He tilted his head in acceptance of that point. "I suppose some of them do."

Gran turned to Mom. "You called your sister and told her to stay off the sailboat?"

Mom nodded. "I did."

"What about you, Bracken?" I asked. "What did you see?"

He turned and studied me a moment. "I don't know how you do that." He shook his head. "It was horrifying. I was there. I saw the hatred in his eyes, the sneer on his face, as he threw the lit beer bottle of gasoline at your magical gallery."

Staring out the window, he said, "You've done so much. You've created this precious soap bubble of fantasy, brightening our dreary days." He turned up a palm. "And someone decides that must be destroyed. More, the artist, the creator of wonder, must be destroyed along with her creation." He blew out a breath. "Who are these people?"

Declan wrapped his arms more securely around me at Bracken's words.

"Could you see his face?" I asked. "I only got a close-up of his mouth and his hand."

"Oh." He looked up at the ceiling and scratched his jaw. "Let's see. He was white, with brown hair and eyes." He patted his own chest. "He had a black denim jacket that was turned into a vest." He brushed his shoulder. "The edges were ragged with stray threads. It had a patch on the left breast that I believe was a name. There was something obscuring the patch, though."

He tapped his index finger on his chin a few times. "I think it was electrical tape, but since it had been affixed to fabric, it was starting to peel up along the edges. I could be wrong, but given the lines visible above and below the strip of black, I'd guess his name is John. Assuming that was his vest to begin with."

Damn. I wished I'd always had Bracken picking up the details in my visions. "Perfect. Anything else about him physically that might make him easier to identify?"

Frowning, he added, "Well, he has a soft sort of face. Round. His eyes are too small and far apart. He has one of those short noses that forces you to look up his nostrils. Weak chin. And he had a little limp. It wasn't noticeable until he ran for the truck, but then he seemed to be favoring his… right leg. There was a hitch in his step."

"Okay." I got off Declan's lap, grabbed my backpack, and sat on the floor at Bracken's feet. I pulled out my sketchbook and put it on the coffee table with my charcoals. Bracken leaned forward to watch me work, making suggestions if what I drew was different than what he remembered. It wasn't perfect, but at the end, we had a close approximation of the arsonist.

"I don't understand, darling," Mom said. "It hasn't happened. How can this help?"

"It's always good to know who our enemies are," Gran said.

"There's that," I said, flipping the page and drawing the stalker. This face, I knew well. "I'll send them both to Osso and he'll send them out to the rest of the group. It's good to have faces and know what the threat is. If we're lucky, someone may even recognize one of them."

Away from Declan's warmth, I felt a chill run down my spine. I glanced out the back window and caught a dark shadow disappearing around the house. I needed to do something to beef up her wards. "Meanwhile, what are we doing about the Swans and their willingness to kill in aid of a sorcerer?"

Mom and Gran shook their heads.

"I know I shouldn't be shocked," Mom said, "given what my sister and niece have done, but I suppose I've become used to thinking of this lust for power at all costs being a Corey failing. That the Swans—or at least two of them—would poison innocents to curry favor is hard for me to accept. We're not living in the Middle Ages."

"She covets your power," Bracken said. "And Mary's. She always has."

"Do we have any recourse?" I asked, taking more time with the familiar stalker's face.

Mom tipped her head side to side. "We can report them to the Council, I suppose."

Gran shook her head at the suggestion. "To a council that fell apart more than a decade ago? What would be the point?"

"What's the Council?" Declan asked.

"Every wicche family has a leader," Mom explained. "Sometimes it's one person, but more often than not, it's a triad, like ours."

"Maiden, mother, crone," I clarified. "Basically, three generations of the most powerful wicches in a family."

Declan nodded, watching me draw.

"It isn't always the most powerful," Bracken said. "Sometimes it's the most sane, or the ones most able to work well with others."

Gran sighed. "True. Some of the most powerful have gone mad with it."

"Okay," I said, "but I don't remember hearing about a council other than the Corey Council."

"It existed for ages," Mom told us. "A representative from each of the old wicche families sat on a council that met regularly. They settled squabbles and dealt with threats to wicche survival. Had the Council not existed, far more of our numbers would have been lost in the Dark and Middle Ages. As it was, most accused wicches were just human women that someone had an issue with."

Gran nodded. "Midwives, early apothecaries who had some knowledge of medicinal herbs, women who refused to marry powerful men."

"Poor women, as well," Mom said. "The vast majority of women burned, drowned, or hanged were humans that some pious person pointed a finger at for their own highly dubious reasons. We know how to hide and when that doesn't work, how to cast the spells that keep us alive."

"In the modern world, the Council seemed less important," Bracken said. "The days of ritual burnings were long gone. Also, as more families intermarried with humans, our power was diluted." He paused and then looked at his sister. "This family excepted, of course."

"Oh, yeah," I grumbled. "We all know about the importance of pure bloodlines."

Gran's back went rigid. "Mock if you must, but notice which family still has real power."

I can't tell you how I knew, as Declan was sitting behind me, but I could feel him bristle. He was as pissed off as I was about my

Gran and Great-Gran making Mom give up Dad because he wasn't a wicche.

Still drawing, I lifted my left hand and wiggled my fingers. "Speaking as a mongrel, I'm plenty powerful, Gran."

She *tsk*ed. "I didn't mean you and you know it."

I sat back from my sketchbook and looked over my shoulder at Gran. "Okay. If you knew that my having a fae father would make me strong enough to survive being a Cassandra, why didn't you let Mom stay with Dad? We could have had more fae blood strengthening our line."

"Arwyn, please," Mom said, shaking her head.

"We are one of the oldest and strongest line of wicches in the world," Gran said. "We respect and value that."

I'd heard this all before and never pushed her on it. Today, I was feeling pushy. "Does it bother you that my last name is Corey, considering my fae DNA?"

Gran blew out a breath. "This isn't helping. We need to decide what to do about the Swans."

Mom stared at Gran with an expression I'd never seen before. If I had to guess, I'd call it a combination of disbelief and disillusionment.

Bracken laid his hand on my shoulder. "My sister was taught by a severe and unbending woman. She may not be able to bring herself to say that she is proud of you and proud to call you Corey, but she is."

I patted his hand. "Deep, deep down, right?"

"Arwyn," Gran said, "you are a part of the Corey Council, and we waited until you arrived before we made any decisions. We're overlooking your werewolf friend while we discuss Council business. I'm not sure how we've leapfrogged from the Swans being in league with your cousin to the status of mixed-blood Coreys. We have problems that touch the entire family that need to be dealt with now. Perhaps we can table the angst for another time."

"I can leave, if you'd prefer," Declan rumbled.

I closed up my sketchbook, put it and my charcoals in my backpack, and then returned to Declan's lap. "I'd prefer you stayed. It saves me explaining all of this later."

He wrapped his arm around me again and we sat together as a team.

"So, are you saying there is no wicche Council anymore?" I asked.

"That's just it," Mom said. "The Council hasn't met in years."

"Are you sure they're not meeting without us?" I ventured. "We're kind of the worst. Maybe they're still meeting and just dropped our names off the list."

Bracken chuckled. "I think you're on to something. I've heard mention of Council meetings off and on over the years. If you're no longer getting an invitation, that could be intentional."

Gran pushed up off the sofa and began to pace. "Who do they think they are, cutting us out of the Council? We led the Council for centuries."

"That could be why," I mumbled.

Bracken glanced at me, mischief in his eyes.

While Gran continued to rant, I caught another swoop of a shadow across the window. There was nothing I could do about this Council issue, but I could try to do something about that dark entity circling Gran's home. I had an idea.

When I stood, Gran paused her tirade, watching me expectantly.

"While you three figure out how we get back in the Council's good graces, Declan and I are going up on the roof."

Mom's brows drew together.

"Gran, I can feel it. I can see it. Something is trying to break through our wards. I'm going to see if I can add a fae ward. Neither a wicche nor a demon should be able to break that."

Declan rose.

"You guys keep it up," I said. "I'll let you know if my tainted blood helps save the day. Again."

Declan dropped an arm around my shoulder and we went out the front door.

TWENTY-THREE

Fae v Demon

When we stepped through the door, I felt a chill.

"I thought demons were hot," Declan said. "I sat near Dave once and started sweating."

I nodded. "Yeah, he runs even hotter than you. I think this cold has something to do with the way they're trying to break the wards."

Stepping out onto the drive, I looked back at the house. The problem was that Gran's home was like a bag of holding, appearing much smaller on the outside than the reality of the inside. Gran's home looked to be a derelict cottage clinging to a cliff. Really, it was a gorgeous three-bedroom, three-bath show-place. The problem was figuring out how to get on the roof when the roof wasn't where our eyes told us it was.

"Any idea how we get up there?" I asked.

He turned his back to me and crouched. "You can be my back-pack and I'll climb. I can't jump, since I can't see where I'll be landing, and I don't want to take off your grandmother's gutters."

I got on and wrapped my arms and legs around him.

He tugged my arm from his neck. "Maybe try not to strangle me." Reaching up, he tried to locate the actual edge of the roof. He followed it around the corner and then came back to the front door. "I have an idea, but be ready to save us if this doesn't work." He picked up Gran's heavy bench with ease and moved it out from under the porch overhang.

"Don't judge me," he grumbled. "This is going to be awkward as hell. She has high, peaked ceilings inside, so I'm assuming this is a peaked roof. If my aim is off and we fall, we'll need some kind of magical air mattress down here."

I wiggled my fingers. "On it."

He pulled me around so I was clinging to the front of him. "By the way, that was a really hot exit line about tainted blood you gave them." He kissed me with a ferocity that made all thought dribble out my ears.

When we finally came up for air, he had one hand under my butt and the other on my face. He opened his mouth like he was going to say something but then closed it, gave me a soft kiss, and slid me back around.

Stepping up on the bench, he reached up, much higher than the edge of the roof we saw, and wrapped his fingers around the side of what I assumed was a gutter. He stepped up onto the back of the bench, his balance perfect.

He flexed his knees and jumped, landing on the steep incline of Gran's slate tile roof—one we could now see. It had occurred to me earlier as I sat in her living room, watching that dark shadow circle the house, that the roof might be vulnerable. We'd never come up here to place a ward. Granted, our wards were for the entire building, extending onto her property, but if that dark shadow was getting to the windows and chilling the air inside, they were breaking down Gran's wards.

"Apparently," I said, "whoever created the original spell making Gran's house look like a cottage didn't extend the spell to the roof."

"Thank goodness," Declan grumbled, "or we'd be risking our necks with every step."

He scrambled to the top, pausing in a valley between two peaks. He helped me down and held on until I had my balance. I did a quick cleaning spell and then found a stable spot to sit. Declan moved out of my way, close enough to grab me if I started to slide, but far enough away to give me room to work.

"The tree cover helps too," I said. "Otherwise, satellite photos would show the roof of a very large house."

Declan nodded, looking up into the undersides of the huge trees surrounding Gran's home.

I took out the octopus bottle, slipped off my gloves, and squirted some ocean water into my hands. Closing my eyes, I placed my wet hands over my face and looked inside, trying to separate out that part of me that was fae.

I had no idea how long I was sitting there searching, but it was long enough to feel completely demoralized. I had no idea how to do this. I could have created a wicche ward, but at this point it felt like little more than a Band-Aid.

A large, cool hand pulled one of mine from my face and held it. I blinked my eyes open and found my father sitting beside me, his hair long and curly again. His bright aqua blue eyes watched me with humor.

"Tell me, daughter. Why are we sitting on a roof?"

I couldn't stop the ear-to-ear grin. He was back. "Hi."

He waited.

"Oh. My cousin and her demon are breaking down the wards on Gran's house. I came up here to create a ward using fae magic, but I have no idea how to do it. Can you help me?"

He glanced around the roof, nodding at Declan. My butt all of a sudden hurt less. I looked down and saw that Dad and I were now sitting on cushions.

"Thanks," I said.

He looked annoyed, but I wasn't sure what I'd done to tick him off. "This is Mary's house?"

I nodded.

"I'd like to help you, daughter, but I have no desire to help her. Perhaps we could just let the demon have her." He shrugged one muscular shoulder. "I can't imagine she'd be much missed."

I gave him my best disappointed look, but he was unmoved.

"Please," I said. "I know she's not your favorite person. Sometimes she's not mine either—"

"That shows good sense," he interrupted, patting my knee. "You get that from me."

"*But* she's still my grandmother and the head of this family. I want her to be safe. Can you show me how to build a fae ward?"

He studied me like he was memorizing everything about me. "Had you been allowed to visit me growing up, you'd have a much better understanding of your fae side. Instead, they kept you from me, denying my hand in my own daughter's education."

He looked down at the roof as though he could see through it into the living room. "The arrogance of wicches is not to be borne."

"I'm a wicche too," I said.

He shook his head. "Nonsense. You're far greater than any of them." He blew out a breath and then looked back at me. I saw the moment he gave in. "All right. We'll protect the sour old barracuda, whether she deserves it or not. This I do for you, daughter, and no one else."

"Thank you." I leaned forward and kissed his cheek.

"I'll guide you through. Remember, we—the fae—don't do spells. We *are* magic. There are no incantations or potions involved. We impose our will on the world—in this realm. In Faerie, the realm interacts with us. Faerie and the fae are—what's the term?— symbiotic. We work in concert with each other. Faerie, through the queen, has its own magic.

"The queen allows us our freedom until she doesn't and then she, as the source of all magic, reigns. Here, though, the realm itself is not magical. It adheres to Science. So in this realm, we impose our magic over the natural world."

A wind kicked up and blew our hair into our faces. "Here," he said. "This is a good example. We want the wind to blow in another direction, so our hair isn't in our faces. This is a small magic."

He took my hand again and I smelled the ocean, felt a wave

capsize over me. "We use the source of our magic," he explained. "For me—and you through me—that source is the immense power of the oceans. Do you feel it?"

I nodded. "I do."

"Good. Think about how it feels to move through the water, the way you propel yourself through that ancient power. The ocean moves as it will and has since the beginning of time, but you are able to slide through it, to make it give way to you."

"But..." I opened my eyes to catch a peek of him through my hair. "Humans can swim in the ocean too."

"Yes. Science," he explained. "Their bodies, being made of water, are buoyant. They can exert their muscles to force their way through. What happens, though, in a storm, when they are swamped by waves?"

"They drown," I answered.

"Precisely. The water is not their home. They may visit for short periods in good conditions, but they cannot survive there. Do you drown?"

I shook my head. "No. If I go too long without breathing, I get a bad headache, but I don't drown."

He made a sound of annoyance in the back of his throat. "Wicche genes are giving you that headache. I'll see later if I can fix that. So the ocean welcomes you. It is as much your home as the land. This is a source of power you can use.

"Back to this damned wind. Feel the ocean moving through your veins, the ancient magic that covers three-quarters of this realm. Feel the wind the ocean stirs up and move it—not *all* of it," he said, his voice suddenly stern. "We can't have you blowing ships off course all over the world because your hair has flown in your face."

I laughed.

"Not a joke, little one. I could do that easily. We have yet to see what you can accomplish. As you are mine, you are quite power-ful. So, no changing the tides or disturbing my creatures." He tapped his broad finger on my knee. "We respect those that live in our realm. We mean life or death to them. We protect what is ours. Yes?"

"Of course," I responded. He may have believed I could change the tides, but I knew that was far beyond my abilities.

"Don't be too sure," he said, responding to my thoughts. "Now, using just a small drop of that power, shift the winds right here, on your grandmother's property, to head southwest so we can see."

I thought about standing on my deck and the wind off the ocean blowing my hair back and then suddenly my hair was off my face.

"Good," he said. "Can you gentle it?"

I wasn't sure how I was doing it, let alone how to ease up on whatever I was doing. I pictured a warm summer afternoon with a little breeze off the ocean. The air warmed and my hair was no longer flying straight back in a gale.

My dad smiled at me with pride in his eyes. "Excellent. Now, as for securing the old bitty's house, we'll do something similar."

He held my hand in one of his and placed his free hand on a slate tile. I mirrored him.

"Wicche wards are very complicated things," he said. "Yes?"

I nodded.

"Again, we don't cast spells," he instructed. "We impose our will."

We *impose* our will. How was the question. Okay, I'd do what I did with the wind. I imagined that huge wave my dad had sent to put out the gallery fire that one of Calliope's minions had set a while ago. I pictured the force of that huge wave capsizing over Gran's house, coating every inch of it in ocean water that had been touched by Dad and me. Our magic, like an electric eel and jelly-fish, swam through the coating.

When I heard a hiss of pain, my eyes flew open. Declan stood on the crest of the roof, looking over the back toward Gran's patio, where the sound had originated.

Dad threw his head back and laughed. "Yes! That did it. You stung him." He put his hand back on the roof and said, "And now your mother, grandmother, and great-uncle can walk in and out of the house."

"Oh. Good save. Thank you." I pointed at Declan. "Can you fix it so Declan is safe too?"

Dad shook his head. "No need. You already accounted for him when you created this ward."

I glanced up and found Declan grinning back at me.

Dad stood and pulled me up, the pillows disappearing. "Good," he said and we were back on the ground near Gran's front door again.

Declan went to move the bench back to where it belonged.

"I look forward to our next lesson," Dad said, and he was gone.

TWENTY-FOUR

He's Not Your Underling

"How cool was that?" I whisper-shouted.

Declan put down the bench and then picked me up and swung me around. "Look who's getting fae lessons from her dad." He kissed me, cutting off my laugh.

"Oh, wait. My backpack!" I looked up on the roof and grimaced. Declan was going to have to climb back up there to retrieve it.

He tapped my back, and I felt it. "Your dad's got you covered."

I took it off and looked inside. Sure enough, the octopus bottle that had been in my lap was now inside the backpack. I picked it up and almost dropped it. It was cold, far colder than the water I'd put in it an hour ago. I popped the top and sniffed. It smelled of the inky black ocean. What did I mean by that? No idea. When I smelled this water, though, I saw deep, dark waters hiding leviathans.

"He changed my water?" I said, awed.

Declan paused and stared at the octopus in my hand. "What do you mean?"

"This isn't the water from beside my deck. Feel it." I put the bottle in his hand.

He held it a moment and then looked up at me with a shrug. "What am I feeling?"

"You don't sense it? It's cold, colder than it was when I first filled it."

He wrapped his fingers around the bottle a moment but then handed it back to me. "I think that's a you-and-your-dad thing. To me, it feels like your water bottle always does."

"I can't explain how I know, but this water is from the deepest part of the ocean, far below where any human has ever explored." I poured some into my palm and the world became clearer and brighter. I shook my head on a grin. "He gave me the good stuff."

I slid my gloves back on, stowed my very valuable seawater, and took Declan's hand to walk back in.

He paused at the door. "We could just jump in my truck and take off. There's no rule that says we have to go back in."

I tugged him down for another kiss while reaching for the door. I felt something akin to static electricity.

"Put your hand on the door," I said.

He did and then looked at me again, waiting for something to happen.

"Interesting," I said. "I wonder if they'll feel it." I pushed open the door and found Mom, Gran, and Bracken standing at the large picture window overlooking the patio, cliff, and ocean.

Mom turned and waved us forward. "We heard a hiss of pain out here, but we don't see anything."

"That was your daughter," Declan said with no small amount of pride in his deep, growly voice.

Bracken turned at that. "Are you hurt?"

"No," I said, waving away the concern. "He means I'm the one who set the ward that burned the dark entity circling Gran's house."

"Oh, darling. That's wonderful." Mom crossed to me and took my forearm, squeezing. We'd discovered lots of ways over the years to hug without hugging. "What did you do, and is that thing gone?"

Declan sat in the club chair again and pulled me back onto his lap. Gran stayed at the window, looking out, but Mom and Bracken moved to the couch.

"I'd love to take full credit," I said, "but Dad showed up and guided me through setting a fae ward."

Mom sat forward, her head snapping to the front door. "Your father's here?"

Declan's thumb brushed my side. He'd noticed too. Mom was a little too intent on Dad's whereabouts. "Not anymore. He must have sensed what I was trying to do, so he just appeared beside me." I turned my head to ask Declan, "Did you see him arrive?"

He nodded. "I was watching you, so yeah. He quite literally popped into existence beside you." He rubbed my leg. "He wasn't there and then he was, but it was like he'd always been there. I didn't smell the ocean until he appeared. I mean, Arwyn always smells lightly of sea spray, but this was more like floating on a raft in the middle of the Pacific."

I grinned. Yep. That was my dad, all right.

"Is it gone?" Gran asked, still looking out the window.

"No idea," I replied. "It doesn't feel as cold in here, so maybe. I wasn't trying to zap whatever that was. I was just trying to keep you safe. Hurting it was a nice perk."

Gran finally turned and brushed nonexistent lint from her sweater. "Thank you." She walked to the fire and twirled her fingers, causing the fire to go out, leaving hot embers. She sat in the rocking chair, straightened her back, and looked at me. "Could you get us some tea?"

"I can—" Mom began, but Gran waved her hand, telling my mom not to get up.

"Arwyn doesn't have a seat anyway," Gran said.

I'd been waiting for the disapproval of my sitting in Declan's lap. I supposed she'd had too much weighing on her to give it to me earlier.

I stood and went to the kitchen. A moment later, I heard the rumble of Declan's voice and then Gran say, "I can assure you, Arwyn was making tea long before she met you."

"With all due respect, Ms. Corey," Declan said, "I'm not a member of your coven. If you don't want me in your den, say so, but I'm Alpha, not your underling."

Shitshitshit. I flew back to the kitchen doorway and ran into Declan's massive back. He reached around to steady me. I couldn't see Gran but eventually, I heard, "Sybil, I want you to speak with Hester. See if the Goodes are attending Council meetings. I want to know if the lesser families have continued without us."

"That *lesser family* shit could be why," I muttered, turning back to the jar of tea leaves I'd just put on the counter.

Declan followed me in and wrapped his arms around me. "Sorry," he rumbled.

Patting his arms, I whispered, "Not your fault. She's used to being in complete control and she's struggling."

"I thought the same," he said. "She's like an aging wolf. She used to be the strongest, but time has worn away at her speed, the sharpness of her claws. Now she growls and bares her teeth to remind others she's to be feared."

Nodding, I brewed the tea, quite content to have Declan holding me while I did it. I'd never thought myself to be a person who'd enjoy easy affection. Perhaps because I'd thought it something I could never experience, I'd told myself I didn't want it.

"Will you be okay if I go?" he asked. "I need food before I head back up to the pack grounds. I'll work with whoever shows up and then sleep—poorly—in the woods, since I'll need to meet with more pack members in the morning."

"I'm sorry," I said, turning in his arms. "You must be exhausted."

"Nah." He gave me a kiss. "I got to sleep in a little this morning and then spend the day with my favorite person."

I laid my head on his chest and tried to soak in as much of him as I could. "You'll be safe, right?"

He kissed the top of my head. "No one's gunning for me anymore. I'm Alpha now. Didn't you hear?"

I snickered. "I think I heard something about that a minute ago." Resting my chin on his chest, I looked up at him. "If you wake up in the middle of the night, know I'm okay. I'll put the same kind of ward I did here on the gallery when I get back. I'll be safe and warm in bed, dreaming of you."

His hands came up to cradle my face. "See that you are." Gaze traveling over me, he added, "Take care of yourself while I'm away."

I grinned. "Will do."

He gave me another kiss and then walked out of the kitchen. I heard him saying goodbye as I loaded the tea cart. When I pushed it out into the living room, I found Gran, staring into the embers, Mom, looking concerned and staring out the back window, and Bracken, smiling and watching me. What had I missed?

I poured and delivered teacups to all before reclaiming the club chair as my own. "So, have we come up with the plan for the Swans?"

When neither Gran nor Mom responded, Bracken filled me in. "We had a question for you first. Do you have cameras inside the gallery?"

"No—oh." I thought about it a moment and then took out my phone, pulling up the app that held all the camera feeds. "I remember telling the security guy that I'd want cameras inside when I opened, but at the time, I was far more concerned with exterior cameras. And then I was trying to get everything ready for opening and forgot to have him come back to install interior ones."

I clicked through the different views and found five different angles inside the gallery. "*But,* Mary Beth was with me for a week getting everything ready and clearly she took care of it because I'm looking at the inside of the Sea Wicche right now. Including a camera angled directly on the café."

"Why would he aim one there?" Mom asked. "Your art is worth far more than muffins and tea."

"Ordinarily, I'd agree, Sybil," Bracken said. "In this case, though, that means we have video evidence of the Swan boy poisoning Arwyn's food."

Mom blinked and shook her head. "Of course. My mind was elsewhere. Yes, that's great news."

Gran studied Mom a moment and then turned to me. "Does the video show him going behind your counter and opening the cases? Sprinkling poison on the food?"

"Checking…" I responded, fast reversing the feed. "And there he is." I got up and went to Gran, sitting on the tall stone hearth beside her rocker.

Mom and Bracken stood behind Gran to look over her shoulder. I hit play and we watched the crew move out the back door. Milo hung back. Melissa paused at the door and looked back. Milo pointed at the café, and she nodded and walked out. It was all exactly as I'd seen in my vision.

Milo glanced around the gallery again, no doubt checking to make sure he was alone. His hand moved to his pocket as he walked toward the café area. From the vision, I knew he'd asked Melissa if he could get himself tea. As I'd already approved that, Melissa had said yes and went out to where the rest of her workers and the plate of honey cookies were.

Milo went behind the counter, pulled the fetish from his pocket, and unwrapped it. Looking out the back door, he slid open a case and sprinkled something quickly on a few items. Sliding the case closed, he checked the back door again. He looked at what was in his hand, turned to the tea jars, yanked the lid off one, dumped in what poison he had left, and then stuffed the fabric holding the poison back into his pocket before going to the sink and washing his hands. When he was done, he walked through the back door and out of camera shot.

"Can you see what he did when he went out on the deck?" Bracken asked.

"Good call," I mumbled, pulling my phone back and checking until I found the deck camera and then reversed the feed until I got to the cookie break. I turned the screen around and we all watched him walk out onto the deck, nod at another worker, and pull out his phone. He sent a quick text and then sat on a bench and laughed at a joke.

"Quite the little sociopath, isn't he?" Bracken mused. "He's just guaranteed someone's death, sent a text to his grandmother, letting her know it's done, and is now enjoying some down time." He shook his head. "It's chilling."

Threats in Too Many Directions

"I'll force a meeting of the Council," Mom said. "You send me that footage and I'll play it at the meeting. They'll be shunned by the wicche families."

"Sure. That's good, but why aren't I pressing charges? I have video evidence and we have the poisoned food." I turned to Bracken. "Declan has it, doesn't he?"

He nodded. "Yes. It's in one of his truck boxes. Given how crafty your raccoon friends are, he worried his dumpster wouldn't be secure enough."

"Perfect." I tapped the screen and called my boyfriend. I got a little charge just thinking of him in those terms. Look at me, with a father and a boyfriend. Who would have ever believed it? Not me, that's for sure.

"Hey," he answered.

"Do you still have the poisoned food in your truck box?"

"Thanks for the reminder," he said. "I completely forgot to get rid of it."

"No," I said, "that's good. I have Milo on video poisoning my food and tea. I'll call Osso, give him the evidence, but also let him know I want to press charges."

Declan was quiet a moment. "Yes. Do that. How long have there been cameras inside the gallery?"

I felt my cheeks redden, remembering times things may have gotten out of hand while he was helping me set up the gallery. "It was sometime in the last week, when Mary Beth was here, getting everything whipped into shape."

He considered. "Okay. We should be fine then. Back to the original question: I have the poisoned pastries and tea tied up in a locked truck box. When you talk with Osso, tell him I can deliver them to him tomorrow, that I'll be up in the mountains tonight. Unfortunately, he's not going to be able to get a hold of me, as I'll be running in my other skin."

"He'll understand, and I doubt it's a big deal as to whether they get the evidence tonight or tomorrow. Okay, drive safely and have a good dinner."

He chuckled. "It's probably for the best that I'll be eating alone. I'll be protein loading and it won't be pretty to watch."

I laughed with him. The man ate a ton, but he was so polite with it, it was easy not to notice that an entire lasagna was gone or that he'd eaten three stacked burgers to my one.

"Okay, love, have a good evening," he said easily, as though my heart hadn't just seized.

"Bye," I choked out and then sat, stunned. He'd called me *love*. I didn't—how was I supposed to react to that?

"Well?" Mom asked, interrupting my internal meltdown. "Does he still have the evidence?"

I nodded, not trusting myself to say words yet.

"I don't know," Gran said. "I'm not comfortable getting human authorities involved."

"I agree with Arwyn," Bracken said, and my confused heart warmed. I wasn't used to having someone jump in on my side. "Detective Osso is a black bear shifter, so he understands secrecy. Also, the most the Council can do is censure them, perhaps shun them, neither of which is commensurate with what they planned and what would have happened had Arwyn not thwarted them."

I got up and walked to the window, my emotions still all over the place. He'd said *love*. "It's not just that they need to be punished for trying to kill people to make me look bad. It's also that if we don't do something, they'll continue to help Calliope destroy this family." I pulled out my phone again. "I need to make sure Melissa and her crew don't do or say anything to tip off Milo that we know."

When I walked back into the living room from the kitchen, Melissa assuring me that nothing would be done until I gave her the go ahead—though she sorely wanted to tear him apart—I found Mom standing and Bracken gone.

At my confused look, Mom said, "Bracken will meet you at home. I told him I wanted to drive you back."

"Oh. Okay." Not gonna lie, I was disappointed. I wanted to ride in Bracken's Bronco, but clearly Mom needed to talk to me. "Gran, let me know if you sense that entity back again."

She nodded but seemed tired as she sipped her tea.

If I'd thought Mom wanted to talk with me, I was wrong. We sat in silence on the drive. "Mom, why did you want to drive me? What's up?"

She was quiet a moment longer and then said, "Nothing. I just wanted to make sure you were okay." There was another long pause and then she said, "It must have been strange, your father just showing up like that."

Ah, now we were getting down to it. "Thank goodness he did. I didn't know what to do."

She gave a vague "Hmm" and settled back into silence. It wasn't long before she pulled up in front of the gallery. She put her car into park but still didn't say anything.

"Just say what you want to say, Mom."

She gave her head a quick shake. "Don't be silly, darling. I'm glad it all worked out." She paused. "It's nice that you're beginning to have a relationship with him."

"I had to talk him into helping me protect Gran. He was all for letting the demon have her."

She turned sharply at that. "He said that?"

"Yep. Called her an old barracuda. He complained that if he'd been allowed to see me as I was growing up, I'd have a much better understanding of my fae side and be better able to use my magic." I watched the play of emotions across her face.

"I see. Did he say something similar about me? I mean, I'm sure he did. He was so angry with me."

"Nope." I picked up my backpack from between my feet. "He didn't mention you." I watched her face fall as she nodded her acceptance. "Of course, I did notice that he had a hard time keeping his eyes off you during opening night."

Her eyes widened and then she quickly shook her head. "No. I did what I did, and I knew the consequences." She gestured to the gallery's door. "Go ahead. I'll watch until you're in." She glanced up and down the road, so I did too. We were both looking for the stalker.

"I don't see his car," I told her.

"Good. You're looking a little tired, darling. See if you can get to bed early tonight."

Mom knew I rarely got more than a couple of hours of sleep a night, but this was our routine. She'd tell me to get more sleep, and I'd agree to try. We both knew it was useless, but we pretended.

I got out. "Thanks for the ride, Mom. Let me know what happens with the Council. *After* I talk with Osso, though."

"I remember." She waved and I closed her door. I flicked my fingers at the gallery door, went in, and locked it behind me.

The gallery was dim, the overhead lights off. A soft, pearly glow of early evening lit the way to the studio door. When I passed the café, my stomach twisted. That poor child would have writhed and died right here and for what? Money? A demon's favor?

When I opened the studio door, my stomach twisted again. Oh no. I ran to the bathroom and was sick. I couldn't get the image of that dying child and his wailing mother out of my head. After I cleaned myself up, I brewed some tea and took it to my chair to drink, hoping it would settle my stomach.

As the light bled from the sky, I shook off my stupor and called Detective Osso.

"Yeah," he answered.

"Always the charmer." I put him on speakerphone, so I could continue to hold my teacup in both hands. I needed the warmth. "I have to talk with you about a poisoning. Are you available tonight?"

"Someone poisoned you?" he growled.

I flicked my fingers and the exterior shutters came down. A shiver went through me. I didn't know why I was feeling so vulnerable, but I was locking everything up tight tonight.

"Not me, no. Someone poisoned the food in my café case so that a human would be killed. I know who did it. I have camera footage and Declan has the poisoned food in a bag in his truck lockbox."

I heard young voices in the background. "Oh, I'm sorry. I didn't think. You're home. We can do this tomorrow."

"Are you in danger tonight?" he asked.

I thought about it, wishing I had a blanket. *Oh, shit.* The cold. I still needed to do the fae ward. What was the matter with my head tonight? "I think I'm okay. Or, at least, I will be once I make another ward."

He grumbled, "Where's Declan?"

"With the pack in Big Sur. My cousin and her friend are causing problems with the pack. He's going to be meeting with them in the mornings and evenings until we deal with our problem."

There was a woman's voice and then he said, "Fine, but call me if you need me. I can be there in ten minutes."

"Thank you and I'll see you tomorrow."

I pocketed my phone, went to the freezer for three muffins, and thawed them in my gloved hands as I walked to the back door. Hopefully, my raccoon friends would visit this evening. I could use some adorable mischief right about now.

The moon was bright overhead, so I didn't bother with the outdoor lights. I put the three muffins in a semicircle in front of the bench closest to my back door and then sat. It was night and the wind was coming in strong off the ocean, but it was still warmer out here than in my studio.

I breathed in the sea spray and tried to center myself so I could create this ward on my own. Instead, I felt a prickling between my shoulder blades. Someone was watching me. I let down my mental blocks, listening. Nothing. I lowered them more and felt Bracken sleeping in his RV.

Was I wrong? Maybe Cal was scrying tonight, keeping tabs on me. I almost rationalized it away, but I felt something to my right, something in the tall grass near the rocks at the water's edge. It was my property, but an area I let grow wild.

Closing my eyes, I did my best to project relaxation and calm while I sought out what was niggling in my brain. The image of a small camera popped up behind my eyelids. *Damn it.*

I stood and walked to the edge of the deck. I needed a tall door here, one that locked. Declan had promised to make doors for each end of the deck, but he'd been so damned busy, he hadn't had a chance to yet.

Movement on the rocks drew my attention. Wilbur's head bobbed in the water but on the rocks, Cecil climbed toward the tall grass. What was happening? Cecil was running a special op for me. His tentacle rose up in the air, wrapped around a narrow pole, and snapped it, dragging the top half of the pole and the small camera attached to it back into the ocean with him.

Once it was gone, the tension in my shoulders eased. I waved at Wilbur and the water where Cecil had disappeared. "Thank you!" Feeling more settled, I went back to the bench, sat to the side, took off a glove, and then remembered the octopus bottle in my backpack. I ran in, retrieved it, and sat back down. Gloves off, I poured the special ocean water into the palm of one hand, rubbed them together, and placed my hands on my face, fingertips on my forehead, covering my eyes.

Deep-sea leviathans swam through my mind again. Breathing deeply, I held that picture in my head and moved my hands to the side of the gallery. I imagined a massive whale breaching and throwing himself onto his side, creating a tidal wave that swamped the gallery and Bracken's RV—and new car because why not?

As I pictured the ocean covering every inch of the gallery and washing out to the property line, I felt water run over the backs of my hands. Imposing my will, I added stingrays and lionfish to swim through the watery ward. I thought of Declan and Bracken, Mom and Gran, Detectives Osso and Hernández, Carter, Hester, Frank, Faith, Aunt Elizabeth and Uncle Robert. I didn't want any of them accidentally hurt.

I'd have to adjust the ward before I opened again next weekend. Until then, I wanted to hold everyone at bay while we tried to find Calliope.

TWENTY-SIX

A Witch Burning

When I opened my eyes, I saw movement and jumped. Otis chittered at his brother for scaring me. "I'm okay. How are you three tonight?"

They sat behind their muffins, watching me, seemingly waiting for the invitation to eat. It didn't escape my notice that Jasper had already taken a bite out of his. Thankfully, I didn't seem to scare Daisy anymore. She stood with her brothers, staring up at me.

"Please eat. I brought those out for you." They each plopped their butts down, picked up their muffins, and began to eat. "I hope you guys are staying safe. I worry about you when there are so many creeps around here."

When they finished, they scampered off and I went in. I checked the freezer for what I could serve for dinner tomorrow night. I had a couple of large lasagnas. In the refrigerator, I found two big steaks, some green beans and asparagus—look at Declan, being healthy. I could make some garlic bread and serve lasagna and vegetables. Good. Done.

I brewed more tea and turned off the overhead lights, just leaving the lamp beside my chair on. I considered watching a show, but I wasn't in the mood. I glanced at my e-reader, but again, couldn't muster the interest.

I could go upstairs, put my hand on the pillow Declan had used earlier, and check on him. No. That felt too much like spying, like what the stalker was doing. I'd checked on Declan once that way because I had to. He would have been shot and killed before the Alpha challenge had even begun. A twinge of guilt got me right in the chest. He'd forbidden me from helping him and I'd never told him that I had. I mean, did I have to? It felt like a deathbed confession was the only reasonable answer.

So I sat in my chair, sipping my tea and trying very hard not to think about what I'd been trying not to think about all day. There was a podcast out there about me.

My stomach dropped. It was middle school all over again. Was I a strong, powerful woman? Fuck, yeah! Did it make me sick to think about someone devoting all this time and energy to talk shit about me? Also yes.

Resigned, I opened my podcast app and searched for *A Witch Burning*. And there it was, right at the top. I clicked on it. Carter was right. The face of the witch being burned looked exactly like me. I wondered if the stalker had fed a photo of me into AI. *Shit.* There were even more ratings now.

I hit play.

"Have you been seeing the signs too? Darkness is overpowering the light. This is what comes of tolerance, of letting people do whatever they want. Evil rises.

"Have you seen it too? My God, we're not blind. False prophets, claiming righteousness and goodness, are leading people from the one true path. Wars around the world. Atrocities. Genocide.

"They call it climate change, but we all know what it really is. The earthquakes and hurricanes, the blizzards and tornadoes, they're God's will. He's trying to shake us up, to get our attention. He wants to punish the sinners. Those who deny the true path. And instead of listening and changing their sinful, unnatural ways, they talk about the planet's temperature rising a degree or two. They're hysterical about the wrong things.

"The world has gone through ice ages and heat waves. It's how nature

works. It's all a big scam, though. One of those shell games. They want us looking at emissions and green energy instead of our own sinful, godless ways. Earthquakes are a wake-up call. It's why we get so many of them in free, liberal, blue California.

"Pandemics? Check. Persecution of Christians? Check. The lawlessness is rampant. All of it are signs from heaven to repent and change our ways. Instead, we embrace godlessness and Satan rises.

"And with Satan comes the witches, his handmaidens. We have to fight for the soul of humanity, and that means burning all the witches!

"How do we do that? By calling them out. We present our evidence, so everyone knows that our actions are righteous and godly. We're God's warriors. When the end of days inevitably arrives, we'll be singled out as the ones who deserve eternal life in the light of God's love. We won't be cast down into Hell with the tolerant ones who lived and let live," he sneered.

"No! Would you walk by a drowning child and say, 'That's his choice'? Of course not. You'd step in and help him. You'd drag him out of the water and breathe life into him. Will it hurt? Probably. But we can't allow the fear of causing pain to still our hands. We are warriors, and in war, there are casualties. If they wanted to stay safe, they would have kept to the path.

"Temptations are put in our way to distract and confuse us. They take many forms. For some, it's drugs and alcohol. For some, it's pornography. For others, it's greed and the pursuit of wealth at all costs. And for still others, it's unnatural, lustful thoughts."

A thump sounds in the background, like he's pounded his fist on his podcasting desk.

"They lure us from the path and the face of God for their own twisted reasons. They know what they're doing, packaging evil in a beautiful face and a short skirt.

"Who among us hasn't seen a pretty young thing waiting for a school bus and had sinful thoughts? That's the Devil trying to tempt us, using weak women to do his will. All the way back to Adam, the Devil has been using women to tempt us, to lead us astray. We have to recognize the

temptation, and we have to destroy it. It's the only way to win back our souls and keep them pure.

"So, this podcast is going to call out the witches among us, to discuss their evil influence, and to help the righteous avoid them. I'm not advocating actually burning the witches. Okay? Are we clear? I didn't say to do it. I just think we need to know who the enemies are so we can protect our loved ones from them."

That was exactly what he was doing. He was wrapping it in religious fanaticism and purity, but what he wanted was for me and anyone like me to burn.

"This isn't a call-in show, but maybe, if I get enough listeners, it can become one. For now, you can go to my Witch Burning website and fill out the form with the information you have on a possible witch, and we can arrange phone calls to discuss your evidence on future podcasts.

"Today, we're going to start with my witch. She's a local artist. Aren't they always those free-spirited, bohemian types? Their lack of rules makes it easier to talk you into abandoning the path. They aren't happy unless they're drawing us in and polluting our souls.

"Even the name of her gallery has witch in it, though it's spelled wrong. Maybe it's plausible deniability while still signaling to other demonic beings that she's one of them.

"She's beautiful, of course. Those old cartoons of ugly witches with long, warty noses and hunched backs make no sense in the real world. We all know beautiful people get special treatment. They can do anything, and the weak among us are so taken with their beauty, we let them get away with it.

"She has a perfect face, bright green eyes, a ton of long, shiny curls that go down to her butt. She's petite. I've stood beside her. The top of her head came to maybe my shoulder. You could pick her up and carry her off, if you wanted. But just to lure us in, she's got an hourglass figure. She hides it under overalls, but I think that's just to make us wonder about what she's hiding.

"It's like that old Hansel and Gretel story, except instead of a house made of candy, she uses her looks and her art to draw people into her trap. And I'm not saying for sure she's a witch. I'm not saying that. I'm

laying out the evidence so you can help me decide what needs to be done.

"Let me tell you a little story. An origin story, if you will. I'd noticed her working on a mural, walking around this big old building that was being remodeled. I thought she was beautiful, so I noticed. There's nothing wrong with noticing. That's what they do, though, how they draw us in. One day, I see her walking around to the back of her gallery and I get a bad feeling. Out of nowhere. I follow her, to talk with her and try to find out why."

I thought about that day. I'd just come home, and this strange man followed me onto my deck. He asked if I was really a wicche, said with hair like mine I had to be. His gaze traveled leisurely over me and I dropped my stuff by my back door so my hands were free to cast spells.

I'd known then exactly what he was thinking. He hadn't been the first predator who'd cornered me with lust and violence in his eyes. For some, I think the fae blood intensifies their obsession. He hadn't followed me to discuss evil in the modern world. He *was* the evil and I'd been dealing with his kind since I was a child.

When he'd moved in and tried to loom over me, I'd flicked my fingers and stopped his breathing for five seconds. If he'd been looking to overpower and abuse a woman, he'd stumbled on the wrong one. So, for all the other women out there who didn't have my magic, I choked him just a little more.

I'd been on the phone with Mom when he'd appeared, and I'd kept the call live so someone would know what was happening. Apparently, she'd called Declan because when I released the man and he'd turned to run, he bounced off the chest of a very angry werewolf.

Declan, eyes wolf gold, had picked up the stalker by his neck with one arm and shook him, threatening him if he ever came back. The stalker wet himself. Declan threw the creep off the deck into the dirt along the side of the gallery and waited until he got up and ran away before he stopped glaring, his muscles bunched and ready to attack.

"It was like she'd been waiting for me to approach her, like a spider in a web. I said 'excuse me' so as not to startle her."

Nope.

"I asked if I could just have a moment of her time."

Like hell.

"And then she dropped her bag and put her hands on her hips, pulling her clothes tight across her chest, trying to distract me. I didn't give in to the temptation, though. I looked into those dead green eyes and said again that I didn't want to bother her. I only wanted to talk."

How much of a liar did he know himself to be? Had he convinced himself of this alternate history or was this whole thing fabricated to soothe his hurt pride, to blame me for his predatory impulses?

"And then she cast a spell on me, trying to kill me. What she couldn't seduce, she had to destroy. I couldn't breathe. She was a good ten feet from me, but she choked me with an invisible hand. I felt her evil hold on me.

"When I finally escaped, her guardian—this seven-foot demon— picked me up off the ground with one hand. I told him she was a witch, and he growled that he was something much worse. I'm telling you. The hair on the back of my neck stuck straight up. I was in the presence of the Devil's own."

He blew out a breath. *"It's all true. I got free of them that day and have been going down rabbit hole after rabbit hole, trying to figure out what happened to me. In hindsight, it's all perfectly clear, but at the time I was trying to convince myself that witches and demons weren't real.*

"I know the truth now. They're walking among us. On the next episode, I'll get more into this witch's background. I've been digging and found some very interesting stuff. I'll even have a few friends and class- mates on to discuss what they've seen. It's disturbing as hell. She should have been locked up a long time ago.

"Okay, that's it for the first episode. Go to my website to let me know what you think and keep your torches lit. We're going to need them."

TWENTY-SEVEN

A Burnt Witch

It felt like the walls in the studio were closing in on me. The next episode was titled. 'A___ is a Witch!' This had to be illegal. I'd ask Mom to talk with the family lawyer. No. Better. I'd sic Mary Beth on his ass.

I wanted to let it go and let someone else deal with the problem, but I couldn't. He was fixated on me, and I needed to be prepared for what he was sending my way. I considered my beautiful gallery that I'd *finally* opened. Was this why I'd had that vision of someone trying to burn down the gallery?

I needed air. I put on my fleece jacket by the back door and went out to the same bench I'd used earlier so I could watch the waves in the moonlight while I listened to his unhinged ravings. I hit play again and put my phone, speaker side up, in my breast pocket so I could hear the podcast over the roar of the wind and waves.

"Welcome back to A Witch Burning. I'm going to be honest here. I wasn't sure how many people would listen or care, but my inbox is already flooded with witch identifications. We're going to get to them all.

"It's great too that so many of you are seeing the signs as well. When I posted the first episode, it got sixteen listens. Now, there are thousands. We're doing something important here, and we're doing it together.

"So, let's get back to the witch that started this journey for me. I'm going to call her A~. We gotta be careful, right? I don't want witch lawyers harassing me. Right? Okay, she lives in this old cannery that she remodeled into an art gallery. First of all, she looks like she's in her twenties. Where the hell did she get that kind of money to buy oceanside property and then remodel this gigantic space?

"She works, but artists are usually too poor to afford a cheap studio apartment. Where did she get all this money to buy prime real estate? I think someone made a shady deal or she's got some demonic sugar daddy setting her up.

"Speaking of which, I told you about that seven-foot monster guardian of hers. He sure acts like her boyfriend, showing up at all hours, often not leaving until morning. Maybe it's sex. Maybe it's Satanic rituals. I don't know. That gallery of hers is locked down tight. There are tons of windows on the ocean side of the building, but they've all been blacked out."

Gee. I wonder why. I had no idea he'd been slinking around this much—because I was working! Shit, I was going to need to go through the security footage so I could give Osso the stalking and trespassing evidence.

My stomach twisted. I hated this so much. This is why I'd been living on my own for years: the weird obsessions some people developed and then blamed on me. They weren't all sexual either. There was a new girl—Emily—in eighth grade who'd stared at me constantly. She'd just moved to town and almost immediately started following me from class to class or positioning herself behind me on track runs in PE. I stopped once to talk with her, but she turned away, trying to pretend she hadn't been following me.

Finally, one day I came out of a bathroom stall and Emily was there. She tried to open the door and flee, but I flicked my fingers and kept the door from opening. She panicked and I tried to calm her while asking why she'd been following me. She was like a deer in headlights, but as she stared at me, her panic subsided. She told me she thought we should be best friends.

Recalling it now, perhaps it was sexual, and she just hadn't come to terms with that yet. What I felt radiating off her in that moment was loneliness, fear, and adoration. Her obsession scared me, but I didn't want to hurt her, so I said she should start walking with me, not behind me, so we could talk.

It had been exhausting. She projected her emotions so loudly, my head was killing me by the end of the day. I also couldn't take all the negativity. I already had so many dark visions and nightmares in my head, the last thing I needed was constant hissing in my ear about how so-and-so likes someone who hates her and how ugly some other so-and-so was.

I could do no wrong, though, and a couple days in she'd started wearing gloves too, like it was a fashion choice on my part, like we were twin trendsetters. Emily was new to town, though, new to school. She didn't know about me, so I was—in her mind— the most popular girl.

I'd told her I didn't like being touched and she was good about not touching me, though she got as close as she could without making contact. We were in the cafeteria at lunch one day and she was unusually quiet. That part was great, but the staring was starting to feel more aggressive. Trying to ignore her, I ate my yogurt, feeling a little sick to my stomach because at some point, that yogurt container had been touched by a deeply depressed person. I'd been happy Emily was leaving me alone so I could work through someone else's depression when I felt a hand on my cheek.

I went down and saw the reason she'd left her last school, the reason for the move to a new town. She'd been cyberbullying a classmate, encouraging others to join in. Her target couldn't take it anymore and tried to end her life. Thankfully, she'd survived and got the help she needed. It all came out then and Emily became a pariah, as everyone was more than happy to tell authorities about the things Emily had done to unmercifully harass the poor girl.

Emily denied it all and her parents were outraged by the accusations. They wanted the school administration to apologize. The principal laid out all the evidence, including all the text messages, emails, online posts. It didn't matter. Emily swore she didn't do it, and her parents backed her up.

When I opened my eyes, I was on the gross cafeteria floor. A teacher was talking on a walkie-talkie about calling my mom and Emily was staring down at me with a look of disgust. She took off the gloves and dropped them where she stood, while I tried to stand with a teacher hovering over me, afraid I was going to drop and hit my head again.

After that, Emily made it her life's goal to make sure everyone knew what a freak I was. The joke was on her, though. My freak status had been established years earlier. I was no longer a hot topic. She got a little traction at first, because I hadn't had an episode in a little over a year. So while everyone agreed with Emily, it wasn't terribly interesting any more.

I still often felt her staring at me, but I was happier having her far away. Of course, since I'd developed early, by eighth grade Emily had a lot of competition from the boys in class who were fixated on my chest. Good times.

"The gallery opening is in just a couple of days, so I'll get to see the inside soon. See what she's been up to. She almost never leaves that place, though. It's really strange. And now she has an old guy living in an RV, parked next to her gallery. He's up all night and sleeps all day.

"Is he a part of it? Witches have those black cat familiars, right? Is he a human familiar? I don't know. I've seen her talking to the water and raccoons. If she hadn't cursed me, I'd think she was just independently wealthy and crazy.

"A woman contacted me right after the first episode aired. She left a message on the website with her phone number. I asked her if I could record our conversation, and she said yes."

There was a soft hiss of white noise and then…

"Hi. You contacted me about the witch I'm going to call A~, is that right?"

"Yes," she said.

It was Calliope. Fuck.

"Can you tell my listeners how you know A~?" he asked.

"Of course. We grew up together. I'm a distant relative. Ar—I mean, A~ has always been off."

"Can you explain how?" he asked. "We want to hear it all."

"Well," she said, "there was a lot of speculation as she was growing up as to who her father was. Her mother never told anyone, so most of the family assumed he was a criminal or addict of some kind, once Ar—A~ started pretending to hear voices and started wearing gloves all the time like a germaphobe, we were all pretty sure her father was mentally unstable."

"Interesting," he interrupted. "Did you ever find out if that was true?"

"No. A~ lived in her own world, though. She drew and painted all the time. Her mom, who's a huge bitch, would coddle A~, never letting anyone question the weird stuff she did. It was like she was trying to force all of us to like her damaged daughter, but it had the opposite effect. No one liked her. We just knew to be quiet about it, you know?"

"Did you ever see any signs of evil in her?"

"Absolutely. When she was little, we were all at the beach together and I saw what could have been the mark of the beast on her." Cal was breathless to tell everyone the things I'd been hiding all my life. After a dramatic pause, she said, *"She has scales."*

He sputtered. "Did you say scales? Like a snake?"

"Exactly like that. A line of scales went around her thigh, like she'd been roped and branded by a reptile."

"Is that why she's always covered up, neck to foot? Is she covered in scales?"

The giddiness in his voice was making me sick. I was a freak show. Yes. Got it.

"Probably. She hates being touched," Calliope told him, *"so I doubt that guy is her boyfriend."*

"Yes," he said and there was a shuffling of paper. "A woman wrote in and said she went to school with A~ and that she refused to be touched. She said she got curious and did it anyway. A~ convulsed and hit the floor. She said A~'s eyes rolled back in her head and she acted like she was being electrocuted. The teachers

moved everyone away from her. Did you ever see her pass out like that?"

"Too many times. They tell the family she's epileptic, but that's not it. It only happens if someone accidentally touches her. That's why she doesn't drive. She never knows when she's going to hit the ground, writhing."

"Do you think she's been marked by the Devil and now if a godly person touches her, she has a seizure?" It was Christmas and his birthday all rolled up into one.

"Now that you say it, I bet you're right. Sometimes she gets a glazed, vacant look in her eye. You just know she isn't in there anymore. Maybe that's when she's communicating with her master."

"That's really—"

The show cut out and I opened my eyes. I didn't remember closing them, but I suppose I'd been trying to hide from what they were saying.

"Why are are you crying, daughter, and why are you listening to that?" My dad was back, dressed in a toga again.

I wiped my cheeks and smiled. Seeing him lifted some of the pressure off my chest. "Hi, Dad."

TWENTY-EIGHT

Under the Sea

He waited.

"Um, there's this podcast. Do you know what that is?"

He thought a moment and then nodded.

Huh. I wouldn't have guessed that. I explained who the man was, his stalking, and what he was saying on his podcast.

My dad sat with that a moment and then said, "A human?"

I nodded.

"I can take care of this for you, daughter, though I don't understand why a weak, cowardly human's opinion should matter to you."

I blew out a breath and tried to decide how to explain it. "The Goddess gifted me with precognition and psychometry. Your genes super-powered my wicche abilities. On one hand, that's wonderful and I'm grateful for all my gifts. On the other, though, I've been considered a freak all my life."

His eyebrows slammed down, his expression filled with rage. "Who would dare insult my daughter?" His massive hands fisted on his knees.

I shrugged. "It wasn't one person. I'm different. I've always been different. I've thought about this a lot over the years. You know how sometimes animals will banish one of their kind when they look too different?"

He reluctantly nodded.

"I think it might be like that. Other wicches see me as a threat. It wasn't that long ago that being accused of wicchery meant torture and death. Humans see me as a strange unknown and that makes them nervous. And then you have those attracted to the fae blood, so attracted but afraid. That combination often merges into violence."

He stood abruptly and went to the railing. "I was assured by your mother that she would take good care of you. That I was to leave you to her so you would be safer in this human world, that my presence would be a danger to you, and now I find out that they've been mistreating you?" His roar was deafening.

My insides shook. He'd wanted to know me, to be a father to me.

He turned and held out a hand, saying, "Come with me. I will show you how you should have been treated your whole life."

I stood and took his hand, unsure of what was happening, but after listening to the podcast, I was happy for the distraction. He glanced at my jacket and then it was gone, my phone along with it.

"They're inside," he said. "You won't need them." He studied me and then laid his hand on my head for a moment. "No more headaches."

And then we were flying over the railing and diving deep into the ocean. My father cut through the water like a dolphin, swimming faster and deeper than I ever could. Before I knew it, we were diving to the bottom of the Monterey Canyon, two and a half miles deep. We were in black water, but my eyes had adjusted and I marveled at the anemones and jellies. We passed a catshark and a flapjack octopus, basket stars and brittle stars, sea cucumbers and sea angels. I was almost positive I caught a glimpse of a vampire squid.

This was one of the greatest gifts I'd ever been given. As we moved farther out into the Pacific, a pod of orcas and a fever of bat rays swam with us, flanking my father. At one point, it looked as though the ocean floor was moving with us. It wasn't until the floor rose above us and breached the surface that I realized we'd acquired a blue whale in our phalanx. I sensed there were even more out there with us, but I couldn't see them.

At intervals, orcas and rays would swim close, brushing against me and then moving back into formation. At first, I'd thought it an accident, but it became clear that there was a coordinated effort amongst them. My father looked back when one ray stayed a little longer than the others, pressing himself against my stomach. Dad raised an eyebrow at the ray, who flapped his wing-like fins in a way that felt like a hug and then moved back with the others.

The orcas leading our party swam straight down. Oh, the blue whale had a calf swimming beside her. Dad and our security detail all angled down into a darkness that proved to be too all-encompassing for me.

If I hadn't felt the strength of his hand, clutching mine, I'd have questioned if I was trapped in a dream of endless black. I'd lost track of time in the vast inky deep. I had no idea how long we'd been diving, but it was somewhere between forever and the blink of an eye.

My mind may have been playing tricks on me, but it looked as though there was light far below us. As that made no sense, I tried to decide if an optical nerve was reacting to the pressure or if something was firing in my brain. We were far, far deeper than humans or even submarines could go. Whatever my father had done before we'd left, he'd taken care of the headache and the pressure that would normally have crushed my body.

I got so turned around in the unending black, though, I wondered if we were actually swimming up toward light. It was the only thing that made sense.

As we got closer to the strange green glowing light, I noticed people swimming close. Merfolk had joined us. Turning my head this way and that, I tried to catch glimpses of whoever was with us.

By the time I'd stopped gawking at our escorts, the green light was closer and taking on a form. It looked like an old-timey gas streetlight.

The whales, orcas, and rays had pulled away from us at some point when I couldn't see, leaving only the merfolk who followed us past the green light, down into a narrow crevasse.

I began to worry I was going to get squished between two rock walls, but we made it through the narrow break. It opened into a gigantic underwater cavern with many narrow cave entrances.

Clinging to the rock walls were every variety of coral and sponge. Brightly colored anemones dotted the carpet of red and purple algae. A bloom of blood red jellyfish bobbed along the outside edge, and everywhere I looked, merfolk were swimming in and out of caves, some stopping to watch us, others carrying on.

Dad led us to the largest cave opening that glowed in the dark, murky water. Something pale caught my eyes and I looked up. A goblin shark swam above us and out the narrow opening between rock walls. When I looked down, I saw an octopus scuttling along the ocean floor, following us toward the glowing cave opening.

We swooped under the lip of the cave and then up, emerging into a pocket of air. Dad climbed out, pulling me along with him. We stood in a huge torchlit cave filled with beautiful antique furniture. Paintings that should have been in museums hung on the rocky walls.

A willowy woman with light blue skin and long green hair moved forward. Bowing deeply, she said, "Welcome back, my lord."

When she rose, my father wrapped an arm around my shoulders. "Cerene, this is my daughter Arwyn."

Cerene's eyes widened and she dropped into another deep bow. "My lady, we are honored to have you with us."

"Thank you very much." I looked around. The underwater

cave looked like a sitting room in Versailles. "Where did all of this come from?"

Dad waved a hand as though it were nothing. "Shipwrecks. My people find all sorts of treasures that they like to bring me." He blew out a breath and made his way between large pieces of ornate furniture. "Come. We can sit over here."

Worried I'd ruin the fine silks with my wet clothes, I scanned myself and realized he'd already dried us. I reached up to feel my hair. It always suffered the most from drying spells. It was still shiny and soft. He'd have to teach me how to do that. It'd save me hours.

"May I bring you and your daughter refreshments, my lord?" Cerene asked.

He nodded, gesturing to a velvet settee. "Can you also ask Mythis to come report his findings?"

"Of course, my lord," she bowed again and moved into the back of the cave, disappearing in the dark.

Where was the light coming from in here?

"There are lanterns set throughout. They're brighter than usual, as you seemed to be having trouble seeing in the dark." Once again, he answered my unspoken question.

"Can you hear my thoughts?"

He nodded. "Of course. As can you. You've chosen to erect mental walls. I have not."

"Doesn't the constant noise, the negative thoughts, the judgments get to you?" They'd made me crazy before I'd learned to build the walls.

He began to shake his head and then said, "I see the problem. You're granting everyone the same level of importance in your thoughts." His hand fisted on his thigh. "This is something I could have taught you when you were young. Why in the realms would we want to know the thoughts of every being? You need to filter, to teach your brain who to focus on and who to ignore.

"You do the same with your vision. Do you pay attention to every single person you see in a day or does your brain assign the vast majority to a background role, while you focus on the ones who matter to you, the ones who spark your interest? The same can be done with thoughts. They can blend into background until you focus on the one or ones who interest you."

I leaned forward. "I would love to learn how to do that."

He gave a nod. His expression was stern, but his eyes betrayed his pleasure. "Then I shall teach you."

A man walked in. He looked like an elf but would probably need to be some kind of water fae to live down here. Dad watched him, eyebrows drawn together a moment before he quickly rose and bowed, pulling me along with him. I mirrored the bow as best I could, unsure of what was happening. I'd thought he was sending for one of his guards. He'd asked for a report but now he was standing and bowing.

The elf was tall and thin, with long white hair, pale purple eyes, an elven sword on one hip, and a dagger on the other. He glided silently across the large cavern. Blinking, I tried to make sense of how his form shimmered in and out of sight, as he appeared to be covering more ground than his strides would indicate. Everything about the elf seemed just a hair off.

My father's boot tapped the side of mine, and I remembered that he, and perhaps this elf, could hear my thoughts. Thinking of nothing proved to be quite difficult, so I focused on the large indigo opal on the elf's finger. For some reason, it made me think of my cousin Sam Quinn.

"So," he began, "this is your daughter."

"It is," Dad said, his head bowed again.

I looked up into his luminous eyes and saw mischief. I grinned, feeling no malice from him—or her. This was a glamour, and they had a feminine feel. I had no idea who was behind it, but they weren't who I was looking at.

"Perceptive," they said, glancing at my father.

Damn. I forgot. My mind was supposed to be blank.

Dad shook his head, and one side of the elf's lips turned up.

"You'll need to work on that, but your father will help you," they said. "Now, what is this I hear about you asking for our help in locating a sorcerer?"

"Yes," I responded. "If it's not too much trouble, that is. My cousin has become a sorcerer. She and her demon are causing immense harm. I can't find her. I was hoping maybe the fae could sense something I couldn't, so I asked for help."

They lifted a hand and cupped my cheek. "I'm considering your request. Perhaps if you first do something for me, I might reciprocate." Their eyes closed and I waited, unsure of what they expected of me.

When they opened again, they were a swirling kaleidoscope of colors and they had become much smaller, my height but slim and delicate. She had silvery hair, high cheekbones, and a bow mouth. She was stunningly beautiful and quite clearly the queen.

As she still had a hand on my cheek, I did my best to drop into a curtsy. Dad bowed low beside me.

"She's quite powerful," the queen said. "Your Goddess has blessed you as well." She pulled her hand back and crossed her arms. "We both appear to have plans for you, child."

She turned to Dad. "You allowed them to keep her too long. You have much to do to teach her to harness and use her magic."

"Yes, my queen. It is my honor to do so," he said.

Her gaze traveled over me, stopping at my gloves. A moment later, they were gone. "Your father can also teach you how to protect your gift, so you don't need those anymore."

My heart leapt and they both swayed, no doubt feeling it. "Truly? I can control it?"

The queen's eyebrows raised in challenge. "That remains to be seen, doesn't it? Will you dedicate yourself to your lessons?"

I thought about that huge order for the Winslows hanging over me and the gallery itself. I'd just have to make it all work. "I will."

TWENTY-NINE

Marital Spats Make the Rest of Us Terribly Uncomfortable

She looked at my father. "Have you touched her skin?"

He shook his head. "Not without blocking, as I assume you just did."

She nodded. "I think it's time we see if her gifts work on the fae." She held out her hands to me. "This experiment is payment for the information you requested."

I took her hands in mine.

A dark, torchlit passage, deep underground, far from the sun. Footsteps. At the end of the passage is a solid wooden door. There is no knob, no hinge. I walk through the door and am in pitch black. A ball of light appears in my hand and is tossed up in the air, illuminating the small cell. A beautiful man lies on a cot, the back of his hand casually thrown over his eyes, as though the light is disturbing his sleep.

He looks around the side of his hand. "Oh. It's you. Come to check on me, have you?"

"Why do you do this?" It's the queen's voice.

He blows out a breath and sits up, leaning back against the cell's stone wall. "Must we rehash this all again? It serves no purpose other than to annoy us both."

She's quiet for a moment. "Did you always hate me?"

He stretches out his legs and crosses them at the ankles, tipping his handsome head to watch her under a swoop of glossy reddish-brown hair. "Questioning all of it, are you?" He makes a mocking sad face. "Poor you." Gesturing around, he adds, "Perhaps we should change places, and you can use your time in this cell to contemplate our marriage. It's rather peaceful down here. Quiet."

"Did you?" she asks again.

He brushes his hair off his face. "Did I? Always hate you? Hmm, that's a tough one." He taps a finger to his lips, every gesture, every word seemingly intended to mock and belittle. "One could argue that you never respected me."

The queen crosses her arms, seething. "Your fragile ego being soothed is more important than Faerie, than my ability to rule? Would you have me abandon my responsibility, my people, to placate your need to preen and playact power you don't possess?" She shakes her head, not wanting to go down that well-worn road again. "Did you ever love me, or has it always been an act?"

His eyelids droop, as though he's having a hard time staying awake. "Your hurt is tedious. Is it my fault I grew bored almost immediately of being little better than a servant? You never wanted a partner. You want adoration by your side and in your bed. Speaking of which, how is that lapdog guard of yours? I'm sure he worships you the way you enjoy."

"You started flaunting other women—no. We're not doing that." She stopped and took a breath. "Can't you hate me in peace from far away? Must you recruit my own people to plot the destruction of Faerie and everyone in it?"

He scoffed. "Your people. Is everything yours then? The entire realm is yours and we're only here because you allow us to be? Don't you think it more likely that this realm is filled with a magic that birthed us all and that you, a delusional megalomaniac, have decided that you are our queen? How marvelous for you."

He rolls his eyes. "You don't suppose that it's because you are the oldest of us and have absorbed the most magic from this realm? You honestly believe this world would cease to exist without you?" He shakes his head. "You're exhausting. Have you noticed that when you visit other realms, nothing bad happens here? It's almost as if we don't need you."

"I created this realm," she shouts, angry sparks ricocheting around the cell.

"And yet you can't destroy me," he says with a smirk. "What does that tell you?"

The queen dropped my hands and stepped back. I blinked through the disorientation that comes from moving from a marital fight in a dungeon to a well-appointed undersea cavern.

"Impressive," she said, but I wasn't sure if she meant it. She sounded irritated. Perhaps, though, her anger in the memory was bleeding over to the present.

She shook her head. "I'm not irritated with *you*, child. That wasn't what I'd intended to share with you—assuming you were able to see anything."

Dad's hand landed possessively on my shoulder. "She meant no disrespect, my lady."

Her chin went up. The colors swirling in her eyes intensified. After a charged moment, she blinked and they were the sparkling lavender of the elf's. "Relax, Manannán mac Lir. Your child is safe with me." A piece of paper appeared in her hand. "My scout found two locations he believes are possibly the home of your sorcerer." She handed me the slip of paper.

Turning back to my father, she said, "I expect updates on her progress." Her gaze fell on me again. Reaching out, she picked up one of my long curls. Her mouth tipped up. "Such a rare and wonderful gift is a child." Her eyes flicked down. "She has your hair and the shape of your eyes. Send her back the easy way so that note in her hand doesn't get wet."

And she was gone.

Trembling, I opened the note she'd given me. It was a tiny, near perfect map of the Monterey Bay with two dots in red along the coastline. This was gold.

Dad looked over my shoulder.

It's a double-edged sword. Dad's voice was in my head. *When the queen takes an interest in you, incredible things can happen. Unfortunately, horrendous things can as well. Were it up to me, she'd never know of your existence. I don't want you caught between the queen and king, losing your life because they can't kill one another.*

A chill ran down my spine.

"I know we offered you refreshments," he said out loud, "but it's getting late, and you need your sleep." *If I learn anything more that can help your sorcerer problem, I'll let you know.* "I'll visit in a few days, and we can begin our lessons."

"Tha—"

He put a finger over my mouth and shook his head. "Never thank the fae." Leaning down, he kissed my forehead. My vision went dark, my stomach dropped, and I was standing back on my deck. After a long moment, I felt steady enough to go in. My jacket and phone were on my worktable. I checked the time. It was after midnight.

Mom and Dad were right. I needed sleep, and though I was exhausted, my brain was racing and I was starving. I heated up a French bread pizza and ate it standing over the sink, my mind on the world down below. When I finished, I headed to my supply closets for a canvas. I needed to paint.

As I pulled out a large canvas, though, I stopped. Declan had once mentioned my painting the raccoon siblings and I'd had the idea of someday making ink drawings incorporating watercolors as a nursery collection. It had been a maybe-someday idea but tonight it felt right.

Ideas raced through my brain. I'd do a set of four tonight. Using watercolor paper, I began filling the white with blues, greens, and indigos as a background base. Once I was done with the fourth, the first was dry enough to begin the line drawings.

I had a set of gorgeous ink pens, the tips more like delicate brushes than hard nibs. As I worked on the first one—the blue whale and her calf—I remembered how much I loved this medium. Lost in the memories of my adventure, I worked far later than I'd intended.

The sun was rising when I stumbled to the couch and fell face-first into sleep.

Auntie Abigail walks around nasty Aunt Sybil's sunroom, checking on the cousins' progress with glamour spells. Colin is the best at it, so far, though my stupid sister Serena is good too. I guess. Pearl is embarrassing, as always. She can't even change her eye color. Colin can make himself look like a movie star.

"You're doing really well, Calliope," Aunt Abigail says, rubbing my shoulder. She crouches down, staring into my eyes, and whispers, "You're the best. Others might have mastered one skill, but you're good at many skills. You just need the right training to find your power."

"Really?" I whisper back. No one has ever told me I was good at magic. My stupid mother always says I'll grow into it soon.

Aunt Abigail nods. "I have a friend I study with, and he told me to pay close attention to you. He thinks you can be one of the best."

"Who is it?" I ask in awe. Finally! Someone else sees it too. I just know I'm destined to rule the Corey Council. And won't they be sorry for all the pats on the head and the laughs at my mistakes. I'll make sure they're sorry. I hope she's not talking about Daddy, though. He's a healer and he already checked. I have no healing skills.

"You'll meet him soon and he'll help you find your power," she tells me.

I give her my best puppy eyes and a hug. The aunts and uncles all think I'm a little doll, so I use it whenever I can. I may not be able to do all the spells stupid Serena can, but she still gets yelled at when I screw up. How could she have let poor little me handle that problem all by myself? It's hard not to laugh when she gets yelled at for something I did.

I whisper in Aunt Abigail's ear, "Will I be as powerful as Arwyn?"

She scoffs. "She's a freak, little one. An abomination. She's not even a true Corey wicche. No one knows who her father is. We're not even allowed to ask," she whispers with an eye roll. "I'm sure he's strong, but I doubt he's a wicche. Have you noticed those scales on her leg?"

I nod my head, eyes wide. "Is her daddy a snake?"

Aunt Abigail laughs. "I wouldn't be surprised. Don't worry about her. It's pure-blooded wicches who have the real power. I'll talk to Gran and Sylvia, see if I can begin private tutoring sessions with you."

I hug her again and mean it this time. "I knew I was special."

Knocking startled me awake, but I was okay with that. I had no desire to spend more time with Abigail and Cal. They worked with demons, but I was the abomination. Yeah, okay.

I reached for my phone to see the time. Too early. More knocking. Ugh. Flicking my fingers, I opened the shutters and then was blinking against the sudden light.

I dragged myself to my feet and went to the door. Osso stared in the window, trying to see me. As my windows were spelled against snoops, he was out of luck. When I reached for the door, he relaxed. He might not have been able to see me, but he could hear me.

"Good morning, detective," I said, trying my best to sound well-rested and alert.

"You look like hell," he grumbled as he walked by me. "No sleep?"

"Always the charmer, aren't you? And I was sleeping before you so rudely woke me up."

He glanced around at the worktable and the couch. "You're the one who wanted me to stop by before work." When I stared at him blankly, he added, "Poison."

"Oh, shit. That's right. It's been a long night." I'd meant to copy the camera footage into a folder for him before he arrived.

Osso turned back toward the deck. "Sounds like Declan."

A moment later, Declan strode into view. He raised a hand to knock, but I called out, "Come in."

When I met him at the door, he wrapped his arms around me and lifted me into the air so he could kiss me more easily. Declan's kisses were magical.

When we broke apart, he looked over my shoulder. "Did you know that Osso was raiding your honey jars?"

Squawking, I made Declan put me down. "What the hell?"

"What do you mean *what the hell*?" Osso grumbled, eating a heaping spoonful of honey. "You call me at home last night. You ask me to see you this morning, and then you're oversleeping and making out. Why do I have to be here for this?" He put the spoon back in for more honey.

"You did that on purpose! You knew you were contaminating the honey and that I'd end up giving you the jar. Well." I flicked my fingers, and the jar disappeared. "Now no one gets honey."

The bear's growl was deep and very loud.

Declan moved in behind me and wrapped his arms around me. "You should probably give him back his honey."

"It's *my* honey." When Osso's growl got louder, I flicked my fingers and returned it, mumbling, "Big baby."

Holding the returned jar closer to his chest, he eyed me warily. Finally, he pulled out his phone, hit the voice memo app, tapped record, and placed it on the coffee table. "Start at the beginning and tell me what's been going on with this guy."

So I did. I had to leave some magical things out of the official report, but when I did, I wiggled my fingers so he'd know there was more to the story. After that, I launched into the story of my stalker. When I got to the podcast and last night's spy camera, Declan's grip on me tightened.

Osso paced around the room as I spoke, finally stopping as the story wound down. Tapping his phone, he closed the app and returned his phone to his pocket. "Fuck," he grumbled. "Now tell me all the parts you left out."

I grabbed my laptop, sat back down on the couch with Declan, and filled in the magical bits while I hunted up footage of the stalker and the poisoner for him.

"An octopus?" he asked, shaking his head. "An octopus took out the camera?"

It took me a moment to realize the rumbling sound I was hearing was Declan growling, low and mostly to himself. I patted his knee. "I'm okay."

"No," he said. "You're not. You're going to have to start coming up to Big Sur with me. I can't leave you here all by yourself."

"You're not *leaving* me" I said. "This is my home. I'm perfectly safe and can handle whatever gets thrown at me. I'm just trying to do that within the legal bounds of human society."

When Declan started to argue, Osso growled, "Fight about it later. Do you still have the poisoned food in your truck?"

Jaw clenched, Declan nodded.

"Can you get it for me?" Osso asked, pulling out his notebook.

Reluctantly, Declan got up and left, his boots heavy on the deck as he went to his truck.

Osso sat on the coffee table beside me and lowered his voice. "He's exhausted, trying to look after the pack and you, whether you need it or not," he said, holding up a hand to placate me. "I get it. You're a bad bitch, but he loves you. If you didn't want a protective boyfriend, you shouldn't have started dating a wolf."

There was that word again. "He doesn't love me," I whispered back.

Rolling his eyes, he moved to my worktable and sat down. "Keep telling yourself that, if it makes you feel better."

THIRTY

Beer: The Breakfast of Champions

Declan came back in and dropped the knotted garbage bag just inside the back door.

"This doesn't look like your usual stuff," Osso said, studying the watercolor and ink pieces I'd done last night.

Declan was clearly still worked up, but he walked to the table to see what I'd done, and my annoyance melted away. He cared and wanted me safe. It was as simple as that. He wasn't the fae king. There was no resentment or jealousy, no desire to stifle me in order to feel more important. He worried about me, and wasn't that lovely?

Declan stood behind Osso and joined his study of the four pieces. His jaw unclenched and his expression softened. He looked up from the worktable. "After what happened last night, *this* is what you painted?"

"Oh," I said, putting my feet up on the coffee table. "You haven't heard the half of last night." I told them all about my father and our journey, the orcas and rays, the whales, the cavern at the bottom of the ocean, and then about the queen. "I doubt she wants me to share what I saw when I touched her, so we'll leave it as I saw something she hadn't intended for me to see, and she gave me a map with two possible spots as Cal's lair."

The men stared at me, speechless.

"I know, right?" Declan was holding his stomach, so I asked, "Are you hungry?"

"What?" he responded.

Osso glanced over at Declan and told me, "You're going to give him ulcers."

Declan moved his hand and rubbed his forehead instead. "Your father took you out into the middle of the ocean, miles and miles below the surface, where the queen appeared and told you she had plans for you?"

I nodded. "That about sums it up."

He went to my fridge. "I need a beer."

"It's morning," I protested.

"Get me one too," Osso said.

"And you're on duty," I reminded him.

Declan slapped a bottle into Osso's palm and then they both popped off the tops and took long swigs.

"And I'd thought a sorcerer was the worst of our problems," Declan said before he downed the rest of the bottle.

"Yeah," I replied, "my dad wasn't happy about it either. He said he really wished the queen didn't know about me."

Osso's head dropped. "Your dad is some kind of fae sea god and even he's afraid of what the queen might do?"

I considered all the dreams I'd had last winter of the insane crap my cousin Sam had been going through because the queen and king had taken an interest in her. They were right. This wasn't good.

Osso stood. "Can you give me copies of the security footage for Swan and the stalker? I'll get the tainted food to the lab. I need proof there was poison before I can arrest him."

I transferred the videos using a files compression service. "It says it'll take about seven more minutes and then you'll get an email with the file."

"Here." He took a USB drive from his pocket. "The D.A. gets nervous about documents that go through outside services."

I took it from him and went to the far side of my worktable. "I have a dongle in here somewhere." I rifled through cords and attachments in my tech drawer. I found one, plugged it and then the drive in and started copying files. It didn't take long. I have excellent computers, considering all the digital images I work with.

Osso stood by the back door, the garbage bag at his feet while he scribbled notes.

I handed him his drive. "Tell your lab to check the peanut butter chocolate chip cookie first. It should save them some time."

He took the drive and put it back in his pocket. "I have a cousin in the lab. I think I can talk her into moving this to the top of the list. I'll get back to you." And he was gone.

Declan stood in the middle of my very long worktable, studying the underwater scenes. "Is this me?"

I'd given one of the mermen a beard and a wolf tattoo on his biceps. "Maybe."

He shook his head, grinning. "Thanks. I love these. They're very different from the rest of your work." He gestured toward the gallery. "And yet it's still you. Each one is its own world. They're so intricate and detailed, but the full image is…charming. They're like those Busy books I had when I was little. Every section I look in, there are little stories going on. You're story-telling in a way that will draw children in and spark their imaginations."

Bubbles of pleasure and pride made their way from my stomach to my chest. I went to him, pulled on his arm, and kissed the top of his cheek, above his beard. "Thank you."

"You should sell prints for people who want your work in their child's nursery but can't afford to pay for your original art." He held up a hand. "It's your art and your decision. I just like the idea of all kids having access to your work, not just the rich ones."

I wrapped my arms around him, and he snugged me in tight. "It was a thought I had last night as well," I said. "My cousin Frank suggested I sell some of my larger photos as five-by-sevens, matted and slipped into cellophane sleeves for those who'd like to own my work but can't pay thousands for it."

Declan nodded. "I like that, and I like Frank and Faith. I met your other cousins at your Aunt Sylvia's wake. They were…not great. These two, though, I was watching them on opening night. They're hard-working, polite, and they honestly seemed happy and proud to be working for you."

"They're both great," I confirmed. "They benefitted from being a decade younger than the rest of the cousins who, no doubt, would have terrorized them." I went to the kitchen. "Are you hungry?"

"Always." He wrapped his hands around my shoulders and directed me to the couch. "I'll make us something for breakfast in a minute. You look beat."

"Jeez, you and Osso are doing great things for my self-esteem today. He said I looked like hell."

Declan sat on the couch and pulled me into his lap, turning me sideways so he could see my face. "Sorry. We're idiots. You're gorgeous." He shook his head. "Insanely so. When you're over-worked and overtired, there's a tightness around your eyes that says you need sleep. My guess is that Osso noticed the tightness too and being the snarly bear he is, put it in the most delicate way he could."

That made me laugh.

"I'm sorry about the way I acted earlier, but I'm worried. There's too much aimed at you and it's making me very nervous, especially when I have to keep leaving to meet pack members in the mountains."

"I can handle myself," I assured him.

He nodded. "I know you can, but that doesn't change the worry. You and I both know you're vulnerable to attack. Someone comes up behind you and puts a hand on your neck? You're down and unable to use your magic to protect yourself."

I couldn't argue the point, but that didn't mean I enjoyed being reminded.

He kissed my temple. "I don't want anything bad to ever happen to you. I realize that's an impossible wish, but I can try to protect you, can't I?"

His earnestness melted my heart just a little more.

"We talked earlier about guards and I said I had an idea." He rubbed my back. "I feel you tensing up. Give me a minute to explain. Okay?"

After some internal wrestling, I said, "Go on."

"There are two wolves. They used to be members of my dad's pack in the Santa Cruz Mountains. After Dad was killed and his son Marcus took over, the wolves' lives were more difficult. Marcus wasn't our father. He was weak. Many of the stronger wolves wouldn't accept him as Alpha and moved on.

"These two, Jake and Tyler, tried to stay. They had been happy there, but the pack dynamics changed. The men have been together for decades. Alexander was a strong enough Alpha to keep everyone in line. Once Marcus took over and other strong wolves left, the ones remaining had issues with gay wolves and made sure their problems were everyone's."

"Assholes," I grumbled.

"Yes. So, they moved down here and applied for the Big Sur Pack. Apparently, the Alpha before Logan turned them away. When Logan took over, they tried again, but Logan and his buddies thought it was hilarious and did nothing to support the men or bring them into the pack."

I grabbed his arm. "But you can, right? Wolves who want to be in a pack shouldn't have to be on their own."

Declan tipped his head. "We'll see. I'm trying, though. I was only made aware of them a few days ago. They have a cabin on a large tract of land in the mountains. I went to meet them and invite them into the pack. One of them, Tyler, seemed ready to try. The other, Jake, told me to fuck off. Given the way they've been treated, I get it."

"We could invite them to dinner," I suggested. "Once they get to know you, how can they say no?"

Declan gave me a kiss. "We'll see. I'm not going to force them. They're both strong, mature wolves. They know what they're comfortable with. I asked if they've been getting more irritated lately. They didn't tell me yes or no, but I got the feeling from Tyler that he was concerned about Jake."

"Did you explain about Cal?" I asked.

He nodded. "I told them we had a sorcerer in Monterey who was messing with the wolves, amping up the aggression. Tyler looked relieved to know there was reason for what they'd been feeling. Again, this is just me picking up on emotion and body language. Neither trusted me enough to tell me anything."

"Okay." I rested my head on his shoulder, suddenly sleepy. "You've extended the olive branch. Hopefully, they'll take it."

Declan adjusted me on his lap so I could nap on him more comfortably. "I'm telling you this," he said, arms wrapped around me, "because I asked if they'd be interested in taking on a side job as personal guards for you until we find and stop your cousin."

Resting my hand on his chest and listening to his strong heartbeat, I yawned. "Good idea." And I was out.

For the second time this morning, I was awakened by knocking. "Go 'way," I mumbled. Declan stretched beneath me, and I knew I was going to have to get up. Stupid visitors.

"Oh. These are the two I told you about," Declan said, standing easily while still holding me. He opened the door. "Good morning. Why don't you have a seat. We'll be right out."

"Is she okay?" one of them asked.

"Yeah. Exhausted. She worked all night."

At that point, knowing more sleep was out of the question, I rolled my head to the side to see our visitors. "Hey."

THIRTY-ONE

Sunshine & Rain

They were tall and muscular, but only one of them smiled. They looked to be extremely fit men in their late twenties, but werewolves were *very* long-lived, so who knew how old they actually were? The one who smiled had light brown hair, mossy green eyes, and wire-rimmed spectacles. He wore a *Dr. Who* t-shirt, blue jeans, and running shoes.

I smiled back. "You're Tyler."

His grin got bigger. "I am."

I turned to his partner and found black eyes, with ridiculously long eyelashes, scrutinizing me—and I was not passing muster. Of course, Declan was still carrying me, but whatever. I wasn't getting anger or disgust from him, just questions. His skin was darker than his partner's, a natural deep tan. He had straight black hair pulled back in a tail and a short beard on his very handsome face. He wore a button-down, black jeans, and black boots.

"Jake," I said. "It's nice to meet you both. Give me a minute, okay?" I tapped Declan's arm, and he put me down. I went to the bathroom to brush my teeth. Declan was right. My eyes looked tired. I did a quick glamour spell to hide that and went out to the kitchen to make a better impression by offering up brownies, cookies, and lemon squares. Remembering I'd been sleeping on Declan, I took off my gloves, went to my backpack for the octopus bottle, and then donned new gloves.

Declan and the guys were still out on the deck. I brought out a loaded plate and found Declan on the bench by the back door, while Tyler and Jake sat on the ocean side. No one was speaking. That couldn't be good.

"Can I offer you something to eat? And I have water, milk, coffee, tea, grape soda, and beer." I held the plate out to them.

Tyler's eyes lit up. "Oh, can I take a few?"

"Please do," I said. Jake was glaring at Declan. *Shit.* What did I miss? "What can I get you to drink?"

"Is it too much to ask for a cup of tea?" Tyler asked.

I laughed. "I think you've forgotten who you're talking to. Wicches are all about tea. Jake, can I offer you anything?"

He barely glanced at me before he shook his head.

"Oh my god! You have to try this." Tyler tried to give Jake a bite of his cookie, but Jake ignored him, still staring down Declan.

I stepped to the side, blocking Jake's line of sight.

He glared up at me.

"Don't do that," I said, my voice low. "He doesn't deserve it, and I won't allow it. Declan is a good and honorable man who is running himself into the ground, helping to level out his wolves so that no one—neither the wolves nor their mates and children—are hurt."

"Arwyn don't—" Declan began, but I put up my hand to stop him.

"This is between Jake and me. You butt out." Out of the corner of my eye, I caught Tyler's eyebrows winging up as he started on a brownie. His calm reassured me that Jake wasn't really going to attack. Not that I couldn't take him; I just didn't feel like brawling today.

"My cousin is a sorcerer," I continued, "and doing what she can to tip the wolves into a violent frenzy. One has already died. If it weren't for everything Declan is doing to look after his pack, there would be more. So I'm not going to let you poke at him. Too many rely on his strength and calm."

"Do you fight all his battles?" he sneered.

Tyler's gaze was going back and forth between Jake and me like a tennis match while he continued to eat. Him, I liked. "Ask yourself," I said to Jake, "what's your goal right now. Are you trying to goad Declan into killing you? Sick of your life? Or were you looking for me to stop your heart? Maybe freeze your lungs? Maybe just toss you over the railing to see if some cold water can snap you out of this sour mood?"

Jake growled and I felt Declan moving in behind me.

"I'm fine," I said.

"I know." He kissed the top of my head. "I was more worried about him." He reached over my shoulder and snagged two brownies. "Plus, I wanted these." He sat back down. "Sorry to bring you guys out of the mountains. I thought this might work, but I see now that it won't."

Following Declan's lead, I ignored the men and went to sit on Declan's bench. "Will you be able to make dinner tonight with my aunt and her family?"

He nodded, taking a cookie. "I told the pack I couldn't meet tonight. I want to be here for the planning, especially now that you have that map. Can Bracken make it?"

Neither Jake nor Tyler had moved.

I nodded. I wanted a lemon square, but I hadn't brought chopsticks or rubber gloves with me.

"Which one?" he asked.

Grinning, I said, "Lemon, please."

He held it for me so I could take a bite.

"She can't feed herself either?" Jake grumbled.

"Shh," I hissed. "We're ignoring you." I took another bite and turned to Jake, eyebrows drawn together. "And what do you mean *either*?"

Tyler raised his hand. "Can I have a lemon too?"

"Of course," I said while continuing to glare at Jake.

"He carries you around. He feeds you. Not much of an Alpha," Jake said, but the challenge I heard in the question was different from the words he said. With any luck, Declan had picked up on that too.

"You live in the mountains," Declan said. "Haven't you noticed the power dynamic in natural wolves? The Alpha isn't some aggressive tyrant. They're just the mated pair who look after the pack. They set the tasks and activities, but the pack works as a family. It's like Arwyn's grandmother being the head of the Corey Council and the matriarch of the family."

Tyler sneaked back over for another lemon square, giving me a grin of thanks.

Jake gave a mean laugh. "So you're saying you want to be our daddy?"

I choked on the bite I'd just taken.

Declan leaned forward and patted my back. "Definitely not saying that. And I'm helping Arwyn because she's wearing gloves and forgot her chopsticks. You've been watching Tyler this whole time, pretending to be pissed at us while happy he's eating something he likes. It's the same for me, although I'm not pretending anger I don't feel. I'm annoyed at the disrespect you're showing my mate, but I understand that you've both dealt with a great deal of disrespect yourselves and you neither know nor trust us."

I stood up. "Sorry! I said I'd get you tea and them Mr. Grumpy-pants made me forget." I'd started to go in when a tennis ball flew across the deck and bounced off the side of the gallery. "Wilbur!" I ducked in my back door, grabbed the orange flippy thing, and used it to pick up the soggy ball.

I went to the railing and scanned the water for his head. "Thanks for your help last night."

"What is she doing?" Jake asked.

Declan ignored him and came to stand at the railing beside me. "Here. Give me that. I'll send it farther."

Tyler stood to look over the railing and watch whatever was going on.

"Ooh, good idea. Did you hear that, Wilbur? Do you think you can catch one of Declan's throws? Hah. We're winning this round." I elbowed Declan. "Do it."

He did and sent it farther than it's ever gone before. With a bark of joy, Wilbur shot out from under the deck and torpedoed through the water after it.

Tyler started laughing. "That was a seal! You have a pet seal?"

Jake stood to see what had tickled Tyler.

"He's not my pet. He's my friend." I lowered my voice. "And a selkie."

"Her father's very powerful water fae," Declan said, and I knew that meant he trusted these two, even if Jake didn't trust us. "He has some of his guards keeping an eye on her."

"Hey, Tyler," I said, "watch this. Good morning, Cecil! How are Poppy and the babies today?" Tentacles swirled and tapped the surface of the water.

Tyler looked stunned. "Is that an octopus?"

Jake's hand went to Tyler's back. He looked as stunned as his partner, though in a grumpier way.

"They're giant Pacific octopuses who are expecting," I told them. "The eggs will take about six months to hatch. I'm looking forward to being an octopus auntie."

"Oh. Sorry to interrupt." Detective Hernández stood on the edge of the deck with an evidence bag in her hand, looking uncomfortable. "I didn't realize you had company."

I waved her closer. "These are friends of Declan's. This is Tyler and Jake." I gestured to each in turn. "Gentlemen, this is Detective Hernández. Sometimes I consult on police cases. Right now, I'm helping with a serial killer." Talking to Hernandez, I said, "And these two are considering being my bodyguards until my cousin is caught, so I guess it makes sense for them to see some of what I do." I turned back to the men. "Detective Hernández is human but aware of us. She works with a black bear detective sometimes."

"Speaking of which," Hernández said, "he told me about the poisoner and the stalker." She glanced at the big men. "I can understand the impulse to have bodyguards, but you're more deadly than they are."

Tyler turned to reassess me. Jake glowered.

"I don't have eyes in the back of my head and when I'm working, I lose track of what's going on around me," I said. "So, what's in the bag?"

She held it up for me to see. "It may be nothing, but we found it in that group of trees where you said he was waiting and watching her."

"A folded-up gum wrapper?" Declan asked.

She nodded.

"Interesting," I said. "I'd invite you in, but there's more seating out here." I sat back down, my legs crisscrossed on the bench seat. I held out a hand for the bag.

"You need a reset," Declan said.

I'd forgotten the kiss he'd given me earlier. Thank goodness one of us was paying attention. I went to the railing, slipped off my gloves, and then stopped, turning to Declan. "Give me a kiss first," I whispered.

Grinning, he stood and did so.

"You make an excellent assistant," I told him.

His eyes darkened. "I've been practicing."

I held my hands over the railing, caught a missile of water, and returned to factory settings, feeling that sizzle in my blood again.

I sat back down and Declan held out a hand for the evidence bag. He pulled open the top and then shook the gum wrapper to the mouth of the bag, to make it easier for me to take. Lifting my ungloved hand, I turned back to Hernández. "The lab has already checked it, right?"

She nodded. "They found a couple of partial prints, but nothing they could identify. And again, we don't even know if that was his."

I picked up the wrapper.

He pulls the stick of gum from his pocket. He's watching the long-haired woman watering her plants. He pulls open the wrapper with his teeth and then slides the stick into his mouth. She goes back in, turns off the lights. As he waits to see her again, he begins folding up the wrapper into smaller and smaller squares.

The sun has set behind clouds. He enjoys surveilling her while hidden in the dark. Shortly after, her garage door goes up. Her Jeep backs out and she drives away as her garage door closes. He considers running for the door before it closes, but he'd be too exposed. If she glances in her rearview mirror, she'll see him. He's excited but not reckless.

He waits a few long minutes, pulls on thin blue surgical gloves, and ghosts his way to the sliding glass door off the patio. Crouching, he pulls a screwdriver out of his pocket, jams it under the door, and lifts it off its track, popping the lock.

He slides the door open and slips in, pulling a penlight from his pocket. The apartment is small but he takes his time, going through drawers and in cabinets, thrilled that she has no idea he's looking through her life, finding out her secrets.

He opens her closet door, puts the penlight in his mouth, pulls off one glove, and slides his free hand along the fabric, allowing himself time to consider what it will feel like when he takes control of her, when he squeezes the life out of her.

He goes to her bathroom and opens the medicine cabinet, his face flashing in the mirror for a brief moment. He studies her prescriptions, disappointed there's nothing more interesting than allergy meds, birth control pills, aspirin, and dental floss in the cabinet.

He checks the time, does one last circuit through the apartment, making sure that everything is where it was when he entered. He decides to screw with her, taking a quart of ice cream out of the freezer and leaving it on the counter to melt. Let her wonder.

He goes to the back door, checks, and seeing no one, slips out and away.

Declan caught the wrapper in the evidence bag as it fell from my fingers. I slid on my glove and closed my eyes, trying to hold on to the reflection I'd seen in the medicine cabinet mirror.

"Did you—" Hernández began, but I held up a hand to stop the question.

"I need my sketchbook and a pencil," I told Declan.

He grabbed them for me and put them in my lap. Trying my best to hold on to the image, I opened my eyes and began to draw.

THIRTY-TWO

What Is Wrong with Me?

I worked quickly, trying to get his face before it faded from my memory. When I finished, I realized everyone was in a circle around me, watching. I reared back. There were too many emotions too close to me.

Declan made a pushing motion with his hand. Hernández, Tyler, Jake, and Bracken all moved to the ocean side of the deck.

"Bracken, when did you get here?" I asked.

"Good morning, my dear. I saw the crowd on the deck and decided to investigate. You were working. I didn't want to disturb you, so I made everyone some tea."

I looked back at the others and realized they were holding my mugs. Smiling at my great-uncle, I said, "Thank you. I promised them tea and kept getting distracted."

He waved away my thanks. "You're busy. I wasn't doing anything—other than taking one of your brownies for breakfast."

"Can I get you a muffin or something? A brownie doesn't seem like enough," I said.

"Perhaps not for these young men, but for an old one like me, it's perfect." He pointed to my drawing. "Now, tell us about him."

So I did.

"He breaks in before he attacks?" Hernández asked, scribbling in her notebook.

I nodded, ripping the sketch out of the book and handing it to her. "I don't know if this is new for him or if he's always done it. He was getting a charge out of being there when she wasn't, though. It made him feel powerful. Leaving the ice cream out was a dick move, but he enjoyed the idea of scaring her, making her question herself and then question if someone had been in her home."

She studied the drawing. "The ball cap will make identification impossible, but how sure are you on the lower half of his face?"

The killer was wearing a black ball cap, his head angle down and a little to the side as he opened the cabinet. "Maybe ninety percent. The jaw is right. The temple, the ear, those are right. It's the nose I'm not positive about. I saw his reflection for a split-second."

"Have you tried checking your visions?" Bracken asked. When I looked up, expression confused, he continued. "Touch the wrapper again, but this time, tell the vision to show you the reflection. It might not work, but it's worth a try."

I nodded, grinning. "It is." I slid off both my gloves this time and held out my hands to Declan. He squeezed water into one palm. I rubbed my hands together, placed my hands on my face, and smelled the deep blue. Keeping one hand on my face, I held out the other toward Declan, who rolled the wrapper out of the bag and into my hand.

When I saw the woman watering again, I thought, *Show me the reflection*. The vision jumped to the bathroom. When he opened the cabinet door, I told it to freeze. I had the nose wrong. It was a bit more bulbous at the end than I'd drawn. I could see part of a black t-shirt and what looked like the top of a tattoo, barely peeking over the neck of his shirt. When I knew I had it, I opened my eyes and dropped the wrapper back into the bag.

I put my gloves back on, picked up my pencil, and motioned

for Hernández to return the drawing. I looked up at Bracken. "Brilliant. Thank you."

He nodded and waited with the others to see what I was going to do.

After fixing the nose, I drew the t-shirt and tattoo. I also shaded his cheek. It was more sunken in than I'd drawn, like he'd lost weight recently. Was he sick?

I showed the revised drawing to Hernández, pointing at the tattoo. "It's low enough that if he wears collared shirts like Jake's, no one would ever see it. I know we can only see the tops here, but I think that's and S and an M."

"That could be a C," she said.

Declan studied the image. "The curve is too tight."

Curiosity was getting to Tyler, so he moved back over to our side and stood beside Bracken, craning his neck to see. Brow furrowed, he motioned to Jake. "Look at this. Is that what I think it is?"

Bracken and Tyler moved back so Jake could get closer. Declan must have explained to them while I was in the vision why I didn't like people crowding around me.

Jake leaned over and stared at it a moment and then started unbuttoning his shirt. He took off one sleeve and showed us his biceps. Tyler put his hand over most of the tattoo, so only the top of the S and M were visible. They were identical.

Grinning in triumph, Tyler dropped his hand, exposing Jake's USMC tattoo. "The letters are drawn in an arc. That's why we can only see the middle two. The killer was a Marine."

"Nice!" I put up a gloved hand and he high-fived me.

"He may not have been one," Hernández said. "He may have just wanted to be one, but it gives me somewhere to look. Thank you." She looked at all of us as she said it, pocketing her notebook. She pulled her phone out of her pocket, read a text, and said, "Osso says the lab confirms poison, so he's picking up Swan now."

"That was quick." I pulled out my own phone and texted Mom and Gran. "We need to be prepared for retribution. There's no way

Milo is rolling on his grandmother and she, I believe, is the power in the family." I looked at Bracken, checking.

He nodded. "I don't know anything about the younger generation, but in my time, Catherine was the strongest of them. The fact that she still heads the family leads me to believe she still is, but that's conjecture on my part."

"Okay, I need to check out this Marine theory. Thanks again," Hernández said, walking away with the evidence bag while texting.

I blew out a breath. "Okay, well, I'm as warded as I can be." I turned to Bracken. "I made a fae ward that Cal should have no power to break. I included your home as well, of course."

"Thank you," he said. "I must admit, ever since you had that vision of a man setting fire to the gallery and my home, I've been having a hard time relaxing." He patted his chest, and I got it. It'd been plaguing me too.

"Fire?" Jake asked, his shirt buttoned up and his arms crossed over his chest.

I nodded. "Yeah, I had a vision—Oh! Bracken, wait!" I ran in my studio and looked on my coffee table, my end table, the kitchen counter, my worktable. Where was it?

Declan stood in the doorway. "What are you looking for?"

"The map," I cried in desperation. "Where's the map?"

He pointed at my pants. "You pulled it out of your pocket this morning."

I patted down my pockets, found it, and almost passed out. What was wrong with me? Running back out to the deck, I said, "Look what the queen gave me." I showed my great-uncle.

Excited, he pulled his notebook out of his pocket and took the poorly drawn map out so we could compare them.

Tyler whispered, "Did she say queen?"

"Yes," Bracken said. "Look. The queen's mark is very close to where the *shades* are indicated here."

"I mean technically," I began, "the map was made by one of the queen's scouts. She just gave it to me because I was able to read her."

Bracken stared at me shocked. "Really? The queen asked you to read her?"

I lifted one shoulder. "She says she has plans for me, which made Dad super uncomfortable."

He patted my shoulder. "I can see why. It's never good to draw the faes' attention, dear, especially not the queen's."

"Arwyn," Declan said cautiously, taking my gloved hand in his. "You're being awfully free with information in front of two people we just met. Are you feeling okay?"

"Hmm?" I looked over at Tyler and Jake. "Oh, they're fine. They'll take the job. Tyler already likes us, me more than you." I elbowed Declan. "Jake is pretending to not like or trust you but the only reason they're here is because Jake *does* trust you and his sudden anger issues scare him. He doesn't want to hurt Tyler, so he's hoping you're more like your father than your half-brother."

The men looked stunned and uncomfortable.

"Sorry. I don't normally do that." I rubbed my forehead. "I'm usually really good about keeping secrets." I turned to Bracken. "Have I been spelled?"

"I don't know," he said, a gentle smile on his face. "I have a suspicion, but I don't know. I don't believe it's an immediate danger, though. That map and finding Cal is the priority."

I nodded. He was right, but I was still uneasy. I had too many secrets floating around in my head to just start blurting them out.

Declan ran a hand down my back. "Hey, what did you see when you read the queen?"

I turned back to him and shook my head. "Oh, I don't think she'd like that. Sorry."

He kissed my forehead. "See? You're fine, just overtired and dealing with too many threats at once. And I already knew the men could be trusted. I wouldn't have introduced them to you otherwise. I just wasn't sure how you felt about them."

"Oh. Phew." I looked at Tyler and Jake. "Do you guys want to stay or is all this too crazy?"

"Hello."

We all turned to the tall, thin woman wearing very dark sunglasses. Orla, our new owl-shifter friend. Glinting in the sunlight, her long, light brown hair was coiled in a bun.

"Is this a bad time?" she asked.

"No. It's a perfect one, actually." I waved her over.

She eyed Jake and Tyler but then ignored them, coming to me and pulling a piece of paper out of the back pocket of her jeans. "I made a map."

"Perfect!" I shouted. "Everybody inside. I'm living in terror of the wind whipping a map out of someone's hand right now."

I went straight to my worktable and put the queen's map down. Bracken put down the poorly drawn one, and Orla placed hers beside the other two. Bracken arranged all three so the shapes of the bay roughly aligned. Orla's map had seven spots indicated. Two of them matched the queen's map.

I turned to Orla. "Can you tell us about your scouting trips?"

She looked at the two unfamiliar men.

"Oh, sorry! Orla, this is Tyler and Jake. They're werewolves," I told her.

Jake's expression darkened but Tyler smiled.

"Gentlemen, this is Orla. She's an eagle-owl shifter."

Tyler's eyebrows winged up. "Really? That's so cool. I've never met an owl shifter." He held out a hand and she shook it.

"Orla," Declan began, "is it okay that Arwyn just told them about you?"

She looked uncomfortable but eventually nodded.

Seriously, what the hell was wrong with me? I touched the sleeve of her thermal. "I'm sorry. I should have asked."

"Should have asked us too," Jake grumbled.

"True," I said. "I should have. I just… I know we're all going to be friends and work together. We're all going to be tangled up in each others' lives, so why not just start now?" I paused to think and turned to Declan, suddenly afraid. "I never get feelings like that about myself." My eyes filled with tears. "What's wrong with me?"

I could see my concern mirrored in his eyes but then they cleared and he leaned down to give me a kiss. "There's nothing wrong. You're perfect."

"Maps, dear," Bracken prompted.

"Yes. Sorry." I shook my head and turned back to Orla. "Your scouting trips?"

She blinked, taking in the chaos compared to her nice, serene life in her bookstore. "Yes. I found seven locations that felt dark. I circled each, rested on tree branches, and observed. I never saw anything specific, but all of them felt dark. Evil."

"Please tell me we don't have seven sorcerers working in the area," I said. That was all we needed.

THIRTY-THREE

You're Shopping?

"The other six could be black wicches or some other type of supernatural," Bracken said.

Ugh. He was right. Sorcerers and black wicches would read as dark. Black magic fed on blood and pain to power spells. Sorcerers added demons to the mix. As for other supernaturals, who knew?

"Wait." I pointed at one of the dots on her map. "Is that an address?"

Orla nodded. "That was a normal house with an address. I memorized it so I could write it down when I shifted. Four of them were structures I could almost see. The warding was strong. The last two were hidden completely. I couldn't see anything but felt nauseated when I flew near. I had to pass over multiple times before I realized what I was feeling was a ward that didn't just hide, it shoved me away."

"These two?" I pointed at her map. When she nodded, I compared them to the queen's map. "The queen's scout picked those two spots as well." I grabbed Declan's wrist and squeezed. "We have two locations."

"And five more to keep on eye on," Bracken warned.

I nodded. "I'll text Osso and ask him to find out who owns that one property we have an address for."

"He'll do that?" he asked.

"With all the work I do for them for free? They can look up addresses for me." I turned back to Orla. "Thank you so much. This is amazing." I glanced at the kitchen. "Can I get you something to eat? I know this is normally your sleeping time, but I'm sure you're hungry. Maybe some tea?"

She was feeling overwhelmed, and I wasn't making it easier for her. "Declan, can you show Jake and Tyler the gallery while I get Orla something to eat?"

"Refreshments," Orla muttered with a nod.

"Sure." Declan waved the men with him and then went through the door into the gallery.

"Holy shit!" Tyler breathed as the door closed.

"I'm sorry, Orla. I didn't mean to bombard you. I just wanted to thank you, and I often do that through my baking. I brew an excellent cup of tea too. If you want to sit down with Bracken, I'll pull together some food."

I couldn't see what was going on behind the dark glasses, but she finally nodded and sat. While they spoke quietly about the maps, Bracken holding all three in his hand, I went through the refrigerator and freezer, pulling out muffins and brownies, sourdough rolls and pecan lace cookies. I had no idea what she liked and wanted her to be happy.

I placed the heaping platter of warmed baked goods and napkins on the coffee table before going back to brew tea. When I returned with three mugs, I was happy to see them both eating.

Orla took the mug with a nod of thanks. "Your baking is far superior to my local bakery. Perhaps I should come buy from you instead."

"Nope," I said. "Your money is no good here. After what you've done for us? You can come by for baked goods any time you feel like it."

She sat stiffly a moment and then nodded with a shy smile. "I'd like that very much."

"So it shall be written. So it shall be done," I proclaimed.

"Is that a spell?" she asked.

Bracken tapped his chin. "I believe she's quoting Yul Brynner in *The Ten Commandments*." At Orla's blank look, he explained, "It's an old movie. He was Pharaoh Rameses." He waited for an expression of understanding. "Arwyn meant that the offer of baked goods was decided."

Orla nodded. "I see. I'm afraid I'm quite tired. I've been going to bed late so I could scout. The food and tea have helped, but I should get going. I don't want to fall asleep on the drive home."

"Oh, let me," Bracken said. "I just purchased a new vehicle and would be happy to drive you home. We wouldn't want you to get hurt." He stood and looked around, patting his pockets. He handed me the two accurate maps, folding his back into his journal. "You should hold on to those, safe behind your wards."

"Good idea," I said, slipping them into my pocket. "Orla, let me get you some food to take with you." I filled up a container and snapped it shut. "These are fine in the freezer for a bit. You don't have to worry about eating it all right away—unless you want to."

I handed her the container. Bracken led her out and down the deck to his Bronco. Deciding werewolves were always up for more food, I took what was left on the platter and brought it into the gallery.

The men appeared to be shopping. Tyler held up a vase and Jake nodded. Tyler handed it off to Declan, who added it to a collection of pieces at the cash wrap.

"Jake, you were too busy being grumpy earlier. Would you like something to eat now?" I held up the platter.

Declan walked over and snagged a muffin. "I saw Bracken and Orla walk by. Everything okay?"

I nodded. "Yep. The poor thing has been missing sleep to scout for us. This is way past an owl's bedtime. Bracken is driving her home so she doesn't fall asleep behind the wheel."

"Good." He finished the muffin in two bites.

Jake and Tyler walked over, Jake holding one of my big wave bowls. The glaze on the inside was an iridescent blue-green. The outside of the bowl base was a matte black, so the wave appeared to be hanging in space.

"Okay," Tyler said, "I thought you were an adorable little badass before, but now? Holy crap. You're an artistic genius! Everywhere I look, I see something I desperately want in my home so I can marvel at it for decades to come."

"Thank you." I held out the platter, embarrassed by the praise. "Muffin?"

Grinning, he took two in his large hand and gave Jake one.

I looked again at what they had accumulated on the counter. "Um, you guys know my stuff is expensive, right?" I grimaced, feeling like an idiot. This is why other people needed to handle selling my stuff.

"We have money," Jake growled, taking a bite and pausing, his eyes closing.

Tyler noticed Jake's reaction too and said, "I told you," to him before winking at me. He picked up one of the pecan lace cookies. "Ooh, pretty." He took a bite and then grabbed a handful off my platter, passing one to Jake.

"I was thinking," I said to Declan. "I'm going to need more chairs for tonight. Do you have any or should I find a party rental —no. Mom has chairs. If I tell her about the dinner and the planning, though, she'll want to be involved. Which, now that I think about it, makes sense. I got the feeling, though, that Aunt Elizabeth wanted it to just be her family at this, like there are some things she's not comfortable sharing with the whole class."

"You're a member of the Council," Declan said, "so that's covered. Your Gran basically put you in charge of hunting down a sorcerer, which is…" He shook his head. "I say go with the original plan and if we decide on something tonight, you can tell your Mom and Gran afterward. You can't tell someone it's their job and then expect a say every step of the way."

"Maybe you can't," I said, patting his arm, "but they definitely can." I started preparing excuses in my head as to why they were left out. "Okay, just us. So, chairs?"

Declan nodded. "Some are folding chairs, but I should be able to find—what—seven, right?"

I nodded. "You, me, Aunt Elizabeth, Uncle Robert, Frank, Faith, and Great-Uncle Bracken."

"Do you want us patrolling the gallery?" Tyler asked.

Jake gave him a sharp look, but Tyler just grinned. Jake glared at his partner for a count of three and then relaxed into a nod.

"Fine," Jake grumbled.

Declan wrapped an arm around me. "Thank you."

"That'd be great," I said, "but it's pretty short notice. Are you available to be here tonight?"

Tyler nodded. "I even packed us a bag so we can stay down here for a few days."

Jake's brows drew together again. "When did you do that?"

"While you were showering. There's a duffle in the truck box." Tyler looked over at Declan. "I had a good feeling about you. You're not Alexander, but that's not all bad. Your dad was a good man and a powerful wolf, but there's no way he would have mated himself to a wicche. He basically disowned his son Michael, who should have succeeded him as Alpha, for marrying a wicche." He paused, eyes widening. "Wait." He pointed at me. "Your aunt?"

I nodded. "My Aunt Bridget. Apparently, when I was about three-ish, I went up to them at their engagement party to tell them they'd have a daughter and that I was sad they'd both die."

Tyler put his hand over his mouth. "Oh, no."

"Oh, yes," I said. "That was my first prophesy. Afterward, I asked my mom for gloves. I didn't like seeing my poor Aunt Bridget being torn apart by a demon. Let's just say it put a damper on the party. It also became clear that I was in fact a Cassandra wicche."

"Wow," Tyler said, shaking his head. "Anyway, back to my point." He looked at Declan. "Alexander appreciated our strength and loyalty to him. We were pack. Personally, though, he didn't want to know about us as a mated pair." He glanced at Jake and then back. "I could be wrong, but you seem to have his strength without his closed-minded arrogance."

Declan didn't say anything for a moment. "You know more about him than I do. They were both killed when I was small. I have feelings of warmth and love at the thought of them, but I don't have any specific memories of either of them."

"Let me look through albums," Jake said. "I'm sure we have pictures we can give you."

I felt Declan's heart race.

"Do you?" He swallowed. "Thank you very much."

Jake nodded.

"We can go to my place and look for chairs. Jake, Tyler, I have an apartment over my workshop and retail space. I'm still mid-construction, so it isn't furnished, but it's all yours until the bodyguarding job is done. It'll save you time driving up and back to the Big Sur mountains."

"Sounds good," Tyler said, nodding at his partner.

"Well, wait until you see it before you decide." Declan turned back to me and my empty platter. "Are you good to go?"

"Yup." I went back through the studio door. "Let me put this down and grab my backpack."

Declan's property was quite literally across the road and down maybe three hundred yards.

Tyler pointed to their loot. "What about?"

"I can get it when we come back. It all needs a lot of wrapping so nothing breaks on the way home. And the gallery is only open on the weekends, so no one will be in to move your things."

We filed onto the deck and I flicked my fingers to lock the gallery up. Leaning over the railing, I called, "You're in charge, Cecil. I'm going over to Declan's for a bit."

Tyler waited to see if anything happened. Sure enough, Cecil's orange tentacle slapped the surface. Shaking his head and grinning, Tyler followed me to the parking lot. Already, Jake and Tyler had split up, one in front of me and one behind.

I really hoped we'd be able to come up with a plan tonight. As much as I liked Jake and Tyler, I didn't want them following me around all the time. A girl needs to have some secrets.

THIRTY-FOUR

A Seahorse Love Token

Tyler went to get his duffle bag and then he and Jake jumped into Declan's truck bed. Declan drove us the short trip over, where construction continued.

"I'm sorry you've been missing your own renovation," I said.

He squeezed my gloved hand. "That's why I have a crew. They're working, whether I'm here or not. Kenji keeps his hand in, and I've got a couple of my pack working on the crew. Come on," he said, opening his door. "You haven't seen it since it was a disaster zone. I want you to see the progress."

I opened my door, slid out, and found three big werewolves surrounding me. I held up my hands. "I'm good, guys. At ease." I felt a prickle at the back of my neck and turned to the road. "That's him."

All three turned, and then Jake started running. The podcasting stalker had his window down and his phone up to record me. Declan's arm went over my shoulder and across my heart. Tyler stood in front of me, so I had to lean around him to see what was going on.

Jake ran across the street, not even pausing to check traffic, which was insane. The stalker's eyes went comically round as Jake grabbed the door and leaned in the window.

Tyler and Declan laughed.

"What?" I asked. Their hearing was ridiculous.

"Jake told him that if he ever saw him hanging around you again, he'd rip off his head and shove it up his ass," Tyler said. "He's very good at growling intimidation. The guy seems to just be whining. Jake told him to get the fuck out of here and never come back."

The stalker floored it, his car fishtailing onto the road. Other drivers had to slam on their brakes and honk. Amid the chaos, Jake jogged back.

"What does he do in real life?" I asked Tyler.

"Jake's a writer and I work in cybersecurity. Both are jobs we can do remotely."

"Nice. Is this gig going to mess up your day jobs?" I tapped Declan's arm around me. "By the way, how much am I paying these guys?"

"A lot," Tyler grinned.

Jake stood beside his partner, like nothing had happened. "I just finished a book. I'm plotting the next. It's head work, so I can do that on guard duty."

"And I'm between projects, so I'm good," Tyler added.

"Everything okay, boss?"

We all turned at the voice and found Kenji with two big men I didn't know. Kenji was a member of the Big Sur pack. When Declan arrived in town, Kenji and Daniel left the pack to follow their true Alpha. Once Declan won the Alpha challenge against Logan, Kenji and Daniel returned to the pack, taking senior positions. I assumed the other guys were the pack members Declan had been referring to earlier.

Declan waved them over. "Kenji, this is Jake and this is Tyler. Have you met them before?"

Kenji shook his head and held out his hand to shake theirs.

"Kenji is my second. He's a lawyer, but his parents own a large construction company. He's done construction work all his life, so he slums to check in on the project occasionally."

"One his sister did the architectural plans for," I added, knowing Kenji would like her work being acknowledged.

His gaze cut to me, and he nodded before returning his attention to Jake and Tyler.

"Behind Kenji," Declan continued, "are West and Joaquin. Both are members of the pack and both are excellent construction workers, which is lucky for me."

They stood straighter at their Alpha's praise.

"And gentlemen," Declan said, "Jake and Tyler"—gesturing to each man in turn—"were members of my father's pack in the Santa Cruz Mountains and are now living in Big Sur. They're deciding if they want to join our pack."

"We're married," Jake growled, clearly waiting for a negative reaction. Tyler stood serenely by his husband, and I couldn't help but smile.

Kenji nodded. "It's always good to have more strong wolves. If you decide to apply, we would be happy to have you run with us."

As West and Joaquin didn't react, Jake said, "And what about you?"

The two men looked at each other and then back at Jake, clearly confused as to why they were being addressed when the Alpha and second had already welcomed them.

"Do you have a problem with us?" Jake elaborated.

The men shared a look again and then both shrugged. Joaquin's eyes widened and he smacked West's arm. "He thinks we're homophobes."

"Oh," West said, nodding. "Yeah no, we don't care."

"Jake and Tyler will be around a lot for a little while. I hired them to guard Arwyn until some current danger has passed."

I tapped Declan's arm again. "You mean *I* hired them, right?"

"Let's go in," Declan said, ignoring my question. "I want Arwyn to see the progress and the men to see the apartment. If it works for them, they'll sleep here when they're not on guard duty."

Declan pulled me along.

"Wait a minute," I protested.

Tyler patted my shoulder on a laugh, taking the lead this time. Jake fell into step behind us.

"We'll talk about it later," Declan said. "We've just started on the retail space. I wanted the workshop done first, then the apartment."

We walked into the retail space. It was wide open and mostly empty. I looked up and the ceiling stole my breath. It looked like what I would imagine the top of a pyramid would look like if one were looking at it from the inside. It started about twelve feet high, at the tops of the walls, and angled up and in to meet in the middle, maybe fifteen feet high. The ceiling was paneled in wood, with the boards all perfectly aligned to create a perfect inverted pyramid.

I pointed up. "It's stunning. What kind of wood is that?"

Declan looked up with me, smiling. "They finished it." He walked around, studying it. "Great work," he said, his voice raised for the others.

His crew, men and women, had filtered in to see what he thought. At his praise, they grinned and nodded, looking up themselves.

"It's reclaimed wide-plank heart pine," Declan finally answered. "I've been refinishing the boards for weeks."

They were a satiny, well-oiled reddish brown. "Please tell me you have more of these boards to use in your apartment."

Laughing, he picked me up and spun me around. "It's happening," he whispered to me. "I have a home."

He put me down and then, noticing a woman, waved her forward. "Cam, tell me where we are." The tall Black woman who looked remarkably like Melissa moved toward us. She wore dark blue coveralls and a bandana over her hair.

"Arwyn, this is Cam. She's the forewoman on the project," Declan explained. "Cam, this is Arwyn." He pointed in the direction of my gallery. "The Sea Wicche."

She nodded at me. "My cousin Melissa said she was boxing up art at your gallery yesterday."

"Yes," I said. "She and her crew did a beautiful job."

She smiled at that and then returned her attention to Declan. "As you can see, we finished the ceiling. The tile guys were here yesterday. The bathrooms, upstairs and down, are done. By the way, the crew are asking if they can use your shop toilet instead of the porta outside."

Declan nodded. "Of course. This is Jake and Tyler. If they like the apartment, they'll be staying up there for a little while. I was hoping the bathrooms would be done. What about the kitchen?"

"There's a microwave and the refrigerator that got plumbed yesterday. The stove is supposed to arrive the day after tomorrow."

"Hey," I interrupted, elbowing Declan. "You didn't ask me what kind to get."

He wrapped his arm around me again. "That's because I just ordered the same model you use."

"Oh. Nice."

"The crew's been focusing upstairs," Cam continued. "West and Joaquin are working on the bookshelves today. Jim and I were just about to put up the lighting fixture in the living room. Do you want to come see?"

Declan nodded, excitement bright in his warm brown eyes.

"Okay, everybody back to work and the shop bathroom is available if you don't want the porta outside," she told her crew before mumbling, "And who the hell would?"

Leading the way, she took us through to the workshop toward a back staircase. The workshop was fully equipped with a wall of tools and freestanding table saws and I didn't know what because I'd just seen one of the merry-go-round steeds leaning against a wall.

I detoured from the group to go see it. This property had been a tourist trap with a dangerous merry-go-round. The whole place had fallen into disrepair years and years ago. Someone bought it maybe a decade ago and went broke, dealing with the crumbling building, the rusty pipes, and shaky foundation. Could they have just torn it all down and started again? Sure. There still would have been a ton of repairs needed to the infrastructure, but there also would have been huge delays, waiting to get all the permits approved for building new construction in an historic part of town. So builders seeing it as a money pit, passed on the project.

Declan worked with Kenji's sister Natsuki to work with what was here while creating a completely new masterpiece.

When I'd seen the carousel animals thrown in a pile during demolition, I'd asked if he could keep the octopus for me. It was the one I'd ridden when I was little. He promised he would, but it looked like he may have salvaged another.

Leaning against the wall was a seahorse. All the paint had been sanded off and the wood treated. It felt so strange to see him naked, without his garish Day-Glo paint. Declan had given him his dignity back. I ran my gloved fingers over his narrow snout. The brass pole was now tarnished, but that somehow fit. He'd been through a lot in his life. He wasn't pretending otherwise.

I turned to call after Declan but found him standing behind me. My eyes filled with tears. "He's beautiful. You've restored his pride. Look at him." I put a hand on Declan's chest and leaned in. "Can I paint him?"

He kissed me and said, "I think he'd appreciate that." He paused. "I know you want to see the octopus, but I wanted to do a test run on one you didn't feel such an attachment to. What if he fell apart once I took the paint off? I couldn't be sure about the state of the wood until I sanded it."

"I get it," I said, smiling up at him. "Thank you for taking care of them."

He took my hand again. "I want you to see the upstairs."

Cam, West, and Joaquin had already gone up. Only Jake and Tyler were waiting for us.

Declan make a hand gesture and Jake and Tyler hung back.

"Ooh, the stairs are that same wood," I said. "I feel bad stepping on it."

"It's all been treated," he explained. "They'll clean off easily enough."

"You should leave your boots on a mat at the base of the stairs so you don't track sawdust—Oh!" Declan had stepped out of the way at the top of the stairs, revealing his new home.

THIRTY-FIVE

Home

It was so beautiful, I teared up again. I'd been expecting a single dude's apartment: white walls, beige carpet, and a huge flat-screen TV. I couldn't have been more wrong. It was a Craftsman flat. The same deep, rich reddish-brown wood from downstairs was used on the floor, in a board-and-batten panel running a third of the way up the walls, and in the pillars and bookcases used to divide rooms.

The walls above the wood were a sunlit ocean blue in what looked like Venetian plaster. The ceiling was a far lighter hue than the wall color and was bisected by matching wooden beams to create a coffered ceiling.

The large first room had a stone fireplace that was open to the room beyond, with a wide casement opening to the right of the fireplace. I wandered into the second room, wanting to see it all. This room—that shared the fireplace—was smaller. Mission-style pendants hung from the ceiling in the center of the open space.

"Dining room?" I asked.

He nodded, appearing wary of my reaction, though I didn't understand why. It was a freaking showplace. I looked through the adjoining doorway and saw the kitchen. The floors were the same gorgeous wood. The cabinets, though, looked like black walnut.

I went in, running my gloved hand over the island countertop. "Brushed stainless steel? I figured you'd do a butcherblock or granite. Something more earthy."

Looking uncomfortable, he said, "Isn't this better for baking and cleanup?"

"Well, sure, but since when do you bake?" It really was gorgeous, the soft brushed silver against the black cabinetry. He'd used that same sunlit ocean blue for the glass tile backsplash.

"Oh, honey," Tyler murmured from the other room.

"This is harder than I thought it would be," Declan said.

"I'm sorry!" I hugged him close. "I haven't said it yet. It's all beautiful! You've done amazing work here. This is, hands down, the warmest, most stunning bachelor pad known to man."

"Oof," I heard from the next room.

"What? Why am I being heckled?" I called out to Tyler and Jake.

"We're going to go wait in the workshop," Jake said.

"Declan, your home is gorgeous. What am I saying wrong?" I squeezed his hand. "The last thing I want to do is hurt you." I put my hand on his cheek. "What am I missing?"

He shook his head and kissed me. "It's not you. I'm the one who's screwing this up." He blew out a breath. "I put in these countertops so you could bake here. I chose the wall and tile colors so it would remind you of the ocean. I built this home for both of us."

I stared at him, stunned. My heart may have stopped.

"Whether you move in or just stay over once in a while, I wanted it to be comfortable and welcoming for you." Swallowing, he added, "What do you think?"

"Really? You want me in your home?" Heart now racing, insides turning to goo, I stared up into his handsome face. "Fair warning, I'm pretty annoying. I'm not even sure how I'd do living with someone." I looked around the kitchen and what I could see of the dining room, trying to imagine us living here together.

"If," I began, "after spending more time with me, you decide this was a horrible idea, tell me and I'll go. Don't resent me in silence. That would kill me."

He kissed the tip of my nose. "I don't anticipate that being an issue, but if it is, you'll be the first to know."

I nodded. "Okay. Good. We'll work out the hows and whens later. Maybe we can keep essentials in both your place and mine so we can stay wherever it's convenient that day."

"Sure," he said, "but it's our place and yours." He took my hand again. "Let me show you the rest."

As we walked back through the dining room, I pointed up at the pendant lights. "How attached are you to those?"

He glanced up with a shrug. "They fit the style of the room, but I don't love them."

I nodded. "Cool. I have an idea for a light fixture that I think would work better."

"You already have a ton of work to do. We have time. A new light can wait."

My chest felt tight. *We have time.* He wanted time with me.

There was a guest bath off the living room. The plaster in there was a lighter green, like shallow water on a sunny day. There were two guest rooms with creamy walls and views of the forest behind Declan's business.

My stomach dropped and I clutched his hand.

"What's the matter?" he asked.

"I can't move in," I told him. "Bracken and I just had this long conversation about being outcasts all our lives and how happy he is to now be with family who understands him. I told him I'd put an addition on the gallery, one very similar to his RV, so he'd have a stable home that was known and comfortable. I can't leave him all by himself again." I blinked back the tears. "I can't do that to him."

"Then we won't," Declan said simply. "We'll figure out an arrangement that works for everyone. I mean, you're not moving across country. I could throw Wilbur's ball and hit the gallery from here. That's your studio and your gallery. You'll be there every day. No one's being abandoned."

Nodding, I wiped my face. "That's true. Sorry. I don't know why I'm leaking so much today." There was too much going on and emotions were running too high, obviously.

"I want you to see our bedroom." He pulled me into a huge room. The board-and-batten paneling in here mirrored the living room. On the outside wall were huge windows overlooking the ocean. The view was amazing.

"That strip of sand, seagrass, and rocks across the road is part of your property. It's obviously too narrow to build anything, but I wanted to make sure no one could throw up a billboard and ruin our view. I asked Natsuki to look up the boundaries of your parcel of land."

Pushing up the window where I was standing, I breathed in the ocean air. I wasn't too far from it. Pointing down the road, away from the gallery, I said, "Do you see those daisies growing on the verge? That's about where my land ends."

I glanced over and realized I'd walked right past another stone fireplace, a smaller version of the one in the living room. "How did you do this so fast?"

He laughed. "I have a good crew, all of whom are suspiciously strong."

Grinning at that, I kept exploring, opening a door and finding a large, walk-through closet that led to a huge master bath. "And I thought my shower was massive." I stepped in, marveling at the blue, green, and indigo glass tiles. "Ha! You already have a hair trap on your drain."

"I know my mate and her incredible hair." He kissed the top of my head and then spun me around. "Well?"

"I love it. I love everything about it."

"Except the dining room light fixture," he qualified.

I grimaced. "They're great lights. I just have an idea for something better."

"Good," he rumbled, wrapping his arms around me and

picking me up off the floor. "I want you to put your touch on all of it. This is our home. It should reflect both of us."

"Done and done." I had a hard time keeping the excited bubbles from fixing a permanent grin on my face. "Tell me the truth," I whispered, not wanting the wolves and bears in the building to hear. "Are you sure about this? I'm a lot. Ask anyone."

He dropped his hands to my butt, pulling my legs around his waist, and then pressing me against the beautiful shower tiles. "Ursula, you may not be aware of this, but wolves mate for life. I have no control over how you feel about me, but I *love* you. I want to be with you and only you, so, yes, I'm sure."

I pulled off a glove and ran my fingertips over his brow and down his nose. I brushed my thumb across his bottom lip and then kissed him until we'd both lost track of time and space. When we came up for air, I said, "I love you, Declan Quinn, and I take you."

He kissed me again and my butt tingled.

I gasped. "How'd you do that?"

Laughing, he gave me another quick kiss and put me down. "Your phone is on vibrate."

"Oh. Right. I knew that." Feeling like an idiot—a ridiculously happy one—I pulled my phone out of my pocket and tapped the screen. "Hey, Hernández. What's up?"

"Can I come see you? I have an idea and something I want you to touch to see if my idea is correct."

"Oh, uh." I walked out of the beautiful bathroom, through the roomy his-and-hers closet, bummed I had to think about murder instead of love and a shared home. "Yeah, I guess. I'm at Declan's workshop right now, but I can be back at the gallery in a few."

"Thank you and sorry to mess with your plans," she said. "I should be there in about ten minutes. If you're not back by then, I'll wait on your deck."

"Sounds good." I disconnected and found Declan in the living room, talking with Jake.

Tyler walked out of one of the guest rooms. "We like forest views anyway." He grinned when he saw me. "You two should be the first to sleep in your bedroom. We told Declan to put the blow-up mattress in one of the guest rooms for us. The bigger question," he began, turning back to Declan, "is whether or not you have Wi-Fi here."

Declan was smiling at nothing in particular, and I felt another squeeze of my heart. "Yeah," he said. "The network is Quinn Woodcraft and the password is Ursula, the number four, and good. All one word and only Ursula is capitalized."

And there went that squeeze again. "I have to get back."

Declan nodded. "We heard. I have them loading up chairs in the back of the pickup. I'll take you back, the men will follow. They're going to run along opposite sides of the road and search for cameras."

I got a little lightheaded at that. It hadn't occurred to me that there were more. I'd thought the one camera I'd found was unusual for the stalker. He seemed to like to film me himself. I needed sleep. My brain wasn't working properly and I had a sorcerer to deal with.

"Oh, shit," I muttered. I needed quiet and calm to get my head on straight. There was too much going on and no time to process it.

"What?" Declan asked, suddenly concerned.

I rubbed my forehead. "I've been so off lately. I'm slow on the uptake and I have a demon to best. I think Cal is getting in." I thunked my head against Declan's chest. "If I can't rely on my own brain, my own magic, Cal wins and more people suffer and die."

He wrapped his arms around me. "So you know what we'll do?"

I looked up. "What?"

"It's time for you to take another swim. The ocean will clear your head and mess with any spells aimed at you."

I grinned. "You're so smart."

"I don't have a demon trying to screw with my head," he said.

"Or a detective pulling him away from what he was doing to find a serial killer," Jake added.

"He also didn't have a new living arrangement and relationship upgrade sprung on him," Tyler said.

Declan rubbed my back. "And you're used to working and living on your own, avoiding your mom and gran, saying hello to your ocean friends. Your life has changed a lot in a very short time. Being overwhelmed is a normal reaction."

He glanced over my head at Tyler and Jake before returning his attention to me. "When we feel that way, we shift and go for a run. For you, it's a swim. Let's get out of here so I can toss you off the deck."

Laughing, I nodded. "Deal."

THIRTY-SIX

What?!

When we got back, I carried two chairs and Declan carried the rest. He didn't like that. He wanted to carry them all, but that was silly. I had two arms just hanging off my body doing nothing. When I came around the corner of the gallery onto the deck, I found Bracken waiting.

He jumped up and took the chairs from me. "Let me, please."

Declan followed closely behind. "Did Orla get home okay?"

"Yes," Bracken said. "Lovely girl was so tired, she fell asleep on the drive. Luckily, she's not a deep sleeper. I left her stumbling into her home to sleep properly."

Flicking my fingers, I unlocked the door and tried to take a couple of the chairs from Declan.

"I've got it," he said. "It's more difficult to split them up now. If you could hold the door open, though, I'd appreciate it."

I did and both Declan and Bracken brought the chairs in and set them up around my worktable.

A thought hit me. "I just remembered." I went to one of my storage closets, the one with household things rather than art supplies, and rooted around until I found a long piece of folded material. "Mom gave me a tablecloth when I moved in—no idea why—but clearly she was thinking ahead."

I flung it over the table and Bracken caught the far end, pulling it taut. The deep grooves from being folded for so long disappeared as he ran his hand along the cloth.

"Thank you."

"You're welcome. It's lovely. Your mother clearly had you in mind when she chose this. If she were to buy one for herself, I imagine she'd lean more toward classic white or perhaps ecru."

I laughed. "You're very perceptive. I believe she does own multiple tablecloths in a variety of light neutrals." I looked more closely at the fabric and my stomach dropped. I walked around to Bracken's end, marveling that she'd done this for me. Pointing at it, I said, "I painted her a watercolor for her birthday years ago. It was the view of the ocean from her front window." I tapped the fabric. "She had my painting turned into a tablecloth." My throat tightened. Why was everything hitting me so hard today?

Declan wrapped an arm around me and kissed the top of my head. "She gave you a little bit of herself and little bit of your childhood to take into your new home."

I looked up at him. "I'm such an asshole. I never opened it. I just thought, what am I going to do with a tablecloth, and put it in the cupboard."

"Stop it," he said. "You're not an asshole. You just hadn't had a need for it before. You should take a pic and send it to her, so she knows that you know."

I pulled out a chair, put a leg up, and started to climb up when Declan caught me around the middle and pulled me down. "You're too tired and I don't want you falling. Hand me your phone. I'll take it for you."

I started to argue and then realized he would get a better shot than me, as he's much taller, so I opened my phone and handed it over. He stepped up, took the pic, and passed it back.

"Thank you." I tapped on the pic and then caught a strange look pass between Bracken and Declan. "What?"

"What what?" Declan asked

I pointed between the two of them. "Why are you two acting weird?"

"I've been weird all my life, I'm afraid," Bracken said, walking around the table. "There isn't much I can do about it now." He patted my shoulder as he went past.

"I didn't mean it that way. You two were just—Oh, Declan, were you able to make those copies for me?"

Nodding, he went into his front pocket. "Thanks for reminding me. I've been carrying these around for a couple of days." He held up three keys to my back door.

I took them from him and then handed one back. "Put that on your key ring." I held out the second to Bracken. "I want you to be able to come in any time you want. You shouldn't have to wait for me on the deck."

He stared at it for a long moment. "Are you sure?"

"Of course. My home is your home." I held it up higher. "Please."

He took it from my hand like it was a priceless relic and then slipped it into his pocket.

"This one," Declan said to Bracken while pointing at me, "is feeling off today, so it's time for an ocean swim."

I put my phone, key, and backpack on the table. After toeing off my sneakers, I slid off my gloves and walked out, passing Jake and Tyler. "Any cameras?"

"Not that we found," Jake said.

I blew out a breath of relief and was therefore blindsided by what Tyler said next.

"We did, however, find a listening device in the ice plant over there." Tyler pointed to the side of the gallery, near where the camera had been. He was holding an electronic device with the bottom hem of his t-shirt.

"What? He's been listening to us?" My skin crawled and my stomach twisted. "He's been—he heard all about you two this morning? My reading for the police. When…" He listened to me and my dad talking about him. I'd had precious few conversations with my father after a lifetime of wondering about him, and this asshole was listening in and taking notes? My stomach flipped again. I ran through the studio and into the bathroom, lifting the toilet seat just in time.

He'd had me under a microscope to review and dissect. He'd heard everything Declan and I said to each other, my talks with the raccoon babies, with Cecil and Wilbur… I was so busy freaking out, I didn't realize that Declan had followed, that he was holding my hair and now pressing a wet washcloth to my forehead.

Empty, I took the cloth, wiped my face, and thumped back, my butt on the tile floor, feeling lost.

Declan crouched down and pushed my hair back. "Can you find him?"

"What?"

"Can you touch the recorder and find him," he growled. "Let me do the rest."

"You can't." I shook my head. "He's human. Do you want Osso and the rest of the Justice League after you?" I grabbed his arm. "No endangering our newly formed plans."

He stood, pulling me up with him. "We have to do something, love. We can't have this creep sneaking around after you."

Nodding, I patted his chest. "Let me think."

When I walked out into the studio, Bracken was looking out the back window and Tyler was waiting for me in the kitchen, the electronic device still held in the fabric of his shirt.

"If it helps," Tyler said, "this isn't a sophisticated device. It does transmit, rather than record locally, but it isn't sensitive enough to hear over the wind and surf. If you were standing near it and talking, he might have heard you. On the deck?" He shook his head. "We all have a tendency to speak quietly, as what we're saying can be problematic if overheard and because we have sensitive hearing. You, less so and the human detective, not at all. Still, if he caught anything, it was probably indistinct murmuring. I've jammed it, so we should be okay, but I'm with Declan. We need to find this guy and stop him."

I nodded, trying to calm my jittery stomach. "Come with me, please." I led the way out onto the deck. I stepped onto a bench and then the railing.

"Arwyn?"

I turned to see Hernández back again. "Sorry. You're going to have to wait a minute. Declan, can you give—holy crap!" I jumped back down and pulled the maps out of my back pocket with a shaking hand. I'd been so close to ruining everything.

I handed the papers to Declan. He felt my hand trembling and squeezed it.

"We're okay," he murmured.

"I'm not," I whispered.

He pulled me into a fierce hug, and I let his body heat settle me.

"Can you ask Hernández to look up the owner of that one address Orla got?" I asked him.

"Of course." His hands went in my back pockets.

"What are you doing?" I asked.

"I'm checking that nothing important is about to get wet." He checked my front pockets and then patted me down. "You're good."

"You enjoyed that a little too much," I muttered.

"Is there such a thing as too much enjoyment?" he responded.

I turned around to step back up on the bench and found myself on the railing, thanks to a very tall and strong boyfriend. I held out my hand to Tyler. "Hit me with it."

He dropped it in my hand. I closed my fingers over it and as I started to feel a vision creeping up on me—even after touching Declan—I dove off the deck. When I hit the water, the vision overtook me.

Wearing all black, he walks along the verge, the gallery ahead. Dim security lights shine down around the building, illuminating the mural. It's all right, though. He knows how to avoid the lights now. He can't see cameras but assumes she must have them. She's paranoid about security, which is ironic since she's the one people should be afraid of.

He tries to keep his mind focused, to stop thinking about how beau-

tiful she is. She cast a spell on him. He knows it. The only way to free himself is to get rid of her. His new friend, the woman who calls him with information about the witch, says the same. The only way any of us will be safe is if we destroy her.

He knows that's right, but he can't help wanting her. It's a compulsion he fights every day. He dreams of having complete control over her, but that's the spell she's put on him. He's never killed anyone before. He knows he has to, but he needs to be sure. It must be a righteous kill.

He feels a tingle go through him at the thought of overpowering her. Before he gets too close to the building, he walks down the short slope toward the jagged rocks at the ocean's edge. His phone's flashlight is turned low. He walks along the rocks and approaches her deck.

When he gets as close as he dares, he plants the gardening pole in a patch of tall seagrass and pulls a small webcam out of his pocket. He uses duct tape to secure it and checks the feed on his phone. Adjusting the pole, he makes sure the camera is pointed at her back door and deck.

He's making his way over hazardous ground when a seal barks loudly behind him. Jumping, he drops his phone and then fumbles in the dark, trying to find it in the ice plant. The seal barks again. It feels closer. He isn't sure why the seal makes him nervous, but it does.

His hand finally lands on a smooth screen. He picks it up, jams it in his pocket, and then pulls it back out for the flashlight. When he does, he inadvertently knocks the compact listening device out of his pocket. Not noticing, he continues back to the road and then to his car.

Show me where he is, I think as forcefully as I can.

He's sitting in a small room. He has a plastic folding table against a wall that's decorated with hundreds of photos of me. His laptop is open, a recording program up. He's wearing professional-looking headphones and has a microphone plugged into his laptop. Right now, though, he's listening.

"Brandon, you promised," Calliope reminds him. "We talked about this. She's evil. You have to send her back to Hell."

He stares at his phone, listening intently, his fists clenched in his lap. "I will. I'm going to do it."

"She won't expect it from you. It's perfect. She won't see you as the threat you are. You have the gun, right? You're ready."

He nods, ignoring that niggling worry he can't seem to shake. "Yes. I'm ready."

"Tonight," she demands, and he feels the push, the drive to get it done.

"Yes. Tonight," he echoes, pulling the gun from the back of his waistband. He's been walking around the apartment with it, getting used to the feel of it, occasionally pulling it out to aim at his own reflection in the mirror. We'll see if that giant of hers is feeling tough with a gun in his face.

Fixated, he gazes at the gun, loving the weight of it in his hand, unaware of the chanting coming through his headphones.

Where? I ask again.

The vision pulls out and I see the Pacific Place Apartments sign.

A large hand dropped onto my shoulder and my eyes flew open. Dad's brilliant blue eyes put me at ease. His long hair tangled with mine in the buffeting waves. Sitting on the ocean floor, I looked up and saw the surface thirty feet above.

Emrys was worried about you. He said you didn't respond to his nudges. His voice was in my head, but I wasn't sure how to talk back.

I thought, *I was in a vision.*

He nodded, so I supposed it worked. *Who was the man with the gun? I caught part of what you were seeing.*

The stalker I told you about. Calliope has been influencing him, pushing him to shoot me.

The water around us churned into a whirlpool. *No one hurts my daughter!* His voice was a roar in my head.

I reached for his hand. Was this what it was to have a father watch over you?

Emrys also told me you've been upset. That's to be expected. Your mother was emotional too. Don't make big decisions right now.

Confused, I tried to make sense of that but couldn't. *I think Cal has figured out how to mess with my head. She and her demon couldn't get in before. Now my brain is scattered all the time, and I keep crying, which is totally not like me. I was hoping if I was in the ocean, they wouldn't be able to touch me.*

Dad closed his eyes, still holding my hand. When he opened them, I felt his anger. *I hear the whispers. They're faint, but I hear them in you. It's because of the wolf.*

Declan? He wouldn't hurt me. He told me he loves me, wants me to live with him. How could he think Declan was helping Cal?

Of course he loves you and wants you close. He's not a complete idiot. I'd have preferred a fae mate for you, but at least he's not a wicche. Dad shook his head. *I wasn't referring to that wolf.* He pointed at my abdomen. *She's getting in through that wolf. Part wolf, anyway.*

THIRTY-SEVEN

Everyone Is a Little Distracted

I'm pretty sure my heart stopped. *What!*

His brown furrowed. This is what comes of mating. I thought you knew. Your mate and great-uncle seem to know.

What? I thought back over the last couple of days: looks between the two of them, grabbing things from me, keeping me from climbing on things... How did they know if I didn't?

Dad patted my knee. *I don't know about the wicche, but a gestating woman's scent changes. It's quite subtle at first, but if he's paying atten-tion—and he seems to be—he'd notice.* Dad placed his hand on my lower abdomen and closed his eyes again. *She's a tiny ball of cells right now. I believe she's going to be a she, but it's far too early to know. Rest assured. She seems to be coming along on her journey quite nicely.*

Your immediate concern is not her, he continued. *It's this gunman and the sorcerer. What are you doing about those threats?*

I tried my best to put babies and motherhood and terror out of my mind to concentrate on the immediate danger. *We're having a planning session tonight. I'm hoping we'll go out afterward to hunt for her.*

He nodded slowly, thinking. *I need you to do something for me.*

I waited.

I'm going to teach you how to project an image of yourself. When you go to confront that sorcerer and her demon, I want you in the ocean where I can see to your protection.

But I'll need to use my magic to overpower her.

Whereas I need you not to die. He put his hands on either side of my head. There was a flash of white in my head and then he was pulling his hands away. *I would have rather you built up the ability to do that on your own, but time is an issue. I won't lose my daughter and granddaughter tonight. The queen will need to understand.*

The strange, scattered feeling I'd been struggling with was gone. My thoughts felt laser focused.

Form a picture of yourself in your head. Down to the smallest detail, it is a mirror image of you.

I did.

Now, picture yourself standing on your deck. You know it like the back of your hand. Picture yourself there. Do you see it?

Closing my eyes, I pictured myself in these clothes, standing on my deck. I nodded.

What do you see?

The tentacles and railing, the beautiful weathered gray wood.

No, he said, his hand covering my closed eyes. *Don't imagine what you might see. Open your eyes up on the deck and tell me what you see.*

What do you mean? I can't. I'm down here. An image of myself can't see.

Magic, daughter. You are made of magic. Do you think I'm sitting here with you right now? No. My physical form is in the ocean north of Ireland, but you can feel my hand over your eyes. You can hear my words in your mind. You felt my magic clear your thoughts, pushing out those demonic voices. Remember, we impose our will over the natural world and our will is magical. Now, on the deck, open your eyes and tell me what you see.

I saw the people I expected standing around, but I knew I wasn't really seeing them. I was imagining what I'd see if I could. I reached up and pulled down his hand to look at him. *I don't know how.*

Of course you do. I just explained it. Project part of yourself above the water onto your deck.

As that instruction felt lacking, I thought about it. Now that my head was clear, it didn't seem so impossible. I'd done something similar before. I'd connected with Declan so I could watch the Alpha challenge and help him not die when Logan cheated.

I felt a twinge of guilt, as I still hadn't told Declan I'd helped after promising I wouldn't. *Shit.* I had to tell him now, didn't I? Never mind. Not thinking about that. Just thinking about projecting part of my consciousness forty feet away.

Hands clasped together, I pushed my magic up and out of the water. I felt myself bobbing on the surface and heard a voice saying, "How is this not freaking you out? She could be drowning."

"Arwyn's fine," I heard Declan say. "She doesn't drown."

Wilbur swan up beside me and tried to nudge my shoulder, but his snout went through me. Right. Okay. I'm here, treading water in the ocean. I can see and hear. My body is real and solid. Seals shouldn't be able to pass through it.

When Wilbur tried again, his snout booped me instead. Okay, magic. Could I cast a spell in this state? Holding my hand under water, I directed a funnel of seawater to shoot straight up. It did. I'd thought if it worked at all, it might go a few inches. Instead, it shot ten feet in the air.

Declan, no doubt noticing the jet of water, leaned over the rail. He saw me and grinned. "Look who's back. We were getting nervous."

"You weren't," I said.

His head tilted to the side. "What did you say?"

It was like those horrible nightmares where you can't scream. I cleared my throat, thought about vocal cords and breath and then said again, "You weren't worried about me."

"I'm always worried," he said, "but I've seen you do this trick before."

I laughed. "You haven't seen *this* trick before."

His brow furrowed. "Are you okay?"

I considered the latest revelations and the fact that he knew before I did. Is that why he invited me to live with him? My heart sank.

He turned around said something to someone and then next thing I knew, he was diving off the deck. When he surfaced and tried to pull me into his arms, I panicked, lost concentration, and was back in my body on the ocean floor.

I heard my name shouted.

You should go, Dad said. *He's afraid something's happened to you. Use your earrings tonight. Let me know what's going on. And practice so you don't drop your shadow when you're distracted or frightened.*

I will. Thanks, Dad. I kicked off and swam up, surfacing beside Declan.

Eyes wild, he grabbed onto me. "You disappeared."

"I did. I'll explain later." Wrapping my arms around his neck, I whispered in his ear. "Why didn't you tell me?"

"Tell you what?" he whispered back, working harder to stay afloat than I had to.

"Dad said I was pregnant and that you knew." Was this the most important thing to be discussing right now? Actually, yes. It was. I'd deal with the sorcerer and the stalker and whatever else got thrown at me. A baby, though, was life-altering and forever.

Could I do this on my own? Yes. I wasn't struggling. I wasn't a teen being preyed upon by a family member or an older neighbor. I was a successful adult who owned my own business. I made good money and worked from home. Did I want Declan in his child's life? Also yes, but I didn't want it to come from a place of guilt and sacrifice.

He pulled back to look in my eyes, his large hand cradling my midsection. "Are you sure?"

I saw wonder and joy in his expression, and a tight, scared knot in my chest began to ease. "Dad says so, but I'll do a test. He says she's just a little ball of cells right now, but he believes she'll be a girl."

His gaze went glassy with sudden tears. "One of those guest rooms will need to be a nursery." He hugged me tight. "And I need to start designing a crib."

"Dad said you and Bracken knew."

He leaned back to look at me again and shook his head. "No. I wondered but was afraid to get too happy about it. You weren't acting like yourself. Your scent has changed, subtly so, but that could have been new hair stuff or soap. When you said you thought Cal had found a way in to mess with you, my heart cracked a little.

"We've never discussed children," he continued. "I had no idea if you even wanted them, given everything you've gone through in life. What if we have another little seer?"

I laughed, suddenly ready to burst. "Well, at least she'll have a mom who knows what's happening and how to navigate. I can teach her all the things I had to figure out on my own."

He kissed me and I gave into the moment of joy. We'd be plotting and planning soon enough. We needed this now.

Wilbur nudged me again. I broke from Declan on a laugh. "Okay. We're going." He booped my stomach and I petted his head. I had a feeling the ocean would be quite protective of me for the next nine months. Wait.

"How long are wolves pregnant?"

Declan's brow creased. "Natural wolves are pregnant for roughly two and a half months. Why?"

"Hmm, wicches are the typical human nine. I have no idea what the fae term is. I need to ask my mom if her pregnancy with me was normal." Wilbur bumped me again. "Okay. Okay. Later. Sorcerer and stalker now."

We swam to the rope. Declan took my arms, moved me to his back, and linked my arms around his neck. "Hold on." He climbed it quickly and we were back on the deck.

Jake and Tyler, who had probably heard our whole conversation, even with the whispering and the sound of the waves, were on either end of the deck, looking out toward the road. Bracken sat beside Hernández.

"There," he said. "She's right as rain. No need to worry. Little Arwyn has always been safe in or near the ocean."

Hernández's naturally tanned skin was looking a little green. "I was watching the water and I kept unconsciously holding my breath, waiting for you to surface." She shook her head. "I didn't realize I had a drowning phobia."

"I'm sorry but I really am fine," I assured her, sitting on her other side. "I don't think I *can* drown. My father even took away the headache I used to get when I went long periods without breathing." I looked past her at Bracken, who seemed fascinated by this new information. "Dad said he didn't know I was having that problem, that the headaches were because of my wicche blood."

Bracken nodded. "Perfectly understandable that he'd resent and blame us. We kept him from his child and children are hard to come by among the fae."

I gave him a suspicious look at that. Dad had said that Bracken knew too. My great-uncle just smiled serenely and leaned back against the bench.

I held out my hand. "Okay. What have you got for me?"

Declan told Hernández and Bracken to move to another bench, that they were too close and might interfere in my reading. He was such a good assistant.

"It's a paper coffee cup," Hernández said. "It was used this morning."

I nodded and she dropped it into my hand.

THIRTY-EIGHT

That's One Question Answered

"Come on! I'm already late for work." The young Asian woman with the patio filled with potted plants is behind the wheel of her Jeep. She's wearing the same white polo and black shorts, this time with reflective aviator sunglasses.

"License and registration," he says, voice bored.

"I was like two miles an hour over the speed limit. Can't you just give me a warning?" She pastes a smile on her face, trying to charm him. "I promise to slow down. Okay? Under the speed limit the whole way."

"License and registration," he says again.

She gives a strangled cry. "I can't afford a ticket. I was literally two miles an hour over the limit. Why are you doing this?"

"License and registration, And I clocked you at five miles an hour over, with your music blasting and your hand on your phone."

She stops rummaging around in her backpack and sits back in her seat. "Uh, no you didn't. My radio doesn't even work, and my phone is in my bag." She pulls it out of the front pocket of her backpack." She points at his chest. "Do you have your bodycam on? I can prove it."

"License and registration. Don't make me say it again and take those glasses off so I can see your eyes."

"Why?" she asks, outraged.

"Because you might be under the influence, and I told you to." The *last few words were snarled as his right hand moved to rest on his gun. "You seem to be confused as to who's in charge right now. License. Registration. Sunglasses. Now."*

She pulls her wallet out of her bag, opens it, and slides her license out of its slot. "What's your name?" she asks

"I'm the one with the badge and the gun who doesn't give a shit how cute you think you are." He gestures for her to hand over her license.

She does, fear now pinching her features. "You can't talk to people like that."

"I just did. Registration."

She leans over to get it from her glove compartment, clearly uncomfortable turning her back on him. As a waitress, she's learned who the dangerous ones are. She hands it to him.

He stares at her license. "Do you still live at this address?"

A chill runs down her spine at the dead look in his eyes. She doesn't want him to know where she lives but she nods.

"Glasses," he reminds her, enjoying the fact that he's broken her. He'd love to backhand her right across that smart mouth of hers. For now, though…She hands him her sunglasses and he drops them to the pavement, stepping on them, cracking the glass and bending the frame. "I'll be back. Keep your hands on the wheel while I'm gone."

He goes to his vehicle, types in her information, and checks her record. She has a few speeding violations. The last was two years ago. He takes out his phone and takes a picture of her license. It's convenient, having the headshot with the address all in one pic. He considers again how much he'd enjoy shutting up her smart mouth for good. He'll think about it.

A text pops up on his phone from Joel. With a growl of annoyance, he taps the message. Joel is short on rent and needs five hundred dollars. The cop swipes and deletes. That's a problem he's going to need to deal with soon.

He goes back to her Jeep, hands her the license and registration cards, and then tells her to slow down before he walks to his cruiser and drives away.

Looks like the bitch is going to be late after all.

Blinking my eyes open, I met Hernández's gaze. "You already know who he is."

She let out a gust of breath. "A cop. *Shit.*" She shook her head. "After I left this morning, I just sat in my car thinking. He knows how to get in and out without leaving evidence, almost like he knows how we investigate. You said he uses a penlight, just like cops. You were really uncomfortable at Gaby's crime scene. Arthur said the cops were bothering you.

"I went back to check the record, to see who was there. One of the patrolmen is the one you already told me to watch my back around. I found a history of authority issues, especially with female superiors or supervisors of color. He was suspended for two weeks. When he came back, I felt more uncomfortable around him. It was like he was seething in silence whenever he saw me."

She rubbed her forehead. "Whatever. I'm a cop. I'm used to men on the force having issues with me. I'm a lesbian Latina. That's three things right there to hate about me. I'm used to ignoring that shit.

"I thought about what you said though. That it wasn't sexual with him. It was all about power, about permanently shutting up the people, especially women, who question his authority. I looked up his record. He was in the Marines for a short time. I knew he'd had an issue with a judge at some point. I contacted a court reporter I used to date and asked. She said that he'd screwed up the evidence chain of custody for drugs found in a dealer's car. The case ended up having to be thrown out. The judge he killed was the one who presided over the trial. The defense lawyer—a white man—ripped the cop a new one and the judge—a Black woman—let it go on. My friend said he was fuming as he stalked out of court and guess which one he went after.

"I did a deep dive on complaints against him and found our latest victim had submitted one, saying he was rude and threatening, destroying her property and making her worried about him having her address."

"Yeah," I said. "That's what I just watched." I relayed what I saw. "I couldn't see him, but I saw white hands and I saw him take a picture of her license. I'm sure hers isn't the only one he has. His photo app probably contains his hit list."

Hernández stared into space a moment. "The text was from someone named Joel?"

I nodded. "He wanted five hundred bucks, and it pissed off the cop."

"Joel was the name of our one male victim." She stood, closing the evidence bag. "I'll talk with my captain. Nothing you've told me is admissible. I need hard evidence, and he's left none at the crime scenes. I snagged that cup from his trash can this morning. I wanted your take on him. We should have enough to subpoena his phone." She put on her sunglasses. "Okay. Thank you for your time. I'll get out of your hair now."

She walked off the deck and around the corner. I wished I could've given her more, but I didn't have the smoking gun.

Declan sat down beside me. "You did everything you could. She's smart. She'll get what they need to arrest him."

"Hopefully before he kills someone else." I tipped my head onto his shoulder, suddenly exhausted.

His arm went around me. "We have about two hours before your aunt and her family arrive. Why don't you go in and take a nap? You haven't been sleeping well and we need you firing on all cylinders tonight."

I never napped, but it sounded so good, I stood and was suddenly dry. "Thanks," I said to Bracken before zombie walking into the studio and up the stairs to my bed. I flicked my fingers, blocking out the skylight, dropped onto my bed, and was out.

I woke to the sound of dishes clinking and hushed voices. The light had changed. I'd actually slept. Sitting up, I realized that one of the hushed voices I was hearing was my Aunt Elizabeth. I stumbled to the half wall and looked over. They were all here.

Declan looked up and grinned. "They just arrived."

"Sorry. I'm sorry. I'll be right down."

Elizabeth and Robert looked up, both smiling. She waved away my apologies. "Your young man has been taking care of us. We're fine. Honestly, I was so happy when he told us you were napping."

Robert rubbed his wife's back. "The way she worries about you working with fire while being perpetually sleep-deprived." He shook his head, laughing. "You sleeping has made her day."

"It has," she confirmed. "Now take your time. We're fine. We haven't been able to spend quality time with Declan before. Robert and I are enjoying grilling him."

They went back to talking amongst themselves and I went into the bathroom. Holy crap! I'd forgotten that I'd been in the ocean earlier and then just fell asleep salty. I jumped in the shower for a super-fast scrubbing.

There was no time for my usual hair routine, so I conditioned, blew dry just long enough for it to stop dripping, and used one of my black terry cloth headbands to keep it off my face. I put on black jeans, a long-sleeved black sweater, matching gloves, and black slip-on sneakers.

When I started down the stairs, Declan glanced over and raised his eyebrows. "You look like an adorable cat burglar."

"That's the point," I said. "We have sneaky things to do."

He gave me a hug and a kiss when I hit the bottom step. "I'm glad you got some sleep," he murmured. "Bracken and I have it all under control."

Elizabeth and Robert were sitting on the couch, Bracken in my chair. Frank and Faith sat at the end of the worktable eating chips and salsa—which I didn't realize I had. I had a severe lack of seating options. It had always been fine because I was the only one here, with the occasional visit from Mom or Aunt Sylvia.

My mind flashed on the new flat Declan had created and my heart warmed. Soon, we'd be able to have a proper dinner party. Wait. I only had a set of six plates and bowls because that was how many had come in the box. There were seven here tonight.

Scanning the table, I saw seven matching plates and utensils. I pulled Declan to my side. "Where did the seventh set of dinnerware come from?"

"Bracken. He brought over one of his and then spelled it to look like yours."

I grinned. "Tricky." I smelled something spicy and delicious, but it wasn't lasagna. "What are we having?"

"I called Mariana's and put in a huge order. Bracken went to pick it up. I put out chips and salsa." He pointed to the worktable. "Your aunt brought bacon-wrapped jalapenos. Sorry. Those are all gone. There was also chicken quesadilla over there." He gestured to where Elizabeth and Robert sat, the plate empty. "I saved some of that one for you." He pulled a plate from the microwave with a triangle of cheesy goodness on it. "I have the pans in the oven keeping warm. I figured we could do dinner buffet style. Put all the aluminum pans across the stove and counter, use some serving spoons, and let people take what they want."

I pulled a thin rubber glove from my kitchen drawer, heated the quesadilla slice in my hand and took a bite. Delicious. "I should sleep more often. You two have it all figured out, and this is so much nicer than the frozen lasagna I had planned."

Grinning, he gave me a kiss. "Good."

"You sure are smiling a lot tonight," I observed, taking another bite.

"Huh," he mumbled. "I wonder why?" His arm slid around me as he looked over the group. "Is everyone ready to eat?"

"Yes," Frank and Faith said in unison.

"Sorry I made you wait," I said again.

"Don't be silly," Elizabeth said, walking over to give me a hug. She knew just how to do it without touching my skin.

Uncle Robert rubbed my shoulder in lieu of a hug, trying to make it safe for me, which I appreciated. "They've only had a few shifts, but the kids are really enjoying working here."

"Thank goodness." I lowered my voice. "If that ever changes, let me know."

He nodded, patted my shoulder again, and moved to stand beside his wife.

Declan took out all the trays and lined them up, peeling off the covers. "Can everyone grab a plate and then come up and take whatever looks good. We have Mexican rice and black beans, some chicken flautas. In this pan we have chicken, beef, and cheese enchiladas. I think the beef is in red sauce and the chicken is in green. Honestly, I'm not sure about the cheese. Here we have a few chimichangas. Those three are beef. These three are chorizo."

He pointed to the last tray and said, "And then we have tacos. These are beef. These are chicken. Carnitas. Chorizo. Shrimp." When he turned, he appeared confused by our stunned faces.

"That's a lot of food," Elizabeth said and then gave him the sweetest smile. "You're so kind providing a feast for us."

"Wolves need a lot of fuel," I said, "and he loves leftovers."

He laughed at that. "I really do. And we have churros and flan for dessert."

I waved everyone forward. "Let's fill up our plates, share some secrets, and come up with a plan to deal with our sorcerer problem."

THIRTY-NINE

Cartography & Churros

My stomach was close to exploding, but I still ate one more forkful of flan. So. Good. I slid my plate over to Declan, who finished the wedge of carmely, custardy goodness in one bite. He was so good at not looking like he was eating as much as he was, probably due to his excellent table manners. The kids were excited about the churros and had had a couple each. Everyone was chatting happily, even Bracken.

I wasn't sure if this evening would prove to be too much for him, but he was hanging in there and seemed content to talk with Robert about his work as a healer for human children. When Bracken's notebook had come out, I was pretty sure we were going to be okay.

"I hate to be a killjoy, but we should probably talk about our sorcerer problem," I said.

Elizabeth nodded, patting my covered arm. "You're right. I think we were all enjoying the company and wishing we could forget about her."

"Unfortunately," Robert said, "avoiding problems doesn't solve them. We need to deal with Calliope, but we also need to stop more from popping up. This family is plagued by sorcerers and black magic practitioners."

"Yes," Bracken said, nodding. "We think we know why." He glanced at me, seemingly checking to see if he could elaborate.

"We're all on the same side," I told him, "and we're showing all our cards. No more secrets. This family has way too many of them."

He looked down a moment and tapped his notebook. "This is so." Taking in the whole table, he began, "We believe there's a demonic grimoire that's passed down from one sorcerer to the next."

"I had a dream," I elaborated. "It was about Abigail singling out Cal for special private lessons when she was a child. She whispered to Cal that her friend had told Abigail to keep her eyes on Cal, that she would be a good candidate for special lessons."

Elizabeth hung her head. "I never saw it. Abby wasn't my favorite sister, but I never saw the evil." With tears glistening in her eyes, she turned to me. "Like your mother was with Sylvia, that's what it was like for Bridget and me. We were inseparable growing up." She shook her head. "Sybil told me Abby hunted Bridget and her little girl relentlessly, finally slaughtering Bridget in some run-down apartment where she and her daughter had been hiding. And now not only did she torture her own sister, she also offered up her niece to a demon."

"Mom and Gran didn't see it either," I assured her. "I've seen visions of the grimoire she's using, but I can't read the writing. Just looking at it in a vision makes my head pound. I asked a half-demon I know about it. He says it sounds like demonic script and that he has heard of an ancient grimoire that's been used in an old wicche family for centuries. Given the disproportionate number of black wicches and sorcerers in this family, it stands to reason the story's about us."

Faith gasped and we all looked in her direction. She pointed at the back door. "A man just walked by."

Declan rose and went to the door. He looked in both directions and then said something we couldn't hear. A moment later, Jake and Tyler stood in the doorway.

"This is Jake and this is Tyler," Declan said, gesturing to each man in turn. "They're wolves like me and they're here to guard Arwyn. There are too many threats directed her way right now. If you ever see something in the gallery that looks scary or just odd, please tell Jake, Tyler, or Carter. They'll sort it out."

"And not just about me," I clarified. "If there's someone bothering either of you, tell them. You shouldn't have to deal with any of that either. Okay?"

Frank nodded, his expression serious. Faith looked relieved and glanced at her brother. I'd have to remind Carter to keep an ear open for what people were saying to the two of them.

Jake and Tyler went back out to patrol. I still had a stalker with a gun who was planning to kill me tonight.

When Declan sat back down, I remembered and grabbed his arm, lightheaded at the thought. "Tell me you didn't still have the maps on you when you dove in the ocean."

He shook his head, gesturing to Bracken. "Your great-uncle is holding them for us."

I blew out a breath. "Thank the Goddess. Bracken, can you show everyone?"

He took his leather journal from the inside pocket of his tweed sports coat. Opening it, he pulled out all three maps, placing them side by side. "This one is a very old hand-drawn map I found decades ago tucked into a book I discovered at an estate sale. The subject matter was the history of this region. As you can see, this one appears to be drawn by someone with a limited understanding of the shape of the bay.

"It's hard to read," he continued, "but the word *shades* is written right here. There's no legend. It could mean anything—"

"Isn't *shades* sometimes used as a euphemism for Hell?" Frank asked. "Or for the souls of the damned in Hell?"

Bracken nodded approvingly, as at a favorite student. "Very good. That's exactly right. We know we've had local sorcerers in our family. We know they need privacy to do what they do. Neighbors would call the police if they consistently heard chanting coming from a suburban home. Not to mention the stench of sulfur."

Bracken shook his head. "No. They need a secret place and once established, it again stands to reason that it would be passed down, like the grimoire itself."

"Could it be in another city?" Faith asked, moving her plate out of the way. "No one has seen Cal in a while. How do we know she's still here?"

Bracken held up a finger, in full professorial mode. "Good question and one we have considered. Calliope has been doing sorcery for years. She was living with her parents while she was practicing her demonic magic. Her workshop can't have been too far because when one of her parents called, looking for her, she was able to make an excuse and return quickly."

He looked at me and I took over, standing up to collect dirty dishes. Declan rose with me and helped. "I checked with Uncle John. I asked him, on average, how long would it take Cal to show up when he called. He told me it sometimes took an hour, but she always had reasonable excuses. For the most part, though, she returned from her errands or the library or visiting a friend—even though she'd never seemed to have friends—within about twenty to thirty minutes.

"I also had a vision of the house. I know it's on the ocean's edge. I saw what looked to be a large home with empty rooms above ground. When I've seen her building spells, working with the grimoire, it looks like she's in a torch-lit basement. I once saw her open a glass patio door, though. Waves hit the rocks and sprayed up just beyond where she stood."

Elizabeth tried to stand to help, but I patted her shoulder. "We're good and you're our guests," I told her. "As Bracken said, the map is far too inaccurate for us to find her, but it did give us a general area. We've driven the 17-Mile Drive multiple times, but neither Bracken nor I felt anything off. So, we asked two other people to help us search for spots along the water's edge that feel dark."

"And that's where it gets interesting," Bracken said, pointing at the two other maps. "Arwyn knows a woman who is an owl shifter."

Frank and Faith shared a look, surprised and delighted.

"We asked if she could scout the shoreline for anything that made her feel wrong or uncomfortable. Orla found seven places. Some could be black magic practitioner or other forms of supernaturals."

Declan and I were back in our seats, the dishes piled in the sink for now.

"These two spots"—he pointed at Orla's map—"she couldn't see, but that was true of these other four. When she tried to fly over these two, though, she felt a push to go away. Both locations made her feel sick. We think they've been spelled so they're not only invisible but repel people."

"That certainly sounds like a sorcerer's lair," Robert said, staring at the maps. "You said two spots. Are there two sorcerers?"

"We hope not," I said. "Just because it's been warded to keep people away doesn't mean it's a sorcerer. It could be a mild-mannered supernatural who used a black wicche to create his wards because he doesn't want visitors, which is fair."

"And what about this map?" Robert asked.

Bracken looked at me.

"Okay, you all know my father is water fae, right?"

Frank and Faith nodded. Elizabeth and Robert shared a look. "We didn't *know*," my aunt said. "I guessed, given your enhanced magic, your affinity for water, the way your hair changes color in it, and..." She glanced down at my leg, where the ribbon of scales was, but didn't say it.

"Okay, hmm, well, in the spirit of no secrets," I said, "I'll give you the condensed version. When Mom was young, the Goddess sent her a prophetic dream. In it, she gave birth to a Cassandra wicche, but her daughter was sad and sickly, terrorized by the visions she saw, ultimately walking into the ocean as a child to end the pain."

Elizabeth gasped at the thought. "She never said."

"Mom spoke with Great-Gran, who told her it was a blessing and that she had to find a man powerful enough to father a Cassandra who could survive."

Elizabeth's hand covered her mouth. "I've never heard any of this," she whispered. "Poor Sybil."

"We're all about secrets around here," I said. "Mom met my dad and they fell in love."

Elizabeth sat up straight. "She loved him? She's never spoken about him. I'd always thought he'd hurt her."

I nodded. "That's what I thought too. All my life she's derailed any conversation about him. I finally forced the discussion, asking if he'd been cruel and hurt her, if that was why she never spoke about him. Nope. She loved him completely and the Council—Gran and Great-Gran—forced her to leave him, to send him away, because they didn't want any more little half-faelings running around, mucking up the pure Corey line."

Frank stood in outrage and went to the window. Robert held out his hand and Elizabeth took it and squeezed.

"The elders were hard and cold," Elizabeth said. "Great-Gran had an issue with my marriage as well."

I looked between the two of them. "But Uncle Robert is from an old and well-respected wicche family," I protested.

Robert held up the back of his free hand, showing me his dark skin. "I wanted Elizabeth to come East and live near my family, but she couldn't leave. She was waiting, praying, for Bridget and Samantha to come home. This family, though, is why I treat human children. The Coreys spurned my help."

He shrugged a shoulder. "They have John, who is a good man and a skilled healer. I work in pediatric neurology. The children and their parents are desperate for my help, so no one much cares about my skin color."

My throat tightened. "I'm so sorry."

He waved away my apology. "It wasn't you, or your mother, for that matter. Your great-grandmother and her siblings were…"

"Cruel," Bracken finished, his gaze far away.

Robert nodded. "That they were."

"So, Sybil had to deal with all the whispers, the looks, the judgment because your Great-Gran didn't want any more fae blood than was absolutely necessary to produce a Cassandra wicche who could survive her gifts?" Elizabeth looked ready to fight.

Declan's hands were fisted on the table. Reaching over, I laid a hand over his fist. It immediately loosened as he opened his hand to hold mine.

"I guess they're just going to have to get used to their precious blood being polluted," Declan said.

Robert glanced over and nodded at us. "They will indeed. No one can make Arwyn do anything she doesn't want to, and they know it."

On an eye roll, I said, "Oh, they try."

FORTY

I'm Telling Dad!

"Try and fail," Robert contended. "They wanted you on the Council as a child. You held out until you were twenty-eight and established in the art world. I thought for sure that bribing you with this gallery would get you on board, but still you resisted."

"Wait a minute." I looked between Robert and Elizabeth. "Do people think I was *given* this cannery?"

They shared a look and then nodded.

I stood, suddenly pissed off. "Serena said something similar once. Who the hell told people that?" I paced between the work-table and the kitchen. "No wonder the rest of the family hates my guts."

When I passed Declan's chair, he snaked an arm out, pulling me to his side.

"This is why all the cousins thought those earrings I was given at graduation were from John and Sylvia. They really do think I'm a spoiled brat who gets whatever I want."

"The earrings you're wearing?" Elizabeth asked.

I nodded, still fuming.

"I was told they were left to you from your Great-Gran," Elizabeth explained. "That they had been made to celebrate a Corey Cassandra."

Faith began to raise her hand and then stopped, no doubt remembering she wasn't in class. "That's not what we heard. We were told that Aunt Sylvia and Uncle John used the money they'd saved for Cal's college tuition to buy them for you, that you'd seen them in a jewelry store and begged Sylvia to get them for you." She shrugged. "They said that you were powerful but unpredictable, so everyone had to keep you happy."

My anger was turning to grief. I didn't want to cry—stupid hormones. I needed to keep myself pissed off. "Just so everyone here is clear, these earrings were a graduation gift from my father—not that anyone told me that. I just found out a few weeks ago that he's wanted to see me my whole life. And *I* paid for this building and all the renovations. Gran bought the property when I was a child—"

"I'm not sure she did," Bracken interrupted. "You told me that story weeks ago and I looked into it, because it didn't sound like something Mary would do. I checked the history of this building. After it was closed in 1971, it languished for decades and then was finally sold to an entity called Mac Lir Properties when you were five."

I went stiff.

Bracken watched me a moment. "I'm not positive, but I believe your father could be Manannán Mac Lir, fae Irish sea god. Didn't you tell me you were about that age when you found the cannery and that pedophile followed you here?"

Elizabeth and Robert went on high alert and Faith looked down.

I nodded. "And Dad told me his name was Mac."

"The name on the deed changed to Arwyn Cassandra Corey when you were about ten. My guess is he noticed you breaking in, exploring, hanging up your art, and he wanted it to be yours."

Declan shook his head in disbelief, looking up at me. "How much did she charge you for this place?"

I felt dead inside. It was one thing to use me and my gifts for the betterment of the family, but now she was stealing from me. "Three million," I whispered.

Elizabeth's eyes went wide. "Mother charged you three million for a gift from your father?"

My eyes filled, but I angrily dashed the tears away as Declan pulled me onto his lap. "Gran said it was easily worth five million, but she'd take the loss and sell it to me for three because she knew I loved it."

"Where did you get that kind of money?" Faith asked, her voiced hushed.

Shaking my head, I gestured around us. "My art. I've been selling my pieces since I was a teenager. Mary Beth, my agent, was in Carmel for another artist's showing. She walked by a tiny gallery on the way and saw one of my paintings in the window. She came to see me and signed me that same day. I was thirteen. She's been selling my work ever since. I do readings too, but I use that money to cover daily expenses. The proceeds from my art sales go into a special account. All I've wanted since I was little is to have my own gallery."

I leaned on Declan when he wrapped his arms around me. "Why?" I whispered.

"Sometimes," Bracken began, his voice somber, "people are alienated from friends and family as a means of control. If they're the only ones showing you love and affection, you'll do anything for their approval. It's like a beaten stray who's finally adopted. That dog will be more loyal, more vicious against threats, than one who has enjoyed love and safety all its life."

"Not my mother," I protested, sitting up straight. "She wouldn't do that to me."

He nodded, not looking entirely convinced. "You're probably right. You two wouldn't have been at odds with one another for so long if she was in on it."

"You should sue for that three million," Frank said from the window. "Destroy her." The rage in his voice made us all turn to him, but he kept his back to us.

Feeling hollowed out, I wanted to crawl back into bed and pull the covers over my head. I didn't want to do this tonight. I didn't want to—wait. Standing abruptly, I looked around the room and then at the maps.

"Oh, no you don't, Calliope. You're not derailing our plans." Suddenly concerned, I watched my cousin a moment and then said, "Frank, why don't you come back and help us plan."

He didn't move.

"Declan," I said softly, moving across the studio toward Frank. "I need my octopus bottle."

He was up and bringing it to me a moment later. I took off my gloves and he poured some ocean water into my palms.

"Hold him for me," I whispered.

Frank spun, enraged, but Declan was too fast. He had his arms around him, pinning Frank against his chest. Robert was up and started to say something, but Bracken hushed everyone.

"Frank, you've been standing over here, looking out the window for a while now. I won't hurt you. I promise. I just need to make sure Cal hasn't made her way past my wards through you."

I laid my damp hands on either side of his face and heard the chanting almost immediately. Gathering my magic, I let it flow through my veins and collect in my hands. I needed to impose my will. Cal had no counter to fae magic. I let the tidal wave build in me. When it was cresting, ready to slam down, I let it pour out of me, washing through Frank, telling it to cleanse Cal and her demon from his mind.

Seawater splashed at my feet. When I opened my eyes, I saw a terrified and drenched Frank staring back at me.

"Wh—what happened?" he asked, his voice shaking.

Robert and Elizabeth ran over, pulling Frank into their arms. They held him close, getting wet themselves.

"Is he okay now?" Elizabeth asked, panicked.

"Yes," I said. "They're getting tricky. I put a fae ward on the building, knowing she couldn't break it, but I exempted everyone here tonight. I didn't want any of you zapped by the ward. Frank was looking out the window and Calliope seems to have figured out a way to sneak past the ward through him."

There was a knock at the back door and then Jake opened it. He nodded to everyone and then his gaze found me. "There were two men in a pickup truck. We clocked them when they drove by slowly. One of them hopped out of the truck with a Molotov cocktail he lit and threw. I tackled him, but he'd already let it go."

He shook his head in disbelief. "It hit the side of the gallery, splashing fire, and then water flooded off the roof, putting it out. There isn't even a scorch mark where it hit."

Declan moved to the door, but Jake held up his hand. "We got it. Tyler got the one driving. Both are on the ground, trussed up with bungie cords we found in their truck bed." He looked back at me. "I called the detective that was here earlier to say we had a couple of arsonists for her."

"Thank you—both of you—very much," I said.

He waved off my thanks. "Your ward did most of the work. I'm going to get back so Tyler's not on his own when the detective arrives." He went back out, closing the door behind him.

"She does love her distractions, doesn't she?" I glanced over at Bracken, who was writing in his journal. "Everything okay?" I asked him, moving back to the table and sitting beside him.

"Hmm? Oh, I don't think anything is okay right now." He wore the barest of smiles. "I think, though, that it *will* be." He finished his note and then turned back to me. "How did you know what was happening with Frank?"

"How do I know anything?" I asked. "I was feeling defeated. I just wanted to crawl into bed and pull the covers over my head, which isn't like me."

Declan chuckled. "You're more the shove-the-big-idiot-who-thinks-you're-a-conwoman-off-the-deck-and-into-the-ocean type."

The memory of our first meeting warmed me, helping me shake off my unease. "Good times. Anyway," I said to Bracken, "I wanted to get out of the responsibility of all this." I gestured to the maps. "I knew then that something was happening to me. Yes, I'm exhausted and have been emotional today, but I *need* Cal caught and that damn book destroyed. Then I noticed Frank had yet to move from the window and him telling me to destroy Gran was totally out of character."

"I said what?" His voice was still weak.

I shook my head as Robert's grip on his son tightened. "It wasn't you," I told Frank. "Cal hates Gran. She thinks she should have been made the Council's third years ago. She believes herself extraordinary and is angry that no one else, especially Gran, recognizes that."

I studied Elizabeth's family a moment. The fear was palpable. "It's okay," I told them. "You don't need to be a part of this. I can do it."

I stood and braced for what would come next. Declan opened his mouth to protest, but I shook my head. It wasn't right to ask people to do something they couldn't. Declan rubbed his forehead but held his tongue.

Elizabeth looked outraged. "You are *not* this family's sacrificial lamb! We weren't prepared. That's all. Now, we will be."

Robert nodded, a fire in his eyes. "She has no idea what we're capable of."

"Mom hasn't paid much attention to my family, which is fine by us," Elizabeth said, looking at Robert. "That means, though, that the rest of the family are unaware of our gifts."

"Fascinating," Bracken said, "and quite smart. What they know, they exploit."

Elizabeth nodded, unhappy with the truth of that statement. "As you know from Sylvia's wake, both Robert and I can speak directly into another's mind. It was a gift of Bridget's and mine. As far as I know, none of the other siblings can do it. Bridget and I used to carry on full conversations, each in our own classrooms, at school." She smiled, remembering.

"After Michael was killed and she took her baby and ran, the link was still there, but she was silent. Sometimes I'd feel her grief, her fear. I'd speak to her, but she never spoke back." She brushed away a sudden tear. "Maybe she worried Abby would think I'd been told about her sorcery and would come after me. I don't know," she said on a shrug. "I doubt Abigail would have noticed. I'm easy to overlook in the family."

"She's an introvert," Robert explained, "in a family that prides itself on back-stabbing and clawing one's way to the top."

Elizabeth smiled at that. "I'm quiet and not even a little competitive. When the others were vying for attention, I was in my room reading. I had Bridget, though, so being overlooked was okay. It meant I didn't have to deal with the fights and tensions. After Bridget disappeared," she said, her voice faltering, "I faded away with her. People would walk right past me and ask Mom if she'd seen me." She gave a bitter laugh. "And most of the time, Mom would say no."

Robert kissed his wife's forehead, murmuring something to her. She nodded, patting his chest.

"When Robert and I fell in love, I taught him my little trick." She tapped her forehead. "I had a kind, loving voice up here again." She gave her husband a kiss. "The point is, Cal will have no idea what gifts we have."

Faith smiled at that. "You saw that Frank can create illusions that look and feel real."

I nodded, remembering the tiny dragon that had walked across my palm.

"What I can do is a little different," she said. She closed her eyes, held up a hand, and rain began lashing the windows. Lightning flashed across the sky and thunder boomed.

Faith was an elemental!

FORTY-ONE

The Importance of Pants

"Holy crap!" I ran into the gallery so I had a wall of windows, forty feet high, to watch the show.

The storm suddenly ended.

Faith held a hand over her mouth. "Oh, no. I forgot! Jake and Tyler will be sopping wet."

Declan laughed. "That was incredible, and they'll survive. Once we tell them—assuming it's okay to tell them—they'll think it's as amazing as we do."

I gave Faith a suspicious look. "When we had that heat wave a couple of weeks ago, was that you in a bad mood?"

She giggled, delighted by our reaction. "No. That was climate change."

"She was kind enough to give us a cool breeze in the backyard, though," Elizabeth said, "so we could have a nice dinner."

I glanced over at Bracken, who was watching the rain droplets meander down the windows. "You don't have to look. It's done now." He had a hard time with my wall of windows because they weren't perfectly square. It was a very old building, after all.

He looked down, tapping his pockets, a sure sign he was agitated. I went to him and took his arm, leading him back into the studio.

He patted my gloved hand. "I'm fine. I just feel as though I've let people down. I disappeared when Elizabeth and Bridget were still adolescents. If I'd stayed, perhaps I could have been of service. At least been a gentle and attentive friend in the family." He shook his head. "It was wrong of me to abandon everyone."

He was speaking softly to me, but Elizabeth must have heard because she came up on his other side.

"Nonsense, Uncle Bracken. We saw how they treated you. It actually felt empowering when you walked away. I hadn't known that was possible. You showed me there was another way." She thought a moment. "Have you ever flown?"

He nodded. "Once. It was miserable."

"They tell you to secure your own oxygen mask before you attempt to help others. That's what you were doing. You had to find your own peace before you could offer it to others."

He smiled and nodded. "I'll try to think of it that way. Thank you."

My eyes went to the table and my stomach dropped. "The maps are gone!"

"No, no," Bracken said. "It's all right. Given Cal's interference tonight, I didn't want to leave them behind." He pulled his journal from his inside pocket again and took out the maps. "I'm afraid we got sidetracked. Perhaps we should get back to business."

I let out a sigh of relief and tried to settle my jangling nerves. Flicking my fingers, I put down the shutters. It felt like we needed all the protection we could get for this discussion.

"Now the third map is interesting," Bracken said, "but I'll let Arwyn explain."

He was allowing me to decide how much to share. "I'm going to give you guys the highlights because the whole story isn't necessary for our planning. My dad came to the gallery opening. Before he left, I told him about the Cal situation and asked if he had any scouts or guards or whatever who could search the shore for demonic darkness."

"Oh," Faith breathed. "Good idea."

"I didn't hear back right away. I know Dad's a big shot and busy, so I figured he just hadn't had time to get to it yet. Anyway, I was sitting on the deck, listening to that horrible podcast about burning me—"

"What?" Elizabeth interjected. "What podcast?"

Declan took over when I paused. "Arwyn has had issues with stalkers all her life."

Elizabeth looked appalled. "Why were we not told?"

Robert glanced at Bracken. "As your uncle said, if she received safety and comfort from someone else, it would weaken the connection to her moth—her gran."

"She was abducted by a pedophile," Declan continued, "when she was three? Four?"

Elizabeth gasped and Faith looked close to tears.

I waved my hand, trying to get us back on topic. "The point is I have another stalker right now. When he confronted me on my deck a few weeks ago, I'd had enough of his ignoring my demands to leave, enough of the creepy looks and innuendo, so I froze his lungs for a few seconds."

"You can do that?" Frank asked, impressed.

I shrugged. "Defensive magic was the first thing I was taught so I could defend myself."

"So you could defend *them*," Bracken murmured.

"After I released him and told him to run, he bounced off the chest of a very angry werewolf who picked him up off the deck with one hand." I shook my head. "He was terrified when he ran, but fear often turns to anger and, in his mind, it was no longer about him trespassing on my property and being a creep. Now the issue was me being an evil witch who needed to be burned at the stake."

"But how did he jump to wicche?" Faith asked.

I got up, went for the pan of churros, and brought them back to the table. I took a bite of one, needing the sugar, and said, "Calliope, of course. I had a vision of her talking on the phone to the stalker, getting him pumped up with evil witch talk. He has a gun and promised Cal to kill me tonight, so everyone needs to take special precautions and no one walks outside until I've checked that the coast is clear."

"What about Tyler and Jake?" Faith asked.

"No one is going to confuse two tall, muscular men with me. If anything, they'll find him before he sees me," I told her. "Remember, wolves have perfect eyesight, even in the dark, and they can smell the metal and gunpowder from…" I looked at Declan.

He tipped his head back and forth. "Depends on the conditions. On a calm night in the forest, maybe a mile. Here, with the high winds and the muddled town scents…definitely farther away than he would need to be to take a shot with a handgun."

Frank and Faith's eyes went wide.

"Your guards are distracted with arsonists right now," Bracken reminded us. "Ones who have already tried to set fire to the building. That gasoline smell would probably blunt the scent of a gun. Now would be the perfect time to attack you."

Recognizing the truth of that, I went to my computer and pulled up the camera feeds on my screen.

Declan stood, muscled tensed. "Did you see that?"

I was standing right in front of the screen, and I hadn't seen anything.

"Fourth camera," he said. "There was a flash of movement just on the edge of the frame."

"Otis?" I stared at the screens but couldn't see anything out of the ordinary, other than Jake and Tyler looming over two trussed-up men on the ground who were struggling and appeared to be cussing out my guards. They were near the front of the parking lot, the opposite side of the gallery from where we were.

"There," Declan said again, suddenly beside me. When I leaned forward to run it back, he put a hand on my arm to stop me. "We need to see where he is now, not a minute ago." He pointed to the camera feed showing the arsonists. "They're the distraction, taking the guards out of play, yelling over whatever noise the one sneaking over here is making."

A chill ran down my spine.

There was a shadow and then a man stepped onto the deck with something shiny in his hand. Declan started to move, but I caught his arm as a huge wave swamped the deck, slamming the man into the outside wall of the hot shop.

I heard a gasp behind me and realized that everyone was now circled around the screen, watching.

When the water washed out, my father was standing on the deck, bare-chested. He palmed the stalker's face and picked him up with one hand. Water flooded out of Dad's hand and seemingly down the man's throat. He held the convulsing man until he went limp and then threw the stalker over his shoulders onto the rocks. Another large wave crashed over the rocks and swept him out to sea.

Dad looked up at the camera and raised a hand in greeting, then pointed down and mouthed *Pants* before disappearing. Everyone stood stunned, but I started laughing and couldn't stop. The others were watching me like I was crazy. I finally stopped wheezing long enough to repeat, "Pants."

I made my way back to the table. "Well, that's one less thing we have to worry about tonight."

Frank pointed at the screen. "Is he dead?"

I nodded. "Most certainly. If he washes ashore, he'll have water in his lungs, and it'll be ruled a drowning. Chances are, though, Dad threw him back in the water so scavengers could feed."

Declan and Bracken accepted this and returned to their seats.

"I'll have Jake and Tyler find his car and ditch it somewhere far from here so his disappearance isn't connected to you," Declan said.

Elizabeth and her family were less used to crazy, deadly shit happening and therefore stood together, looking warily at the screens.

"Sorry. This is what it's like to be in the thick of it. I'd feel worse if he hadn't come here to kill me. Don't forget, I've already read him. I know exactly what he planned to do with me, so you'll excuse me if I don't mourn my torturer. And just so you don't think I'm a callous nutjob, I wasn't laughing about his death. I was laughing at my dad. The first time he rode a wave onto my deck, he was naked. I told him I'd be much more comfortable if he at least put on some pants. Tonight, he made sure I noticed that he was wearing pants." I couldn't stop grinning.

"Well," Elizabeth began, ushering her family back to the table, "if he was planning to hurt you, then it's good that your father took care of him. That's what parents do."

Once everyone was seated, I resumed story time and told them about my visit to the bottom of the sea.

Stalker forgotten, Elizabeth and her family hung on every word, rapt. When I got to merpeople, Faith gasped.

"Long story short, it was the fae queen in disguise. She eventually revealed herself to me and gave me that map," I said, pointing.

"As you can see"—Bracken took over the telling—"Both the queen's map and Orla's overlap on these two spots as Calliope's possible lair."

"Wait," Elizabeth whispered, leaning forward. "You met the fae queen?"

I nodded. "She is the most beautiful being I've ever seen in my life and exudes so much power I was feeling lightheaded in her presence.

"The point is," Bracken continued, "that the same two places were identified. We need a plan to investigate both."

"We have a boat," Robert said. "We could sail to both locations, see if we can find a way past the wards."

Faith sat up straight. "I could call up a storm. It might be warded to be invisible, but we'll notice if rain bounces off nothing."

"And I found a spell in that grimoire you borrowed," Bracken said, "that I think can get us past a ward."

I looked at everyone assembled. "Can we do this tonight? Maybe we just look for properties, but if we find it, are we ready to go in?"

"I'm afraid we have to be," Bracken responded somberly. "She's figured out how to use us against you. A man died tonight because she pushed and pushed him to kill you. Two more men are headed to jail for attempting to burn you and your gallery to the ground." He picked up the maps. "These are a gift. We need to act on them before it's too late."

FORTY-TWO

Double the Fun

Robert stood. "He's right. Am I terrified something will happen to my wife and children? Yes, but I feel it too. It's all falling together tonight for a reason."

Elizabeth stood as well. "We'll go to where our boat is docked and sail her back. The water is deep enough for us here, isn't it?" She pointed out the back window to the deck.

"It is," I said. "I can also calm the waters to make it easier."

Robert nodded and checked his watch. "Our slip is close. Prep work needs to be done. We can probably be back in thirty to forty-five minutes."

"We can text you when we're on our way," Frank said. The teens looked nervous but determined.

"I'll call Mom," I said. "We'll need both of them. The three are a power all our own. We'll put aside what we discussed earlier tonight. We need to work together to battle a demon. Questions can be asked tomorrow. All right?"

I waited until even the most reluctant—Declan and Bracken—nodded.

"Also," I said, unsure of how this would be received, "I made a promise to my dad that I'd be in the water when this all went down. It's where my power is its strongest."

They shared looks, appearing confused as to what that meant.

"Remember, the ocean is my father's domain. I can't drown. Okay?"

Declan gave me a sharp look, but the others nodded.

"You guys take off and I'll call Mom." I blew out a breath and tapped my phone. It rang a few times.

"Hello, darling," she answered.

"Hey, Mom. Can you go get Gran and bring her here? We have Cal's workshop narrowed down to two locations. Robert, Elizabeth, and the kids are getting their boat and we're going to go—"

"No, Arwyn," she interrupted. "Remember your vision was of Elizabeth and Faith flying out of the boat and into the ocean. She promised they'd stay out of the water."

"Mom, you and Gran said I had to find Cal. Well, that's what I've done. We're not arguing about this. We'll need the three to break through her wards. Will you get Gran and help or not?"

Declan, who could, of course, hear both sides of the discussion, pulled the phone from my hand. "You need to get ready and practice. I'll talk to her."

Nodding, I blew out a breath and handed him the phone before going out the back door and over the railing. I didn't have long to practice. Treading water, I closed my eyes and shoved out the hurt and betrayal. I thought of the ocean, the force of the waves, and pushed my magic onto the deck.

It took a few tries. Okay, more than a few but I had a lot on my mind. I opened my eyes, staring at the open door to my studio. Declan's voice was raised, so I went in.

"She's been working her ass off trying to make you two happy, taking on all the danger while you pass judgment, always finding her lacking in some way. She's a fucking miracle, but you two never fail to find fault."

He paused, listening, and then said, "No. I'm not. She just found out some hard truths tonight that broke her heart, but she's still getting ready to battle a demon." He paused again. "Guard dog? Yeah, hilarious. Just know Arwyn has a very protective wolf in her corner now. And unlike you, I'll always be on her side. So, are you going to come back her up or are you just going to let the rest of us risk our necks?"

He listened a moment and then threw the phone, but I flicked my fingers, catching it. Bracken was just moving his hand, no doubt to do the same, when they both turned to the open door.

"Arwyn?" He was staring right at me but didn't seem to see me.

I looked down and didn't see myself either. "Can you hear me?"

Both continued to stare through the doorway.

I thought of vocal cords again and cleared my throat. "What happened?"

He walked right through me onto the deck. "Ursula, where are you?"

I pushed harder and heard a sharp intake of breath. When I turned toward the sound, I found a wide-eyed Bracken.

"How did you do that?" he asked.

"Can you hear me?"

He nodded.

"Oh, good. I got that working," I said.

Declan stood in the doorway, looking astonished. Pointing behind him, he said, "You're in the water. How are you here?"

"I know, right. This was what my dad was teaching me earlier. He wants me in the water and sending this shadow out to deal with Calliope."

Bracken blinked. "But can you do magic in that state?"

I flicked my fingers and the lights went out. With a shrug, I turned them back on and said, "Looks like."

"Are you an apparition or physically here?" Bracken walked closer and put a hand on my cheek.

We approach a grand double door that looks weatherbeaten. Bracken has the demon blade in his hand. He thrusts it forward, popping a ward. The door clicks open and he reaches for the doorknob.

Terror floods my system and I try to stop him, but he's already touched the knob. Convulsing, smoke rises off him, along with the acrid scent of burned hair. He's blown back into the courtyard. Declan and I run to his crumpled body. His skin is charred, his expression grotesque. Dead.

On a huge intake of breath, I opened my eyes and stepped away from Bracken's hand. "You can't come with us."

"Don't be silly," he protested. "Of course I'm coming."

"No." Sudden tears flooded my eyes. "You can't. If you come, you'll die."

He stilled a moment and then said, "But if I don't, who will die in my stead?" He paused, patting his pockets absently. "I know not to touch your skin, yet I felt compelled to do it just then. I could have touched your sleeve to know if you were corporeal, but I touched your skin. Was I influenced to do that, so you'd see what you saw? What if my not going weakens our side and Declan dies instead? What if it's little Faith?"

He shook his head. "We have a plan and it's a good one. They're clearly nervous or they wouldn't be trying so hard to derail us." He pointed at Declan. "He never loses his temper and yet he's yelling and throwing phones. No. We're not changing the plan now. We have them spooked, which means we're on the right track."

My phone buzzed. Declan went to the couch to get it. "Can you open it in this state?"

"I guess we'll find out." I reached for it. "If it slides through my hand, try to catch it."

He nodded, looking more than a little unsure of this new development.

The face recognition software on my phone recognized me, so that was good. I checked my messages. "They're there and getting the boat ready. They'll text again when they set sail."

"Good. Fine." Declan took my phone back and put it on my worktable. He looked between the two of us. "He's right. I don't trust myself. I just yelled at your mother." His head went up. "Hernández arrived."

I pushed him toward the door. "Go. She knows you, and being near other wolves might help how you're feeling. We have some time."

He looked between Bracken and me, walked onto the deck, and leaned over the railing, no doubt making sure I was still there.

"The ocean is where I'm safest," I reminded him.

Nodding, he headed around the gallery to where Jake, Tyler, and Hernández were.

Bracken and I stood in silence.

"I don't want you to die." I wiped at my face. "We have an agreement. We're building you an apartment so you can stay here with me," I whispered.

"Yes," he said, his expression softening. "But things change. You're starting a family." When I stilled, he smiled gently. "You forget. I notice patterns and breaks in patterns. Don't get me wrong. I want to be here to meet the little one, who I know will be extraordinary, like her mama, but we all need to work together to stop Cal now if we want that happy future. You know that. If I'm feeling the pressure, you certainly must be."

My shoulders slumped. "I feel it."

"So, tell me what you saw so I know what to avoid."

I blew out a breath. "We're approaching the house—"

"We're going to find it," he said triumphantly.

Nodding, I said, "You use the demon blade to break a ward. It pops open the front door. You touch the handle, and it seems to burn you from the inside out. It was horrible."

"I'm sorry you had to see that." He pulled the sheathed blade from his tweed coat pocket. "I was sure I'd need this tonight." He slipped it back into his pocket. "We'll just have to make sure none of us touch any doorknobs tonight."

"I wonder if I can." I looked at my gloved hands. "We should do an experiment. Go get one of my steak knives. Let's see—"

"What the hell?" Declan roared, storming back in. "We're not seeing if we can stab you. What is going on?"

I jumped. I'll admit it. "Dude, settle down. We were just talking." I rolled my eyes at Bracken.

Declan looked toward the deck again. "That's your mother's car."

"Oh." We needed them, but I felt chewed up and spat out at the moment. "Hey, give me a kiss. Let's see if you null my powers in this form."

A heavy sigh, a quick head shake, and he was leaning in for a kiss.

When he pulled away, my fingertips went to my lips. "I felt that. It was almost like a real kiss." We stared at each other as we both considered other types of experiments.

Bracken cleared his throat. "Still here."

My phone buzzed again. I went over and checked it. "They're on their way. Frank says ten minutes."

Mom and Gran walked in the back door. Both, at least, were dressed for a night sail. I'd half expected trousers and heels.

"Arwyn, for goodness sake, tell us what's going on," Mom said, still eyeing Declan with more than a little animosity.

I waved them in and then stood in the doorway so I'd see the boat coming.

"Here," Declan said, pulling me back in. "I'll go out. I have better eyesight than you do. You talk with your family."

"Good call." I went back in but stopped short. "Wait. What happened with the arsonists?"

"Arsonists?" Mom repeated. "Bracken, what is she talking about?"

While he explained, I caught up with Declan. He was leaning against the railing, looking down at the real me.

"Are you okay?" I asked.

"Yeah. It's very weird, standing here talking to you while I'm watching you bob in the water down there." He studied the me on the deck a moment. "You don't have the hair right. This is more of an all-over brown." He pulled one of my curls. "And it's not soft enough. Your hair is an amazing mix of colors. It's like every hair is a touch different from the one beside it." He rubbed the coil between his fingers. "Maybe because my sight is better, I know what it should look like. You can't duplicate what I see because you don't see it the way I do."

I looked down with him, considering the hair flying around my head up here versus what I could see on the real me down there. He was right. This was weird. "I'm going to need a strong conditioning pack tomorrow."

Laughing, some of the tension left his shoulders. "At least I know for sure this is you." He wrapped an arm around me and looked toward the marina. "I see lights in the distance. That's probably them."

"Been a pretty big day, huh?"

He met my gaze. "It's been a lot. I'll give you that."

"So? Arsonists?"

He looked back out over the water. "They were arrested. Jake and Tyler went in to give their statements. I told her if we survived tonight, we'd send her the security footage tomorrow."

I leaned my head against his chest. "Bracken insists on coming."

"I heard. We'll need him. No one spots details like he does. And my guess is he's hell on maps too. We'll watch out for him. You and I both will."

"No doorknobs! If at all possible, don't touch *anything*," I told him, squeezing my arm around his waist.

"I heard that too. Have you been practicing your magic?"

I held out a hand and a ball of blue fire rolled on my palm. "What would you like me to do?"

He thought about that. "Can you levitate?"

"Only one way to know." I stepped away from him, the fire evaporating. The spell for levitation was ready in my mind. I felt my magic thrum through me—the me in the water. My fingers flicked—below water and above—and I was hovering a foot off the deck.

Declan laughed. "That answers that question. Yes, you can, even after kissing me." He pointed over the water. "See them?"

I saw tiny lights reflecting on the waves. "Yep."

"You're going to need to get out of the water so you can get in the boat."

"Right. On it."

FORTY-THREE

A Fox in the Hen House

We watched me swim toward the rope. Declan moved to help me up.

"Darling, I still don't know what this plan is. Bracken hasn't told us," Mom said.

I looked up at Declan from the water, forcing the other me to jump off the deck. I didn't want to disappear in front of Mom and scare her to death. When he started pulling me up, Mom leaned over the railing.

"For goodness sake, Arw—how did you get to the rope so fast? He was pulling before you went over?" Clearly confused, she kept looking between the two of us.

Declan gave the rope a final tug and then grabbed hold of me and lifted me over the rail. "You good?"

I nodded, scared witless about what was coming.

Looking around Declan's shoulder, I noticed Gran standing in the doorway, watching us. Her expression was strange, almost calculating.

"They're getting close," Declan warned.

I turned and held out a hand, imposing my will on the water. *I need you calm so my family is safe. It will only be for a brief period and then you can rage as you wish.*

The strength and speed of the waves slowed, allowing Robert to steer his boat beside the deck. I added an invisible bumper to the deck so it wasn't wiped out if the ocean decided to ignore me. I saw a seal head pop up and knew Wilbur had come to find out what was going on.

"Dad knows what's happening," I called. "It might get stormy tonight. Please keep an eye on things for me."

He nodded, barked, and dove under the water.

"Your father knows, but I don't?" Mom looked both outraged and hurt.

"I told you that man would be trouble," Gran said.

When Mom's head whipped around, Gran ignored her. "I'm the head of this family, girl," she said to me. "What is it you're trying to do?"

Any answer was cut short when Robert called, "Coming alongside."

Declan grabbed the rope Frank threw. The ocean had calmed but I was pretty sure more than one wicche was working on making sure that big sailboat didn't smash into the deck.

"Let's get everybody on," Robert shouted.

Declan turned back to me. "You need your coat."

"I'm okay," I said.

"You're shivering now, and we'll be sailing for a while before you go back in."

I flicked my fingers, drying myself off and giving myself horrible, static-filled curls. Blech. "Mom, you go first. Declan can help you."

"I'm fine on my own and I don't appreciate all the secrecy," she said, stepping up on the bench. Frank gave her a hand and she stepped up on the railing before leaping over onto the deck.

"Oh!" A new thought hit me. "Bracken, put the maps in a plastic baggie so they don't get wet."

"I was ahead of you on that one." He held up his journal in one bag and the maps in a smaller one. He also had my coat under his arm. "No need to get sick," he said, handing it to me. He was also wearing a heavier coat himself.

"What map?" Gran demanded.

"One of the bay," I replied, being purposely vague. To Bracken I added, "And the other?" I was worried he'd forgotten the demon blade in his tweed jacket.

"Don't be stupid," Gran interrupted. "The boat's navigation system already has the area mapped out."

Bracken nodded wordlessly, patting the front pocket of his coat. Good. He knew not to say it either. He was all about patterns and he was noticing what I had. Gran was not herself tonight.

I waved her forward. "You're next, Gran. Declan, can you help her on board?"

He moved forward but Gran walked past him, climbing first the bench and then the railing, as Mom had.

Bracken went next, a little unsteady in the wind. Declan was there to grab his arm and help him up.

"It's just us," Declan said. "Do you need anything?"

"Courage would be good," I muttered, knowing he'd hear me. "Also, keep an eye on Gran. Something's off there."

Nodding, he took my hand and we stepped up onto the bench. Declan hopped to the railing with the balance and ease of a mountain goat. Before I could move to the rail, he was picking me up and leaping across before putting me down on deck.

I looked back at my beloved gallery, worried about what Cal might do before I returned. Flicking my fingers, I locked up and dropped the shutters. Robert put the engine in gear—or whatever the correct term was for a boat—and got us away from the gallery.

I closed my eyes and reached out for my connection with the sea. *Thank you for your help. Please continue as you were.*

The boat rocked as a huge wave hit the deck, sloshing over and washing up the side of the gallery. Robert, Frank, and Faith did all the work while the rest of us tried to stay out of their way. Bracken stood with Robert, showing him the map and discussing the first stop.

I sat beside Gran, with Declan on my other side. Mom and Elizabeth sat on the opposite bench.

"Why the rush?" Mom asked. "We could have taken tomorrow to talk and plan and then headed out, once we all knew what was happening."

Elizabeth opened her mouth to speak, but I gave a quick shake of my head. This wasn't the time for explanations, especially when it felt like the enemy was listening.

"We're approaching the wicching hour, Mom. There's powerful magic in that." As casually as possible, I pulled my glove down, exposing my wrist. "Gran, do you remember where I got these earrings? Faith was asking."

Faith and Frank turned sharply at that, watching me while still pulling ropes and putting up sails.

"What?" Gran asked, sounding annoyed. While she looked at my ears, I moved my hand as close to hers as I dared without actually touching her.

Mom moved. My eyes darted to her but instead of saying anything, she was staring intently at my wrist with a look of horror.

"These earrings. I got them for my high school graduation. Do you remember who gave them to me? There are conflicting reports." Under my words, I paid very close attention to what I was sensing. Dark, roiling evil and the smell of sulfur made my stomach twist. Chants echoed in my head. *Fuck.*

She rolled her eyes. "It sounds like you should be paying closer attention, then doesn't it? I can't keep track of every gift given and received in this family." She shook her head on a huff of annoyance.

I pulled up my glove. "I guess getting old has messed with your memory."

Gran turned slowly, a very un-Gran-like grin plastered on her face. "What was that, dear?"

I called up a wave to knock her off her bench. It capsized over the side, knocking Declan and me down and drenching us all.

Hand out, I used my magic to hold her in place. "Help me!" I said to Mom and Elizabeth. "Don't let it move. Declan, hold it down."

I held my other hand up, shouting "Bracken!" but he was ahead of me again. The blade was already flying toward me. I swept it out of the air and came down just as Declan was thrown off in a burst of flames. His clothes were on fire but I was already slamming down, the blade in my hand and then in its chest.

Gran morphed into a hideous man with boils on his neck. He wailed as his skin broke apart in fissures of fire. One ear-piercing screech and he popped out of existence. In his place, he left a scorch mark on the polished deck.

Bracken was beside me. I handed him the blade and crawled to Declan. The front of his shirt was singed, sections burned off, and his skin blackened beneath.

No, no, no. Anguish rolled through me. "Robert!" I shouted. "We need you! Declan's been hurt."

The pain had him scowling. "I'm fine," he said, pushing up to a seated position. "You know I heal fast."

Robert was beside us, pushing Declan back down. Faith took over at the wheel as Frank finished bringing up the last sail. We started flying across the water as Robert held his hands over Declan's torso. I sat on the deck beside him, worrying over him and getting in the way. Declan, for his part, bore it all stoically.

Faith kept turning around and watching us. "Did we just kill Gran?"

I shook my head on a sudden laugh. "No. That was a demon wearing a Gran suit." I looked up at Mom. "Is that who came out of Gran's house?" I was sure I'd feel it if one of the three died. I hadn't felt anything. If he'd been in Gran's house, though, how could she be okay?

Mom paused, her brow furrowed. "I'd told her on the phone that we were in a hurry. When I drove up, she was standing outside the door, locking it. At least, that's what it looked like she —he—was doing." She pulled out her phone and tapped Gran's number.

"Put it on speaker," I told her. We'd have a hard time hearing it, but Declan would know if it sounded like her.

It rang and rang. When it switched to voicemail, I patted Mom's knee. "We'll reach out to her."

"Do you think…" Mom began. Her voice caught on the thought of her mother being killed by a demon.

"I didn't feel anything," I told her. "Did you?"

She shook her head.

"Then we'll try to reach her," I said, slipping a glove off my hand before holding it out to her.

She took it. *Goddess, please show us our third. We're afraid she's been hurt by dark forces.* My stomach swooped and then my mind felt like it was racing through the night sky. My consciousness hovered over Gran's house. It was dark, no light shining out from her windows. *Gran? Are you here?*

Mom? My mother called.

Mom and I were in here together, our thoughts entwined.

Sybil? Gran's voice was reedy and tentative. It was like she didn't really believe she was hearing us.

Mom, where are you? Are you okay?

The perspective dropped and we were looking through Gran's back window, into her darkened living room. And there she was, looking smaller and more frightened than I'd ever seen her before. Barely lit by the moonlight, she looked pale. Arms wrapped across her chest, she was visibly shivering.

My Gran, who didn't have a frightened bone in her body, was shivering. *What happened?*

Tears rolled down her face. *That big dog has been pacing in front of the window all day, staring, howling, whispering.* She tapped her head. *His voice has been in here, reminding me of every mistake I've ever made, highlighting every character flaw, telling me exactly how he'd already killed everyone in the family, saving me for last. The images were in my head. Each and every one of you tortured and killed.* A sob escaped before she put a hand over her mouth. *Are you both really there? Are you alive?*

I never thought I'd see my grandmother broken.

Yes, Mom. Arwyn and I joined to find you. The demon posed as you. I picked him up and took him to Arwyn's. We got on Robert's boat to go find Calliope. Arwyn knew it wasn't you. I was so worried about what we were walking into, and that damn wolf of hers yelling at me, that I didn't notice it wasn't really you. Arwyn did, though, and she killed it. It went out screaming, fire consuming him from the inside.

Something was niggling, trying to get my attention. It was like a mosquito buzzing near my ear and I wanted to swat it away.

What? Gran rubbed at her mouth, her fingers trembling. *She killed him? How in the world did she do that?*

She had—

I tugged hard on Mom to keep her from answering. *No!*

FORTY-FOUR

Here Comes the Rain

*W*e know your demon is dead, Cal. What have you done with Gran?

Gran looked outraged for a moment and then laughed, shifting into Calliope. *Caught me.* She glanced over her shoulder onto the floor. *Currently Gran is bleeding out and powering this spell. We'll see if you find us before she dies. Spoiler: We're not here.* With a smirk, she disappeared.

I let go of Mom's hand, experiencing a moment of motion sickness as I was dropped back into my body.

Mom's eyes were wide. "Arwyn."

I nodded. "I know."

Robert was back at the helm. Declan sat on the deck with me, his chest red. Sections of skin had burned off, but he didn't seem like he was in pain.

"It looks worse than it is," he said. "Your uncle dealt with the burns and used a pain-numbing spell on me, which I appreciate."

I rubbed his leg, reassuring myself he was okay. "Can everyone hear me?" When I saw lots of nods, I said, "Okay, so, Mom and I joined to spectrally look for Gran. We went to her house. I was worried that if a demon was there, he may have hurt her."

Elizabeth wrapped her arm around Mom's shoulders.

"We found Gran standing in the dark of the living room, trembling, telling us about how she'd been terrorized all day by a hellhound and visions of our deaths."

Mom stared into her hands. She'd picked up a demon and brought it to us and then believed a sorcerer who was pretending to be her mother. Something was wrong. Mom was normally far more suspicious and distrustful than this.

"It was nagging at me, though," I continued. "Gran is Gran. She doesn't hunch or tremble. I knew the demon had been destroyed. That only left one culprit. Sure enough, Calliope showed herself. She said she had Gran, had used her blood to power the spell joining the Three."

"So," Faith began, sitting beside her mother, "we need to get Cal, destroy the grimoire, and rescue Gran?"

"That about sums it up." It was interesting how none of us wanted to use the word *kill* for Cal. There was no rehabilitation for her. She, along with the book, needed to be destroyed, but she was still our cousin, our niece.

"If I can direct your attention," Robert called back, "we're coming up on the first spot. I know this area well. When Bracken showed me the map, I knew exactly where he meant because I've often wondered why no one's built here. It's a large plot of land, right on the water. It never made sense to me as to why some millionaire hadn't snapped it up and built a mansion." He looked over his shoulder at us. "I guess we know why now."

"Maybe we know why," I said. "It's one of two possibilities." I checked Declan's wounds again. It was hard to tell in the dark, but his chest looked a little less red.

He rubbed his huge mitt of a hand over my knee. "I'm fine and I'll be ready when it's time to go."

"When I go in the water, you can use my coat. You must be freezing." The poor guy didn't even have a whole shirt.

His eyebrows rose. "Are you seriously under the impression your clothing will fit me?"

"I meant you could use it as a blanket." I gestured to his chest.

"Just sort of lay it on yourself so your burn is out of the salty wind."

He leaned forward and kissed me. "Thanks for the thought, but if you're in the water, it means I'm getting off the boat."

"Good point." I started to take the coat off now, but he stopped me with a shake of his head.

"All right, Faith," Bracken said, "I believe it's time for a storm."

Faith stood up and moved to the front of the boat. Mom watched her go, brows furrowed. She didn't know we had an elemental in the family.

Holding her father's hand, finding that anchor, Faith closed her eyes, lifted her other hand, palm out, and made a slow pushing movement. We were hit by a few drops, but the rain clouds quickly moved on and hovered over the rocky, forested land, set between two large homes with manicured lawns that ran to the water's edge.

"Frank?" I called. "Can you give us some cover in case anyone is looking?"

He nodded, his fingers twitching at his side. "Sorry. I meant to do this sooner. I can't make us invisible, so this is more of a chameleon spell. We'll blend with the ocean."

"That's perfect," I told him.

Mom turned to Elizabeth, whispering, "Why didn't you tell me?"

Elizabeth sighed. "There are lots of reasons, too long to get into right now. Suffice to say, I saw how they treated Arwyn. They knew she was gifted and resented her for it, terrorized her for it. You knew too, but you didn't stop it. If you wouldn't protect your own child, how could I trust you to protect mine?"

Mom reared back as though she'd been slapped. "I—of course I protected Arwyn."

Elizabeth just raised her eyebrows. "You don't honestly believe that, do you?"

I couldn't look at my mom and see that hurt, bewildered expression on her face. Instead, I scanned the shore and noticed something moving in the dark. I stood unsteadily on the rocking deck and went to the front of the boat, trying to get a feel for what was out there. More than likely it was a deer, confused by the sudden rain, but just in case, I got down and crawled out to the bow, wanting to be as far away from the emotions behind me as possible.

I let my guard down a bit and focused on where I had last seen movement.

Curiosity. Hunger. He sees us and knows we're the ones causing this storm but is unclear as to why.

I was pretty sure I recognized what he was. I lifted a hand in greeting and thought I saw movement in return.

"At ease, Faith. That's not her." I got up and walked back. "He's a supernatural. I think a vampire, but I'm not positive."

Faith's eyes went wide, her gaze darting back to the shore.

Robert turned the boat around and headed back across the bay. Elizabeth pulled a juice box out of her bag and handed it to Faith, who had sat down beside her. While I was at the bow, Mom had moved so she was no longer sitting near Elizabeth. At some point, they'd need to have a longer discussion, but now wasn't the time.

"You're going to have to do that again in a few minutes and probably for longer," Elizabeth said, kissing her daughter's temple. "Great job."

"Thanks." Faith glanced around, seemingly embarrassed by the mothering. "Did you bring us candy bars too?"

"I could use one of those as well," Frank said, maintaining the chameleon spell.

"You can take a break too," I told him. "She can't see this far out. Maybe just hide our running lights from view. Robert, tell us when you start to see detail on the shore. Frank can hide the boat again."

Frank slumped in his seat and took the candy bar from his mom. "Please tell me you brought us more than one each."

She handed him a juice and said, "I have more." She looked in her bag. "I also have protein bars."

Nodding, he reached for one of those as well.

Robert looked over his shoulder, saw his children eating after expending so much magical energy, and cut the engine before bringing down the main sail. He was giving them time. Robert and Elizabeth were changing generational patterns. It made me hopeful for the future of this family.

Toxic behaviors had become the norm for Coreys over the ages. No wonder so many of us turned to black magic and sorcery.

"Why have we stopped?" Mom asked.

"He's letting Frank and Faith recuperate before pushing them again." I often had to remind myself, when my mom did something that appeared cold and unfeeling, that it was most likely because she was repeating how she'd always been treated and didn't realize another way was possible.

With a short nod, she sat back, watching how Elizabeth pulled out bottles of water for each of her children. Mom stared at the bag a moment, as though unclear as to how her sister fit so much into it before her expression cleared. She, like me, had figured out that Elizabeth had spelled her purse, making it a true bag of holding. Who knew how much stuff she carried around on the regular in that small, tasteful bag.

Once the teens were done, Frank and Faith worked together to put the main sail back up and Robert got the boat moving faster again. Once done, Frank sat beside his mom, turned in his seat, and put one dark hand on the light wood at the edge of the boat. Eyes closed, he blew out a slow breath. After a moment, he nodded.

Bracken unsteadily got back up to talk with Robert, who had the map clipped above the wheel, beside his navigation instruments. Robert pointed at the map and then at a spot on what looked like a computer tablet.

Faith looked down at me, as Declan and I were still sitting on the deck. "It's going to be this one, isn't it?"

I saw the fear in her eyes and wished I could tell her everything would be okay. "I think so, yes."

"And you, Uncle Bracken, and Declan are going to try to break in?" She leaned in harder against her mom.

I nodded.

"I'm going too," Robert said.

"What?" Elizabeth's voice was pitched high. She was doing a good job of appearing relaxed for her children, but she was terrified. "You need to drive the boat," she protested.

The two shared a look and then Robert said, "You heard Arwyn. Your mom is bleeding out. They need a healer."

I shook my head. "Wait. No. I didn't see you in my vision. Only Bracken, Declan, and I go in."

He barely glanced at me before putting his focus back where it belonged, the sea ahead. "You had that vision before you knew your Gran was dying. It would probably be different now."

My visions didn't rely on what I knew. He was right about one thing, though. We were going to need a healer.

Declan and I shared a look. Neither was feeling good about this new development. Robert had a family, a beautiful, loving one. We didn't want to do anything to ruin that.

Elizabeth straightened her shoulders, every nightmare scenario no doubt racing through her mind.

"Can you captain the boat?" I asked. "Frank and Faith will be busy."

She pasted on a smile that looked sickly around the edges. "Of course. We all can." She stood, stowing her bag under her seat, and went to the wheel, where Robert and Bracken were checking the map against the dark shoreline, looking for the spot.

"There!" Bracken pointed to a black void between two houses that had dim lights in their windows.

Declan stood and pulled me up with him. He had the best eyes on the boat, so he could provide confirmation. Head pivoting like he was at a tennis match, he growled, "That's it. It doesn't want me looking at it, so it keeps pushing me away."

"Orla said the same. It kept pushing her off course." Now that we'd actually found it, my heart was in my throat. I'd be fine in the water. Declan, Bracken, and Robert were the ones who'd be risking their lives.

"Okay, Faith," her father said. "We need to make sure. Give us a storm."

Elizabeth took over the wheel and held Faith's hand while her daughter called up a beaut. Her nerves must have been getting to her because hail bounced off my head before Declan blocked it, palming my skull.

"Sorry!" she called.

"Don't worry about us," I told her. "We're fine. Focus on what you're doing."

Her braids bobbed as she nodded, pushing the storm toward the void in the shoreline.

FORTY-FIVE

Follow the Leader

"I hadn't considered how difficult it would be to see rain spatter in the dark," I whispered, not wanting to distract Frank and Faith.

Declan grinned at that, taking my hand and pulling me toward the bow of the boat. His eyes went wolf gold, and then, like I had earlier, he went out as far as he could. As he had excellent balance, he didn't have to crawl.

He returned a minute later, nodding, his eyes darkening to their usual warm brown. "It's there. The hail helped me see it."

Faith's eyes were still closed, but she smiled.

"Should she keep the storm going?" Elizabeth asked.

I shrugged. "Cal knows we're coming. Now she knows we've found her. I say let it taper off so others don't notice as well. With any luck, the people on either side slept through it."

Faith dropped her arm and blinked her eyes open. The poor thing looked exhausted.

I patted her shoulder. "You did your job. Thank you. It's our turn now. Sit down. Relax for a bit."

Robert pointed ahead. "The house next door has a dock. Use that so we can get off, then move back. I want you close enough to see us but not close enough to get hit by anything. We have no idea what she'll do when she's cornered." He turned to his son. "I'm sorry to ask for more, but can you extend that chameleon charm to us when we go ashore?"

Frank's expression was strained but he nodded.

Elizabeth brought the sailboat alongside the dock, nice and easy. Robert jumped off and then helped Bracken. Declan gave me a big kiss, grabbed the front of my jacket, and said, "Stay safe." His hand trailed over my stomach as he turned and hopped onto the dock.

"Arwyn? What are you doing?" Mom said. "They can't do this without you."

"I know. I made a promise, though, and I'm keeping it." I took off my coat and handed it to her before diving overboard. While the sailboat moved away, I let myself drop to the ocean floor. It was deeper here than I'd thought it would be.

Already pushing out my magic, I opened my eyes on the dock beside the men as the real me felt myself hit the sandy, rocky floor.

Declan ran his hand down my arm and nodded. "Say something."

"The water is deeper here than I'd thought," I said.

The men shared a look and Declan shook his head at me.

Damn it. What was it with me and talking? I focused on my throat, my breath. I knew how to talk, but trying to walk my other self through doing it was frustrating. I tried again. "The water here is deep."

"It is," Robert agreed.

"Good. Um, is it a problem that I can see all of you guys just fine?" Maybe the boat was too far away. I didn't know how close Frank needed to be for his spell to work.

"It's because we're all together in the bubble of his spell," Robert explained. "Someone looking out a window from this house here wouldn't see us."

"Oh, cool. In that case, I'll add a muffling spell." I flicked my fingers. The two wicches nodded. Declan looked unsure, so I clarified. "Meaning we can talk amongst ourselves and those outside this bubble won't hear us."

"Nice," he said.

"Okay, I'm in the lead," I said, heading off toward the spelled property.

"Why is that?" Declan argued, walking beside me.

"Because you can be killed. I can't—at least I don't think so. Assuming Cal doesn't go scuba diving with a big knife, I'll be fine." I patted his arm. "I'm not really here, remember?" I pushed him behind me and he fell back.

"You look and sound so real, it's hard to remember," he said.

"True," Bracken chimed in.

As we neared the end of the manicured lawn and headed toward what looked to me like a thick bramble of dense bushes and tall trees, I heard Robert call, "Wait."

Turning, I found Declan far back. Robert was trying to pull him along, but Declan, eyes wolf gold, appeared rooted to the spot.

"I can't move," he growled, "but don't you think about going without me."

I walked back and studied him a moment, considering. "It seems like her spells are especially difficult for shifters. None of the wicches had issues with looking at the property, but you did."

Hands fisted, biceps bulging, he ground out, "You're not leaving me."

I stared up into his super sexy scowl and said, "You're cute when you're angry."

"Arwyn."

I held up a hand. "Let me think a second." I turned to the other two men. "How are you guys doing with this ward?"

Bracken shrugged. "I hadn't noticed anything." He looked at Robert. "Are you experiencing discomfort as well?"

Robert nodded. "It's not as bad for me as it is for Declan, but it feels like I'm pushing through a wall of molasses."

"I think I know what it is, then," I said, and Bracken nodded. "As my great-uncle here is probably holding the only demon blade in the human realm, we need to think of something different to get you two through. Let's see if fae magic helps."

Just like when I had built my new wards, I pulled from the ocean I was sitting in and let it swirl within me. When I held up my hands, I realized I was so used to gloves being a part of who I was, I'd put them on my shadow as well. Pulling them off, I dropped them into oblivion and then touched both Robert and Declan's hands.

Both were suddenly sopping wet, as though a huge wave had swamped them. Declan blew water out of his mouth and Robert wiped at his eyes.

"Sorry about that," I said, shocked it had worked. "Can you move now?"

Declan yanked his foot up and started forward, with Robert following.

I walked to the bushes and forced my way through until I found a tall stone wall. "I don't believe this is real," I called back. "It's a powerful ward, though, that will take precious time to unwind. And my guess is that all those sticker bushes I just went through are there to cut and bleed anyone who gets too close, helping to power the ward."

Bracken pulled the blade from his pocket. "This is hardly a noble use for this blade, but it is apparently necessary."

Pushing my way back through the bushes, I stopped him and held out my hand. "May I? It can't take my blood because I'm not here right now."

"Of course." He handed it to me. "That makes more sense."

As I wasn't sure what would happen, my movements were tentative at first. The blade cut through the bushes like a hot knife through butter. If anything, the bushes almost seemed to cringe away from the blade. After I cut a doorway through, I handed the blade back to Bracken.

It was very weird walking through a green doorway. Looking left and right, I scanned the path before turning back to assess the men on my quest. "I'm afraid this is pretty narrow. Bracken and I should be okay, but Robert and especially you, Declan, are going to have trouble. I don't want to leave you out there, though—"

"We stick together," Declan said.

I blew out a breath and looked down the narrow passage again. "Okay, let me see if I can find a weak point in this ward for us to burrow through. Unfortunately, that means you guys are going to need to do whatever you can to touch neither the sticker bushes nor the wall. I haven't touched the wall, but my guess, based on the dead birds and squirrels I see rotting on the ground around it, is that it's electrified in some way."

Robert and Declan shared a glance and then moved forward.

"Robert and I can do a blunting spell," Bracken suggested, "to try to make the bushes less of a problem. Declan, you bring up the rear."

Holding one hand a few inches from the wall ward, I walked between it and the bramble, with the men following slowly behind. When I made it to the front of the property and the wall cut to the left, I continued, right past what looked like a tall wooden gate. At one point in its history, this property must have been visible to the public.

"The Shades," Bracken said.

I stopped and looked behind me. Bracken pointed to a black metal plate affixed to the stone wall. Really old properties in Carmel and Monterey often didn't have addresses. They had names.

I smiled. "You were right. It was the name of the house."

"Sorry," Bracken said. "I didn't mean to distract you."

Declan was walking by that section that looked like a gate, trying to see through slats.

"That looks like an entrance but it's not."

He nodded and went back to sliding sideways between the wall and thorns.

The bushes were a little thinner on this side of the property. I looked out one of the holes in the foliage and saw what appeared to be a narrow dirt driveway. It was covered in overgrown bushes and trees. I doubt those driving down the road on the other side of all this bloodthirsty vegetation even realized there was a house back here.

When I got to the other corner, I finally felt a hole in the ward, much like that hole in the bushes. It was enough of a weakness, I thought I could unwind what was here and push through.

"Give me a minute. I might have found our way in." I held up both hands, closed my eyes, and felt my way through the spell. It was a bit like finding a hole in a sweater. I could either pull the threads tight and reweave it or pluck the threads out and unravel it. I was working on unraveling.

"Let me help," Bracken said. "The spell I found in your borrowed grimoire should work well here."

Working together, we snapped through the ward like we had scissors. I stepped through the break in the wall, Bracken behind me, followed by Robert. Declan had to squeeze his way through. One of his shoulders brushed the live ward and zapped him like an electrical fence. Robert was there, pulling shirt fibers from the wound and healing what he could in the moment.

I hugged Declan as gingerly as possible. "I'm so sorry you keep getting hurt. It's not fair."

He pulled me in tight and kissed the top of my head. "If someone has to get hurt, it's better that it's me. I heal faster than wicches." He looked over the top of my head. "I thought it'd be bigger."

I turned, keeping an arm around him, and saw a run-down hovel that looked like one good wind would knock it over. "You can't believe what you see. This is an illusion on the off chance someone gets past the wall. You saw the hail bouncing off the structure. Did it look like this?"

He shook his head, but it was more like a wolf shaking off unease than a simple no. He gently tapped the top of my head. "Smart."

"Okay, everyone walk where I walk," I said. "I'm back in the lead. There are more wards."

We moved slowly over the dirt yard. I almost walked face first into a ward, but I caught myself at the last minute. "Bracken. I think we need that blade again. I smell the faintest trace of sulfur."

He stepped up beside me and thrust the blade into the air before us.

A sonic boom knocked the men off their feet. I helped Bracken up, the blade still tight in his hand. Declan helped Robert up, who in turn put his hands over Declan's ears to no doubt stop the ringing. When he was done, he did the same with Bracken.

"Can you heal yourself?" I asked. When he didn't respond, I figured I had my answer. I wasn't a healer, but I went to him, held his hand, and called for help. *Please, Goddess, help Robert to hear. You know what we're doing, why we're here. We have to stop Cal. Please, Blessed One, forgive me for not saying this well. We need your help to right the wrong one of our family has committed. And Goddess, one more thing. Please hold my Gran in your hands until we're able to retrieve her.*

Robert blinked when I let him go, snapping his fingers by his ear. "No one told me you were a healer."

Relieved, I said, "I'm not. I asked the Goddess to help us, and she did. The Goddess healed you, not me." I studied the other two. "Are we good?"

Declan was smiling at me. Bracken, brow furrowed, said, "You know the Goddess doesn't usually do what we ask of her, right?"

I shrugged and started moving again. "I'm not about to question good fortune. Come on. There's worse ahead. Let's get to it—oh!" I swung back around and pointed at Robert. "Do not touch any doorknobs. They're cursed to kill us in horrible ways. In general, try not to touch anything in there. We have lots to do now." I looked up and gauged the position of the moon. "It's the wicching hour. Let's move."

FORTY-SIX

Wicching Hour

Finally, the real house. It was a huge stone and plaster affair that might have been beautiful in its heyday, but now it looked as though it was in the final stages of a painful and terminal disease.

Vines crawled up the crumbling walls, like the earth itself was doing what it could to pull the house into its grave. The windows, like sunken eyes, with dark, moldy circles under them, stared sightlessly out. Just being near it sent a chill down my spine.

I paused and studied the dirty tiles beneath my shoes. "This was in my vision."

Bracken moved up beside me. "This is where I died?"

I nodded.

He patted my shoulder. "Not to worry. I promise not to touch any doorknobs. In fact, just to be safe"—he pulled out a pair of my gloves and put them on, handing pairs to Declan and Robert as well—"I thought we could all wear gloves. A fellowship of handwear, as it were."

I leaned in and kissed his cheek, something the real me couldn't do without visions.

He went a bit pink around the ears and waved off my thanks

while Robert and Declan did their best to fit my gloves on their hands.

"At least they're stretchy," Robert said.

Declan held up his hands and it was hard not to laugh. He was able to yank them down to about mid-palm.

"They look good on you," I told him.

Grinning, he rolled his eyes at that. The humor left him, though, as he looked up at the cancer we were about to enter.

Moving slowly, I approached the front door, waiting for the tingle of a ward nearby but not feeling it. "The lack of another ward is making me very nervous," I whispered.

"We have gone through quite a few," Robert said. "She has to get in and out herself, doesn't she?"

"The wards would be set to her," I said. Sometimes I forgot that everyone else wasn't protected by a million wards. Some, thankfully, got to just live their lives. "Cal can walk through them and turn doorknobs. She's the key that opens and locks them."

When I got to the doorstep, I felt a last line of defense. I turned to Bracken and held out my hand. He placed the blade in it and then pulled Robert and Declan back. I put the knife tip in the keyhole and this time, it sounded like a soap bubble popping.

Backtracking down the steps, I handed off the blade and then flicked my fingers, trying to open the door with magic. Nothing happened.

"I could kick it down," Declan said.

I shook my head. "I'd prefer you kept both your legs."

I suddenly realized I was getting very hot. My legs and butt felt like they were on fire. I looked at the men, who were calmly staring back at me.

"What's the matter?" Declan asked.

"Don't you feel it?" I turned and looked around, now in a real panic. "I'm on fire!"

I felt my real self get yanked in the water and the heat began to dissipate.

"What's happening?" Declan tried to grab my arm, but his

hand went right through me. "You're flickering in and out. What is it?"

I held up my hands, asking for a minute while I focused on what was happening underwater.

An octopus was dragging me away from where I'd been sitting, where the ocean floor was now red and glowing, like lava was about to burst out of the ground. The octopus was joined by a buddy; they each took an arm and dragged me behind rocks covered in anemones and sea stars.

Out of the sand where I'd been sitting the head of a hellhound emerged, teeth first. He climbed out, his red glowing eyes scanning the area for me. *Shitshitshit.*

Before I had a chance to throw a spell, two great white sharks dove down and ripped it apart. The water was filled with the black liquid that ran in a hellhound's veins, but then the water swirled it into a funnel and the black was gone.

Suckers covered my body as the octopuses worked together to hide me. *Thank you.* Deciding everything was under control for the moment, I went back to the men. When I looked around, I saw Declan running for the break in the wall.

"Wait!"

He kept going. I smacked Robert. He flinched away from me and then shouted to Declan, who was already trying to squeeze through. Thankfully, he stopped before he got burned again.

I focused on making myself heard and tried again. "Where are you going?"

He jogged back with his arms open. "What do you mean where am I going? You said you were on fire and then disappeared."

"Oh. Right. Sorry about that. In my defense, I was. She sent one of her hellhounds after me. An octopus and his buddy dragged my body away from the Hell portal opening beneath me. They're actually covering my body right now, no doubt making me look like coral. Anyway, a couple of sharks killed the hound and I'm back."

Robert turned to Declan. "Is it always like this?"

Declan rubbed his hands over his face. "Far too often."

Robert shook his head and studied me again. "We had no idea. I always thought of you as Elizabeth's artistic niece who kept to herself."

"Hell, that's better than most of them think of me, so I'll take it. Meanwhile, we need to get in, and wicche magic isn't doing it. Move back, guys. Calliope has had too much time to prepare for us."

Imposing my will over the natural world, I pulled on the ocean around me and flung my hands at the door. If it hadn't worked, I would have looked damn stupid. As it was, a huge wave knocked down the doors and flooded the floors beyond.

"Well done," Bracken said, patting my shoulder. "If I'm not mistaken, everywhere the ocean has touched is now yours." He extended his hand, inviting me to go first.

Eyes wide, Robert looked like he was frozen in place. When I waved him forward, he blinked and swallowed.

"Okay now?" I asked.

Still mute, he nodded.

I stepped through the doorway and was hit by a horrible stench.

Following closely, Declan grimaced. "It's mold, candle wax, blood, and shit." His eyes lightened and his long, razor-sharp claws slid out through the too-small gloves. He surveyed the room and then pointed at a door to the right. "It's coming from behind there."

"I feel like we should check this floor, just to make sure nothing is sneaking behind us but—"

Robert flew up in the air. For half a beat, we all stared up, trying to understand what had just happened, then I made out the outline of a monstrous spider clinging to the high ceiling. It appeared to have stung Robert with a paralytic because he stopped struggling. Declan leapt, claws out, as the spider began to cocoon his prey.

I lifted my hand to help, but Bracken pulled me away.

"It's a diversion," he said. "Declan will kill it. You and I need to find Cal."

A spider leg hit the wet floor and sizzled in the ocean water. Bracken was right. It killed me to do it, but Cal had to be stopped and I had to trust Declan to hold his own.

Bracken reached for the doorknob and then stopped himself with a headshake. His hands moved in a spell. The doorknob turned and the door popped open. He looked down into the dark and then back at me. "Here we go."

I took the lead again, heading down the stone steps. Declan was right: The stench was overwhelming down here. Even in this form, I felt bile rising. I heard skittering around us, but I didn't want to know what it was.

At the base of the stairs, we saw three doors. Around the edges of one, torchlight flickered and I heard the low murmur of chanting. We didn't have time to check and battle whatever was behind all these doors.

Closing my eyes, I drew from the ocean and asked for my phosphorescent friends to help. My head fell back as I asked the Goddess for assistance as well. As a wave crested within me, I let go and a huge wave splashed up the walls and went under the doors.

The dark door behind us now glowed phosphorescent. The flickering light and chanting had been a ploy. Bracken and I moved to the now glowing door. I flicked my fingers, but it didn't open. Bracken tried his spell and again, nothing. He pulled the blade out of his pocket and ran it along the seam of the door where a latch would be.

The door swung in. Soft glowing light from the wet floor cast strange shadows in the dark room. Copying the queen's move, I made a ball of light in my hand and tossed it up toward the ceiling. The ball burst, splashing light around the room. Gran was crumpled in the corner, seemingly thrown there and forgotten.

The concrete floor dipped in the middle, where I assumed there was some kind of drainage. I didn't want to think about what needed to be hosed down in this room. Gran, at least, was on the far side, so she wasn't lying in water.

What I could see of her arm was covered in bleeding cuts. Her clothes were dirty and rumpled. Her hair had fallen from its bun. I sensed movement, though. She was breathing. Stepping in, I braced for an attack. The room seemed empty but for Gran and a worktable with a grimoire, a ceremonial bowl filled with a foul liquid, and an athame. Calliope's ceremonial dagger was covered in blood, no doubt Gran's.

I only felt one person in the room, so while Bracken approached the book, I went to Gran, laying my hand on her shoulder. "Gran? Can you hear me?"

She rolled over and I was staring into Cal's face. She lifted a hand and Bracken flew into the air, hitting the stone ceiling before dropping in a heap beside the worktable.

I wanted to run to him, but knew I couldn't turn my back on her. "What have you done with Gran?"

She rose slowly, grinning. "You know the old bat never trusted you. Why do you care what I do to her?"

I circled to the side, trying to block Bracken, who I hoped would be okay. I let my guard down and braced for the cacophony of overlapping thoughts and emotions. My head pounded, but I sensed pain behind me. He wasn't dead. "Maybe because, unlike you, I'm not a psychopath."

She shrugged. "Sticks and stones. My friend says he wants to work with you." She rolled her eyes. "I told him we didn't need you, but he thinks with your fae magic, we'd be unstoppable." She smiled slyly. "Wouldn't you like to get even with all the horrible cousins who made your life miserable? Come on. You know you hate them as much as I do."

She may have been trying to talk me into joining her on the dark side, but she was thinking about some kind of hidden chamber behind me. I also felt Robert's fear and Declan's rage as they battled whatever was up there.

Her right hand fisted—the motion she used for casting

spells—but I was still trying to figure out what was in the hidden room. It was important to her, and she wanted whatever she'd secreted in it kept away from the rest of the world. The spell she sent at me took the wind out of me and made me stumble back a few steps, but I shook it off, much to her shock.

The spell smelled of blood and death. That asshole had just tried to kill me.

Flicking my fingers, I sent back a spell, freezing her lungs. Her eyes widened as she tried to draw in a breath.

"You don't honestly think you're better at this than I am, do you?" I taunted. "I was learning defensive magic when you were still whining that you couldn't perform a simple cleansing spell."

Both hands fisted, she sucked in air and sent another one at me. My head vaguely hurt and I thought I heard breaking glass somewhere. It was a good thing I was far away from this room. She'd learned some nasty spells.

But then again, I knew quite a few as well. Fingers moving slowly at my side, I wove a net around her heart and squeezed. She jolted, eyes wide.

Sputtering, hand to chest, she gasped, "You can't—Corey curse…"

I shook my head. "Cal, you're an idiot and a shitty wicche. That curse was created to punish sorcerers like you, not the good guys hunting you."

Declan's roar reverberated through the house before it was cut off.

Cal's sneer was triumphant. "And there goes the boy toy."

I'd inadvertently dropped my spell on her when I heard that roar of pain. *Oh, nononono.* Please. Not Declan. I turned to run upstairs but came face to snout with a hellhound.

"Kill her!" Cal shouted, dark glee in her voice.

I needed to get upstairs, but I couldn't leave Bracken on his own with these two. And where the hell was Gran?

Drool dripped from the hound's razor-sharp teeth. His growls shook the room. Red, glowing eyes pinned me to the spot as he tried to burn a hole through my soul.

The hound sprang and snapped, biting off part of my left arm. The shock kept me rooted to the spot and he crunched and swallowed my arm from the elbow down. I stared at the ragged edges of what was left, while Cal jumped up and down behind me.

Huh. I hadn't considered that something could happen to this form. It stung like I'd shoved my arm in a hornet's nest, but it wasn't agonizing, and I wasn't bleeding. Mostly because I wasn't actually here. This was all so weird.

Couldn't I just put it back on? I envisioned my arm and then there it was, back where it belonged.

"No! How did you—" she screeched

The hound was having none of it. When she started screaming, he jammed his snout in my gut and flipped me over his head.

I banged my head on the ceiling and ended up splatting on the worktable, which would have been fine if I hadn't landed palm down on the grimoire.

A series of wicches through the ages flash through my mind, each poring over the grimoire, chanting demonic spells while the cries of their victims are ignored. The same demon stands over each. Hundreds of wicches appear and fade, while one demon oversees their studies. Finally, as the images slow, I recognize Aunt Abigail. The demon disappears behind her. A new one stands behind Cal and then he changes too. Cal looks up from the book, no demon behind her, as she blows out the candle.

I shook off the vision, afraid of what I'd find, but it had only been a moment. The hound was still turning to come after me. Out of the corner of my eye, I saw Bracken move. Snatching up the athame, I dove off the table over the top of the hound while flinging the dagger at Calliope.

Please, Goddess…

When I hit the ground, the monster hound pounced, crushing me to the filthy floor. *Damn.* I knew I wasn't really dying but this hurt like hell.

Suddenly, the weight was gone and the room was filled with

horrible wailing, reverberating off the stone walls. I pushed up and rolled over to see what was happening. Dark shadows rose from the floor and swarmed Calliope. Her body crumpled to the ground, but her soul stood, eyes wide with horror as the demonic shadows dragged her away.

The hound was gone and Bracken was leaning over the work-table, blood running down the side of his face from a gash on his temple. He'd stabbed the demon blade through the heart of the grimoire and saved us all.

FORTY-SEVEN

The Song of the Dead

I stood and rushed to him. "Are you okay?"

Bracken's expression was grim but determined. "I will be, especially now that I know this is dead." A black ooze radiated out from where the demon blade had been plunged in.

"Dead? Was it living?" I asked.

"I believe so," he said. He yanked out the blade, waved a hand to clean it, and then sheathed it and put it back in his pocket. "It was filled with the twisted souls of our own who had sold themselves for more power."

"Arwyn!" Declan roared.

"We're here and we're okay." I met Bracken's weary gaze. "Are we okay?"

He let out a breath and nodded slowly. "I believe my sister is dead, though."

I flinched. "What? Why?"

He gestured around us. "Do you sense her?"

I listened intently. Declan and Robert were coming down the stairs and...that was it. There were no other thoughts in this building.

"I'd feel it, though. I'm sure I would. I was one of the three." How could she die and me not feel it?

Declan burst in and picked me up, crushing me to him. "Thank goodness you're all right."

"I'm still underwater," I reminded him.

Laughing, he gave me a quick kiss. "I'm well aware. But you wouldn't be here if you weren't okay there."

"Ah, good point." I patted his chest, a request to put me down. Robert looked like he'd been chewed on. I caught his eye. "How about you? Are you okay?"

He blew out a long breath and finally gave a nod. "I'm alive. I may never sleep again, but I'm still breathing. I heard Elizabeth cry in my head while we were dealing with the spider. I need to go make sure my family is okay."

I nodded. "Please, go. Check on them. Bracken and I have something we need to do here."

Robert nodded and then headed back up the stairs. Declan stayed with us, like I knew he would.

"Bracken thinks Gran is dead. I don't sense anyone else in the house with us." I held up a finger. "*But,* Cal was thinking about a hidden chamber over here." I gestured to the side wall. I went back to the doorway, looked out into the short hall, and threw a ball of light at the ceiling. The walls were definitely off.

"This rock, dirt—whatever it is—is too thick to just be a wall. Gran may have been hidden in a compartment here. That might be why I can't feel her." I waved Bracken over. "We'll do this together."

Limping, he made his way slowly across the room. "Together, then." He took my hand and then we put our free hands against the rough earthen wall. Our magic combined and brought down the false front.

There, cuts all over her body, was the frail form of Gran. The force of the loss hit me like a truck. My brain froze. My lungs seized. I dropped, trying to catch my breath as my real self raced through the water. When I hit the ocean surface, I heard Mom wail. She'd felt the loss of our third as strongly as I had.

Dad was in the water looking up at her, sharks circling the sailboat. I had a moment to put two and two together. The land between the house and the water was torn up, like a huge rototiller had been used. Sharks were circling the boat. That asshole Cal had sent more hellhounds at Mom, Elizabeth, and the kids.

Robert stood at the water's edge, eyes wide, watching the distinctive dorsal fins cutting through the water around his family.

In the next moment, a strong arm scooped me up. Dad, holding both Mom and me, put us down in that foul room of death and terror. Shadow-me disappeared. Mom shrugged out of her coat and covered her mother with it.

She looked back at me, tears streaming down her face. "Arwyn?"

I went to her. We clasped hands and sang the song of the dead for Gran, asking the Goddess to take Mary into her loving embrace. Gran wasn't perfect. No one was, but she'd worked and sacrificed her whole life to look after the Corey coven.

A phrase came to me: *Whoever destroys a single soul destroys the whole world.* The evil we do echoes on into eternity. All those wicches I'd seen in that vision, they'd twisted the soul of our family, heedless of those the echoes would touch, would hurt.

Gran was a hard woman because strength was needed to survive. She'd kept this family thriving when other wicche families had splintered and lost their power.

In addition to my prayers for Gran moving on, for her peaceful rest, I prayed for Mom, who now inherited the mantle. She was now the head of the Corey clan. She'd been preparing for it her whole life, but it was different when you had to do it on your own.

As our song came to an end, Mom hugged me to her. I pulled Bracken into the hug. He'd lost his sister today. Estranged or not, he'd lost another member of his family.

Mom wiped her face and turned to Dad. "Mac, can you take her for me? To her home? We need to care for her now."

Nodding, he disappeared with Gran.

Mom squeezed my hand. "You'll stand with me, won't you?"

"I will," I said.

She nodded, clearing her throat and straightening her shoulders. "All right then. We'll need a third. Perhaps Elizabeth…"

I shook my head. "She's happy in her quiet life with her wonderful family. Besides, we need a maiden. Mother and—sorry—crone are covered."

"What do you—" she looked sharply between Declan and me.

"It's still very early," I told her. "Dad says she's healthy and though she's not technically a she yet, he believes she will be."

"You told your father before me?" She was a jumble of emotions right now, but hurt seemed to be leading the way.

"No. He told me."

Her eyes got wide and then she huffed out a laugh. "I'd forgotten. I found out about you from him too." She looked between Declan and me. "So, you ignored my advice and tied yourself to this…wolf."

"Mom," I warned.

She waved away my concern. "Fine. What do I know? At least you'll make beautiful babies. How could you not? Look at you two." She air kissed my cheek. "This is good. Thank you for telling me. Death was answered with life. Okay. A maiden, then."

We looked at each other and both said, "Faith."

Mom glanced at Calliope lying in the corner, her eyes open and unseeing, the athame sticking out of her chest, and shook her head in disgust. "Let's get out of here."

Bracken pointed at the grimoire. "I don't feel comfortable leaving this here."

I thought a moment. "Anyone have a phone on them that works?"

Mom pulled hers out of a pocket.

"It's a good thing I memorized his number." I dialed and hit speaker.

"Do you know what time it is?" A very growly and annoyed voice filled the room.

"Pleasant as always. I found that book we were talking about before. I'd really appreciate it if you could dispose of it properly."

"Give me a minute. I've got those damn meringue cookies Sam loves in the oven. I'll be there in…three minutes." Click.

I stared at the phone. "Why the hell is he complaining about the time if he's up baking? Jeez." I handed it back to Mom.

"Did you just call a demon on my phone?"

"Yeah, but he's only half a demon and he's baking one of my recipes." I flicked my fingers, causing the grimoire to float. "Let's go upstairs. The stench down here is going to make me hurl."

"Arwyn, really," Mom chastised. "That's no way for the second in this family to talk."

When we got to the main floor, Mom closed and sealed the door with a flick of her fingers, cutting off the smell. When she went to the front door and reached for the knob, Bracken, Declan, and I all yelled, "No!"

She jumped.

"Sorry, Mom. The doorknobs are cursed to kill." I looked at Bracken, unsure. "Do curses disappear when the sorcerer and demon are gone?"

Dave popped in beside me. "No," he answered. "That's how people get hit by ancient curses. Use your head." He checked our hands. "So, where's the—" And then he saw it hovering behind me. "Good call not touching it." He shook his head. "I don't miss that smell. Fucking sorcerers are savages."

Mom said, "But aren't you—" At his glare, she stopped talking.

He studied the grimoire, touching the black ooze. "Looks like someone has an ancient artifact they're not supposed to have." He stared at Bracken, someone he'd never met before. "So you know, that item glows to my kind. You need something stronger than a leather sheath to hide it. Also, there are many who wouldn't think twice about killing an entire town to get a hold of that."

"How do we hide it?" I asked.

He blew out a breath. "There's nothing in this realm that'll hide it. I'm not sure how long you've had it, old man, but you're living on borrowed time."

Bracken finally responded. "I have the proper box for it. I don't use it if I need to carry it on a day like today."

Dave shook his head on a chuckle. "Good on you then. Someday I'd like to hear the story of how you procured that, but not today. The one who's in charge of keeping track of those is very high up and he's been pissed for centuries that one of them disappeared from under his nose."

Bracken's gaze turned speculative. "I'd be more than happy to tell you how I ended up with this item, if you'd be so kind as to let me interview you about Hell."

Dave's eyes slid to me.

"Dave, this is my Great-Uncle Bracken. He's a researcher of both human and supernatural history and I trust him with my life. Bracken, this is Dave, half-demon, half-Corey wicche, and cook at The Slaughtered Lamb."

"Dave? As in Daeva?" Bracken looked at me. "Do you know his real name?"

"No, she doesn't, old man, and she doesn't need to." Dave suddenly took more of an interest in Bracken than the grimoire in his hands. He turned to me, "Do you know he's not full wicche?"

I glanced at Bracken and realized that everyone but Dave and me were frozen. "What did you do?"

"Just having a private conversation," he said. "I'm not saying don't trust him. I'm just saying he's not how he presents himself. I'm calling him *old man* because that's a glamour he's wearing, and I want him to know that I know."

"I meant what I said before," I told him. "I trust him."

Dave shrugged a shoulder. "I'm not saying you shouldn't. Given my parentage, that'd be pretty hypocritical of me. I just want you to be aware."

"He did say that he didn't believe his father was his father. He thought that was why he'd been spurned by his family."

Dave nodded. "He's probably right about that. Lots of secrets in this family. They may believe his father is another wicche, but I think fae."

I stared at Bracken. "Really? He's wicche and fae too?" He felt like even more of an uncle to me now.

"Did you already know that?" Dave asked to the right of me.

Bracken blinked. "I've wondered."

Dave smirked. "Were you listening to the whole conversation?"

Bracken ignored the question and turned to me. "Does this change things between us?"

My eyes filled with tears as I quickly shook my head. I went to him and held his gloved hand. "We said we were alike. Now we're even more so."

He looked down, smiling. When he lifted his head, he was young and so handsome. He blinked and went back to my old great-uncle. "This guise is more comfortable for me now. It's what I'm used to seeing in the mirror. Someday, when it's time for Bracken to die, I'll reappear as a long-lost cousin."

I squeezed his hand. "Perfect. Just don't go away for real."

"Okay," Dave said. "Move back to where you were standing so I can get rid of this thing. It feels like maggots are crawling over my hand."

I went back, Dave lifted the spell, and he walked to the far side of the room, stepping over a huge spider leg. "Here we go." Fire burst from his hand and the grimoire went up like an explosive. Dave's clothes were blackened, but he was fine. When there was nothing but ash left, he brushed off his hands and looked around.

"I'd recommend torching the whole place and cleansing the soil. You can never sell this property, and you have to keep it hidden. If this place passes into the wrong hands, you'll end up with a serial killer who keeps his victims in the basement." Hands on his hips, he scowled around him. "You all get out. I'll burn it down and see what I can do about pulling the curse out of the ground." He seemed to be talking to himself now. "I can see if my father wants to help. He enjoys ridding the human realm of our interference." He glanced over at us. "Why are you still here? I just said I was burning it down."

"We're going." I grabbed Mom and we all headed to the patio doors as flames began to race up the walls.

FORTY-EIGHT

New Beginnings

Elizabeth and her family waited at the dock on the sailboat for us. As we approached, she looked behind us, her brow furrowed. "Where's Mom?"

My mom shook her head.

Elizabeth grabbed Faith's hand. "I—I can't wrap my head around Mom not being here. She's…indomitable. How could she be dead?" Her eyes filled with tears as Frank led her to a bench. He and Faith sat on either side of her, their arms around her.

"Fire!" Frank said, staring back at Cal's house.

I nodded. "A friend is burning it to the ground for us."

He looked alarmed for a moment and then seemed to realize that was for the best, slumping back and holding his mother's hand. "Sorry," he murmured to her.

Robert piloted the boat back to the gallery while the rest of us sat, lost in a haze of thoughts.

We made plans to have dinner again in a few days, once we'd decompressed, to discuss the night. Under cover of dark, Declan, Mom, Bracken, and I hopped quickly off the boat and back onto my deck while they sailed away.

We stood for a moment and stared at one another.

"I should tend to your Gran," Mom said.

"Not tonight," I told her. "You stay here with us and then we'll tend Gran together tomorrow."

Dad appeared on a bench. "That makes good sense, Sybil. Your mother is safe in her own home. She'll be okay until you get there."

Mom looked torn, but at Dad's words, she nodded, her shoulders slumping.

I turned to Bracken. "Do you want to stay with us?"

He shook his head. "That's a kind invitation, but I have an artifact to store and then I'd like to sleep for a very long time."

"Sounds good. Mom, you should stay here. Don't go home all alone." It hadn't hit me before, just how huge and empty that house was with Mom living there on her own.

Dad stood. "Your mother and I have things to discuss. She won't be alone."

I gave him a hug. "Thank you for your help tonight."

He nodded and then held out his arm for Mom to take. Bracken shuffled off to his RV and Mom and Dad walked around the gallery in the opposite direction, leaving Declan and me staring at each other.

"There were so many times tonight," I began, "when you could have understandably walked away, but you never did. You stuck by me, getting cut and burned, fighting a damn monster and dealing with curses. It hit me when Robert asked you if it's always like this. I can't tell you it'll be smooth sailing from here on out, because that's never been my life."

"Shh." He wrapped his arms around me and kissed me. "I told you. I love you. You're my family. And I turn into a wolf. I lead a pack of others who also turn into wolves." He shook his head. "If you can handle my crazy, I can handle yours."

I squeezed him as hard as I could. How'd I get so lucky?

"Come on," he said, rubbing my back. "Let's get cleaned up, and you need a conditioning pack for your hair."

I laughed. "I really do."

We went up and showered, getting cleaned up, dirty, and then cleaned up again. Being the responsible Alpha, he remembered to send a message to the pack, letting them know the sorcerer was gone and everyone should sleep in.

As the sun was beginning to rise and we were tumbling into bed, I thought we'd sleep for days. Unfortunately, it felt as though I'd just closed my eyes when I heard a knock on the back door.

Declan grumbled, "No," and tightened his arm around me.

The knock came again,

"Go 'way," he growled.

When I heard my phone vibrating on the worktable below, I gave up and got up. I pulled on sweatpants and a hoodie, slippers, and my gloves. My hair was still wet and probably looked stupid, but I was too tired to care. If you knocked on my door at the butt crack of dawn, you got what you got.

Squinting one eye, I made out Hernández's silhouette. I opened the door and squinted some more.

"Oh. Sorry. I didn't realize you'd still be sleeping," she said, pushing her sunglasses up on top of her head.

"Why would I not be? It's only—" I looked over her shoulder and found it far too sunny for early morning. "Never mind." I waved her backward. "Let's go out there. Declan's sleeping."

"No, I'm not," he growled.

"Well, you should be," I shouted back, closing the door behind me.

Hernández and I sat down on a bench. It was a glorious day and for the first time in centuries, we didn't have a sorcerer in the family and there was no demonic grimoire waiting to corrupt more. It was a good day.

"Rough night?" she asked, the corners of her serious mouth turning up.

I nodded. "Not in the way you mean, though. We found the sorcerer." I shook my head. "It was a lot. Remind me to tell you someday when we have time. Suffice to say, the sorcerer, her demon, and the spell book are all gone. Unfortunately, so is my gran."

Hernández sat up straight. "Arwyn, I'm so sorry. I shouldn't have made a joke."

I smiled, soaking up the rays. "Yes, you should have. You don't relax and joke nearly enough. So, are you visiting because of the serial killer or the stalker?"

She scratched her nose. "Both, actually."

I turned to her. "Did you get him?"

She knew I meant the killer. "I did. And, yes, he's the cop you warned me about when I was here arresting our last serial killer."

"I'd prefer not to think of them as ours," I muttered.

She stretched out her legs, crossing them at the ankles. "Harding was recently suspended for two weeks because of far too many civilian complaints and then pulling his gun on you. Unfortunately, he seems to have used that time to amp up his issues with unnecessary force to begin stalking victims.

"The judge who presided over the botched trial witnessed his humiliation and therefore needed to be punished," she continued. "The woman with the patio full of plants submitted a pretty damning complaint against him. My friend Gaby, with the floral couch, reported him for harassment and the repeated use of ethnic slurs. The man—Joel—didn't fit the pattern. He wasn't a woman of color."

"The one who wanted money?" I asked.

She nodded. "Yes. He worked part-time in records and did some IT stuff around the station. We discovered that the reason Harding's complaints weren't flagged earlier was because Joel was going into the system to delete complaints or to alter them so the civilian seemed like a crank. Those two carried the same prejudices, and Joel was more than happy to help his buddy Harding even the playing field, as they saw it."

"Jeez."

"Yep. Unfortunately for Joel, he started to ask for loans in a way that sounded very much like blackmail. So Harding's in jail as we collect more damning evidence against him, and Joel's in the morgue." She lifted her face to the sun. "We found the pictures on Harding's phone and some keepsakes from the murders. We're hopeful he goes down for all four murders."

The wind off the water was chilly, so I stuffed my hands in my pockets. "Sometimes there is justice. Sounds like we have two fewer killers in the neighborhood today."

We were quiet for a bit. "I'm sorry about your gran," she said.

My throat tightened and tears rushed in to blur my vision. I'd been doing so good, not thinking about it, about the loss of her. It was all so complicated and gut-wrenching. She was my Gran, the one I'd always turned to as a child when Mom had seemed cold and unfeeling. Knowing I'd been manipulated, even robbed, was devastating. I couldn't make it make sense. I'd felt warmth and affection from Gran. I was sure of it. And yet… She was a complicated woman, raised by cruel elders—if Bracken was to be believed, and why wouldn't he be?

She'd been raised to always put family first, to protect and promote Coreys. Did she steal from me? It sure seemed like it, but I also knew that Gran was the one family members went to when they were in trouble and needed help. Sometimes that help was financial.

My guess was that she had an account the three million went into and out of which came the loans she gave others. Maybe she'd originally thought of me as the half-faeling guard dog who could protect and benefit the family and then, eventually, learned to love me. Maybe. Someday, I'd ask Mom, but I wasn't ready for the answer right now.

"And I'm sorry about yours," I said to Hernández, patting my face and soaking up the tears with my gloves.

She gave me a sad almost-smile. "Thanks."

"Wait," I said, sitting up straight. "What day is it?"

"Wednesday."

I slumped back down. "Oh, thank goodness. I thought I was going to have to open the gallery soon." I shook my head. "How is it only Wednesday?"

"Don't you want to know about your stalker?" she asked.

I gave her a Declan-worthy scowl. "What about him?"

"A body washed ashore early this morning. Drowning victim named Brandon White."

"Brandon," I repeated. "That's his name."

"I'm told they went to the address on his ID and found a small room with a card table and podcasting equipment. The walls of that room were covered with pictures of you, this gallery, and articles from fringe websites about demons and witch burnings."

I blew out a breath.

"Arthur went to check out the apartment, rather than sending a uniform. He wanted it documented and processed with the fewest cops aware of it. He said White's car was in his designated parking spot, so he doesn't know how he ended up in the ocean."

Not wanting to think about that room, I got up and went to the railing. "Hello, Cecil! Good day, Poppy." I watched the water and smiled when I saw a tentacle. "I don't know how to feel about any of this," I told her. "I don't wish harm on people, but he was obsessed, and with the prodding of my cousin, had a gun he intended to use."

"I was just about to tell you about the gun," she said, sounding frustrated that I, yet again, knew before she told me.

"I had a vision. He was supposed to kill me last night."

The silence was charged. "Arwyn, I know you can control water. Did you drown him?" Hernández walked to the railing beside me.

I stared her in the eye and shook my head. "I didn't kill him. I wasn't sure what I was going to do when he showed up, but we were out dealing with my cousin all night, and I forgot about him." I wasn't going to tell her I knew my father was the one who had drowned him. He'd been protecting me, and it wasn't as if the police could do anything about the fae.

"Okay. I can see you're exhausted. I'll let you go." She moved toward the end of the deck and then spun. "I almost forgot. The arsonists from last night are in jail, as well, and I need the security feed."

"I'll send it to you when I'm more awake," I promised.

"Good. And that other one." She pulled out her notebook and flipped the pages. "Milo Swan has been arrested. Arthur already has the security feed for that one. Swan is claiming innocence, and his grandma is shouting that Coreys have always been jealous of Swans. I'd watch out for that one if I were you. She's nuts. Anyway, we got him dead to rights, so her shouts aren't going to amount to much. I just wanted you to be prepared if she takes the fight to you."

I nodded. "Got it."

"Oh." She tapped her forehead. "One more thing. The podcast has disappeared. Osso tried to pull it up and it was gone. Like it had never existed."

I stared at her, confused. Dad?

"Go back to sleep." She checked her watch. "But get me the arsonist footage by one, okay? I can stall things that long."

"Will do." I waved and walked back in, finding Declan on the couch rather than in bed. "What are you doing down here?"

"Listening to the updates and sketching plans," he said, with one of my sketchbooks and a pencil in hand.

"Oh, yeah? What are you sketching?" I sat beside him and rested my head on his shoulder.

"The baby's going to need a crib," he said, showing me his idea.

"I thought—" I looked again. "I thought you'd continue with the Craftsman design."

He shook his head. "Not for our little sea princess. This is actually something we can both work on. You'll paint the room, and it will be gorgeous. For the crib, though, I want this tall, carved wood backboard with ocean animals. And then see here and here?

That's where I'll make cutouts and you can blow glass inserts, so the jelly looks translucent, and the wave looks like water."

"The light will stream through." I grinned up at him. "It's beautiful. I especially like this wolf right here. Why is he underwater? We don't know, but he's looking out for you."

With a kiss he said, "Always."

Keep reading for an excerpt from
WICKED WICCHE, book four of the
Sea Wicche Chronicles

CHAPTER ONE

In the Past, She's Been a Nasty

I thought longingly of the cool air skating across the waves outside. Soon. I wiped a drop of sweat off my chin, glad my mass of curls was piled high on my head. I couldn't take more heat on my neck and back. Using my torch and tongs, I pulled and shaped tentacles on my latest glass octopus. I'd been commissioned for a very large order and had been working every day, trying to get it done early.

With our latest—and hopefully last—sorcerer in the family taken care of and the demonic grimoire destroyed, I had time to just work. Unfortunately, I also had time to think, as my mind often wandered when I was creating something I'd done countless times before.

I was a murderer.

Was it necessary? Yes. My cousin Calliope and her demon had harmed and killed many. They had to be stopped, and I was the one there to do it. It had to be done. I knew that. I couldn't make peace with it, though.

I didn't worry the Goddess was angry with me or that the Corey curse would be triggered because I'd killed one of my own. It wasn't a fear of being punished. It was a feeling of being irretrievably marked. I'd carry it forever. I'd taken a life.

I kept telling myself it had to be done. Cal would never have stopped. She'd killed her own mother and grandmother, but now I was a murderer too. That moment—when I'd leapt over the hellhound and thrown the athame at her—haunted my nightmares.

When my boyfriend—my mate? My significant other—Declan, the werewolf Alpha of the Big Sur Pack, slept with me, the nightmares were silenced. Unfortunately, the pack was still dealing with the aftereffects of a sorcerer prodding them into rages. The morning and night runs continued a few times a week. He thought in another month or so, they would be settled enough to go back to once a week runs. Until that happened, I was dealing with nightmares I had a hard time feeling I didn't deserve.

A shadow slid across my peripheral vision. Turning, I found my great-uncle standing on the deck outside. "Don't open the door!" I shouted.

A cool wind now could crack the glass. He waited, studying the accordioned glass doors while I finished curling my last tentacle. During the remodel, I'd had my contractor put in special doors that could be opened all the way for maximum air circulation.

I put the octopus in the annealer to cool down and then took off my work gloves and went to open the doors to cool myself off. "Sorry about that. I couldn't let cool air in."

"Not to worry. I know not to open the door. I've been thinking, though," Bracken said. "I'd like doors like these on my apartment."

"I love that idea." I tipped my head up to the wind. "Declan said his crew could come over and build your place as soon as they're done at his—which shouldn't be too long."

"Sounds perfect," he replied. "That gives me time to decide if I want them to duplicate my RV completely or if I should make some changes." He glanced at my no doubt very red and sweaty face. "Can I get you something to drink?"

"I'm okay. You'd consider changes?" Bracken had trouble with new things. The fact that he was considering altering the home he was used to was amazing. He'd once told me he feared that his world was becoming smaller and smaller, that he'd end up trapped in a tiny room somewhere. This would be a huge step in a healthier direction for him.

"I think I'd like a larger living room. When you and your mother visited, you had to share that small bench." He paused, considering. "Possibly big enough for a couch, so I can have visitors from time to time."

He gave me a surreptitious look. "Perhaps—if you're comfortable—I could babysit. Only if you think your child would be safe with me, of course. And I understand completely if you're not comfortable." He shrugged a shoulder, feigning an equanimity he wasn't feeling.

I caught his eye and smiled. "I have complete faith in you. It's still really early yet."

He stood a little taller. "Then I think I'll need a bigger living room. Maybe even a playroom for when she visits me."

My throat was suddenly tight, but I nodded. "Great idea."

He stared at the waves for a moment. "Maybe you could paint the walls, so she knows it's her room."

I cleared that tight throat and said, "I absolutely could do that. When I'm further along and it feels safer, I'm going to paint an underwater scene in the nursery at Declan's. In your room, I can do a forest scene, since her daddy's a werewolf."

"That sounds lovely and restful," he said with a wistful smile. "Good for nap time."

I moved to the nearby bench and sat, with Bracken following. "I've been meaning to ask. Do you know if werewolf babies have a shorter gestation period? I asked Mom and she said she was pregnant for the normal forty weeks with me. Declan told me natural wolves were pregnant for about two and a half months. When you were researching werewolves, did you ask about the length of pregnancy?"

He thought a moment. "I didn't ask—though you're right. I should have. I do recall Alexander, Declan's father, making a comment about his mate's pregnancy." He tapped his lip, lost in memory. "I don't recall what he said, but it made me think that Quinn wolves—the origin line—were closer to natural wolves in this." He patted my leg. "Let me check my journals and do a little digging. I don't know that I'll find anything, but at least there are two healers in the family who can track your pregnancy and perhaps give you a better estimate."

"Thank you. I'm trying to get this order of glass octopuses done as soon as possible because I don't know how all of this is going to affect me."

He stretched out his legs. "Understandable."

"Are you sure you wouldn't like your apartment at Declan's?" I wanted to move into the gorgeous home Declan had built for us, but I didn't want to leave Bracken behind, not after he'd been alone for so long. He finally had family again.

He shook his head. "That's your new home for your new family. I love it here. The beauty and constancy of the ocean calms my mind, and your Cecil and Wilbur bring me joy. Besides, it isn't as if you're far away or that you won't be here most days. When the gallery is open, the little one can stay close by with me—unless your mother pulls rank and takes her," he added on a smile.

With a sudden jolt of panic, I grabbed his arm. "Don't let anyone take her, not without my seeing them." I tried to shake it off but found I couldn't. "Demons can shapeshift. So can the fae." My heart was racing. "Too many have come after me all my life, and that was before the queen said she had plans for me." I squeezed harder. "What if that plan involves my child?"

He patted my hand. "You forget," he said, his voice low. "I have a great deal of power myself, and I would never let anyone steal or hurt your child."

My eyes flooded with tears and I shook my head, looking up

and blinking. "Sorry. My emotions are all over the place. Stupid hormones."

Declan raced around the corner of the gallery, making Bracken and me jump. "What? What happened? Are you okay?"

"You could hear my heart beating from your place?" How had I not known that?

He shook his head. "I wish. I was walking over to have lunch with you when I heard it." He gestured behind him. "I was at the road." He crouched at my knee. "You've been crying too." He looked between Bracken and me. "What's going on?"

Bracken stood and patted my shoulder. "I'll let you two talk. I need to go through my journals and see if it I can find that answer for you." He strolled away and Declan took his spot, wrapping his big hand around mine.

"I didn't mean to scare you." I leaned my head on him, suddenly tired. "We were talking about his new apartment." I looked up at him and smiled. "He wants a bigger living room so people can visit, and a playroom for this one." I patted my stomach.

Declan's eyebrows rose. "He does?"

The stupid tears rushed back when I nodded. "He was saying he'd keep her close when the gallery is open, unless Mom comes and pulls rank, taking her."

Declan grinned, stretching out his legs.

"But then I panicked," I told him. "We've seen how demons and the fae can alter their appearance to look like anyone. What if one of the king's assassins pretends to be Mom and takes our child from Bracken?"

He wrapped his arm around me and pulled me in tight. "We'll have to ask your Dad about that. I'm sure he can come up with a ward that protects his grandchild. And while you and the little one are here, next to the ocean, you have his guards keeping watch too." He kissed the top of my head. "If you and I can't keep her protected, I don't know who could."

Nodding slowly, trying to make myself believe it, I said, "That's true. And Bracken is more powerful than a normal wicche. He promised he'd never let anything happen to her."

"She's going to be surrounded by protectors. We can ask Tyler and Jake to continue working security on days like today, when you're working here alone."

I waved away the suggestion. "They have jobs. They can't drop everything just because I'm nervous."

"Sure they can." He stood, pulled me up with him, and walked into the hot shop. "They'd thought the job would be a lot longer than one day when they agreed to guard you." He looked at the completed octopuses. "Did you get more done this morning?"

"Three. They're in the annealer."

"No wonder you're tired." He led us into my studio. "You need a break. And last time I heard, you had a few months to finish that order. You don't have to push so hard."

I plopped down at my worktable. "I'm not sure what's going to happen and when. That's what Bracken is checking. Is this pregnancy nine months? Two? Somewhere in between?"

I'd left all the doors open. The gates at the ends of the deck hadn't gone up yet; Declan was carving something special. Until then, I'd added a fae ward about halfway from the front of the gallery to the back that made people want to turn around. My friends and family could get through, but it was designed to push away the random person who was too curious for their own good.

If I was on my own, I'd probably lock up on the off chance someone got past my wards. As Declan was with me and had excellent hearing, I figured I'd enjoy the cool breezes. I seemed to be running warmer these days.

Declan went through the refrigerator and pulled out our Thai leftovers from last night's dinner. While he heated the food, I got up and went to the bathroom to clean up. Looking in the mirror, I saw the telltale tightness around my eyes that said I was getting less sleep than usual.

After doing a quick glamour spell to hide the tightness, I went back out. Declan had food on the worktable and was dishing it onto two plates for us. I got a couple of napkins and some drinks before sitting down, suddenly ravenous. Declan easily ate three to four times as much food as me, but you wouldn't notice unless you were paying close attention. He had excellent table manners and never shoveled it in.

I took a bite and realized he was looking at me, not eating. Eyebrows raised, I chewed and waited.

"You don't have to hide the exhaustion from me. I'm sorry I've been away so much and you're left here with the nightmares."

Shaking my head, I swallowed. "You have a responsibility to all those pack members to keep them and their families safe."

"I have a responsibility to you and the little one too, and you need sleep."

I nodded and he finally started eating. Being a werewolf meant burning through a ton of calories every day. He needed to eat. "Maybe I'll take up afternoon napping," I told him, glancing over my shoulder at the couch. I'd been joking, but that actually sounded really good.

Declan's head came up and he looked toward the hot shop. "Someone's coming." He paused, listening. "I think that's Hernández's walk."

Sure enough, a minute later, Detective Hernández was standing in the back door of the studio. "Sorry to interrupt your lunch. This shouldn't take long."

I waved her in. "Would you like some leftover Thai?"

"Smells great," she said, "but I'm good. I won't mess up your meal. Please, keep eating." She pulled out the small notebook that was always in her pocket. "When I'm closing up a case, I go through my notebook, pull out all the pages related to that case, and file them. When I was doing that for this last one—Officer Harding—I found the note about that address you wanted me to check."

She looked up with a guilty expression and shook her head.

"I'm sorry. We were in the thick of it and I completely forgot to do it earlier."

"That's okay," I said. "We know you're busy."

Declan nodded, steadily making his way through the pile of food on his plate.

"I looked it up this morning and now I'm worried I should have done it a week ago when you gave it to me."

When I'd asked Orla, our new owl-shifting friend, to check the coastline for possible sorcerer lairs, she'd found seven. One was Cal's house. One was a vampire's. Four were invisible, and one was a normal house in an ordinary neighborhood that had an address.

"The owner of the property is Catherine Swan."

I sat up straight at that. The Swans were another old wicche family. They didn't have Corey-level power, but it wasn't for lack of trying. Catherine was the head of the Swan coven. Bracken said she'd been trying to spy on and steal from us since he was little, wanting to be as powerful as Gran had been.

And just that quick thought of Gran caused my breath to catch and my chest to tighten. I kept forgetting. Gran couldn't be gone. Of course she was still here, guiding the family, keeping us all in her sights. It was hard to imagine her not at the helm.

I'd recently learned that Catherine Swan had been working with Calliope, trying to curry favor and gain strength. She'd even had her grandson Milo poison my pastries in the gallery, hoping someone dying here would wreck me and help Cal get the upper hand. If the poison had killed me, all the better.

"Swan?" I looked at Declan. "This isn't good. I need to tell Mom. Is she a black magic practitioner now?"

"That's the other part," Hernández continued. "Catherine owns the house, but Milo and his sister Milena are the ones who live there."

I pushed away the plate and rested my head on the table. "I hate dark wicches."

• • •

WICKED WICCHE: THE SEA WICCHE CHRONICLES *WILL BE out 3/31/2026*

Acknowledgments

There are times in life when escape is particularly important. That doesn't mean we don't strive to do what's right, to help those in need, to fight for those who can't. It just means that sometimes we need a break, a place to recharge so we can fight again. I hope my books serve as a reprieve before we go out and get into more good trouble.

Thank you to my wonderful family for always supporting me on this grand adventure! Being a full-time writer is a dream come true. Thank you to my incredible critique partner C.R. Grissom, who has over the last sixteen years read everything I've ever written. She's a wonderful writer, funny, insightful, and ridiculously supportive.

Thank you to Peter Senftleben, my extraordinary editor. He has the enviable knack of getting to the heart of the story and then helping me to see my own work through a different lens. Thank you to Susan Helene Gottfried, my exceptional proofreader who always knows exactly where the commas go (unlike myself).

Thank you to the remarkable team at NYLA! You've made every step of publishing a little easier with your wit, compassion, and expertise. Thank you to my incomparable agent Sarah Younger, the fabulous Natanya Wheeler, and the incredible Cheryl Pientka for working together to make my dream of writing and publishing a reality.

Dear Reader,

Thank you for reading **Wicching Hour**. If you enjoyed Arwyn and Declan's third adventure together, please consider leaving a review or chatting about it with your book-loving friends. Good word of mouth means everything when you're a writer!

Love,
Seana

Want more books from Seana?

If you'd like to be the first to learn what's new with Arwyn and Declan (and Sam and Clive and Owen and Dave and Stheno…), please sign up for my newsletter *Tales from the Book Nerd*. It's filled with writing news, deleted scenes, giveaways, book recommendations, first looks at covers, short stories, and my favorite cocktail and book pairings.

Arwyn's next adventure is **Wicked Wicche.** It will be arriving in the spring of 2026. Stay tuned for more…

If you're a Sam Quinn fan, **The Mermaid's Bubble Lounge** will be out October 7, 2025.

What else has Seana written? Well, I'll tell you...

The Slaughtered Lamb Bookstore & Bar
Sam Quinn, Book 1

Welcome to The Slaughtered Lamb Bookstore and Bar. I'm Sam Quinn, the werewolf book nerd in charge. I run my business by one simple rule: Everyone needs a good book and a stiff drink, be they vampire, wicche, demon, or fae. No wolves, though. Ever. I have my reasons.

I serve the supernatural community of San Francisco. We've been having some problems lately. Okay, I'm the one with the problems. The broken body of a female werewolf washed up on my doorstep. What makes sweat pool at the base of my spine, though, is realizing the scars she bears are identical to the ones I conceal. After hiding for years, I've been found.

A protection I've been relying on is gone. While my wolf traits are strengthening steadily, the loss also left my mind vulnerable to attack. Someone is ensnaring me in horrifying visions intended to kill. Clive, the sexy vampire Master of the City, has figured out how to pull me out, designating himself my personal bodyguard.

He's grumpy about it, but that kiss is telling a different story. A change is taking place. It has to. The bookish bartender must become the fledgling badass.

I'm a survivor. I'll fight fang and claw to protect myself and the ones I love. And let's face it, they have it coming.

The Dead Don't Drink at Lafitte's
Sam Quinn, Book 2

I'm Sam Quinn, the werewolf book nerd owner of the Slaughtered Lamb Bookstore and Bar. Things have been busy lately. While the near-constant attempts on my life have ceased, I now have a vampire gentleman caller. I've been living with Clive and the rest of his vampires for a few weeks while the Slaughtered Lamb is being rebuilt. It's going about as well as you'd expect.

My mother was a wicche and long dormant abilities are starting to make themselves known. If I'd had a choice, necromancy wouldn't have been my top pick, but it's coming in handy. A ghost warns me someone is coming to kill Clive. When I rush back to the nocturne, I find vamps from New Orleans readying an attack. One of the benefits of vampires looking down on werewolves is no one expects much of me. They don't expect it right up until I take their heads.

Now, Clive and I are setting out for New Orleans to take the fight back to the source. Vampires are masters of the long game. Revenge plots are often decades, if not centuries, in the making. We came expecting one enemy but quickly learn we have darker forces scheming against us. Good thing I'm the secret weapon they never see coming.

The Wicche Glass Tavern
Sam Quinn, Book 3

I'm Sam Quinn, the werewolf book nerd owner of the Slaughtered Lamb Bookstore and Bar. Clive, my vampire gentleman caller, has asked me to marry him. His nocturne is less than celebratory. Unfortunately, for them and the sexy vamp doing her best to seduce him, his cold, dead heart beats only for me.

As much as my love life feels like a minefield, it has to take a backseat to a far more pressing problem. The time has come. I need to deal with my aunt, the woman who's been trying to kill me for as long as I can remember. She's learned a new trick. She's figured out how to weaponize my friends against me. To have any hope of surviving, I have to learn to use my necromantic gifts. I need a teacher. We find one hiding among the fae, which is a completely different problem. I need to determine what I'm capable of in a hurry because my aunt doesn't care how many are hurt or killed as long as she gets what she wants. Sadly for me, what she wants is my name on a headstone.

I'm gathering my friends—werewolves, vampires, wicches, gorgons, a Fury, a half-demon, an elf, and a couple of dragon shifters—into a kind of Fellowship of the Sam. It's going to be one hell of a battle. Hopefully, San Francisco will still be standing when the dust clears.

The Hob & Hound Pub
Sam Quinn, Book 4

I'm Sam Quinn, the newly married werewolf book nerd owner of the Slaughtered Lamb Bookstore and Bar. Clive and I are on our honeymoon. Paris is lovely, though the mummy in the Louvre inching toward me is a bit off-putting. Although Clive doesn't sense anything, I can't shake the feeling I'm being watched.

Even after we cross the English Channel to begin our search for Aldith—the woman who's been plotting against Clive since the beginning—the prickling unease persists. Clive and I are separated, rather forcefully, and I'm left to find my way alone in a foreign country, evading not only Aldith's large web of henchvamps, but vicious fae creatures disloyal to their queen. Gloriana says there's a poison in the human realm that's seeping into Faerie, and I may have found the source.

I knew this was going to be a working vacation, but battling vampires on one front and the fae on another is a lot, especially in a country steeped in magic. As a side note, I need to get word to Benvair. I think I've found the dragon she's looking for.

Gloriana is threatening to set her warriors against the human realm, but I may have a way to placate her. Aldith is a different story. There's no reasoning with rabid vengeance. She'll need to be put out of our misery permanently if Clive and I have any hope of a long, happy life together. Heck, I'd settle for a few quiet weeks.

Biergarten of the Damned
  Sam Quinn, Book 5

I'm Sam, the werewolf book nerd owner of The Slaughtered Lamb Bookstore & Bar. I've always thought of Dave, my red-skinned, shark-eyed, half-demon cook, as a kind of foul-mouthed uncle, one occasionally given to bouts of uncontrolled anger.

Something's going on, though. He's acting strangely, hiding things. When I asked what was wrong, he blew me off and told me to quit bugging him. That's normal enough. What's not is his missing work. Ever. Other demons are appearing in the bar, looking for him. I'm getting worried, and his banshee girlfriend Maggie isn't answering my calls.

Demons terrify me. I do NOT want to go into any demon bars looking for Dave, but he's my family, sort of. I need to try to help, whether he wants me to or not. When I finally learn the truth, though… I'm not sure I can ever look at him again, let alone have him work for me. Are there limits to forgiveness? I think there might be.

The Viper's Nest Roadhouse & Café
Sam Quinn, Book 6

I'm Sam, the werewolf book nerd owner of The Slaughtered Lamb Bookstore & Bar. Clive, Fergus, and I are moving into our new home, the business is going well, and our folly is taking shape. The problem? Clive's maker Garyn is coming to San Francisco for a visit, and this reunion has been a thousand years in the making. Back then, Garyn was rather put out when Clive accepted the dark kiss and then took off to avenge his sister's murder. She was looking for a new family. He was looking for lethal skills. And so, Garyn has had plenty of time to align her forces. When her allies begin stepping out of the shadows, Clive's foundation will be shaken.

Stheno and her sisters are adding to their rather impressive portfolio of businesses around the world by acquiring The Viper's Nest Roadhouse & Café. Medusa found the place when she was visiting San Francisco. A dive bar filled with hot tattooed bikers? Yes, please!

Clive and I will need neutral territory for our meeting with Garyn, and a biker bar (& café, Stheno insisted) should fit the bill. I'd assumed my necromancy would give us an advantage. I hadn't anticipated, though, just how powerful Garyn and her allies were. When the fangs descend and the heads start rolling, it's going to take every friend we have and a nocturne full of vamps at our backs to even the playing field. Wish us luck. We're going to need it.

The Bloody Ruin Asylum & Taproom
Sam Quinn, Book 7

I'm Sam, the werewolf book nerd owner of The Slaughtered Lamb Bookstore & Bar. My husband, Master vampire Clive, has been asked to go to Budapest to interview for a position in the Guild, a council of thirteen vampires who advise the world's Masters. The competition for the recently vacated spot is fierce. I worry about Clive, as it quickly becomes apparent that the last person to hold the position didn't leave voluntarily.

Ever the supportive wife, I'm tagging along. I researched Budapest and had a long itinerary of things to do. That is, I did. When we arrive, we find out that the Guild headquarters is in the ruins of an abandoned insane asylum. Awesome. If there's one thing I love, it's being hounded by mentally unstable Hungarian ghosts.

Let's just say this isn't the romantic getaway I'd been hoping for. With Clive in top secret meetings and a bunch of creepy Renfields skulking around corners, nowhere is safe. I want to help Clive because I know he really wants the job, but the other Guild members are ancient and scary powerful. Between you and me, I thought Vlad would be taller.

Wish us luck! We're going to need it.

The Mermaid's Bubble Lounge
Sam Quinn, book 8

The vampire Guild is in shambles. My husband Clive and I might have given more than a few Masters their final deaths—allegedly —so it's fallen on us to fix the problem. Mostly on Clive, that is, as he's the Master vampire. I'm Sam Quinn, werewolf book nerd and owner of The Slaughtered Lamb Bookstore & Bar.

Vlad (yes, that one) and Cadmael are the houseguests no one would want, but we're trying to grin and bear it because the Guild must be rebuilt, and we must make haste as rogue vamps are becoming a big bloody problem.

Finvarra, the fae king who had it out for me even before I helped cause his brother's death, is coming to do what none of his assassins have managed: end me in as painful a manner as possible.

In other news, Stheno and Vlad have been hooking up and we're all a little afraid of those two together.

————

Bewicched: The Sea Wicche Chronicles
  Sea Wicche, Book 1

We here at The Sea Wicche cater to your art-collecting, muffin-eating, tea-drinking, and potion-peddling needs. Palmistry and Tarot sessions are available upon request and by appointment. Our store hours vary and rely completely on Arwyn—the owner—getting her butt out of bed.

I'm Arwyn Cassandra Corey, the sea wicche, or the wicche who lives by the sea. It requires a lot more work than I'd anticipated to remodel an abandoned cannery and turn it into an art gallery & tea bar. It's coming along, though, especially with the help of a new werewolf who's joined the construction crew. He does beautiful work. His sexy, growly, bearded presence is very hard to ignore, but I'm trying. I'm not sure how such a laid-back guy got the local Alpha and his pack threatening to hunt him down and tear him apart, but we all have our secrets. And because I don't want to know his—or yours for that matter—I wear these gloves. Clairvoyance makes the simplest things the absolute worst. Trust me. Or don't. Totally up to you.

Did I mention my mother and grandmother are pressuring me to assume my rightful place on the Corey Council? That's a kind of governing triad for our ancient magical family, one that has more than its fair share of black magic practitioners. And yes, before you ask, people have killed to be on the council—one psychotic sorceress aunt stands out—but I have no interest in the power or politics that come with the position. I'd rather stick to my art and, in the words of my favorite sea wicche, help poor unfortunate souls. (Good luck trying to get that song out of your head now)

Wicche Hunt: The Sea Wicche Chronicles
  Sea Wicche, Book 2

I'm Arwyn Cassandra Corey, the Sea Wicche of Monterey. Want a psychic reading? Sure. I can do that. In the market for art? I have all your painting, photography, glass blowing, and ceramic needs covered in my newly remodeled art gallery by the sea. Need help solving a grisly cold case? Unfortunately, I can probably help with that too.

After more than a decade of being nagged, guilted, and threatened, I've finally joined the Corey Council and am working with my mother and grandmother to hunt down a twisted sorcerer. We know who she is. Now we need to find and stop her before more are murdered.

The evil the sorcerer and her demon are doing is seeping into the community. Violent crimes have been increasing and as a result Detectives Hernández and Osso have brought me another horrifying case. I'll do what I can, because of course I will. What are a few more nightmares to a woman who barely sleeps?

Declan Quinn, the wicked hot werewolf rebuilding my deck, is preparing for a dominance battle with the local Alpha. A couple of wolves have already left their pack to follow Declan, recognizing him as the true Alpha. Declan needs to watch his back as the full moon approaches. The current Alpha will do whatever it takes to hold on to power, including breaking pack law and enlisting the help of a local vampire.

And if Wilbur, my selkie friend is right, I might just be meeting my dad soon. Perhaps he'll have some advice for this wicche hunt. I'm going to need all the help I can get.

Wicching Hour: The Sea Wicche Chronicles
  Sea Wicche, Book 3

I'm Arwyn Cassandra Corey, the Sea Wicche of Monterey. My new art gallery is finally open, my boyfriend is the new Alpha of the Big Sur pack, and my sorcerer cousin is still on the loose. It's been a lot. I'm just sayin'.

Detectives Hernández and Osso are asking for my help again. Bodies have been found torn up in the woods in a manner that has those in the know thinking werewolf. Declan, as Alpha, will need to investigate his pack and help hunt the killer.

We're narrowing in on Calliope and her demon. She can't hide forever, and my uncle might just have the map to where she's been holed up. If it's the last thing I do, I'll make her pay for her treachery.

Did I mention there's a new podcast, hosted by a human, who is coming dangerously close to telling the kind of secrets the supernatural community kills to keep quiet? His latest season is about a certain artistic wicche.

Oh, and I finally met my dad. Like I said, it's been a lot.

Wicked Wicche: The Sea Wicche Chronicles
Sea Wicche, Book 4

Arwyn, our favorite artist and Sea Wicche, is trying unsuccessfully to deal with two new descriptors: murderer and mother.

The gallery is open, and the sorcerer is gone. Arwyn and the whole Corey clan should be celebrating. Instead, they're mourning a huge loss and now dealing with the Council of Wicches over a poisoning.

Lessons have begun with Dad. All the things a little faeling should have already learned, Arwyn is now being taught. And just in time, as the queen—cryptically and rather terrifyingly—told Arwyn that she has plans for her.

While trying to juggle all of that, and work on a huge order of glass octopuses, Arwyn is also drawn into another deadly police investigation. Send Arwyn your good thoughts because she really needs a nap.

Titles by Seana Kelly

The Sam Quinn Series

The Slaughtered Lamb Bookstore & Bar
The Dead Don't Drink at Lafitte's
The Wicche Glass Tavern
All I Want for Christmas is a Dragon (short story)
The Hob & Hound Pub
Biergarten of the Damned
The Banshee & the Blade (short story)
The Viper's Nest Roadhouse & Café
The Nocturne's Gatekeeper (short story)
The Bloody Ruin Asylum & Taproom
The Mermaid's Bubble Lounge

The Sea Wicche Series: Bewicched: The Sea Wicche Chronicles

Bewicched: The Sea Wicche Chronicles
Wicche Hunt: The Sea Wicche Chronicles
Wicching Hour: The Sea Wicche Chronicles
Wicked Wicche: The Sea Wicche Chronicles

About Seana Kelly

Seana Kelly lives in the San Francisco Bay Area with her husband, two daughters, two dogs, and one fish. When not dodging her family, hiding in the garage to write, she's working as a high school teacher-librarian. She's an avid reader and re-reader who misses her favorite characters when it's been too long between visits.

She's a *USA Today* Bestselling Author and is represented by the delightful and effervescent Sarah E. Younger of the Nancy Yost Literary Agency.

You can follow Seana on Instagram, TikTok, and YouTube for posts about books, dogs, and writing in general. She loves collecting photos of characters and settings for the books she writes. As she's also a librarian, you can expect lots of book recommendations too.

instagram.com/seanakellyrw

youtube.com/@SeanaKelly-RW

tiktok.com/@seanakellyfw

bookbub.com/authors/seana-kelly

pinterest.com/seanakelly326